"So we shall work together?" Linnet asked.

"Aye, I am all for joining forces," Jamie said, still hoping this would include more tonight than scheming on the queen's behalf. Tomorrow he would worry about the consequences.

Her eyes grew wide as he closed the distance between them to stand a hairbreadth from her. As he lifted his hand to cup her cheek, she backed away.

"I told you once," she said, her voice sharp with anger. "I will not have you touch me and regret it after." When he opened his mouth to deny it, she held up her hand. "I will choose a lover who is not so harsh in his judgment of me."

He clenched his jaw at the thought of her with another man. "So, it is a lover you are seeking again, and not a husband," he bit out. "Tell me, what are you looking for in the man you choose this time?"

She raised her eyebrows and blinked those wide, innocent blue eyes at him. "Who is to say I expect to find all I want in one man?"

Praise for Margaret Mallory
KNIGHT OF PLEASURE

"4 Stars! A riveting story...Such depth and sensuality are a rare treat."
—*RT Book Reviews*

more...

"Fascinating...An excellent historical romance. Ms. Mallory gives us amazingly vivid details of the characters, romance, and intrigue of England. You're not just reading a novel, you are stepping into the story and feeling all the emotions of each character...*Knight of Pleasure* is amazing and I highly recommend it."

—TheRomanceReadersConnection.com

"Marvelous...a terrific fifteenth-century romance filled with intrigue." —HarrietKlausner.wwwi.com

"An absolute delight...captivating...Combining a luscious romantic story with a fascinating look at an intriguing time in history, Mallory captures her readers' attention...I look forward to the next book in the series, KNIGHT OF PASSION." —FreshFiction.com

"If you like heated romance sprinkled liberally with royal politics, you can't miss this book."

—RomanceJunkiesReviews.com

"Thrilling, romantic, and just plain good reading...an enjoyable, historically accurate, and very well written novel."

—RomRevToday.com

"A beautifully written tale, allowing us to spend a night or two of pleasure engrossed in the story of Isobel and Stephen...Their romance is extremely satisfying for us to experience while the historical background makes the tale so much richer. A fantastic job." —SingleTitles.com

"Isobel almost jumps from the page as a fully developed character whose strengths and weaknesses make her seem extraordinarily real. Readers will rally behind her."

—MyShelf.com

"Lovely...your own heart weeps with all the issues that are keeping [Isobel and Stephen] apart."

—HistoricalRomanceSociety.com

"Mallory opens readers' eyes to the world of King Henry V... detail-enriched...bringing alive historical facts and sur-roundings...I thoroughly enjoyed reading the fascinating and scintillating exchanges between Isobel and Stephen and watching as both characters grew in both love and maturity." —CoffeeTimeRomance.com

KNIGHT OF DESIRE

"Spellbinding! Few writers share Margaret Mallory's talent for bringing history to vivid, pulsing life."

—Virginia Henley, *New York Times* bestselling author of *The Decadent Duke*

"An impressive debut...Margaret Mallory is a star in the making."

—Mary Balogh, *New York Times* bestselling author of *At Last Comes Love*

more...

Knight of Passion

MARGARET MALLORY

FOREVER

NEW YORK BOSTON

This book is a work of fiction. Names, characters, places, and incidents are the product of the author's imagination or are used fictitiously. Any resemblance to actual events, locales, or persons, living or dead, is coincidental.

Cover illustration by Franco Accornero

Forever
Hachette Book Group
237 Park Avenue
New York, NY 10017
Visit our website at www.HachetteBookGroup.com.

Forever is an imprint of Grand Central Publishing. The Forever name and logo is a trademark of Hachette Book Group, Inc.

Printed in the United States of America

First Printing: June 2010

10   9   8   7   6   5   4   3   2   1

This book is dedicated to my children,
Emily and Jeff, who are the joy of my life and
make me proud every day.

Acknowledgments

I am grateful to everyone at Grand Central Publishing for their support, especially my insightful editor, Alex Logan. It's lucky for us both that she has a sense of humor. Special thanks also goes to Claire Brown for another gorgeous cover. As always, I want to thank my agent and friend, Kevan Lyon, for her sage advice and constant support.

A big thank-you goes to my friends and sister—Anthea, Ginny, Jessica, and Cathy—whose comments on the draft manuscript saved my editor much needless suffering. I am in awe of the generosity of other romance writers and am very grateful for it.

I appreciate every single person who e-mailed to tell me they loved one of my books. You make the months alone with my laptop worthwhile.

Thanks to all the friends and family who have thrown themselves into supporting the only author they know. My biggest thanks goes to my husband, who helped me through an incredibly busy year.

"Were I a man, a duke, and next of blood,
I would remove these tedious stumbling-blocks
And smooth my way upon their headless necks…"

—Eleanor Cobham, Duchess of Gloucester
Henry VI, Part 2, Act 1, Scene 2

Prologue

"What if we get caught?" Jamie said, glancing up and down the palace corridor.

Getting caught was precisely the point, but Linnet was not going to tell Jamie that. She looked up at him through her lashes and said, "Don't you want to?"

The way his eyes went dark made her breath catch.

"You know I do," he said, brushing the back of his fingers against her cheek.

Her skin tingled from his touch. If she did not take care, Jamie could make her forget her purpose.

She felt a twinge of guilt for not telling him. None of the other young men at court would care what her reasons were if she dragged one of them into an empty bedchamber. But Jamie would refuse her if he knew. That stubborn sense of honor—misplaced though it may be—was one of the things she liked best about him.

"Everyone is attending the celebrations," she assured him.

The feasting that began with King Henry's triumphal entry into Paris with his French princess was continuing without pause through Advent.

"But the guest who has this chamber could return at any time," Jamie said.

He sucked in his breath as she ran a finger down his chest.

"If you are going to be a frightened mouse," she said, "I can find someone else."

Jamie's boyish sweetness was gone. He gripped her arm and jerked open the bedchamber door. Before she knew it, she was inside the bedchamber with her back pressed against the door. Jamie kissed her long and hard.

"Don't ever say you will go with another man," he said, taking her chin in his hand. "Don't ever say it."

"You are the only one I want." This was the truth, but she regretted telling him. He would read more into it than he ought.

"'Tis the same for me," he whispered and rested his forehead against hers.

She closed her eyes and breathed in his scent as she leaned against him. He could be such a tender boy.

But she did not know how much time she had. "Now," she whispered in his ear. "I want to do it now."

When she rubbed her hand up his cock for good measure, he made a sound between a growl and a moan and lifted her from the ground. Men were so predictable, so easily managed, there was almost no challenge in it. Still, Jamie's reaction was gratifying.

As he carried her to the bed, Linnet gave herself a moment to savor the thought of how angry Alain, her "father," was going to be. That man would rue the day.

From the moment Jamie laid her down and started kissing her, she forgot about Alain and her plans for revenge. This part she could not control, did not even try. A fire had raged between them since the day he arrived in Paris with the king. No matter how often they sneaked away to be together, the fire only burned hotter. She gave into it with abandon now, as she did every time.

Afterward, she lay in Jamie's arms, wishing the contentment of the moment could last. It never did.

"I've sent a letter to my parents," Jamie said, rubbing his cheek against the top of her head. "I expect my father will grant me a small estate upon our betrothal."

Her heart began to race. "Betrothed? You haven't spoken to me of betrothal before."

"Did I need to?" She heard the smile in his voice. "After what we've being doing, I thought it obvious."

"But you never told me. You never asked me."

"I see I have committed a grievous error," he said, sounding amused. "All right, let me ask it, then. My darling Linnet, love of my heart, will you wed me and be my wife?"

"Nay, I will not."

"What?" Jamie sat up and leaned over her. "I am sorry if I offended you by not speaking plainly before. You know I love you."

"Men say that all the time."

"But I mean it," he said, rubbing his thumb across her cheek. "And I shall still love you when your beauty is no more than a memory traced upon your face."

They had left the bed curtains drawn. In the sunlight from the tall window, she took in the strong lines of his handsome face, the intense expression in the violet-blue eyes. She swallowed. She hadn't meant to hurt him. Why did he not tell her these things before?

She reached up and cupped the side of his face with her hand. "You will always be special to me as my first lover."

"First lover!" His fingers dug into her arm. A moment later, he released her and flopped back down on the bed. "How you enjoy torturing me with your teasing! Sometimes you go too far."

Why do men never believe what you say? They persist in believing "no" means "perhaps," and "I despise you" means "I want you to write me bad poetry."

"I do not wish to be a wife," she said to Jamie. "I could not bear having a man tell me what to do all my life."

Jamie laughed. "As if I would dare try."

"You would. It is what men do."

He turned on his side, his dark hair falling across his eyes. "Let us pretend you are serious. What else could you do? I cannot see you as a nun."

She batted away his hand as he reached for her breast. "I may make a brief marriage."

"A brief one?" he said, raising his eyebrows.

"Aye, to a very old man who will leave me a wealthy widow," she said. "Or, I may become a famous courtesan."

The bed shook with Jamie's laughter.

"I am trying to be honest with you," she said, slapping his shoulder.

"You are beautiful enough to become the most famous courtesan in all of France," he said, pulling her on top of him. "And you know it very well. But enough of this foolishness. We must make our plan."

She may as well be speaking to a turnip. She pushed

away from him and sat up, wrapping her arms around her knees. In sooth, she could not imagine letting anyone else touch her the way Jamie did. But her plans required independence and money of her own.

Whenever her resolve weakened, she thought of the men who robbed her grandfather blind when he grew feebleminded toward the end. They were men he'd done business with for years; men he'd trusted and loaned money to in hard times. Not an hour after he died, these same men stripped their house in Falaise of valuables. Because of them, she and her brother, Francois, were stealing food to survive even before the English siege began.

One day, she would return to Falaise and destroy every one of those men who stole from them and left them to starve.

"Do you think your father will object to our marrying?" Jamie asked, startling her from her thoughts.

"Aye, he would," she said absently over her shoulder, "because the devil's spawn has already chosen a husband for me."

Jamie jerked upright beside her. "He intends to pledge you to another?"

"After ignoring me and my brother for most of our lives, Alain thinks he can play father now and tell me what to do." Alain sorely underestimated her. "He only claimed us because his legitimate sons are dead."

Jamie gripped her arm. "Who is the man he wants you to wed?"

"That snake Guy Pomeroy."

Jamie raised his eyebrows. "Your father aims high. Sir Guy is close to the Duke of Gloucester, the king's youngest brother."

"'Tis not for my benefit, you can be sure," she said, rolling her eyes. "I hate the way Sir Guy looks at me. I swear, I would put a blade in his heart before I let him near me."

"You are mine to protect now." Jamie took her hand and kissed it. "I know you loathe your father, but he must be dealt with. It will be awkward if he has already spoken with Sir Guy, but that cannot be helped."

"I have taken care of it." She had to tell Jamie now. He would be so angry he might not speak to her for days.

"Let me do this," Jamie said. "I know what assurances must be given, what pressures can be brought to bear. Your upbringing was . . . irregular. I understand these things better."

"Think about what you are saying, Jamie," she said, raising her hands in exasperation. "I am a bastard and a merchant's granddaughter. I was not raised to live the kind of life you want."

"You are of noble birth," Jamie said in a firm voice. "Everything is changed now that your father has claimed you."

"I am not changed," she said. "What you need is a dull English noblewoman who will be happy to share the boring life you are looking forward to."

"Linnet, you cannot—"

She lifted her hand to stop him. "I know how it will be. Each summer, you will come to France to fight with your glorious king. Then, each winter, you will return home to get your wife with yet another child, settle disputes among your peasants, and spend the evenings telling tiresome stories of your victories by the hearth in your hall."

"It is a good life," he said, laughing. "It only seems dull to you because you do not know it."

She took his face in her hands. "You will be furious with me, but there is something I must tell you."

"First you must promise not to speak to your father of our marriage before I do," Jamie said.

He leaned forward to kiss her but froze at the sound of voices just outside the door. As the door scraped open, he threw the bedclothes over Linnet and turned his body to block the view of her from the door.

She scooted up next to him and called out, "Good day, Alain. How fortunate you brought Sir Guy with you; he's told me many times he wished to see me naked in bed."

Both men stared at them slack-jawed for a long moment. Then her father roared, "God's blood, Linnet, what have you done?"

"Surely," she said, widening her eyes, "I need not explain it to you?"

"You said she was a virgin," Sir Guy spat out, then slapped Alain hard across the face. "I should have known a whore would beget a whore."

Sir Guy was a powerfully built man, and his violence startled her. When he turned to Jamie with murder in his eyes, she put her hand on Jamie's shoulder.

"I won't forget this," Sir Guy said in a voice so full of menace Linnet's stomach tightened. "You shall pay dearly for this one day, James Rayburn."

Jamie threw her hand off his shoulder. For the first time since the others entered the room, she looked at him. Jamie's eyes were fixed on her, wild and accusing. She heard, but did not see, Sir Guy slam the door. Sir Guy and her father did not matter anymore.

"You planned this. You wanted them to find us," Jamie said, his voice cracking. "You only went to bed with me to make your father angry. I thought...I thought you loved me."

The air went out of her, and she could not speak. God have mercy, what had she done?

"You've ripped my heart from my chest," Jamie said in a harsh whisper. "I am the world's biggest fool."

Jamie slid down from the bed, swept up his clothes from the floor in one arm, and started toward the door.

"I shall whip you within an inch of your life, girl," Alain shouted. His face was purple, his fists clenched.

Jamie grabbed Alain by the front of his tunic and lifted him off his feet. "I am tempted to murder her myself, but I will kill you if you lay a hand on her for this," he said, the threat in his voice as sharp as the edge of a dagger.

Heaven above, Jamie was magnificent, stark naked and furious.

"If you were not such a horse's arse, she would not have done it."

Jamie was defending her, which meant he was already halfway to forgiving her. She would explain it all to him. Then they could go on as before.

Jamie picked up his clothes again and walked to the door. He opened it and turned. "Send word if there is a child," he said to Alain. "I shall be in England."

Chapter One

London
October 30, 1425

The stench of the Thames made Sir James Rayburn's eyes water as he rode through the angry crowd. The "Winchester geese," the prostitutes who worked this side of the river under the bishop's regulation, would not do much business today. The men filling the street were not here to seek pleasures banned inside the City; they were spoiling for a fight.

Earlier, Jamie had crossed the river to gauge the mood within the City of London—and found it on the verge of riot.

The crowd grew thicker as he neared London Bridge. Men glared at him but moved out of the way of his warhorse. As he pushed through them, his thoughts returned to the evening before. There had been far too many men-at-arms at the bishop's palace.

Over supper, Jamie had tried to discern the bishop's intent in bringing so many armed men to Winchester Palace. Under the bishop's watchful eye, however, none of the other guests dared speak of it. Instead, they pressed Jamie for news of the fighting in France.

He obliged them, telling them of the recent battle against the dauphin's forces at Verneuil. As he warmed to his tale, the ladies leaned forward, hands pressed to their creamy bosoms. He liked to tell stories. Just when he had begun to enjoy himself, Linnet's words came back to him.

What you need, Jamie Rayburn, is a dull English wife who will be content to spend her evenings listening to you recite tiresome tales of your victories.

After all these years, Linnet's ridicule still rankled. He had brought his story to an abrupt end and left the bishop's hall for bed. Damn the woman. Five years since he'd seen her, and she could still ruin his evening.

Calling him boring was the least of Linnet's crimes against him. No matter that he was three years older and she was not quite sixteen at the time—next to her, he'd been a babe in the woods. It embarrassed him to recall how he had worn his heart on his sleeve back then. While he professed eternal love and adoration, Linnet used him without a shred of guilt or regret.

After the debacle, he left Paris at once in the hope of reaching England before his letter. But nay. He had to suffer the additional mortification of telling his family he and Linnet were not betrothed after all.

Someone should have told him that men value a woman's virginity far more than women do themselves. He had mistaken the gift of hers as a gift of her heart—and a pledge of marriage. Never again would he let a woman humiliate him like that.

That did not mean he'd sworn off women. In sooth, he had bedded any number of them in his determination to wipe Linnet's memory from his mind. Most of the time he succeeded.

Thinking of her now put him in a foul mood. God's beard, he could not breathe with all these people hemming him in. Judging by Thunder's snorts and flattened ears, his horse felt the same.

"We've seen enough," Jamie said, patting Thunder after the horse snapped at a fool who got too close.

With his untimely death, their dear and glorious King Henry had left a babe heir to two kingdoms. The Duke of Bedford, the dead king's eldest surviving brother, had the difficult tasks of governing the French territories and prosecuting the war there.

While Bedford was occupied in France, two other members of the royal family vied for control of England. The power struggle between Bedford's brother, the Duke of Gloucester, and their uncle, the Bishop of Winchester, had been simmering for months. Now that their dispute had spilled over into the streets, however, it was far more dangerous. Jamie must send a message to Bedford at once.

As Jamie turned his horse to return to the bishop's palace, someone grabbed hold of his boot. He lifted his whip but checked his arm when he saw it was an old man.

"Please, sir, help me!"

The old fellow's eye was purple with a fresh bruise. From his clothing, Jamie guessed he was not a part of the rabble, but a servant of some noble household.

Jamie leaned down. "What can I do for you?"

"The crowd separated me from my mistress," the man said, his voice high and tremulous. "Now they've taken my mule, and I cannot reach her."

Sweet Lamb of God, a lady was alone in this mob? "Where? Where is she?"

The old man pointed toward the bridge. When Jamie turned to look, he wondered how he had missed her. London Bridge was three hundred yards long, with shops and houses projecting off both sides. But in the gap created by the drawbridge, Jamie had a clear view of a lady in a bright blue and yellow gown sitting astride a white palfrey. She stuck out from the horde around her like a peacock atop a dunghill.

"Out of my way! Out of my way!" Jamie shouted, waving his whip from side to side above the heads of the crowd. Men flung themselves aside to avoid the hooves of his horse as he forced his way forward through the throng.

As he rode up onto the bridge, he heard the familiar sound of an army on the move. He turned and saw men-at-arms marching up the river from the bishop's palace. God's blood, the bishop had even sent archers.

Jamie had heard a rumor that Gloucester intended to ride to Eltham Castle to take custody of the three-year-old king. Evidently the bishop feared Gloucester's intent was to usurp the throne, for he had decided to stop his nephew at the bridge by force of arms.

God help them all.

But in the meantime, Jamie needed to rescue the fool woman caught between the forces of the two feuding royals in the goddamned middle of London Bridge.

The mass of people caught on the bridge began to panic as word spread of the men-at-arms marching toward them. As Jamie pushed his way over the first part of the bridge, their shouts echoed off the buildings that connected overhead.

He was still twenty yards from the lady when he heard her scream. Hands were grabbing at her, attempting to pull her off the horse. She fought back like a savage, striking at them with her whip.

Someone caught hold of her headdress. Despite the noise on the bridge, Jamie heard the gasps of the men around her as a cascade of white-gold hair fell over her shoulders to her hips.

The air went out of him. There was only one woman in Christendom with hair like that. Linnet.

And she was in grave danger.

"Do not touch her!" he roared. He raised his sword and pulled the reins, making Thunder rear to clear his way.

He pushed forward through the seething mass. As he fought his way the last few yards, he heard Linnet's voice over the clamor, cursing the men in both French and English.

A burly man gripped her thigh with a filthy hand, and murder roiled through Jamie. Just as Linnet raised her whip to bring it down on the man, she looked up and saw Jamie. Their gazes locked, and all the sounds around him faded away.

In that moment when she was diverted, the burly man caught her arm that held the whip. Another man yanked at her belt. Over the thunder in his ears, Jamie heard her bloodcurdling scream as they pulled her off her horse.

"Hold on!" he shouted.

She was hanging off the side, clutching at her saddle with both hands. God help him, she would be trampled to death in another moment. Her horse had remained remarkably steady until now. With its rider unsaddled, however, it was wild-eyed, tossing its head and sidestepping into the crowd. Jamie's heart went to his throat as Linnet swung sideways and slammed against her horse's side.

The men, whose hold was snapped by the horse's movement, were grasping at Linnet's skirts as the horse flung her from side to side. She was hanging on by one hand when Jamie finally broke through to her. With one sweep of his sword, he slashed the two men as he leaned down and caught Linnet around the waist with his other arm and lifted her up onto his horse.

Praise God, he had her! Now he just had to get her off this damned bridge before arrows started flying.

"My horse!" she said, twisting to look over his shoulder.

Without warning, she leaned over the side of his horse with both arms outstretched. Was the woman mad? He gripped her tighter as she reached out to catch hold of her horse's loose rein with her fingertips.

She sat up and gave him a triumphant grin as she held it up in her hand. Good God, she hadn't changed a bit. She was happiest in the midst of tumult and trouble. He wouldn't be half surprised to discover it was she, and not Gloucester, who had caused the riot.

"You gloat too soon," he said through clenched teeth. "We could be killed yet."

Her eyes flicked to the side, and she brought her whip down on an arm reaching for her horse's bridle. He turned his horse and shouted at the crowd, "Get off the bridge! Get off the bridge!"

The panicked mass of people surged against them like rolling swells against a ship at sea. Linnet ignored his repeated command to "let go of the damned horse and hold on." He had to hold her tight enough to leave bruises on her ribs, while she slashed at people who tried to grab her horse's reins.

She felt so slight against him. It seemed a miracle she had been able to fight off those men and stay on her horse for so long. But anyone who touched her now would be a dead man. Jamie was a battle-hardened knight. Now that he had her, he had no doubt he could protect her from the rabble.

Flying arrows, however, were another matter.

By a miracle, he managed to reach the end of the bridge a hairbreadth before the bishop's men blocked the way. Then he rode east along the river, away from the bridge and the crowd, until his heartbeat returned to normal.

They were a quarter mile down the river before he spoke. "What in God's name were you doing on the bridge? An idiot could see that was no place to be today."

Linnet turned around to look at him. This time, with the danger past, his heart did a flip-flop in his chest. In addition to everything else she was, did she have to be so beautiful? It was the curse of his life.

"'Tis nice to see you, too, Jamie Rayburn." She cocked her head and raised an eyebrow. "After all this time, I expected a better greeting."

He fixed his gaze dead ahead and grunted. God in heaven, how could she be so cool after what had just happened on the bridge?

When she leaned lightly against him, his chest prickled with sensation. Lust and longing took him like a fever. He should put her on her own horse now. He wanted to pretend she was too distressed to ride alone, but the thought was ridiculous. This one small weakness he would allow himself. It meant nothing.

"I heard you were with Bedford in France," she said.

"Hmmph."

"When did you arrive in London?"

"Yesterday."

After a long pause, she said, "Are you going to tell me what you are doing in England?"

"Nay."

"Or ask why I am here?"

"Nay."

He felt her sigh against his chest. Against his will, he remembered other sighs, other times...

He had to get rid of her. "I trust your servant will make his own way back. Where shall I deliver you?"

"The bishop's palace," she said. "I can find someone there to escort me to my lodgings."

Good. It was best he not know where she was staying. Not that he would seek her out, but a wise man avoided temptation where Linnet was concerned.

Taking a longer route to avoid the mob, he worked his way back to the bishop's palace. Even over the stink of the city and the river, he could smell the tangy scent of citrus in her hair. The memory of burying his face in it hit him like a punch to the gut.

As soon as he saw Linnet safely inside the palace, he left her.

He went at once to the bishop, who accepted his offer to help mediate the dispute with Gloucester. For the rest of the day, the crisis kept him far too busy to dwell on his encounter with Linnet. He and the other emissaries traveled back and forth across the river eight times, attempting to forge a compromise. It was late in the night before the two feuding royals finally agreed to terms.

Jamie fell into bed exhausted. With the country on the brink of civil war, he had managed to push all thought of Linnet aside while he was awake. But near dawn, he was tormented by a dream of her. Not the annoying, sentimental sort of dream he often had in the early days after he left Paris. Nay, this was a raw, sensual dream of her writhing above him, crying out his name. He awoke gasping for air.

He needed a woman, that much was clear.

But first, duty called. The Duke of Bedford had sent him home from France with two tasks. Last night, he had fulfilled the first by sending Bedford his report on the conflict between Gloucester and the bishop.

This morning, he must attend to his second assignment: keeping the young, widowed queen safe in the crisis. He owed this duty not just to Bedford, but to his dead king. But perhaps he could combine duty with pleasure. If past experience was any judge, one of the ladies at court would be happy to be his bedmate for a time.

He started the six-mile ride to Eltham Palace as soon as he broke his fast. Shortly after he arrived, he was taken to the queen's private parlor. As he entered, Queen Katherine, a fragile-looking woman of twenty-four, rose to greet him.

"Your Highness," he said, dropping to one knee.

When he looked up, he caught the flicker of sadness in her eyes and knew he reminded her of that awful day at Vincennes, outside Paris. He was one of the knights who had carried the dying king into the castle, where the queen waited for him.

"I am so very pleased you have come, Sir James," she said, holding her hand out for his kiss. She looked past him and smiled. "As I believe my friend is also, no?"

He turned to follow the queen's gaze.

Linnet swept past him to stand beside Queen Katherine. With her stubborn jaw and her chin tilted up, she looked more regal than the queen. And here he was on his knees, groveling at her feet once more.

At the queen's nod, he got up.

"My friend says you would not tell her what brings you back to England," the queen said with a coquettish smile. "But you dare not refuse me."

"I have come at the behest of the Duke of Bedford, who is concerned for your comfort and well-being." He could not tell her of Bedford's other charge to him.

"He has always been kind to me," the queen said in a soft voice. She did not need to add, *unlike Gloucester.*

"I have an errand of my own, as well," Jamie added, surprising himself. "I have come home to marry."

Linnet's quick intake of breath was gratifying.

The queen clapped her hands. "How delightful!"

"I have so many tiresome tales of my victories to tell," he said, "that I really must take a wife."

The queen laughed, though she could not have understood the jest. Turning to Linnet, she asked, "What sort of lady should we find for our handsome James?"

Linnet looked at him with her direct, ice-blue eyes and said, "I think he should please himself."

Oblivious to the edge in Linnet's voice, the queen clasped her hands together and beamed at him. "Tell us, Sir James, what lady would please you?"

"A dull English lady," Jamie said, turning to meet Linnet's steady gaze. "The kind who makes a virtuous wife."

Chapter Two

Linnet dug her nails into her palms to fight back the sting in her eyes and kept her expression passive.

A virtuous wife, indeed.

How could Jamie be so cruel as to deliberately insult her? And to what purpose? Was it not enough that he deserted her five years ago without a backward glance? After swearing his undying devotion, he had left without giving her a single chance to explain.

She'd had her reasons for what she did. Good reasons. Who was he to judge her? Jamie grew up in the bosom of a large and politically powerful family, with devoted parents who looked out for him. She had been a young girl with few choices.

To take control of her fate, bold action was required. She did what she had to do. Jamie did not even try to understand.

She had succeeded in avoiding marriage to that lecherous, devil-eyed Guy Pomeroy. And then, before Alain could marry her off to someone else of his choosing, she acted quickly to arrange a marriage for herself.

Just like that, she got herself out from under Alain's

thumb. 'Twas most satisfying. Alain had been appalled and outraged in equal measure, but there was nothing he could do. The man she chose was too powerful. Her twin brother, Francois, had argued bitterly with her over the marriage, telling her she was cutting off her nose to spite her face.

But it had been worth it. All her plans were falling into place. Except for this awful ache that pressed on her heart whenever she thought of Jamie Rayburn, there was nothing she would change.

She stared at him as he spoke to the queen, trying to find the tender young man she once knew. This Sir James had the same long dark hair, the same striking midnight-blue eyes. Each feature was familiar; yet, he was not the same.

He was all hard angles now. It was not just that his face was leaner, his body more muscular. Jamie always had the confidence and fearlessness he showed on the bridge yesterday. But before, there had also been a sweetness to him that he sometimes showed her. There was no trace of that in the man before her.

He was telling the queen about yesterday's events in the City. Apparently, he was unaware of Queen Katherine's astonishing lack of interest in politics.

The queen gave him a pleasant smile and picked up her skirts. "'Tis time for us to join the others for dinner."

"Your Grace, we must speak now," Jamie said. "Gloucester will be here in two hours."

The queen stood stock-still, staring at him with wide eyes. "Gloucester is coming? Here to Eltham?"

"Under the compromise with the bishop, your son is to travel to Westminster with Gloucester. However, they will be escorted by men trusted by both Gloucester and the bishop."

"You speak as if the king were a grown man and not a child of three," the queen said in a pinched voice. "But if that is what they have decided to do, there is nothing I can do about it."

Jamie met the queen's gaze squarely; they all knew she was powerless in this fight.

"Shall I be permitted to accompany my son?" Since the Council had ordered a separate household be set up for the king, the queen could no longer presume she would travel with her son.

"You are invited to come to Westminster," Jamie said. "But it is suggested that when the king returns to Eltham a few days hence, you remove yourself to Windsor Palace.

"You will be safe there from the turmoil here in London," Jamie added in a softer voice. "The king will join you in just a few weeks, for the Council has decided Christmas Court will be held at Windsor this year."

The queen picked up her skirts again and brushed past Jamie on her way to the door.

Usually it was Linnet who attempted to alert the queen to the risks and realities around her. Her friend, however, preferred not to hear about events she felt helpless to influence. If she could not avoid unpleasant news altogether, she pushed it aside as quickly as she could.

Linnet drew in a deep breath and attempted to walk past Jamie as the queen had done, but he caught her arm.

"What are you doing here, Linnet?"

She jerked her arm from his grip. "I thought you did not wish to know."

"I have a duty to protect the queen from every sort of danger," he said. "Tell me why you are here."

She glared at him. "Because she asked me."

She turned and marched toward the door. With his longer strides, he reached it first. He stood in front of it, arms folded across his chest, blocking her way.

"Why did she ask you?" he said. "And why did you come?"

"Because I am her friend, and she is friendless here," she said, clenching her fists. "They have taken her only child from her care, and she cannot even choose his nursemaids. They treat her so poorly, it is almost as if they believe she is in league with her brother, the dauphin."

Linnet's heart fluttered as Jamie leaned closer.

In a low voice, he asked, "Is she?"

"Of course not!" she said, taking a step back. "Our French princess was raised to never have an opinion, to avoid conflict at any cost, and to do exactly as she was told."

"That has served her well," Jamie said. "I hate to think what you might be teaching her."

"I would not let her make the mistake of supporting the dauphin," she hissed at him. "A poorer excuse for a king I hope to never see."

"So you are the queen's confidante?" Jamie asked.

"I am exceedingly fond of her, and I do try to advise her..." Linnet raised her hands in the air. "But when I warn her she must walk a careful line between Gloucester and Bishop Beaufort, she responds by asking what they are wearing now in Paris."

She took a deep breath and made herself stop speaking. With the news that Gloucester was about to arrive, she was out of her mind with worry about the queen. And then, Jamie's pointed remark about virtuous wives had upset her further.

"What you said was unfair," she said, her eyes hot on his. "I never said you were boring. I merely said I did not want that kind of life."

His eyes sparked blue fire, and she had the satisfaction of breaking through his facade of calm control. Jamie could make nasty allusions all he wanted, but he did not expect her to speak directly about what happened between them five years ago.

He clenched his fists and leaned forward, as if to shout in her face. She hoped he did. Instead, he stepped back. With his jaw tight, he stretched his neck, tilting his head from side to side.

When he spoke, his voice was as calm as pond water. "We had best join the queen for dinner."

She refused to take the arm he offered. The walk down the stairs and the endless corridor took forever.

"I am surprised you are still looking for a wife," she said to goad him. "Surely you found another innocent virgin to seduce into marriage."

He grabbed her arm and spun her around. "I did not seduce you, as you know damned well."

"Hmmph." She turned her head and tilted her chin up. She could not contradict him; that did not mean she had to agree.

He released his grip on her arm and blew out his breath.

"What method will you use to get a wife then?" she asked as they resumed walking down the corridor. "Since you are unlikely to win her with your excessive charm, I assume you will have your family arrange it?"

"That is the customary method," he bit out. "But I have reason to hope Bedford or his uncle will suggest an appropriate lady."

He must have impressed Bedford, indeed, to have the royal family facilitating a match.

"An appropriate lady, meaning a very rich one?" she asked in her sweetest possible voice. "And virtuous, of course."

The muscles of Jamie's jaw tightened, and he kept his eyes straight ahead.

"Rich and virtuous. Qualities to *satisfy*"—she paused over the word—"any man, I'm sure."

They had finally reached the hall, so she left Jamie without a backward glance and went in search of Edmund Beaufort. Young, handsome, brilliant—and unmarried—Edmund was the brightest hope of the next generation of Beauforts. And Linnet had an urgent need to speak to him.

When she spotted him, she wanted to groan aloud. How many times had she warned the queen to avoid showing favor to this particular young man, above all others? But nay, Queen Katherine must go straight to Edmund with a bright smile, take his arm, and invite him to sit in the seat of honor beside her.

Linnet could have slapped her for being so stupid. Nay, the queen was not stupid. She simply had a flirtatious nature. After a girlhood in a convent and marriage to the glorious King Henry, it was only now coming into bloom.

Linnet would wager all she owned that Edmund Beaufort had been instructed by his uncle to woo the queen. No doubt, Edmund found the queen charming and pretty, for she was. But he was a Beaufort; it was a calculated move. If Edmund became the young king's stepfather, he could yield untold influence on the boy for years to come.

The prospect of that occurring would send Gloucester into apoplexy. If rumor of the queen's flirtation with Edmund had reached Gloucester's ears, that would explain why he had acted so rashly, raising that fervor in London.

Nearly everyone else was seated, so Linnet hurried to take her place at the end of the high table. Ignoring the attempts of the men on either side to engage her in conversation, she kept watch on the queen and Edmund.

The saints preserve her! The queen and Edmund were staring into each other's eyes. When the queen fed Edmund an oyster with her fingers, Linnet put away her eating knife. She had to get Edmund away from Eltham before Gloucester arrived.

Jamie, who sat at the other end of the table, was also watching the queen and Beaufort—with a sour expression on his face. Suddenly, his gaze shifted, and their eyes locked. Why did Jamie Rayburn have to be here now? She would not let the tumultuous emotions he provoked distract her.

Nor did she intend to listen to any more of his damned insults. She broke the gaze and stood.

She walked behind the high table and whispered her excuse in the queen's ear. "If my dinner companion attempts to put his hand on my leg one more time, I am sure to cause a scene." Raising her voice enough for Edmund Beaufort to hear, she said, "Will you forgive me, Your Grace, if I escape for a short ride?"

"Of course," the queen said, "if you promise to tell me later which one it was."

Linnet straightened and met Beaufort's gaze before she left.

Just outside the entrance to the hall, she stopped a squire. "Could you deliver a message for me?"

The squire stared at her with wide eyes. "I am happy to be of service, m'lady. Anything you ask."

He sucked in his breath as she leaned closer. "Count to one hundred," she said next to his ear. "Then go tell Edmund Beaufort I await him in the stables."

She straightened and put a finger to her lips. "Don't let anyone else hear you give him the message."

As soon as the meal was finished, Jamie went to find Edmund Beaufort. The compromise that was reached last night would be blown apart if the queen made a fool of herself with Edmund Beaufort in front of Gloucester. After a quick search of the castle, he caught sight of his new squire, Martin.

"Help me find Edmund Beaufort," he said.

The lad turned a bright shade of red. What was the matter with him?

"Have you tried the stables?" Martin asked.

"Why? Did you see him go there?"

"He was heading in that direction," Martin said. "He seemed in a hurry."

"Perhaps the man had the sense to leave on his own," Jamie said, more to himself than to his squire.

Martin cleared his throat. "I don't believe his thoughts were on leaving."

"Why do you say that?"

Martin looked pained. "I cannot tell you."

God's beard. "Then I shall find out for myself," he spat out.

Jamie wondered if he had made a mistake in taking on Martin as his squire. He'd done so only because the knight the lad had been serving died in France.

As he stalked to the stables, his mind returned to Linnet—and her nasty remark about a wealthy and virtuous wife being sufficient to "satisfy" him. Perhaps he should have told her he also wished for a wife who could make him forget his name in bed. But only one woman had ever been able to do that.

The moment he walked through the door of the stables, he saw the very one. Linnet stood with her back to him, stroking and talking to the white palfrey she had ridden on the bridge.

He held his breath as she took the horse's head between her hands and kissed its forehead. Now he knew why the horse would follow her through a riot.

Jamie stepped into the shadows as Edmund Beaufort came out from the interior of the stable with a page who was leading his horse. Linnet turned and gave Beaufort a dazzling smile.

So it was Linnet who had brought Beaufort to the stables. Jamie would have to ask Martin how he knew.

"Thank you," Linnet said to Beaufort. "Leaving Eltham now is the only wise course."

Beaufort took her hand. "Come with me."

"I cannot leave the queen alone with Gloucester," she said, laughter tinkling in her voice. "He'd eat her alive and toss away the bones."

"Before I go, I must tell you," Beaufort said, lifting her hand to his lips, "you are the most exciting woman I have ever known."

"I can hardly count that a compliment, sir, when you are but nineteen and have spent the last seven years as a hostage."

Beaufort laughed. "'Twas a gilded jail. I was not completely deprived of female company."

"Cavorting with dauphinists, were you? For shame. Just wait until I tell your uncle."

The blood roared in Jamie's ears. He remembered how often he had been wrenched with jealousy in the weeks they were together in Paris. How many times had he watched other men approach her? Being in love with a beautiful woman had been hell on earth. He'd borne it without killing anyone only because he believed Linnet would never go with another man. Fool that he was, he had believed she loved him.

Edmund Beaufort spoke again. "I do love the queen—"

Linnet interrupted him with a snort.

"But she is a bit...simple. If I could marry whom I wished, I would choose you."

Jamie wanted to vomit.

"Was it your great-uncle Geoffrey Chaucer who taught you to speak with that silver tongue?" Linnet's voice was laden with sarcasm.

"If you were my mistress, you could advise me," Beaufort said. "Think of all we could accomplish together."

"And I am sure listening to my advice is all you have in mind," Linnet said, giving Beaufort's arm what looked like a hard pinch. "Come, Edmund, you must be gone now."

Suddenly, Beaufort had Linnet flattened against his chest. With a wicked smile, he said, "My price for leaving is a kiss."

"Beaufort," Jamie said, stepping out from the shadows. "The lady gives you wise counsel. You should go quickly."

The scoundrel gave a deep sigh before releasing her.

"I beg you to consider my proposal," Beaufort said in a low voice as he brought Linnet's hand to his lips yet again. "*Adieu, ma belle. Adieu.*"

As soon as Beaufort went to join his men-at-arms waiting outside the stable, Jamie said, "I would advise you not to become entangled with Edmund Beaufort."

Linnet turned wide eyes on him. "Entangled with Edmund?"

"I suppose you will say you were only flirting with him to protect your friend?"

"Someone had to get him to leave." She shrugged. "'Tis dangerous for the queen to flirt with Edmund, but there is no harm in my doing it."

"And if flirting is not enough to divert him from the queen, what then?"

She put her hands on her hips and glared at him for a long moment. Then she turned and called out to two stable lads who were forking hay on the other side of the stable.

"Could one of you saddle my horse for me?"

Both lads came running. In the blink of an eye, the damned horse was saddled and ready.

"When you see the queen, tell her I will meet her at Westminster tomorrow," she said to Jamie as she pulled on riding gloves. "Don't leave her alone with Gloucester."

Jamie followed her out and watched as the two boys jostled each other to help her mount her horse.

When she was on it, Jamie asked through clenched teeth, "Where shall I tell the queen you've gone?"

"I have matters to attend to in the City," she said.

Matters involving Edmund Beaufort and a bed? Blood pulsed in his head and hands.

"Private matters," she added, to twist the blade, "that are of no concern to you."

He watched as she galloped off after Beaufort on her white horse. Damn the woman.

Chapter Three

Linnet strode through the wool merchant's house, her heart pounding in her ears. The smell of the river seeped through the walls and permeated the air, carrying with it a flood of memories.

As she moved from room to room, she gave instructions to the clerk trailing behind her.

"Sell that... and that," she said, pointing to an ornately carved chair and a side table as she passed. Most of the furniture had not belonged to her family, and so she did not want it.

This had been their London house. For as long as she could remember, she, Francois, and their grandfather had stayed here when their grandfather made his twice-yearly trip to trade with the London merchants. It was never grand like their houses in Falaise and Calais. Still, it seemed much smaller and shabbier than in her memory.

As with most merchant houses, her grandfather had conducted his trade on the ground floor. The kitchen was behind the house, and the family's solar and bedchambers were above the shop.

Linnet paused on the threshold to the solar. She smiled,

remembering the evenings she and Francois had spent playing chess or backgammon on the floor by the coal brazier.

"Anything you wish to keep in this room?" her clerk asked.

A footstool in the corner caught her eye. She swallowed against the lump in her throat as she recalled lifting her grandfather's feet onto it at the end of a long day.

"Send that to my new house," she said.

"The stool, m'lady?" The clerk looked up from the sheet of vellum he carried and raised his thin white eyebrows. "'Tis in very poor condition."

At her nod, he put his nose to the sheet and scratched another note. She left him in the solar to step into the adjoining bedchamber.

Her throat closed, and she could not breathe.

Suddenly, she was eleven years old again, hiding under that heavy, dark oak bed with her brother. Hearts racing and holding hands, she and Francois had watched the men's feet move about the bedchamber. Sweat broke out on her palms as she remembered the men's voices, arguing over who would take what, and the silver end of a cane pounding on the floor.

She turned around so quickly that she jostled the old clerk and had to catch him by the arm. "Why don't you rest here in the solar, Master Woodley, while I go up to the attic? 'Tis unlikely there is anything there worth keeping, and the stairs are steep."

"Thank you kindly, m'lady," he said, bobbing his head.

She left quickly, knowing he would not sit in her presence.

The walls and low ceiling closed in on her as she climbed the narrow steps to the two tiny rooms under the roof.

None of this was turning out quite as she'd expected. For five long years, she had worked diligently to achieve her goals. First, she married Louis to gain the funds and independence she needed to restart her grandfather's business. Working through her brother, she had gradually built her trade in cloth.

Then she was ready. Her first attack was in their home city of Falaise, where they had retreated after losing everything in London and Calais. In half a year, she destroyed the trade of the "dear old friends" there who had taken advantage of her grandfather in his long illness.

As she had suspected, the men in Falaise were not the ones who had orchestrated the demise of her grandfather's business. They were merely the vultures who picked at the remaining pieces left in Falaise.

From Falaise, she followed the trail of guilt to her grandfather's former business partners in Calais. Those men were more sophisticated and clever. It took her four years to grow her business sufficiently to take them on one by one. Each of the Calais partners had taken a share of her grandfather's trade and property. None of them, however, received the lion's share.

When she finally had one of them in debt to her up to his ears, he confessed. A London merchant had been behind the scheme to ruin her grandfather's business. The men in Calais never knew the London merchant's name; all communication had been through intermediaries.

The queen's letter asking Linnet to visit had come at an opportune time. The two of them had formed an unlikely friendship during the months Linnet spent in Paris before she escaped her father's care. From the start, she felt protective toward the naive princess who came to the decadent court straight from the convent.

Linnet would do her best by her friend. But while she was here in London, she also intended to discover the identity of the shadowy figure who was her greatest enemy.

Finding him would be difficult, of course. London merchants resented foreign merchants and would protect one of their own. But she had the very finest Flemish cloth to be found in London. To get his hands on it, a London merchant might be willing to forget that she was both a foreigner and a woman.

Mychell was one of the men whose voices she heard from under the bed that awful day. But he was only a lackey, a bit player in the scheme. He was not clever enough to plan the demise of a business with interests from Normandy to Flanders. This house had been Mychell's reward for the part he played. She should feel triumphant throwing him out.

But she did not.

Mychell did not know who had driven him into debt until yesterday, when they met to sign the deed. She swallowed back the bile in her throat as she recalled her meeting with the greasy-haired rodent.

"If you just give me a little time," he had said, sweat breaking out on his brow, "I shall be able to pay."

"Time will not help you." She leaned across the table and pounded it with her fist. "Do you not know who I am?"

Startled by her outburst, Mychell sat back in his chair and stared at her. She could tell the moment he recognized her, for his eyes widened with surprise—but not a trace of shame.

"Shall I leave you as much as you left two orphaned children?" she asked him.

"'Tis not my fault your grandfather died in poverty," the man protested.

But she knew better. She had a gift for figures. It took her years to piece it all together, but she knew exactly how much had been stolen from them and how. They started with shorting payments and claiming goods were not delivered and moved up from there. The death knell came when they intercepted her grandfather's huge annual payment to the weavers in Flanders, which ruined relationships he had built over a lifetime.

Even as a child of ten, she had known something was wrong with the accounts. When she shared her suspicions with her grandfather, he was too good-hearted to believe his friends would steal from him. The theft grew more and more blatant. But by then, her grandfather was far too confused to understand.

"Do not bother to deny it," she spat at Mychell. "I heard you dividing up the spoils. You could not even wait for us to leave London to do it."

Linnet looked around, startled to find herself on the small landing at the top of the stairs. How long had she been standing here? She shook her head to clear it of the wretched man.

On either side of her, the doors led to the matching rooms that she and Francois had slept in. She pushed open the one on the right and ducked under the low frame to enter her old bedchamber. The same narrow bed filled most of the cramped space under the sloping roof. How often had she opened that shutter to watch the stars as she made up stories of knights and princesses? Back then, she never expected to meet a princess, let alone befriend one.

She shook her head again. What was wrong with her today? She did not come up here to dream, but to find something. In their hurry to leave London that night, she had forgotten her most prized possession.

There was little chance of it still being where she hid it, but she had to look. She dropped to her knees beside the bed and slipped her hand between the mattress and the ropes. Nothing. The musty smell of the straw made her sneeze as she reached farther. Grunting, she pushed her arm in all the way to her shoulder. Still nothing.

She got down on all fours and stuck her head under the bed. It was too dark to see a thing under there. She sat up coughing—and nearly choked when she heard the sound behind her.

C-r-e-a-k.

The thin blade she kept up her sleeve was already in her hand as she jerked her head around to look. The top of the old chest at the end of the bed slowly lifted to reveal a girl with a headful of springy red curls.

"Saints above," Linnet said, slapping her hand against her chest. "You startled the wits out of me!"

Apparently, Mychell had forgotten one of his belongings when he moved out this morning. The girl, whom Linnet guessed to be seven or eight, pushed the trunk lid all the way back and stepped out.

"Are you the one who has taken our house?" the girl asked.

What was she to say to that? Linnet sat back on the floor and wrapped her arms around her knees. Finally, she said, "This used to be my house."

"Was this your bedchamber as well?"

Linnet nodded.

Tilting her head, the girl asked, "What are you looking for?"

"A polished steel mirror." After a pause, she added, "It was all I had of my mother's." Odd, that she felt she needed to justify herself to this little girl.

The girl held her gaze and then walked around to the other side of the bed.

"I moved it," she said as the top of her red curls disappeared from view. A moment later, she popped back up with the long-lost mirror in her hand.

"Thank you," Linnet whispered when the girl brought it to her. She ran her finger over the familiar bumps of the flowered pattern on the back, which was black with tarnish.

She took a deep breath and gathered herself. Attempting a smile, she asked, "What is your name?"

"Lily."

"You are a remarkable girl, Lily."

"'Tis what my sister says." The girl's bright smile faded, and her gaze drifted to the side. "My brothers call me other names."

"How many brothers do you have?"

"Lots." The girl made a sour face that made Linnet suspect the boys took after their father. The poor thing.

Linnet reached through the slit in her gown to fish out a coin from her pouch. "I can see you are good at hiding things, so keep this safe from your brothers." *And from that filthy, moneygrubbing father of yours.* "It is payment for returning the mirror."

When she took Lily's hand and placed a gold florin in her palm, the girl gasped.

"And here is my ring." Linnet twisted it off her little finger and put it in Lily's other hand. "If you are ever in trouble, show this to my clerk, Master Woodley. He will find my brother or me, and one of us will help you."

Lily closed her fingers over the ring and nodded. Clearly, this was a girl who had learned to expect trouble. Linnet gave Lily directions to her clerk's rooms and made her repeat them twice.

"Your family will return soon," Linnet said as she got to her feet. "Wait for me downstairs, and I will take you for a meat pie while we wait for your father."

When Linnet entered the solar, her clerk's eyes flew open and he fumbled to his feet.

"Tell Mychell to meet me in an hour to hear my offer," she told him. "If he gives me what I want, I will forgive the debt and let him keep the house."

The clerk put his hand to his chest, as if her words pained him. "But the man has nothing left of value."

She smiled at him. "I did get the stool."

"How should I have known the thieving maggot would breed like a rabbit?" she complained to her brother that evening. "I cannot throw his wife and children out onto the street."

She and Francois were relaxing with her best wine in the house on the Strand she had purchased the week before.

"Revenge is proving more complicated than you antici-pated." Francois lifted his glass to her with a sparkle in his eyes. "Perhaps now you'll have the sense to leave jus-tice to God."

She smiled at him over the brim of her cup. "You know me better than that."

He gave a long-suffering sigh. "Linnet, you are good at business. If you were not set on using your trade for revenge, you could make a fortune."

"I intend to do both," she said. "'Tis difficult here in London because of the lock the guilds have on trade. But I have a plan now."

"I beg you, do not tell me yet," Francois said, putting his hands up. "Let me enjoy one more hour of peace."

They grinned at each other, then Linnet squeezed his hand. "How lucky I am to have you for a brother."

They sat in comfortable silence, their feet propped up on their grandfather's stool, watching the burning coals in the brazier.

After a while, Francois said, "I hear Jamie Rayburn is in London."

"He is." Linnet took a long drink of her wine. "I have seen him."

"More than once, I hear tell."

She rolled her eyes. "What do you do, bribe the servants? Sleep with the queen's ladies-in-waiting?"

Francois winked and shrugged one shoulder. "Whatever I must." He picked up the flask from the small table between them and poured more wine into their cups. "How is he?"

"Vile."

Francois threw his head back and laughed. "I take it he did not fall at your feet this time."

Linnet slapped her brother's arm.

"He did play the dashing knight, braving a violent horde of Londoners to rescue me from the bridge," she said, fighting a smile. "I was managing quite well without his help, but he did look magnificent."

Francois sat up straight. "You were on London Bridge the day of the riots?"

"As you can see, I am none the worse for it," Linnet said with an impatient wave of her fingers. "But you should have seen Jamie—*Sir James*, rather. He charged across the bridge like Saint George toward the dragon."

"That does not sound too vile to me," Francois said.

"He was horrid afterward. And even worse when he came to Eltham."

"Poor man," Francois said, shaking his head. "After all his effort to avoid you in France, he comes home to find you here."

When she failed to laugh, Francois turned and gave her a penetrating look. It could be both good and bad to have a twin who could read you like a book. She turned her face away to make it more difficult for him.

"I am sorry if he was unkind to you," Francois said in a soft voice. "The two of you tore each other apart. By the saints, I could never see the cause for it."

"Well, 'tis clear he places all the blame on me," she said.

"Five years gone, and he is still that angry."

"Aye, he will hate me forever."

"Nay, he *wants* to hate you," Francois said, raising his forefinger and smiling. "That, my dear sister, is not the same thing at all."

Chapter Four

*P*raise God, the queen had agreed to leave for Windsor in two days. Jamie would rather fight a dozen battles than remain at Westminster Palace.

From morning till night, he traversed the dangerous no-man's-land between Gloucester and the London merchant guilds on the one hand, and Bishop Beaufort and the Council on the other. The two camps were locked in a struggle for control over the kingdom—and a child-king not yet four years old.

Jamie felt out of his element in this palace fight. Give him a sword in his hand, any day. Still, he was doing his best to keep the queen from being trampled in the melee.

If that was not more than enough trouble for any man, Linnet was here. She moved between the camps with ease, courted by men from both sides of the conflict. And Jamie had to watch it.

He turned to find two of the queen's French ladies-in-waiting hovering nearby. Though both were vaguely attractive, he could never remember which was which.

"Good day, ladies," he said and bowed. "May I escort you to the table?"

The women would likely starve before one of the other men would take them. How could anyone suspect these silly women of being spies?

"*Merci*, Sir James," the ladies twittered as each took an arm.

He took his seat between them for another insufferably grand meal. When he looked up, he saw that his ill luck was holding. In this gathering of notables, both he and Linnet were seated "below the salt," at tables perpendicular to the high table. She sat directly opposite him.

And Edmund Beaufort, whose status surely afforded him a place at the high table, was sitting next to her.

"Do you see that gown on Lady Eleanor Cobham?" one of his dinner companions said, leaning forward to whisper across him to her friend. "If she sneezes, her breasts will fall out."

"And that headdress," the other replied in a low voice. "A high wind, and she shall be carried out to sea."

Jamie pulled at the neck of his tunic and wondered if he could leave now without insulting them. To avoid looking at Linnet, he turned his attention to the high table and saw that the ladies did not exaggerate about Eleanor's gown. But then, Eleanor never had been subtle.

Her lover, Humphrey, Duke of Gloucester, sat in the seat of honor next to the boy-king. Though it was not yet noon, Gloucester was soused. He had won this round against his uncle and was celebrating. Because Gloucester was Protector and Defender of England, the bishop's threat to use force to prevent his crossing the river could be interpreted as treason. Consequently, the bishop had been forced to apologize for the confrontation on the bridge.

But Jamie thought Gloucester celebrated too soon. Gloucester was full of bombast and bluster, but he lacked his uncle's perseverance. While he was here making a drunken fool of himself, the bishop was across the river plotting his next twelve moves.

Jamie would put his money on the bishop every time. 'Twas fortunate, indeed, that Bishop Beaufort's interests coincided with the kingdom's.

Jamie felt sorry for the queen, who sat on the other side of her son, looking pale and cowed. It annoyed him to see how Gloucester's gaze kept settling on Linnet. He reminded himself, yet again, that she was not his concern. If any woman could fend for herself, it was Linnet. Besides, her brother was here. Francois was used to the onerous task of looking out for his sister.

"Why is Lady Eleanor looking at Linnet as if she'd like to put poison in her soup?" one of his companions whispered.

Behind her hand, the lady on his other side said, "She has a stare that would shrivel plums to prunes."

Apparently, Gloucester's mistress had noticed his wandering eye as well. Knowing what he did about Eleanor, Jamie found that even more worrisome. He would have to warn Francois.

Gloucester rose from his chair, drawing the attention of everyone in the hall. "Sir Guy! Welcome!" His voice rang out as he raised his cup in greeting. "Come join our fine feast!"

God help him, did he have to deal with that horse's arse Pomeroy as well?

Although he and Pomeroy did their best to avoid each other, the circle of noblemen around the Lancaster royals was small. Consequently, Jamie had seen Pomeroy several times both here and in France. But he had not been in the same room with both Pomeroy and Linnet since—

Since that day in Paris when Pomeroy found the two of them in bed.

Jamie glanced at Linnet. She had gone deathly pale.

Sir Guy strode to the center of the room and swept a low bow before the high table. After greeting the royals, he turned and dipped his head to Linnet. Linnet's mouth tightened; she did not return the courtesy.

While everyone was watching Pomeroy take his seat at the high table, Linnet got quietly to her feet and left the hall. Edmund Beaufort did not go with her.

With Linnet gone, Jamie thought he could relax and concentrate on his food. But the queen's lady on his right—*Joan? Joanna?*—kept touching his arm and giggling in his ear. Then the other one began to rub her foot up his leg. He began to sweat.

A short time later, Francois appeared at his side. Francois did not say a word, but jerked his head toward the door.

"Excuse me, ladies," Jamie said and got up at once to follow Francois out. As he passed the table where Martin sat with several other squires, he caught Martin's eye and nodded.

As soon as Jamie and Francois were away from the prying ears of the hall, Francois said, "Pomeroy just left the hall. I fear he followed my sister."

"Then we must find her first." Jamie turned and waved to Martin to follow them.

"I told her not to do it, but she would not listen," Francois said as they started down one of the long, dark corridors. "'Twas like stepping on a venomous snake and then poking a stick at it."

Apparently Linnet had done something to Pomeroy in addition to arranging for him to discover her in bed with Jamie. "How did she poke a stick at him?"

"You did not know?" Francois turned cornflower-blue eyes on him that were the exact same shade as Linnet's.

Damn, it was unnerving how much the two looked alike.

"Linnet married Pomeroy's uncle. His great-uncle."

Jamie's stomach went sour imagining an old man's hands on her.

"She had Pomeroy sweating every moment for fear his uncle would get her with child." With a sideways glance, Francois added, "You see, Pomeroy was his heir."

"I swear, your sister walks into trouble every chance she gets," Jamie said, picking up his pace to a trot.

"The worst part is that she believes she can handle trouble alone," Francois said.

"Go straight," Jamie said as they came to an intersecting corridor. "I'll take Martin and look down this one."

As Jamie moved down the dim corridor, opening doors, he told himself he was lucky Linnet had refused him five years ago. If she were his wife, he would be an old man by now.

With her heart pounding in her chest, Linnet walked as quickly as she could without running outright. She turned down a corridor, though she had no idea where it led. She was not even sure which part of the palace she was in now. Her only plan was to put as much distance as possible between her and Pomeroy.

As she came to another corner, she glanced over her shoulder. No one was behind her, praise God! She blew her breath out as she rounded the corner.

And then she ran headlong into Pomeroy.

In an instant, his arm was locked around her waist and his hand was over her mouth. She kicked and tried to bite him as he backed through the nearest door. When his hand slipped from her mouth, she drew in a deep breath to scream. Before she could get it out, a knife was at her throat.

Panic pounded through her veins.

"Can I not have a private word with you without all this fuss?" Pomeroy said next to her ear.

He smelled of onions and dank sweat covered by a heavy, sweet scent that made her gag.

"Can I?" he said, and she felt the sting of the blade against her throat.

She nodded.

He dragged her across the room to the far wall, next to three tall windows. Rain and wind beat against the windows, like the storm raging inside her. Gripping her chin, Pomeroy studied her in the dim light, as if taking in every curve and shadow.

"As exquisite as ever," he said on a long breath. "God is a jester to give this much beauty to such a worthless creature."

She willed herself to regain her calm. Somehow, she must outwit him and get away.

"I have a bone to pick with you, my dear," he said.

"You might," she agreed in a tight voice. Then she let her anger get the better of her and added, "But I am sorry for nothing."

He gripped her chin tighter, and she flinched in spite of herself.

"I believe you are sorry—sorry you failed to steal my inheritance," he said, his spittle hitting her face.

"If I had wanted to take it, I could have."

His eye twitched. "What are you saying?"

When she did not answer, he spun her around, twisting her arm behind her back.

"Tell me."

When she shook her head, he twisted her arm until sweat broke out on her forehead.

"I took herbs so I would not get pregnant," she gasped.

He turned her back around to face him. Her arm tingled and ached as the blood flowed back into it.

"And all this time, I thought my uncle was too feeble to raise his banner," he said in a mocking tone. "Still, you must have had to work hard to get it up."

"Don't be disgusting."

"You've no notion what I am capable of," he said, his dark eyes snapping. "Take off your headdress. Now."

"I will not. Ouch!" She held on to it as he tugged at it with one hand, ripping her hair out by the roots and making her scalp burn. "Ouch! Ouch!"

When he wrenched it off her head, hairpins flew across the room and bounced on the floor. He gave her a hard shove in the middle of her back, causing her to stumble and fall forward on her hands and knees. Then he grabbed her by the hair and roped it around his hand. Tears burned the back of her eyes as he jerked her up to her knees.

The musty smell of his private parts in front of her face made her nauseous. She clawed at his hand—but stopped when the edge of his blade touched her cheek.

"I know how to tame a demon harlot."

The blade stung, and she felt a drop of blood slide down her cheek. She started to shake uncontrollably.

"Now you are going to do for me what you did for my uncle." He nudged her with his knee. "Untie the laces of my chausses."

Chapter Five

Jamie opened the door, and his heart dropped to his feet. Pomeroy had Linnet on her knees before him, her hair twisted like a rope around his fist. The edge of his blade lay against the perfect alabaster skin of her cheek. It was not difficult to discern what the devil's spawn was trying to make her do.

Jamie drew his sword but put his arm out in front of Martin. "Steady," he said in a low voice. "If we startle him, he might cut her."

Pomeroy had not heard them come in over the pounding rain outside the window. Jamie stepped a few feet forward and cleared his throat loudly.

Without moving his blade from Linnet's cheek, Pomeroy turned. His eyes widened when he saw Jamie. After a pause, he said, "You are always where you should not be, Rayburn."

Jamie raised an eyebrow. "I assume the lady's answer was nay."

"She is no lady, as you well know," Rayburn spat out. "But you will have to wait your turn."

Jamie wanted to slice out Pomeroy's tongue and feed it

to the dogs for that remark. Instead, he said with deliberate casualness, "You are a braver man than I."

As Pomeroy watched, Jamie drew a coin from the pouch at his belt and flipped it into the air. "I'll wager a gold florin she will bite that tiny cock of yours right off."

For a moment, it looked as if his taunt had worked and Pomeroy would come after him. Linnet's shriek was like broken glass against his nerves as Pomeroy jerked her to her feet by her hair. Rage throbbed at Jamie's temples. If Pomeroy did not have a blade against her throat, he would be a dead man now.

Jamie was done playing games. "You hurt her again, Pomeroy, and I swear you will not leave this room alive."

Sir Guy must have sensed he meant it, for he began easing toward the door. One false move, and Jamie would have him.

"I don't like being threatened, Rayburn," he said. "No matter what tricks she does for you, she is not worth the trouble this will bring you."

Linnet's eyes were wild and her jaw set, a dangerous combination. Jamie hoped to God she would not do something stupid.

"You two, stand over there." Pomeroy pointed with his chin to the wall farthest from the door. "Stay back and move slowly."

Jamie nudged Martin. As they moved toward the far wall, Pomeroy and Linnet skirted the room in the opposite direction until they reached the door.

"She is a sorceress," Pomeroy said, his eyes full of fire. "She has the power to call on demons and make men do as she wills."

Jamie put his hands out, palms up, in a calming gesture. "Just let her go, Sir Guy."

"I warn you, Rayburn," Pomeroy said. "You shall not live if you interfere with my plans again."

With a sudden move, Pomeroy shoved Linnet to the floor and fled out the door.

Jamie ran to Linnet, who lay in a heap on the floor before the door. Falling to his knees, he gathered her in his arms. She collapsed against his chest, shaking and weeping.

"My squire will stay here with you," he said into her hair. "I shall return as soon as I can."

"Nay, do not leave me," she said, clinging to him.

"I cannot let that swine get away." The blood was pounding in his veins. "I must go after him now."

"Do not leave me," she wailed. "Please, Jamie, do not go."

Every muscle screamed to run after Pomeroy and tear him limb from limb with his bare hands. But with Linnet weeping and clutching at his tunic, he could not leave her. He sighed and wrapped his arms more tightly around her.

"I will do it," Martin said with one hand on the door.

"Halt!" Jamie was not about to let his new squire get killed going after Pomeroy alone. "I will deal with him later. Go find her brother Francois. Tell him I have his sister and that she is safe."

As soon as the door closed behind Martin, Jamie reached up and slid the bar across. He wanted no more surprises.

Linnet's body shook with sobs as he enfolded her in his arms again. "'Tis all right now. I am here."

As he rubbed her back, the silken strands of her hair

fell over his hands. It smelled of citrus and spring, just as he remembered.

"Promise you will not go," she said, her breath hot against his neck.

Linnet never admitted to needing anyone. Never begged him to stay, even when he left Paris. She was always so strong. He'd never seen her like this.

And it undid him.

When she acted strident and independent, he could resist her. When she was angry, as she had been at Eltham, he could keep his distance. But seeing her vulnerable like this broke down every barrier he had.

Before he knew what he was doing, he was holding her lovely face in his hands and kissing her forehead, her cheeks, her eyelids...

And then, at long last, his mouth was on hers. Outside the window, the wind blew harder and the rain pounded against the ground, echoing the thundering of his heart as he gave himself to long, deep kisses.

Kissing Linnet felt as it always had: both a familiar coming-home and wildly erotic. It was as if nothing had ever changed.

He broke away to bury his face in her neck and breathe her in. The smell of her skin filled him...and he was a lost man.

Five years of trying to forget her, gone in one breath. Every woman he had touched to wipe away her memory was forgotten. There was no one for him but her. There never had been. There never would be.

He kissed her again. Though her face was still damp with tears, she kissed him back with a fierceness that sent his blood thundering in his ears and pulsing through every part of him. Her fingers grazed the bare skin of his belly beneath his loosened shirt. He gasped as the surge of lust nearly blinded him.

They fell to the floor, tearing at each other's clothes, seeking the skin beneath. Her throat, her breasts, her thighs, her jaw. Every part of her was both familiar and a rediscovery. He reveled in the smell of her hair, the exquisite line of her throat, the perfect breasts that filled his hands. He had to have her, to own her, to make her his again.

"'Tis been so long." Her voice was rough with longing in his ear. "Please. Now. I cannot wait."

Oh, aye. Now.

They went from memory, their bodies joining with a violent, pent-up need for each other. All he knew in life was this passion between them—a passion so hot it burned his eyelids and scorched his soul.

Being inside her like this was all he wanted, all he was. Pounding, thrusting. She held on to him, her legs a vise around his hips, her hands clutching his hair. When she screamed, he exploded in a climax that was near death.

He could barely keep from collapsing on top of her and crushing her with his weight. Somehow, he managed to fall beside her and roll over onto his back. His ears rang. He was light-headed, dazed, gasping for air.

Good God. Sex like that could kill a man.

He crossed an arm across his forehead and stared at the ceiling.

Christ, what had he done?

He could not look at Linnet. If he did, he would want to pull her into his arms... to feel her head resting on his shoulder... to run his hands over her back... his fingers through her hair...

Nay, he could not look at her now and say what he must.

"This will not happen a second time," he said at last. "I'll not play your fool again, Linnet. I'll not do it."

He pulled his braies and chausses up from around his knees and sat up. Damn, he hadn't even taken his boots off. He pulled his shirt and tunic over his head, then got to his feet. With his back to her, he tied the laces of his chausses.

Over his shoulder, he said, "I'll take you to your chamber and bring your brother to you there."

Praying she did not need his help with her own clothing, he finally turned around to face her.

God help him. With her flushed cheeks, disheveled hair, and skirts in disarray around her, she looked well-used. And every man's dream in the deep of night.

She was attempting to hold her gown over her breasts as she struggled to get her arm through one sleeve. As his gaze slid over her bare shoulders, he cursed himself for his weakness. Touching her was dangerous, but what could he do? He could not walk her through Westminster Palace half-naked.

He swallowed and offered her his hand. "Let me help."

One moment, Linnet felt deliciously glorious, stretched out like a cat on the floor with her arms above her head. The next, she was stricken, nauseous with hurt, and clutching her gown to her chest to hide her nakedness.

After the firestorm of passion that exploded between them, Jamie simply got up and dressed. No last kiss or touch. No soft word. Nothing but the harsh statement that he would not be made a fool again.

Outside the windows, the rain had grown into a storm, casting a dark pall over the room. She was grateful for the loud drum of rain that covered her labored breathing.

When Jamie offered his hand, she ignored it and continued struggling into her gown. Damnation! 'Twas impossible to get into it alone. Fighting back tears, she stumbled to her feet and turned her back to him.

He helped her into her sleeves and then swept her hair aside to fasten her gown. Each time his fingers grazed her still-sensitive skin, unwelcome sensations rippled through her. She wanted to scream at him, but she could not trust herself to speak yet.

By the time he finished, she had control of herself. She slapped away his hands when he attempted to help her with her shoes. Finally, she was dressed so she could leave this wretched room. Between Pomeroy and Jamie, it would be forever etched in her mind. If she never returned to Westminster Palace, it would be too soon.

"Do you remember Owain ap Tudor?" Jamie said as he walked beside her down the narrow corridor. "He was one of King Henry's squires of the body."

He spoke as if making polite conversation at dinner in a hall full of people. As if he had not been inside her not ten minutes ago. As if nothing earth-shattering had happened between them.

Well, she could play this game as well as he.

Concentrating to keep her breathing normal and her voice steady, she said, "You mean the handsome Welshman with the devil in his eyes?"

"I suppose so," he said with an edge. "He calls himself Owen Tudor these days. He will be meeting us at Windsor with a letter commending him to the queen's service."

"I shall look forward to seeing Owen," she said, deliberately using his Christian name. "The company of a good-humored man of charm and wit will be immensely refreshing."

As they turned onto the main corridor, she saw her escape: Francois and Jamie's young squire were coming toward them.

But she was not going to leave it like this. Nay, she was not. She would not let him walk away without a word, as if it had not happened. She grabbed Jamie's arm, jerking him to a halt. When he turned toward her, she slapped him across the face, hard.

"Don't you ever touch me again and then regret it, Jamie Rayburn." She was so angry her vision blurred. "Don't you ever do it."

She picked her skirts up and left him where he was.

She did not look back.

Chapter Six

"Wait here," Linnet told her clerk.

It had not been easy to find the herbalist. She and Master Woodley had spent the better part of an hour lost in the backstreets of London.

There was no reason to hide that she was seeking the old woman's help. Many people came to her, as Linnet's grandfather had, for headache powders or a salve for aching joints. All the same, Linnet glanced up and down the lane before going through the door of the small shop.

The gloom of the interior did nothing to alleviate her unease. As her eyes adjusted, she took in the rows and rows of tiny bottles and jars on the shelves that filled the wall on one side of the room. She stepped closer to see them better. The bottles were filled with every color of liquid. Curious, she picked up one that was thick with dust. Clearly, an unpopular remedy, but for what? She twisted the stopper off to take a sniff.

"Have a care with that, you foolish girl!"

Linnet jumped at the voice behind her and turned to find the oldest woman she had ever seen shuffling toward her.

"Curiosity can kill as surely as a blade," the woman hissed as she wrapped her gnarled fingers around Linnet's hand. "This potion is for warts and will burn your hand like boiling oil if you spill it."

Linnet put the stopper back in the bottle with care. "Sorry, I did not mean to..."

"Snoop? Bah. Of course you did."

The old woman took the bottle from Linnet and put it back in its place on the shelf.

"Kill a man if poured into the ear," the old woman muttered, then nodded, as if having a conversation with herself.

Linnet reconsidered her quest. Suppose the old woman gave her the wrong herbs, and she became lovesick over a goat or grew an extra finger? It was known to happen. Although her grandfather spoke highly of this woman's skills, that had been many years ago.

"'Tis a problem with a man that's brought you here," the old woman said.

Linnet drew in a quick breath. "Do you have the sight?" It was often the case with women who dealt in herbs and magic.

"What other reason brings a young woman aglow with good health to me?" the woman said. "'Tis always a man causing her trouble of one sort or another. But I'll not complain. If men behaved as they ought, I'd have no food on my table."

Linnet smiled as she thought of buying the potion for warts and pouring it into Pomeroy's ear. Unfortunately, life was never that simple.

"If you've come seeking magic to do harm, you can turn yourself about and go." The woman made a circular

motion with her spindly finger and then pointed to the
door. "I trade only in healing herbs and love potions."

"I have come for two remedies, both to good purpose."
Linnet sidled up to the woman and said in a low voice,
"I want the herbs that keep a woman from getting with
child."

Jamie could pretend it would not happen again, but a
woman had to be pragmatic. Their passion had exploded
like oil spilled on a cooking fire. No matter what their
intentions—or how angry she was with him at present—
the risk of their emotions raging out of control again was
too great for her to take the chance again.

She had started her bleeding this morning—as if her
mood was not foul enough after Pomeroy and Jamie. But
she would not rely on luck a second time.

"I warn every woman, the herbs will nay prevent every
pregnancy. Never stops them, though," the old woman
said, shaking her head. She pointed to a large cloth bag on
the floor. "This one you boil, then soak the piece of wool
in it that you use to block the womb."

Linnet raised her eyebrows. If she and Jamie ended up
in bed again, it was hard to imagine them stopping to do
all that.

"Works best if your man's predictable, if you know
what I mean." The woman pursed her lips into a mass of
wrinkles, then said, "The sort who wants an extra cup of
ale and a cozy after Mass on Sunday, reg'lar as rain.

"But if you've a young man, as I'm guessin' you
have"—Linnet jumped as the old woman jabbed her side
with a pointy elbow—"then you'll be wanting the oil of
pennyroyal or wild carrot seeds."

Linnet had heard that a woman could bleed from

every orifice and die from taking a few drops too many of pennyroyal.

"The wild carrot, please."

The old woman nodded, apparently agreeing with her choice. "Now tell me what else you've come for," she said, raising one scraggly eyebrow. "I'd wager a ha'penny 'tis a strange one."

Linnet leaned forward and spoke in a low voice. "Do you have something that works the opposite of a love potion? A potion that will cause a woman to find a man—a particular man—unappealing?"

She thought of Jamie's midnight-blue eyes... and then of how the hard muscles of his stomach felt under her fingertips.

Unappealing might not be strong enough.

"The potion must make him repulsive. Repugnant. Abhorrent."

The old woman gave a high-pitched cackle. "If one medicine does its work, dearie, you'll not need the other. So which is it you want," she said, chortling and waggling her head from side to side, "to prevent the bedding or just the begetting?"

"This one is for a friend," Linnet snapped. This was not entirely a lie; the queen could use a dose to keep her from Edmund Beaufort.

The old woman wiped her eyes on her dingy apron. "Tell your 'friend' to confess to the priest and stop fornicating with a married man."

"He is not married," Linnet said, growing more annoyed.

"All the same, 'tis the work of the devil, and I'll not do

it. I am a God-fearing woman, I am." Her head bobbed, and she added in an undertone, "Unlike some I know."

The woman groaned as she leaned down to lift a large cloth bag onto the table that held her weights and measures. "I'll get the wild carrot seeds for you."

"Let me help you with that," Linnet said, rushing over to lift the bag for her.

"Ah, you're a good girl," the woman said. "Not like that other highborn lady what come here."

"Who was that?"

"If I'd known she meant to use that love potion on a Lancaster—and a married one at that," the woman said, ignoring Linnet's question, "I swear by the bones of Saint Peter, I'd never have given it to her."

"A Lancaster? Which one?" Linnet asked.

The woman shook her head. "I can see warning you about curiosity a second time is a waste of my breath. 'Tis in your nature, just as evil is in others."

Linnet disregarded the shiver that went up her spine and leaned across the table on her elbows. "Come, tell me. Who did she give the potion to?"

"Never say where you heard it." The old woman glanced toward the door, then said in a raspy whisper, "She used it on Gloucester himself, to take him from that foreign wife of his. May God forgive me."

Linnet sucked in her breath. "You mean Eleanor Cobham?"

"Aye. She's a bad'un, I tell you. Her and that priest who follows her like death."

She motioned for Linnet to lean closer. "Then she comes back, asking for the other kind, same as you. 'Tis a dark art, I tell her, but she don't care. She's one who wants what she wants."

"What did she do when you refused her?"

The woman began scooping wild carrot seeds from the large bag into a small one. "I hear she went to Margery Jourdemayne."

"So this Margery can make a potion that renders a man repulsive?"

The old woman fixed Linnet with her bulging eyes. "Put that thought out of your head. Better to fornicate with that married man of yours than dance with the devil."

"I told you, he is not married—"

"But he ain't married to you either, now is he, dearie?"

Linnet had nothing to say to that.

"You can be sure I never taught that sort of magic to Margery when she was my apprentice." As she put another scoop of wild carrot seeds into the small bag, she mumbled, "Sorcery! Consorting with the devil!"

Linnet leaned back. "Surely not."

"Just mind you don't cross either of them two women," the old woman said as she tied the bag closed with her gnarled fingers. "Birds of a feather—and they are sharp-beaked ravens who would pick eyes from the dead."

The woman stopped what she was doing to stare at nothing Linnet could see. After a long moment, she said, "I wonder what others have joined their coven..."

Covens? Consorting with the devil? Linnet eased the small bag from the woman's fingers. "Thank you kindly for the herbs. How much for the bag?"

"Three silver pennies."

Linnet gave her two extra coins for her trouble.

"Take my advice, dearie, and toss the herbs in the river on your way home." The woman patted Linnet's hand. "A beauty like you—your man is sure to wed you once he gets you with child."

Linnet made her escape.

"I am sorry to keep you waiting so long, Master Woodley," she said when she found him in the tiny lane outside the shop.

She looked over her shoulder as they walked. "Did you see anyone watching the shop while I was inside? Or anyone in the lane who did not seem to belong here?"

Perhaps it was just the strange old woman and her gossip, but Linnet felt a prickle of unease at the back of her neck, as if someone were watching her.

"I saw no one out of the ordinary for this neighborhood, save for a priest who passed." He cleared his throat. "And you, of course, m'lady."

Master Woodley was always precise and accurate, excellent attributes. "I am certain you are the best clerk in all of England."

"That may be," he said, sounding peeved. "But I am too old to serve as your protector as well. If you insist on going to every unsavory part of the city, you need a strong young man to accompany you."

How thoughtless of her! Master Woodley did look tired.

"You may hire a young man as big as an ox for me when I return to London," she said, taking his arm

more for his benefit than hers. "*If* you promise to make
Francois pay attention to the accounts while I am gone."

Master Woodley drew in a deep breath and shook his
head. "The second task is by far the more difficult one."

She patted his arm. "I know you will do your best."

Chapter Seven

Jamie sat on his horse waiting for the queen and her entourage to board the barge that would take them up the Thames to Windsor. As he watched Linnet, he congratulated himself on his decision to make the journey by horse. Spending an endless day in an enclosed barge with her would have been uncomfortable for them both.

She appeared to be giving instructions to an elderly man—the very one who had sought his help the day Linnet was caught on the bridge. After bidding the old man farewell, she joined the other ladies on the wharf. She was the loveliest of them all, in a deep blue-gray cape and hood with silver-gray fur trim that framed her face.

He touched his cheek, remembering the slap, and felt a twinge of guilt.

If she was traveling with the queen, why was she taking the queen's hands and kissing her cheeks? A horse whinnied, and Linnet turned to look up the bank. Following her gaze, Jamie saw none other than his own squire leading a pure white palfrey up the path.

Nay. She would not do it. She would not ride with them all the way to Windsor.

Martin swept her a low bow and went down on one knee to help her mount. For his excessive gallantry, Linnet gave the lad a smile that must have warmed him to his toes. She swung up onto her horse with the grace of a natural rider.

All the other ladies had the good sense to travel by covered barge. It was a full day's ride to Windsor. And November, for God's sake. Jamie had told Francois he would bring her horse for her. But he could see that Linnet was back to her stubborn, independent self.

What a sight she made on the high-strung palfrey. As she rode up the hill toward him, she looked like a fairy queen come to tempt lowly mortal men. He glanced at the men gathered to make the ride to Windsor. Judging from their rapt faces, her magic was having its usual effect.

"Let us be off," he called out to them. "We've a long day ahead." That was the God's truth.

Since they could both be at Windsor for weeks to come, he would have to get used to being around her. He fell in beside her, deciding to set the tone now. They would be courteous to each other. No intimate conversations, just formally polite.

"You've a fine horse," he said, making his attempt at banal conversation. He should have stopped there, but somehow he could not help adding, "Not so fine that you shouldn't have left her on the bridge in the riot. But a fine horse, nonetheless."

"She is special," she said, smiling as she leaned forward to pat her horse's neck.

He forced himself not to think of those long, slender fingers grazing the flat of his stomach. But that only made him think of them stroking his thigh . . . or clenched in his hair as she cried out . . .

"Your uncle Stephen found her for me," she said.

Found who? He nearly asked the question aloud before he remembered they were talking about her horse.

"Stephen did?" The traitor. All the members of his family who had met Linnet in France remembered her fondly. But then, they did not know her as he did. He unclenched his jaw to ask, "So you've seen Stephen and Isobel?"

"Aye. They were in London when I arrived a few weeks ago."

Of course Stephen and his wife would see Linnet.

"Speaking of kin," he bit out. "I learned that you and Pomeroy are related."

"I would hardly call it that."

"Christ's blood, Linnet, did you have to marry his uncle? Was there not some other wealthy old man you could have ensnared?"

"There were others," she said in a pleasant voice, "but Louis was the best."

Louis. Through clenched teeth, he asked, "How was he best?"

"*He* had a sense of humor."

"Hmmph."

"'Twas a good arrangement," she said with that annoying little smile on her face. "We both got what we wanted."

"I can guess what he wanted," Jamie muttered, not quite under his breath.

She shrugged one delicate shoulder. "He wanted a young wife to flaunt before his friends."

"As I recall, you wanted a brief marriage," he said. "I take it this ideal husband of yours complied?"

She was an effortless rider, sitting tall but at ease in her saddle. To watch her, you would never guess she had rarely ridden as a child—unless you counted riding in a carriage or cart, which he didn't.

"What I wanted," she said, her gaze fixed on the road ahead, "was funds to start my business, a house in Calais, and a foothold in the Flemish cloth market."

Francois had mentioned something about Linnet taking up their grandfather's trade.

"Francois said you challenged Pomeroy to a duel." She turned to fix him with that determined look of hers that said she meant to get her way. "You must know how utterly foolish that was. I insist you withdraw the challenge."

"A man cannot let that sort of brutish behavior go unpunished," he said, though he felt a bit queasy about his own behavior toward her.

Evidently her thoughts traveled in the same direction for the look she gave him would sear the bacon crisp. He refrained from reminding her that she had been every bit as passionate as he.

"Pomeroy did not harm me," Linnet said.

"He did." Seeing the thin line on her cheek where the devil's spawn had cut her set his blood boiling again.

"A scratch is nothing," she said. "You cannot murder a close ally of Gloucester over it, when killing him might set off a civil war."

How he had burned to take his sword to Pomeroy right there in the Great Hall at Westminster. But she was right that any spark could ignite the conflict between the feuding royals into violence. And so, Jamie had issued a challenge for Pomeroy to meet him in single combat at a place outside the city.

Yesterday afternoon, he rode to the appointed place a mile and a half outside the city and waited for Pomeroy.

Three hours he waited.

When Jamie stormed back into the palace, ready to run the cockroach through on the spot no matter the consequences, Pomeroy was gone. He had left London for his estate in Kent. If Jamie did not have a duty to stay near the queen, he would have followed Pomeroy.

For now, he had to content himself with sending a message to Kent renewing his challenge. He left it to Pomeroy to name the place and time. Eventually, he would teach Pomeroy the lesson he needed.

"It is not your place to defend me," Linnet said, bringing Jamie back to the conversation at hand. "I can take care of myself."

Jamie snorted. "I have seen how you do that. What can you be thinking, traveling about London with no one but that ancient man for an escort?"

It drove him half-mad to think of it, 'twas so foolish.

"Master Woodley is a very useful man." She spoke primly and sat even straighter on her horse. "I've never had a better clerk."

"You use a clerk for protection? For God's sake, Linnet, don't play games about this. Pomeroy is a dangerous man."

She looked off into the distance with narrowed eyes for a long moment. Then, in a low voice he barely caught, she said, "Why can he not let it go?"

"Let what go?" Jamie asked. "There is something more to this business with Guy Pomeroy, isn't there?"

She gave him a sidelong glance. After a pause, she said, "Sir Guy accused me of killing his uncle with sorcery."

"The loathsome swine!" There was no more dangerous charge to level at a woman. "But I heard your husband was old as . . . uh, quite elderly."

"Louis was three score and ten and in poor health, so no one took the accusation seriously." With a roll of her eyes, she added, "Sir Guy even accused me of using a love potion to persuade Louis to wed me in the first place."

Pomeroy was a fool. Linnet had no need of love potions. She could blow her breath into bottles and sell it.

"You'd best tell me what else you did to him," Jamie said. "Surely, I deserve to know the entire story before I kill him."

"You have not forgiven me for that day in Paris, so why should he?" With that, she spurred her horse and cantered ahead, splattering mud on him in her wake.

Damn, must she always bring up their past?

Jamie sank into a sour mood as the men ahead jockeyed for position, each trying to ride next to her. If an ox lay dead in the road, they would ride right over it unawares.

Martin, who must have been trailing behind them all this time, drew up beside him. Jamie ignored him; he wanted to be left in peace.

But peace was not to be his this day.

Martin cleared his throat. "Sir James?"

"I've told you that you may call me Jamie," he said without taking his eyes off the group of riders in front of them.

Whatever Linnet had just said, all the men were laughing. What a pleasant journey this was going to be. He would be watching horses' rear ends and men making fools of themselves over Linnet all the way to goddamned Windsor Castle.

"Sir, may I speak plainly?" Martin said.

Jamie turned to find his squire looking at him with a painfully earnest expression. "Just say it, Martin, and be done with it."

"I am grateful, sir, that you accepted me as your squire after my liege lord was killed in France," Martin said, his voice high with tension. "But I was raised to believe that a knight must always show respect to ladies."

Jamie blew out his breath. His young squire must have seen Linnet slap him yesterday. 'Twas no playful slap either.

"Is it your custom, sir, to offend ladies?" Martin asked. "For if it is, I shall have to seek my knightly training elsewhere."

As if Linnet's presence was not torture enough, now he was saddled with young Galahad here. Surely God was punishing him.

"As far as I know, Lady Linnet is the only woman in whom I inspire violence." Though Jamie was not yet twenty-four, this young squire made him feel a hundred.

"I hope you did not give her good cause to strike you," Martin said, his voice stiff with reproach.

The saints preserve him, Martin sounded ready to pull his sword. Oddly, it both amused and cheered Jamie to see such chivalry in his young squire.

"Things are not that...simple...between this particular lady and me," Jamie said, his eyes on Linnet again.

They rode in blessed silence for a time before Martin spoke again.

"Sir?"

This time, Jamie turned to find Martin gaping at him, his eyes wide and blinking, as if he had entered a brightly lit room from the dark.

"Are you saying, sir, that you are in love with her?"

Chapter Eight

Jamie was throwing dice with the guards in the gatehouse to relieve his boredom—and to avoid running into Linnet. Through the arrow-slit window, he could hear the splash of drops hitting the puddles on the ground below. The rain was finally easing up after a week of downpour.

He should have kept his cock in his braies. Each time he saw Linnet, he remembered the smell of her skin, the feel of her hair sliding through his fingers...

The man next to him elbowed him in the ribs. "Take your turn."

Jamie threw the dice and lost again.

Windsor Castle was enormous. All the same, he crossed paths with Linnet at every turn—at dinner in the hall, walking across the upper ward, passing on the stairs. He was always edgy from seeing her—or anticipating that he might. This near-constant state of arousal could not be good for a man's health.

The guards shouted over someone's lucky roll. Without looking to see who it was, Jamie tossed another penny on the table.

He liked the way she rode her horse, fearless at a

full gallop. He enjoyed the clever things she said at dinner—and that flash in her eyes when she teased him.

"Are you playing, Rayburn?"

He took the dice thrust in his face. As he rubbed the worn dice bones between his thumb and fingers, he thought of the smoothness of Linnet's skin.

How he was going to survive weeks in the same castle without falling into bed with her again, he did not know. He could only pray Bedford would take a fast ship from France and relieve him of his duties here.

His squire appeared behind him and tapped him on the shoulder. Speaking in a low voice so as not to interrupt the game, Martin said, "Sir James, a man has come to the castle asking for you."

"Keep my money," Jamie told the guards as he got up. "You'd win it anyway."

Martin trailed behind him down the circular stone stairs.

"He says he is a friend of yours," Martin said.

The lad sounded skeptical. As soon as Jamie stepped out onto the muddy ground outside the gate, he understood why.

He roared with laughter. "Owen Tudor, is that you beneath all that mud?"

"You know damned well it is," Owen said, his even white teeth making a bright line in his dirt-streaked face.

Jamie's hand made a wet smacking sound when he slapped his friend on the back. As he shook the mud off it, he said, "Did you have a good night's sleep with the pigs?"

"My horse stepped into a hole in the downpour. Next thing I knew, I was sitting on my arse in a puddle a foot deep." Owen wiped his face with his sleeve, which relieved his sleeve of more mud than his face. "'Tis lucky I didn't break my neck."

"You've come to see the queen?"

"Aye," Owen said. "Your father gave me a letter recommending me to her service."

"Well, you can't see her like that," Jamie said, grinning. "I fear the maids will murder me if I bring you inside."

He turned to his squire. "Martin, go fetch soap and towels. I am taking him to the river to get cleaned up."

"But sir, the water is freezing."

"This man survived the winter siege at Mieux," Jamie said, slapping his friend on the back again, despite the mud. "He can survive a dunking in the Thames in November."

"I've not been this filthy since the siege," Owen said with a laugh.

"Praise God you don't smell as bad as you did then."

"'Tis because I bathed in your family tub just last week," Owen said. "With your pretty sisters washing my back."

"Like hell they did," Jamie said. "I expect my father locked the older girls in their bedchambers until he raised the drawbridge behind you."

"I never got closer to them than thirty feet," Owen said with a grin. "By the by, your entire family threatens to come here if you do not pay them a visit soon."

"I am anxious to see them, too, but I cannot leave Windsor yet."

"Your parents hinted they had something important to discuss with you." Owen elbowed him. "Don't suppose they've finally found some poor girl to wed you, do you?"

They walked along the path by the river in companionable silence, looking for a good spot. The rain had stopped, but the path was slippery with mud.

Jamie looked over his shoulder to be sure Martin had gone, before saying in a low voice, "Linnet is here."

Owen turned to stare at him, the whites of his eyes showing against the mud. "Linnet? The same Linnet whose name no man dared mention to you for five years?"

"The very one."

After a long pause, Owen said, "Has she a husband now?"

Jamie shook his head.

"You bedding her yet?"

Jamie did not answer.

Owen laughed. "I can see you have, you devil."

Jamie shrugged.

"Ha, I knew it!" Owen said. "You two could never keep your hands off each other."

That was true enough, but it had been more than that for him back in Paris. Jamie stopped and looked out across the river. He took a deep breath and told himself he would not let it happen again—and he did not mean just the bedding part.

"I have bad news for you, Jamie boy," Owen said. "She seems to be the only one who will do for you. Instead of fighting against it, why don't you fight for her this time?"

Jamie snapped his head around and glared at Owen.

"Aye, I said fight for her. But for God's sake, Jamie, fight dirty this time." Owen raised his muddy fist in the air. "Fight hard. Fight to win."

"As a Welshman, you may be willing to chain a woman to your hearth, but we English are more civilized."

"I can see I shall have to speak plainly, since you are but a slow-witted Englishman," Owen said, shaking his head. "Last time, you left the field."

"After what she did, how—"

"Ach!" Owen said, dismissing his objection with a wave. "The other man found you in bed with her, not the other way around. What is your complaint?"

"She deceived me, scoffed at my good intentions, and made a fool of me." Not to mention, ripping his heart from his chest.

"You know nothing about women! Your problem is that you feel you must be truthful," Owen said. "Believe me, if I loved a woman as you do—and do not even attempt to tell me you do not—I would find a way to keep her."

Jamie put his weight behind a shove that sent Owen sliding down the slippery riverbank. Owen waved his arms wildly, trying to catch his balance before his feet went out from under him and he disappeared over the bank.

"Enjoy the water!" Jamie shouted as he clapped the dirt from his hands. "Catch me a fish while you're in there."

He heard a muffled string of curses coming from below.

Now that was satisfying. He'd feel even better if he could find an excuse to throw a few punches.

"Sir James!"

Jamie turned to see Martin coming down the path with an armful of towels and went to meet him.

"Thank you, Mar— *Aaugh!*" The air went out of him

as Owen grabbed him around the knees and slammed him to the ground.

Jamie lifted his head, blinking mud from his eyes. Muck oozed between his fingers.

"James, tell this lad it was all in good fun before I have to hurt him."

Jamie turned to see Owen lying faceup with Martin's foot on his chest. Better still, the point of Martin's sword was at Owen's throat. The sight struck Jamie as so hilarious, he rolled over on his back, laughing.

Making the same mistake Owen had earlier, he wiped his face on his muddy sleeve. "Lord above, there is even grit between my teeth!"

Martin saw that he had misjudged the threat and sheathed his sword. This was a mistake, however, because his foot was yet on Owen's chest. Owen sprang up, sending the lad flying backward.

That was when the mud fight began in earnest.

Linnet peeked around the door of the buttery. The queen's back was to her, and she was peering intently at something out the window.

"Whatever are you doing here, Your Grace?" Linnet said.

The queen jumped back, looking like a dog caught dragging the family roast from the table.

"One of your ladies-in-waiting told me I'd find you here." Linnet had thought the woman was jesting. "I came to ask if you were ready to go to the hall for dinner."

"You must see this," the queen said, crooking her finger.

Linnet joined her at the window. It afforded an unobstructed view of the Thames, which ran along this side of the castle. On the river's edge, three men were shouting and tossing one another about in the mud.

"They strike each other with such violence that at first I feared they meant to kill each other," the queen said without turning away from the scene. "But amid the grunts and shouts, I hear them laugh."

Linnet wondered just how long the queen had been watching. "Of all things...," she murmured, then narrowed her eyes. "Is that..."

"Aye, your Sir James is one," the queen said.

"He is not my Sir James."

"The slighter one may be his squire," the queen said. "But who is the third one?"

"I cannot tell with all the mud on him."

Linnet's mouth fell open as the men suddenly began stripping their clothes off. In contrast to the rest of their bodies, their hindquarters looked remarkably clean and white as they ran toward the river. Judging by how they pushed and shoved one another, this was a race. Linnet heard the splashes as the three hit the water.

"But it is winter!" the queen said, gripping the window ledge. "They could freeze to death."

The queen was not concerned enough, however, to pry herself from the window to call for help.

"They are fine, I'm sure." Linnet chuckled as the men splashed and dunked one another in the water.

"How lucky men are," the queen said in a wistful voice. "To be so free..."

"Free, indeed," Linnet murmured as the first two men

walked out of the water with no apparent concern for their nakedness.

The queen pretended to cover her eyes, but she was looking through her fingers. The laugh died in Linnet's throat as Jamie emerged, water streaming off his sleek, muscular frame. She sighed as he stopped to shake water from his long hair.

"Merciful God, is he not beautiful?" the queen whispered.

Truer words were never spoken. When Linnet tore her eyes away from Jamie to turn to the queen, she realized her friend had not been speaking of Jamie. The queen's hand was pressed to her chest, and she had eyes for none but the stranger. Linnet took another look at the man, this time giving him a thorough perusal, head to...hhhm... toe. He had a fine build and a jaunty air, but he was no Jamie Rayburn.

She shrugged. To each his own.

"Wait, I believe I do know who he is," Linnet said. "'Tis Owen Tudor. He was one of the king's squires of the body. Do you remember him?"

"I am sure I have never laid eyes on him before," the queen said in a soft voice.

This was not good. After Edmund Beaufort, the queen could afford no more entanglements. Linnet felt sad for her friend. After three years of widowhood, the queen was a very lonely woman. And what was worse, she was full of romantic notions.

Everyone seemed to expect her to be content to mourn the glorious King Henry for the rest of her life. But she was young, and she had already been a widow longer than she had been wed. Unfortunately, any relationship would threaten the men vying for control of her son. The episode with Edmund Beaufort was proof of that.

As she observed the queen's dreamy expression, Linnet felt a shiver of apprehension.

"Your Highness," she said, touching her friend's sleeve, "let us go to dinner now."

Chapter Nine

Linnet's spoonful of soup was halfway to her mouth when the three men strode through the entrance, filling the hall with a burst of vibrant male energy. With their hair slicked back from their faces and their glowing good health, they drew every eye in the room. Slowly, Linnet set her spoon back in her bowl without tasting her soup.

Jamie's wet hair was black, which made his violet eyes all the more striking. When they met hers, the air crackled down the length of the room between them. A high-pitched sound came from the back of her throat as the vision of him standing naked on the riverbank, water streaming down his muscles and glistening on his skin, filled her head.

Desire darkened his eyes, as it did every time he looked at her. It would be so easy to be drawn into that burning passion again, but she made herself remember Jamie's regret after his passion was sated. No amount of pleasure was worth the pain of that.

She broke the gaze. She would not be shamed by him. If lust was all he felt for her now, she would not have him.

Linnet devoted herself to cutting her venison as Jamie strode up to the high table with Owen. Then, recalling her duty, she turned to glance at the queen. Saints above! The queen was staring at Owen with that dreamy expression again—right here in the hall, in front of everyone.

"Your Grace, I beg forgiveness for interrupting your dinner," Jamie said with a low bow. "I was unavoidably detained."

Linnet choked on the piece of venison in her mouth. She shot another glance at the queen, but her friend appeared oblivious to the absurdity of Jamie's remark.

"With your permission, I wish to present my friend, Owen Tudor," Jamie said, extending his arm toward Owen. "He served your husband, our most dear and glorious King Henry."

The queen blushed faintly as Owen gave her an elegant bow—no doubt she, too, was recalling the men's recent naked state. Owen rose from his bow with a broad smile that held frank appreciation, but not an ounce of awe.

The queen blinked at him, her mouth forming a perfect "O."

"Your Grace," Owen said in a deep, resonant voice. "If it pleases you, I ask your permission to give your steward a letter recommending me to your service."

While she waited for Queen Katherine to murmur politely and defer the request to her steward, Linnet set her mind to the matter of Owen Tudor's employment. Just what position would give the green-eyed Welshman the least contact with the queen? Falconer might do. The queen hated hawking.

Better yet, "Keeper of the Royal Sheep." Linnet smiled to herself as she pictured Owen on a very distant hillside. If the queen owned no sheep, Linnet would suggest to the steward that he buy her some . . . on the Isle of Man.

Queen Katherine spoke, startling Linnet from her thoughts. "Would 'Keeper of the Wardrobe' suit you?" the queen asked in a breathy voice. "I have need of a good man for that position."

Good heavens! There could be no worse choice. For any high-ranking noblewoman, the purchase and maintenance of her household's clothes and jewelry consumed a great deal of time and money. But for a queen, these were formidable tasks, indeed. If the queen wished to, she could spend countless hours with Owen.

This was a disaster in the making.

Linnet caught Jamie's eye and mouthed, *Do something!*

When he drew his eyebrows together in a puzzled expression, she stamped her foot under the table in frustration.

"You do me great honor," Owen said, keeping his eyes on the queen's, rather than dropping his gaze as he should have. "There is nothing that would please me more, Your Grace."

The handsome devil was bold, and he had too much charm by half.

"I shall do my best," he said, "to fulfill your every wish as keeper of your wardrobe."

Her every wish. Linnet rolled her eyes, but noticed that the queen's chest rose and fell in a deep sigh.

Linnet's head was pounding by the time dinner was finished.

When she went to the queen's rooms to speak with her later, she was barred from entering. The queen, she was told by the guard, was not to be disturbed.

That had never happened before.

When she went down to the hall for supper, she learned the reason.

"I spent the afternoon with my new clerk of the wardrobe," Queen Katherine whispered to her before they took their seats at the table. "There is so much to be done! I should have had someone in the position long ago."

"The entire afternoon?" Linnet said, hoping she had misheard.

"'Tis a relief to have Owen's assistance," the queen said, smiling as she gazed off into the distance.

"*Owen?* Should you not address him as Master Tudor?"

The queen gave a light laugh. "When did you care about such things? So far as I can tell, you do precisely as you please most of the time."

"But I am not the queen of England," Linnet whispered. "Nor am I sister to the pretender to the French crown!"

Her friend gave her that benign princess smile she used when she waved to the peasants from her carriage. Then someone caught her eye, and she raised her hand.

"*Master Tudor,*" the queen said as Owen joined them. "I was hoping we could continue our discussion over supper."

The queen took Owen's arm. As he led her away, she winked at Linnet over her shoulder.

Supper was more of the same, with Owen spreading charm like a farmer spreads manure—and Queen Katherine wallowing in it like a happy hog.

Late that night, Linnet visited the queen in the royal apartments. The queen, who kept late hours, was still dressed.

"What are you doing walking about the palace in your

night-robe?" the queen asked, her delicate brows arched halfway up her forehead.

"My bedchamber is but a few doors away," Linnet said. "I could not sleep and hoped we might talk."

"Of course."

One look from Linnet, and the French ladies-in-waiting remained behind as she followed Queen Katherine into her private parlor.

Gowns and lengths of colorful fabrics hung over every bench and chair. The queen and her new clerk of the wardrobe had been busy. Linnet was trying to think of how best to bring Owen up, when the queen did it for her.

"What do you know of Owen Tudor?" the queen asked as she fingered a length of silk the color of ripe strawberries.

"I understand he is from an old Welsh noble family," Linnet said. "His father was a Welsh rebel who was in hiding for many years."

"Then he is no one of importance," the queen said, her expression thoughtful.

Linnet wondered what the queen meant by that. A moment later, the answer came to her like a thunderbolt.

"Your Grace, may I speak plainly?" she asked. "I feel I must, out of concern for your safety."

The queen sighed and nodded.

"While Owen Tudor does not present the same danger Edmund Beaufort did, that does not mean he is safe for you."

"What harm can you find in Owen?" the queen asked. "He is no one."

"I must warn you, Owen's lack of powerful connections will not prevent him from having powerful enemies should you become ... involved ... with him."

"I only met the man today." Queen Katherine gave her an indulgent smile. "He is my clerk of the wardrobe, that is all. You worry yourself too much."

Linnet felt a trifle better, until her friend added, "I am certain both Gloucester and the bishop would consider whom I choose to befriend to be beneath their concern."

"Pray, do not provoke them, Your Grace," Linnet said. "Those two have much at stake. Who knows what they might do?"

"But they can have nothing to object to," the queen persisted.

Linnet touched her friend's arm. "I know it is unfair. Eventually, they are bound to allow you a discreet relationship—perhaps even a second marriage. But not now. Not now, when the fight for control is so intense."

"How long before it is safe for me, can you tell me that?" the queen demanded, showing more defiance than Linnet had ever seen from her before. "How much longer must I wait? Three more years? Five? Ten?"

The queen drew away from her.

"You are not a mother—you cannot know what it is like to have your son taken from you," the queen said, her eyes filling with tears. "Am I to be permitted no one? No husband, no children, not even a lover? Am I to be an old woman before I can have the simple things that every other woman in the kingdom may have?"

"You must be patient," Linnet said, though the queen's words had taken the wind out of her.

"What would you do?" the queen demanded. "Would you let them deny you everything you wanted?"

Linnet did not answer, because they both knew she

would fight tooth and nail for what she wanted. Still, it was not the course she wished for her friend.

Jamie was alone in his bedchamber when he heard the knock at his door. Since there was no one he wished to see, he ignored it and continued writing his letter to his parents. His mother had been wise to insist all her children learn to write: *One day you may need to send a message that not even your clerk should see.*

When the knocking persisted, he cursed under his breath and set the letter aside. Whoever had come was damned impatient. He stopped to stretch on his way to the door.

When he opened it, his mouth went dry at the unexpected sight of Linnet at his bedchamber door. Her hair hung in a loose braid over her shoulder like a thick chain of white gold.

And she was dressed in a night-robe.

Oh, aye. If she had come for what he thought, he was more than ready. All his plans for resistance vanished like mist under a summer sun. She had that determined look on her face that he loved without reason. If she was determined to have him, he was equally determined to give her what she wanted.

"Close the door," she said as she swept past him. She stopped in the center of the room and turned to face him.

Without taking his eyes off her, he reached behind him to shut the door. He swept his gaze over her, taking in every inch of her from head to feet, and everything in between.

Why had he been trying to fight this? With her here and dressed for bed, he could not recall a single reason.

She folded her arms under her breasts and lifted her chin. "I hope we can put aside our differences to save the queen from him."

"Save her?" His mind had not yet caught up with the conversation. "From whom?"

"From that sly friend of yours, Owen Tudor, of course."

He looked longingly at the white skin of her throat showing in the V of her robe, then followed the enticing curve of her breasts beneath the cloth.

"You came to discuss the queen?" he finally asked, hoping it was not true.

She leaned forward, clenching her fists in the folds of her robe. "Did you not take an oath to protect her?"

The queen. Linnet was speaking about the queen.

"Owen is a good man," he said, struggling to concentrate. "He will give his loyalty to the queen."

"If that is all he gives her, I shall be happy." She pressed her lips together and tilted her head back to glare at the ceiling. After taking a deep breath, she brought her fierce gaze back to him. "Jamie. Did you not see how the queen looks at him?"

He shook his head.

"Men! You see nothing." She took another deep breath. "As you are blind, I shall tell you. Her Highness looks at Owen as if she would like to lick honey off his skin."

Jamie opened his mouth, closed it, and then swallowed. After a long moment, he said, "She likes him that well, does she?"

"No one is considering licking honey off you, Jamie Rayburn, so cease looking at me that way at once."

That was a damned disappointment.

"This is a serious matter," Linnet said. "I tell you, the queen is very close to doing something foolish."

"Owen is no fool," Jamie managed to say, though he was imagining Linnet naked on all fours over him, running her tongue down his chest, licking honey. "He is a flirt, but he would take it no further."

"I hope you are right," she said, and her shoulders relaxed a bit. "But if he is even seen to flirt with her, more might be read into it. There are too many people at Windsor, to hope rumors will not travel to Gloucester or the bishop."

He nodded. "Both men have spies here."

"I suspected as much," she said. "I will do my best to convince Queen Katherine to be sensible. Will you warn Owen to keep his distance?"

"I will caution Owen and keep my eye on him."

"So it is agreed we shall work together?" she asked.

"Aye, I am all for joining forces," he said, still hoping this would include more tonight than scheming on the queen's behalf.

Tomorrow he would worry about the consequences. Her eyes grew wide as he closed the distance between them to stand a hairbreadth from her. When he lifted his hand to cup her cheek, she backed away.

"I told you once," she said, her voice sharp with anger. "I will not have you touch me and regret it after."

When he opened his mouth to deny it, she held up her hand. "I know you, Jamie Rayburn, so do not try to lie to me."

Would he regret it? Surely it would be better to have

her in his bed, rather than to think about bedding her all the time. A thousand times better.

"I will choose a lover who is not so harsh in his judgment of me," she said.

He clenched his jaw at the thought of her with another man. "So it is a lover you are seeking again, and not a husband," he bit out. "Tell me, what are you looking for in the man you choose this time?"

She raised her eyebrows and blinked those wide, innocent blue eyes at him. In a falsely sweet voice, she said, "Who is to say I expect to find all I want in one man?"

Chapter Ten

Linnet glanced at the queen's ladies, stitching and talking quietly by the brazier on the other side of the parlor. When one of the Joannes—there were three of them—caught Linnet looking at her, the woman made a sour face.

Linnet accepted the ladies' resentment of her close relationship with their patron and did not hold it against them. They had no life beyond their position in the queen's household. Further, they disapproved of her familiar manner with the queen.

Linnet turned back to the window and watched the rain pelting the river below. What could have possessed Jamie and Owen to ride out to hunt on a day like this?

In sooth, she understood their restlessness. She, too, found it trying to be trapped indoors for days on end. If she were in London or Calais, she would be too busy to notice the dismal weather. But here at Windsor, she had little to occupy herself. She was never one to sit for hours doing needlework. Being motherless had at least spared her that.

Linnet started when she felt a hand on her shoulder. She looked up to find Queen Katherine standing beside her.

"'Tis dull without them, is it not?"

"Without whom?" Linnet asked, though she knew perfectly well who her friend meant.

The queen gave a light, lilting laugh. "Come, Linnet, I see you in conversation with that handsome Sir James Rayburn every time I look."

Linnet bit her lip. Was she using her concern for the queen as an excuse to spend time with Jamie? 'Twas a dangerous business, that, and she suspected he was doing the same.

"Do not attempt to tell me I am imagining what I see between you," the queen said.

Linnet pressed her lips together.

"Pray, do not deny it. The air is so hot between you, I fear you will singe the tapestries. They are quite valuable."

"I admit there is a base attraction between us," Linnet said in a tight voice, "but nothing more."

Queen Katherine squeezed Linnet's shoulder. "It would be such a delight to plan a wedding."

A wedding? "Your Highness, I fear I must disappoint you."

"You never disappoint, Linnet."

Linnet put a hand over the queen's. "You are too kind to me. But I assure you, there is nothing between Jamie and me now, nor will there be."

"Would you care to make a wager on that?" the queen asked, her eyes twinkling.

Linnet said nothing; she was far too good with money to lay a wager she might lose.

"I knew it," the queen said with a wink.

Something might happen again between her and Jamie Rayburn, but it would not be a wedding.

"Now, I have something to divert you until our favorite men return." The queen held out two sealed parchments. "Your letters. A servant just brought them up."

"Thank you," Linnet said, breaking into a wide smile. If she did not count the time she spent with Jamie—*which she certainly did not*—the favorite part of her day was reading Master Woodley's daily missive sent up from London.

"Reading your clerk's letters seems dull work to me," the queen said, patting her arm. "I shall sit with my ladies for some needlework and gossip."

Linnet hurried to her chamber to read her letters in private. As soon as she saw her brother's familiar script on one of them, she missed him. She was too anxious to take the time to light the lamp. Instead, she stood by the narrow window, where she had to strain to read in the stormy afternoon light.

She read the letter from her clerk first. What a good man Master Woodley was. He had sold most of the prized Flanders cloth she had brought to London—and at a very fine price. As she expected, he had made little progress on his other assignment. After so many years, tracing where her grandfather's property had gone—and into whose hands—was a difficult task.

She set his letter aside and took up Francois's.

My dearest Linnet,
Your ancient Master Woodley hounds me without mercy. I beg you, dear sister, return at once to res-cue me from him and these damned accounts.

Locating the persons you asked me to find was no challenge for a man of my talent. I must warn you, however, that speaking with them will prove considerably more difficult. I shall explain when I see you. Is that sufficiently tantalizing to bring you back to London?

I cannot be answerable if you do not soon relieve me of the relentless Master Woodley.

With great affection,

Your most devoted brother,
Francois

Poor Master Woodley. She hoped Francois was not exhausting him with his antics. She stared at the sheets of rain outside the window as she tried to guess at the meaning of Francois's intentionally mysterious message.

Clearly, Francois had found Leggett and Higham, two men she hoped could help unravel the mystery of what happened to her grandfather's profitable business ten years ago. Leggett was the one merchant in London she knew she could trust. When her grandfather's creditors were closing in, he came to their house in the dead of night and helped them get out of London. He had even paid their passage on the ship to Calais.

If that swine Mychell was to be believed, Higham was one of the men who had been in their London house that day she and Francois hid under the bed. Mychell said it was this Higham who carried the unusual silver-tipped cane she remembered.

She did not expect to recognize the men's voices after all this time, but she would remember until her dying day that silver claw pounding on the floorboards.

Mychell told her that he and this Higham received their instructions from the third man, whose name they never knew. But Mychell was lying. Whoever had the cane was the man giving instructions that day. Now that Francois had found Higham, she intended to discover if he was another intermediary or the man behind it all.

It was time for her to make a trip to London.

Jamie wiped the rain from his face with his sleeve. Damn, it was coming down hard.

"There's no game," Owen said as he pulled his horse up to ride next to Jamie through the brush. "Animals have the sense to stay under cover."

Jamie had insisted they go hunting, despite the freezing rain. He needed to get away from the castle or go mad. Every time he saw Linnet in the hall, he found himself speculating over which man she had taken as a lover.

Or men. Blood pounded in his ears every time he recalled her saying she might require more than one.

Fortunately, there were few noblemen or wealthy merchants at Windsor in this lull before Christmas. But since Linnet made it clear she was not looking for a husband, she could just as well dally with any of the myriad clerks, grooms, hawkers, and guards. There was an abundance of such men at Windsor.

"Why the sour look, my friend?" Owen said.

"The damned rain is running down my neck."

"'Tis more than this foul weather," Owen said, wiping the rain from his eyes with his gloved hand.

"Quiet. Too much talk will scare the game."

"So Linnet has kicked you out of her bed, has she?" Owen said with a wide grin.

"That is none of your business," Jamie snapped. "But while we are talking of women, I have a warning to give you."

Owen made a face. "Come, Jamie, I already swore to you I did not touch one of your pretty sisters."

"Not with my father at home, or the birds would be pecking at your swollen body in the marshes below our castle wall." Jamie laughed, his mood finally lifting.

"My body pecked by birds is a humorous notion, is it?" Owen leaned between their horses to punch Jamie's arm. "I am not so foolish as to risk William FitzAlan's ire."

"You should fear my mother no less. I warn you, she keeps her dagger sharp and is not afraid to use it."

"'Tis lucky, then, that I've no interest in deflowering virgins." Giving Jamie a broad wink, Owen said, "I like a woman who knows what she's about, if you know what I mean."

Indeed, Jamie did.

Owen's remark about his sisters had diverted Jamie from what he meant to say. "The woman I must warn you about is Her Highness, Queen Katherine."

"Has she suggested she is not pleased with my work in some way?" Owen asked, playing innocent.

"'Tis more that she seems a bit too pleased."

Owen's hand went to the hilt of his sword. "What are you accusing me of, Rayburn?"

"I accuse you of nothing," Jamie said, ignoring the gesture. "But where the queen is concerned, perception alone could get you hanged."

"'Tis bad enough I let you persuade me to come out in

a gale for sport," Owen said, shaking the water off his hat. "But I must put up with another lecture?"

"I am telling you, Owen, they may punish the queen by putting her away in an abbey, but as for you"—Jamie turned to point his finger at his companion—"Gloucester and Beaufort would be quarreling over who had the better right to stick your head on a pike on London Bridge."

"Let us go back," Owen said, turning his horse. "A man can only take so much abuse and keep his sense of humor."

"Fine." Jamie guided his horse around a tree stump to reach higher ground for the return ride.

"Come, Jamie, who would believe the queen would have me anyway?" Owen complained. "I am her lowly clerk of the wardrobe—and a Welshman besides."

"Linnet says anyone who sees the way the queen looks at you will suspect you've shared her bed."

"Linnet says this; Linnet says that," Owen said, sounding cheerful again. "Tell me, why have you not found another woman to take your mind off that one?"

"Not another word about Linnet."

"I was speaking about other women," Owen said. "There are others about, you know. Dozens of them, right here at Windsor."

Why had he not found another woman? Of course, he had thought about doing so. His cock was up so often, he could not help but think of finding a better way to relieve it than with his hand.

In sooth, it would be an easy matter to acquire an occasional bedmate. More than one pretty woman had signaled an interest. But with Linnet here, he simply could not see them. All other women were lost in her shine.

It was hard going for their horses slogging through the wet underbrush, but the rain diminished on their return. Just as they neared the castle gate, the sun broke through the clouds.

"I believe I see the very lady you did not wish to speak about."

Jamie barely heard Owen. His attention was fixed on Linnet, who stood outside the gate, the wind flapping her cloak, watching their approach.

"What has happened?" Jamie asked her as soon as he dismounted. "Is something amiss?"

"All is well at the castle," Linnet answered. "I was anxious to see you."

Jamie's heart did a flip in his chest. Linnet was anxious to see him. More, she was admitting it. Before he could think what to say to her, she turned to Owen, who had also dismounted.

"Owen, I've come to ask if you will take me to London with you," she said, crushing Jamie's burst of pleasure like an ant beneath her heel. "I expect you have purchases you need to make for the queen's wardrobe."

Owen furrowed his brows. "I was not planning on it, but I suppose you are right."

"We should go soon." Linnet put her arm through Owen's and began walking him through the open gate. "The queen will want new gowns for all the feasts during Christmas Court. You can have no notion how many are required, and..."

Jamie followed, leading both horses like a damned groom. What was Owen up to, walking so close to Linnet and leaning down to her like that? She was not one of those women who spoke in a feathery whisper. Owen could hear her well enough without crowding her like that.

"As it happens," Jamie called up to them, "I have business to attend to in London as well."

And that damned Owen laughed.

Chapter Eleven

"Do you think it all right that we left the queen and Owen on their own?" Linnet asked, not for the first time.

"I do," Jamie said, because there was no point in her fretting about it now that they were in London.

Linnet planted a hand on her hip and scanned the crowded hall at Westminster Palace with a murderous look on her face. "I should have found Owen and strangled him when he failed to meet us at the dock."

Jamie exchanged a glance with her brother, Francois.

"Lucky for Owen he is a full day's ride away," Francois said in an undertone.

"In fairness to Owen," Jamie ventured to say, "it was the queen who sent a servant to tell us she could not spare Owen."

"Along with Owen's shopping list," Linnet huffed. "As if I have time to do Owen's errands for him."

"But you love to buy and sell fine fabrics," Francois said. "That is what you do."

Linnet shrugged, showing no sign of being mollified.

She did have unerring good taste. She looked especially lovely this afternoon in a rose-colored gown made of a rich material that shimmered in the light when she passed a window or lamp. While her attention was fixed on the crowd of people who always seemed to congregate at Westminster, Jamie took advantage of her distraction to take in every enticing curve and elegant line.

Linnet turned abruptly and caught him in his thorough perusal.

"'Tis a lovely gown," he said, lifting his hands. God in heaven, there was no harm in looking, was there?

"I am going to speak with the Mistress Leggett," Linnet said to Francois, "since I cannot speak to her *dead* husband."

As Linnet spoke, she gave Jamie a sidelong glance that sent another shot of lust through him.

"I did find Leggett for you," Francois said, not bothering to hide his amusement. "He was in the same churchyard as Higham."

"'Tis a pity Higham has no widow." With that, she turned and disappeared into the colorful silks and velvets of prosperous merchants and nobles.

Jamie had always liked Francois and was happy for the opportunity to talk alone with him. "So your sister has become a merchant, has she? Becoming titled and a wealthy widow to boot was not enough for her?"

"She regrets the title, as it comes from our father," Francois said.

Jamie was well aware of the lengths Linnet would go to make that man suffer. Though her father deserved her scorn, Jamie could not help feeling a bit of sympathy for a man Linnet was determined to punish to his dying day.

"Oddly enough, it will be Linnet who saves our father's estates," Francois said. "She received only a modest marriage portion, but she has multiplied it several times over."

"If she gained so little from Pomeroy's uncle," Jamie said, "why the devil did she marry the old man?"

"I believe," Francois said in a careful tone, "she liked him."

So he had been thrown over for an old man and a small marriage portion. It was insulting.

"Her husband also had useful connections in Flanders," Francois added.

What could Jamie's offer of undying devotion be next to that? God in heaven, how much longer did he need to remain in this stifling room?

"Where is Gloucester?" he asked Francois. "I should pay my respects before I leave to visit the bishop."

Not that he felt much like seeing the bishop either. From the frying pan into the fire, that was.

"Gloucester? I expect he has some lady with her skirts up behind a door." Francois turned his head from side to side as if he expected to spot Gloucester's bare behind in the midst of a tryst right in the hall.

"But, is that not his mistress just over there?" Jamie said, tilting his head in the direction of Eleanor Cobham.

"Eleanor is far too clever to censor Gloucester." Francois leaned closer. "But God help the lady should Eleanor find out who she is. Rumor has it she poisoned the last woman he dallied with."

Jamie had no trouble believing it of Eleanor. "I heard nothing of a murder."

"Not for lack of effort," Francois said in a low voice. "The woman was in bed a month—long enough to cool

Gloucester's interest. They say she still can eat nothing but porridge."

"Good Lord."

"Of course," Francois said, "there is no proof Eleanor did it."

They stood side by side, scanning the crowd in silence for a time. Jamie was looking for Pomeroy—the swine had yet to respond to his challenge to meet in single combat. Though Jamie was itching for the fight, he was relieved not to see Pomeroy here today. He did not want Pomeroy anywhere near Linnet.

Jamie noticed Eleanor had moved into a dark corner, where she was talking with four men in clerics' robes.

"Is Eleanor conspiring with churchmen now?" he asked.

"They do look as if they are up to no good, don't they?" Francois said with a laugh. "Gloucester and his mistress have some interesting acquaintances."

"Who are they?"

"That one with the high forehead and exceedingly long nose is a famous alchemist from Oxford," Francois said. "Gloucester is a great supporter of philosophers, as well as artists."

"Is not alchemy art?" Jamie asked. "The art of deception?"

"Aye, they turn your silver into their gold," Francois said, and they both laughed.

"The man with the pointed beard standing next to Eleanor is Roger Bolingbroke, an Oxford scholar in astrology," Francois said. "The one next to him is Thomas Southwell, a physician and canon of Saint Stephen's Chapel here at Westminster Palace. And the last one—the one who looks like a weasel—is John Hume, a clerk in Gloucester's household."

It did not surprise Jamie that Francois knew everyone. If Francois was swept ashore in a strange land, he'd know half the criminals and be invited to sup at the king's table within a week.

"Gloucester and his mistress have a fascination for all the ancient mystic arts." Francois leaned close to add, "I hear they even consort with necromancers."

"Conjurers of the dead? You cannot mean it."

In an all-too-familiar gesture, Francois lifted one eyebrow and shrugged his shoulder.

"You share too many mannerisms with your twin," Jamie said. "'Tis irksome."

"Just so long as it annoys you, rather than makes you want to kiss me," Francois said and puckered his lips.

"Good God, Francois." Jamie punched his shoulder, hard.

From the corner of his eye, Jamie saw Eleanor walk quickly out of the hall with a furtive glance over her shoulder, as if she hoped no one noticed her leave. One of the clerics she had been talking with appeared to catch someone's eye across the hall. Then, in quick succession, the four clerics left the hall.

Francois swore an oath under his breath. Jamie forgot the clerics as he followed Francois's gaze to Linnet. She was surrounded by a circle of men, wealthy merchants by the looks of them. As he watched, she took the arm of a short, well-fed man in an orange-and-violet-brocade tunic and matching hose that made Jamie's eyes hurt.

"Not the alderman," Francois muttered. "I swear, she'll be the death of me . . ."

Jamie knew he should not ask, but he could not help himself. "What has you worried this time?"

"She is set on finding the man who ruined our grandfather."

"What will she do when she finds him?"

"Trust me, you do not want to know," Francois said, before he set off through the crush of people to waylay his sister.

Linnet usually had little difficulty getting information from men. Every merchant she approached today, however, evaded her questions. Their palpable unease made her believe she was getting close. Whoever was behind her grandfather's ruin was someone the others did not wish to cross.

Even that dragon, Mistress Leggett, seemed frightened. She grabbed Linnet's arm and yanked her into a dark alcove behind a pillar.

"Pray, use what little sense God gave you, girl," the woman said in a harsh whisper. "Let sleeping dogs lie."

"My grandfather was robbed," Linnet said, jerking away from the woman's huge, hamlike hands. "I promise you, I shall have justice for him."

"Would your grandfather want to see your body floating down the Thames?" Mistress Leggett said, her jowls shaking. "I am warning you for his sake, because he was a good and honest man: *Leave this be*."

"If your husband were alive, he would help me."

"You know nothing, girl," the woman said. "My husband was part of it. But when they were planning to take you and your brother, that troubled him, see?"

Could she have been wrong about Leggett? She remembered a cane pounding on the floorboards by the bed as one of the men shouted, "Where are the children?" The cane had an unusual silver end in the shape of a lion's paw.

"So he comes to me," Mistress Leggett continued, "and I tell him that if he ever wants a warm bed again he must sneak you out of London and put you on a ship."

Linnet blinked at the enormous woman. "Thank you for saving us—but what did they want with us?"

Mistress Leggett glanced toward the hall before she answered. "They had a notion someone would pay ransom for you."

Alain would not have paid ransom for them, for his legitimate sons were still alive then. But how had the men found out about their nobleman father? Their grandfather must have let the secret slip to one of his "friends" after he grew feebleminded.

"Do you know the names of the others?" Linnet asked.

"All I know is that some powerful merchants were involved." Mistress rested a heavy, clammy hand on Linnet's shoulder. "And that is all you need to know as well."

When Mistress Leggett left her, Linnet took a deep breath. There was one other person in the hall who might know something useful. Her clerk, Master Woodley, believed that if a vast quantity of Flemish cloth had changed hands without proper payment ten years ago, Alderman Arnold would know of it.

When Linnet found the rotund alderman and cornered him, he broke out in such a sweat that she feared he might expire at her feet. She bit her lip as she watched him dance from foot to foot. Who could be powerful enough to put fear into an alderman? What she needed was an ally who was more powerful than her enemy.

"Excuse me," the alderman said and backed away from her as if she held the point of a blade to his soft belly.

When he was some distance from her, he signaled to someone across the hall. She rose on her toes, straining to see who he was looking at, but there were too many people to guess which one it was.

From the corner of her eye, she followed him as he worked his way around the edge of the room until he reached the arched doorway that led to the privy palace. Then, with a quick glance over his shoulder, the alderman left the hall.

Linnet pushed her way through the crowd, not caring if she stepped on a few toes. By the time she made her way to the vestibule outside the hall, the fat alderman was gone. The cold air felt good on her skin as she stepped through the outer doors to peer out into the darkness toward the privy palace.

She heard footsteps on the flagstones, but the sounds disappeared as she followed them down the covered walkway past Saint Stephen's Chapel. She entered the next building by the closest door and found herself in a corridor dimly lit by thrush lamps. The building seemed empty—which only heightened her suspicions. Why would the alderman come here except to meet someone in secret?

She followed the corridor around a corner and saw two hooded figures in long black robes in front of her. When they halted by a door on the left, she drew back quickly. She waited until she heard the creak and swoosh of a door, then peeked around the corner.

She caught sight of the edge of a robe disappearing through an opening on the right. Odd, she had not noticed a door there before. She waited a few more moments, but when they did not come back out, she tiptoed down the hall to listen at the door.

But there was no door on the right.

She glanced up and down the corridor to be sure no one was coming, then ran her fingers along the paneling. She smiled when she found what she was looking for— the outline of a secret door. If she had not known where to look, she never would have seen it.

She pressed her ear to the panel, but heard nothing.

Now, how to open the door? For several frantic minutes, she felt along the panel, pressing every few inches, trying to find the release. Frustrated, she stood back and glared at the panel with her hands on her hips. She gave the panel a good kick that hurt her toe.

Damn, she should have brought Francois. He had a knack for this sort of thing. As she turned to go, one side of the panel moved out from the wall a quarter inch. Her kick must have sprung the device. Dropping to her knees, she pried the panel open a couple of inches with her fingertips. When she paused to listen, she heard very faint voices in the distance.

Whoever had gone through the secret door did not appear to be waiting on the other side, so she eased it open and slipped inside. The door clicked shut, and panic choked her until she found a handle behind her. As soon as she lifted up on it, she felt the door start to give. She could get out, praise God!

She stood still until her thundering heart slowed enough for her to hear. The voices were louder from here, but still muffled and distant. Gradually, shapes emerged as her eyes adjusted to the darkness.

Merciful God! She flattened herself against the door as she realized she stood at the top of a long flight of stairs. The staircase dropped steeply through a tunnel built of stone blocks into a deeper darkness below.

This must be an escape route leading to the river. Relations between England's royalty and the powerful London merchants were often uneasy; any one of the prior kings could have foreseen the need to be able to escape Westminster unseen.

She thought again of the alderman's odd behavior and the other merchants' unease with her tonight. If the alderman was one of the caped figures she was following, she had to find out whom he was meeting in secret and why. Perhaps she should go back for Francois...Nay, that would take too long—she could miss her chance.

She opened the door a crack so that a thin line of light shone along its edges. Taking a deep breath, she eased one foot down to the next step.

A shiver went through her as she heard the old herbalist's voice in her head, telling her curiosity was in her nature...just as evil was in others. She would go but a little way, just far enough to hear the voices a bit more clearly—or see where the tunnel came out. If she kept a safe distance, she could come to no harm.

Holding her arms out to brush the walls on either side to keep her balance, she took the steps one at a time. The darkness grew deeper and the smell of dank earth grew stronger the deeper she went. Finally, her feet hit the dirt floor.

She peered into the black passageway before her. Her

mouth was dry with fear, though of what, she could not say. The voices were louder here, but still muffled. It was hard to tell how far away they were. She looked back over her shoulder. The dim light at the top of the steps seemed a long, long way off.

She licked her lips. Should she go back? Every muscle tensed, screaming for her to run—but she might never get another chance to find out what this was about.

After the alderman's strange behavior, it seemed quite possible his business down here had something to do with her. So far, all her efforts to find out who had ruined her grandfather had come to naught. If whatever was down here could shed light on that, she had to know.

She would just go far enough to see who the voices belonged to and hear the words they were chanting. For it was a chant, she could tell that now. It sounded like monks...and yet not.

She was beyond the reach of the light from the top of the stairs now and had to feel her way along the passage. The walls here were damp, rough-hewn rock, as if the passage had been cut through sheer rock face.

She rounded a bend and suddenly the chanting was louder, insistent and repetitive, and there was light up ahead. She could make out the words now: "Come to us. Come to us. Come to us."

As she drew closer, she saw that the passage opened into a room that extended to the left. She could see only a small part of it from where she stood, so she took a step closer. Through the opening, she saw candles on the floor and dancing shadows.

Fear shot through her, making her knees weak and her head feel light. Every child grew up hearing the stories:

sorcerers and witches consorting with the devil; stolen children never seen again; horned demons called up from hell; dark rituals of bloody sacrifice. Her palms went clammy as all the tales she had scoffed at as a child raced through her head.

With her heart pounding in her ears, she dropped to her knees and crawled forward. She had come this far. She was going to see what was in the room before she fled back down the passageway and up the steps.

Just one peek. She sucked in her breath as something crawled over her hand. Over the stench of damp earth, she smelled incense, and beneath that a tangy, musky odor. She inched forward, craning her neck to the side to see farther inside the room.

She caught glimpses of dancing figures in capes moving in and out of the part of the room within her sight. They appeared to be dancing within a ring of candles on the floor. She crawled a little closer. All at once, she saw that the figures did not wear hooded capes as she first thought. They wore masks and the hides of animals.

Mary, Mother of God, protect me. Mary, Mother of God, protect me.

There could be no doubt what this was now. She was witnessing a sabbat, a ritual meeting of witches. Their chanting pulsed in her blood and throbbed in her ears.

Mary, Mother of God, protect me. Mary, Mother of God, protect me.

Linnet could see the edge of a table covered in black cloth at the center of the circle. Pressing against the wall of the passageway, she scooted forward, then got up on her knees to see what was on the table. Her mouth fell open, and she sucked in her breath. She was rooted to the ground, too shocked to move.

A woman lay on the table. A stark naked woman.

Of course, Linnet had seen other women partially undressed—even naked briefly—as they changed clothes in a shared chamber. But that was nothing like what was before her now.

The skin of the woman glistened with oil, and her nipples were erect. Dark tendrils of her uncovered hair fell over the end of the table nearest Linnet. She lay on her back with the soles of her feet together and her knees splayed apart.

And all she wore was a mask.

Linnet knew intuitively the woman was not here against her will. Whatever was taking place here, she was a willing participant.

A tall figure in a wolf's mask and hide appeared from the other side of the room holding a bowl aloft. As he approached the table, the others began to chant, "Goddess, Goddess, Goddess."

The wolf-man stood at the end of the table where the woman's feet were drawn up sole-to-sole close to her body. Slowly, he lowered his outstretched arms over her until the bowl rested on her belly. Then he dipped his fingers in the bowl of dark red liquid.

Linnet knew she must leave at once. This was the devil's work, for certain, and she should not see it. Even so, she could not tear her eyes away as the wolf-man touched drops of what looked like wine on each of the woman's nipples. Linnet swallowed, feeling her own nipples tighten unaccountably.

The woman on the table moved her lips to the chant,

rocking her head from side to side. A line of the deep red liquid curved down the glistening skin of the side of the woman's breast.

The chanting grew louder and more insistent as the wolf-man dipped his fingers in the bowl again. This time, he dripped the red liquid onto the sensitive spot between the woman's legs. Three times he repeated the ritual, dripping the liquid onto the woman's nipples and between her legs. Each round, the chanting in the room pulsed louder and louder, an ancient sound from pagan times.

Linnet let her breath out when one of the fur-clad figures came forward to take the bowl from him. But it was not over. The wolf-man leaned over the woman and lowered his masked face to her breast, where he had dripped wine. The woman moaned as he gave a sucking kiss to her nipple.

As he lowered his mouth to her other breast and kissed it, the chanting grew louder until it pulsed in Linnet's body. The dancers' movements were frantic, twirling and flailing, casting unearthly shadows against the walls.

Linnet held her breath as the wolf-man took hold of the woman's ankles. Then, as Linnet knew he would, he slid the woman's feet apart and leaned down to place the last kiss between her legs. As he did so, the woman tossed her head and chanted.

Mary, Mother of God, protect me. Mary, Mother of God, protect me. Linnet prayed even as she was rooted to the ground, unable to take her eyes from the scene before her. She was horrified, and yet there was a dull ache between her legs. It was as if some primeval force held her there and would not let her go. Three times, the wolf-man did the ritual kisses.

Then, in a sudden movement, the man straightened and swung his arms out, flinging back the wolf skin. He was naked beneath it, his member engorged. Linnet gasped and finally scrambled to her feet.

But then, the eyes behind the wolf mask met hers and held them, as if he had known she was there in the dark watching all along. Her heart pulsed in her ears in rhythm with the pounding chant. The wolf-man kept his eyes fixed on hers as he grasped the woman's thighs and thrust forward.

Linnet screamed and ran blindly into the darkness. With one hand banging against the wall to guide her, she stumbled through the passageway. The chanting followed her, vibrating off the walls and pressing in on her from all sides.

Mary, Mother of God, protect me. Mary, Mother of God, protect me.

At last, she saw a dim light high above her. She imagined the masked figures of hideous demons chasing her, grabbing at her feet, but she did not look back. Fear choked her as she lurched up the steps toward the light.

Chapter Twelve

After a clandestine meeting with the bishop next door at Westminster Abbey, Jamie returned to the palace. He was weary of politics. Intent on escape, he avoided the Great Hall, which was still crowded, and headed for the privy palace. Most of Gloucester's guests were Londoners and would be returning to their homes tonight. Consequently, the guest wing was nearly empty—and blessedly quiet.

As he neared his guest chamber, running footsteps broke the silence. With his hand on the hilt of his sword, he followed the sound to the corner ahead—and saw Linnet. She was looking over her shoulder and running hard right at him.

"Ahhh!" Linnet gave a piercing scream as he caught her.

Her eyes were as big as platters, and her chest rose and fell in rapid breaths, as if she had been badly frightened. And she was utterly filthy.

"Linnet, what has happened to you?"

She opened her mouth as if to speak, but then only shook her head.

Mother of God. Keeping his voice calm with an effort, he asked, "Are you hurt?"

When she shook her head again, relief poured through him.

"Come, my chamber is right here," he said, guiding her with an arm around her shoulders. "We will get you cleaned up, and then find Francois."

Her headdress was askew, and a dozen tiny braids had come uncoiled and fallen loose from the nets on either side of her face. How could a woman be such a mess and look more beautiful than ever?

"I had a small fright," she said, her voice unnaturally high. "But I am all right now."

"I am sure you are," he said as he opened his chamber door and brought her inside.

He had forgotten that both his manservant and Martin would be in his chamber. They jumped to their feet and gawked open-mouthed at Linnet, but had the grace to look away when she tilted her chin up and stared them down.

"Go now," Jamie said in a low voice and tilted his head toward the door. The two murmured their hope that the lady was unharmed and filed out.

His manservant stuck his head back through the door to say, "The pitcher of water by the brazier should be warm now."

Jamie nodded his thanks. With his free hand, he picked up the pitcher on his way to the wash table.

Steam rose as he poured the water into the basin.

"Oh, my!" Linnet said, looking down at herself for the first time. And then she laughed, of all things.

Lord above, there was no woman like her.

The water turned brown and gritty as she washed

her hands. While she wiped them on the small towel he
handed her, he took the basin to the window and tossed
the dirty water out.

He poured more water in it, then stood back and
watched as she washed her face. It was an intimate activity to witness—something she did every day, alone in her
bedchamber. Water dripped from her long slender fingers
as they caressed her cheeks and forehead. With her eyes
closed, she reached her arm out. He handed her the towel
again, as if he always shared this routine with her.

When she looked up from the towel, her skin was damp
and glowing. And she was smiling at him.

He took the towel from her to wipe a drop from her
chin.

"You've smudges on your neck as well." He dipped the
edge of the towel in the basin and took his time dabbing at
a long streak of mud that ran from beneath her ear and—
God help him—down across her collarbone. He swallowed. This was dangerous country. But he already knew
he was not going to turn back.

He dipped the towel in the water again. Her breathing
grew shallow as he wiped at another streak marring the
perfect white skin just above her bodice. His own breathing quickened as he saw how her nipples pressed against
the cloth.

"Your gown is heavy with mud and past saving, anyway," he said. "You'd best take it off and wear my cloak to
leave the palace."

She nodded and turned around for him to undo the buttons. He undid them slowly, praying this was going where
he thought it was. He should ask her what had happened,
how she got so filthy.

But if she did not care to discuss it right now, neither did he.

His mouth was dry as he eased the gown off her shoulders. This was wrong, he knew it. He might regret it later, but no man was made to resist this kind of temptation. At least for him, Linnet was the apple in the garden. The one great passion he could not resist.

He stood still, aching to touch her. Every part of him throbbed with need as she pulled the gown down over her breasts and hips. It fell to the floor with a wet swoosh.

When she turned, her lips were parted. His breath caught at the sight of the pink tips of her nipples showing through the thin white cloth of her chemise. When he returned his gaze to her face, she was looking at him with wide blue eyes, in that direct way she had, as if he were the only man in the world for her.

"Jamie...," she whispered, leaning toward him.

He pulled her against him and crushed his mouth to hers. God, how he wanted her. Her hands gripped his hair, and her mouth was open, tongue seeking his. His desire grew into a raging inferno.

And she was as inflamed as he. When she locked her arms around his neck, he did not care if this was heaven or hell. He clamped his hands on her buttocks and pressed her against his throbbing shaft. Right now. He wanted her right now.

Nay, he wanted her naked first. He pulled away, breathing hard. Her lips were swollen from his kisses.

"Your chemise," was all he could manage to say.

She nodded and reached down her side for the hem.

"Slowly," he said and dropped to his knees beside her. He ran his hands up her bare thigh as she eased the cloth up out of his way. Closing his eyes, he rested his head on her hip as he rolled her stockings down, inch by inch. She tugged at the chemise to free it, and his face touched bare skin.

"Touch me," Linnet said above him, and it was all he wanted to do.

It was always like this between them. A shared lust that allowed for no embarrassment. No denial.

She quivered as he ran one hand up the inside of her thigh. When he touched her center, she was already hot and wet, and he thought he might explode. She leaned forward against the wash table, gripping it with both hands as he moved his fingers over her sensitive nub. When she dropped her head to rest her forehead on the table, he nipped at the smooth rounded flesh of her buttocks with his teeth.

He thrust a finger inside her, and she gasped. His throat tightened. Oh, Lord, she was going to come quickly the first time.

He'd been wanting to taste her since he first dropped to his knees, and he wasn't getting up until he did.

"Turn round and lean your back against the table," he said.

Without a word, she did as he asked. Her chemise had fallen down so he pushed it up to her hips to reveal the golden triangle of hair.

He looked up at her. "Will you be too cold if you take your chemise off?"

In one motion, she crossed her arms, pulled it over her head, and dropped it on the floor.

Her breasts were as beautiful as ever. He covered them with his hands. She groaned as he finally put his mouth to her. No other woman tasted like her. What did the priests know about women, to preach that this was a sin?

"Aye, aye," she said in harsh breaths as she tangled her fingers in his hair.

His shaft throbbed as he licked and sucked. Every sigh and groan told him she was closer. He wanted to hear her scream with pleasure, to know no other man could do this for her.

He stuck his finger in her as he worked the sensitive spot with his tongue. How he loved it when her breathing changed like this. He knew her, could read her body as if it were an extension of his own.

Her cries as she climaxed were the sweetest sound a man could hear.

"My knees are weak," she said, her voice breathy, weak. "I will fall..."

"I've got you."

He put an arm behind her knees and swung her up across his chest as he got to his feet. When she put limp arms around his neck, he gave her a deep kiss to remind her he was a long way from being finished.

She gave him a languid smile and raised an eyebrow. "You are not going to regret it this time, are you?"

He shook his head and carried her to the bed.

After the weeks of denial, his hunger was so great it made him shake. He made love to her as if it were the first time and might be the last. Their passion for each other was bottomless and heedless.

Afterward, he lay with her sprawled on top of him, with only one thought in his head: *This is what I want.*

She is what I want.

Why had he been fighting it? This was how it should be.

Owen was right. If she was the woman he wanted—and she was—he should stay and conquer, not leave the field.

He ran his hand down her back and cupped her bottom. As she sighed and moved against him, he smiled to himself. The effort to win her would be a good deal more pleasant than trying to resist her had been. Aye, this would be no penance at all.

Linnet would find that he could be every bit as determined as she, once his mind was set. And it was set on her.

Pride is a terrible thing. He wanted to leave her sated. He wanted to make certain that the next time she wanted a man, she could think of no one but him. He wanted her to sit by her window and long for him, ache for him. To dream of him, despite herself. To know that no other would ever satisfy her completely.

He wanted her to suffer as he did.

Jamie lay propped up on one elbow, watching her.

Without opening her eyes, Linnet took a deep, satisfied breath and murmured, "I cannot lift my arms."

She looked as though her body fit the mattress like warm wax on the candle holder.

When she cracked her eyes open, he could not help giving her a wide grin. Then he blew on the damp skin between her breasts, down the center of her chest.

"That feels...heavenly," she said, closing her eyes again.

He blew again, making her sigh.

"If we are to have an affair again, as it appears we are," he said, "this time, it will be on my terms."

Her eyes snapped open. "Terms? You speak as if we were enemies settling a war between us."

"You are always insightful. Now, do you want to know the terms?" She drew in a sharp breath as he paused to flick his tongue over her still-sensitive nipple. "Or shall we end it here?"

He could not be sure if that was a flash of hurt in her eyes or just surprise. Regardless, he was not making the mistake of showering her with romantic professions of love this time. Nay, he was a wiser man. And he was out to win.

"I cannot say," she said, lifting an eyebrow, "until I know the terms you propose."

"First rule: no other men during the course of our affair."

She must have felt at a disadvantage lying down, for she sat up and wrapped her arms around her knees. "Then no other women either."

"Agreed. Rule two: When one of us wishes to end it, we will simply advise the other."

She rolled her eyes. "Will it be sufficient just to tell the other person, or must this be done in writing?"

He smiled. "Either method will do."

"Any other terms?" she asked, sitting straighter and sounding very prim.

"Just one more." He held her eyes as he ran his finger slowly down the length of her arm. "I know there are herbs you can take to prevent conceiving a child."

"'Tis no guarantee," she snapped, then turned her head to glare at the tapestry on the wall—a particularly gruesome one of a bleeding saint with a chestful of arrows that was unlikely to help her mood. In a low voice, she muttered, "Just like a man, thinking a drink of herbs could be foolproof."

"All the same," he said, keeping his tone easy. "Will you do it?"

He did not want her to feel trapped into marrying him. Nor did he want to always wonder if a child was the only reason she did so. There would be time for children later.

"I don't want you thinking I did it on purpose, should something happen." She lifted her chin. "Still, you need not fret. If I did conceive, there are other herbs I could take that have a more certain effect."

Her words sent a flash of anger through him that almost made him forget the game he was playing. Somehow, he managed to keep his features smooth and not shout at her.

"Or," she said, "I could simply return to France without ever telling you."

You could try, but I'd catch you before you ever made it to the damned ship. He gave her a broad smile that he suspected looked more wolf-like than complacent.

"Perhaps I will save us both a lot of trouble, *Sir James*, and end this." She got down from the bed, scooped up his clothes from the floor, and tossed them at him. "I shall let you know what I decide."

He ran his gaze over her slowly, wishing she was in the mood for another tumble. With an inward sigh, he watched her march across the room stark naked to grab his cloak from the back of the door. Her eyes were snapping as she turned and wrapped it tightly around herself.

Linnet was most definitely not in the mood for another tumble. Still, he had cause to be well pleased. Her fury was a very good sign.

He hid his smile as he dressed. Then he picked up the towel they had used earlier and began to wipe the mud from her shoes. Good Lord, where had she been today? They smelled of river marshes.

He did the best he could with them, then dropped to his knees beside her. "Here, give me your foot."

She snatched the slippers from his hand and headed for the door. "Let us go."

"Linnet," he said, catching her arm, "what happened to you earlier, before . . ."

"Nothing happened tonight." She turned and looked him in the eye to be sure he caught her meaning. "Nothing that mattered."

As she stormed out the door ahead of him, he heard her say, "You bastard," under her breath.

Jamie walked down the hall with her, cocksure of himself. He had Linnet right where he wanted her. Or soon would have. Ha! She would not hold out a day before she crawled into his bed again.

He would take his time, pretend he had no expectations for the future. His mistake before had been to pressure her and tell her exactly what he wanted. This time, he would worm his way into her heart until she could not imagine life without him.

It was like laying siege. It took patience. And steady bombardment helped, he thought with a smile. But eventually, the walls would be breached, and the gate opened.

By Saint Wilgefort's beard, she was going to be his. Linnet would never even know how it happened. But when this was all over, Jamie intended to be her lover *and* her husband.

Chapter Thirteen

Linnet sat on the window seat in her solar, knees pulled up and chin resting on her arms, thinking dreamily of the last three days and nights. She let out a deep sigh, feeling more content than she could remember.

When Jamie arrived at her door the morning after their fight, she meant to slam the door in his face. But somehow . . . she could not.

The sight of him would turn a nun's heart to mush. With eyes the color of deep-blue velvet, in striking contrast with his dark hair, and the strong lines and planes of his face, Sir James Rayburn was the sort of handsome that caused even staid matrons to turn their heads as they passed him on the street.

She'd had a weakness for Jamie Rayburn since she was a girl of fifteen, and it was not likely to change. There was something solid and reassuring about Jamie that drew her even more than his looks. He never boasted, but he walked with a confidence that said he was not afraid of any fight—and that he would choose the side of right, no matter the odds.

So when she saw him filling her doorway, the anger

burning in her chest drained out of her into a puddle at her feet. She should have taken offense at the presumption of the bag slung over his shoulder. Instead, she appreciated the unambiguous message: Jamie had come to her house intending to stay.

Her skin had prickled as Jamie's gaze burned over her, head to toe and back up again. Then, without a word, he had kicked the door shut behind him, grabbed her wrist, and headed for the stairs. She made not a word of protest. With an unerring sense of direction, Jamie passed the other rooms and led her straight to her bedchamber.

Her heart beat hard in her chest as he crushed her in his arms and gave her a deep kiss against the back of her bedchamber door. Soon, they fell to the floor. That first time, they never made it to the bed.

Three days later, she still had burns on her knees. But she was not complaining.

Francois had disappeared, and her two servants had the sense to stay well out of the way, so they had the house to themselves. They made love until they were too weak to move, then lay in bed talking and laughing. Each afternoon, they managed to go out for two or three hours to take care of their separate errands in London.

On the first day, she beat on Alderman Arnold's door until a servant informed her that the family had left the City for their estate in Kent. She was told the same at the Guild Hall, so she let the matter rest.

For all her effort, she seemed no closer to discovering who was behind the scheme that destroyed her grandfather's business. In time, she would find the alderman and force him to answer her questions. In time, she would discover the man behind it all. But just this once, she allowed herself to set aside the burden she carried. She let herself have this one gift, while it was offered.

Today was their last day in London, so she wished Jamie would hurry back from his visit to the bishop. She had returned an hour ago from meeting with Master Woodley.

At the sound of the door, she turned, a well of happiness surging inside her chest. But it was Francois, not Jamie, who walked into the solar.

"Where have you been?" she asked.

"Here and there," Francois said with a shrug. He stopped and narrowed his eyes at her. "But what has happened here? You seem...different."

It could be trying at times to have a twin.

"Different?" she asked, to avoid answering his question. "How do you mean?"

"Happy. Content. You are never truly either, so something remarkable must have occurred. Did you murder one of the men you are after or..." He looked around the room sharply, then back at her. "'Tis a man. You've got a man here."

Linnet folded her arms across her chest.

"Who is it?" His stern expression melted into a broad grin. "'Tis Jamie Rayburn, isn't it?"

She shifted her gaze to the ceiling.

"Any other man, and I would feel compelled to beat him or some such thing. But Jamie is a good man." Francois grabbed an apple from the bowl on the table, sat down beside her, and put his feet up. "You should have married him the first time around."

"I assure you," she said in a tight voice, "marriage is not on Jamie's mind this time."

"And this annoys you." Francois cocked his head, a smile playing at the corners of his mouth. "How very interesting."

He took a large bite of the apple with his straight white teeth. His eyes sparkled with amusement as he crunched it.

"I am not annoyed by it," she said. "I have no time to have a lovesick fool dogging my every footstep."

"Mmm-hmm," Francois said between bites.

"I'll slap that irritating little smile off your face if you do not stop it," she snapped.

As soon as she said it, she knew she sounded exactly as she had at ten. When she met Francois's eyes, they both burst into laughter. She could never stay angry with him for long.

After their laughter had died, Francois said in a quiet voice, "I suspect that if you want something more from Jamie Rayburn, all you need do is tell him."

"Ha, that is all you know about it," she said, flicking her hand in the air. "Jamie is quite content with things as they are. As am I. You know there are things I must do."

No husband—particularly Jamie Rayburn—would allow her the freedom she needed to pursue her plans.

"For God's sake, Linnet, leave it be," Francois said, losing his easy manner.

"I just need a little more time."

"Five years of your life ought to be enough."

She had accomplished a great deal in five years, but she chose not to say it.

Francois took her chin in his hand and leaned close. "You are keeping something from me, aren't you?"

She met his gaze without blinking. It was difficult to

keep anything from her twin, but she was determined not to tell him about going down the hidden passageway and finding the witches' cabal. Jamie had goaded her into telling him most of it, and that had caused her enough grief. She did not need a second scathing lecture.

The fact that she had come away from the adventure unharmed would not appease Francois any more than it had Jamie. She needed Francois's help with her plans. If he knew about this, he would be even less inclined to give it.

"You cannot keep a secret from me, so why attempt it?" Francois said. "Besides, I know the absolute worst about you, and I still love you. The best outweighs the worst by a thousand times."

"I have nothing to tell."

"Come," he said, giving her his most charming smile, "confess to your brother."

"Perhaps I will, if you will tell me about the woman who kept you from home the past three days."

Francois gave her his cat's smile. "A man must keep some secrets from his sister."

She gave him a matching smile. *And vice versa, brother dear.*

Jamie was whistling to himself as he walked up the Strand to Linnet's house when someone grabbed his arm from behind.

"Francois." Jamie dropped the point of his dagger from the base of Francois's throat and sheathed the blade. "Surprising a man like that could get you killed."

Francois, to his credit, had not blinked an eye.

"All this about you having no serious intentions toward

my sister is a lie, is it not?" Francois asked, his eyes drilling holes through Jamie.

Jamie was a brother, too, so he respected Francois's right to ask the question. More, he felt a surge of sympathy for Francois's having a sister like Linnet to keep watch over. Three of his sisters put together would never be as much trouble.

"I mean to make her my wife," Jamie said. "You won't tell her, will you?"

"Not a word, my friend," Francois said, slapping him on the shoulder. "Not a word."

"We need to talk," Jamie said. "Let us find a public house where we can have a cup of ale."

"You want me to give you advice on how to get around my hardheaded sister?" Francois said with a grin.

"Aye, and I need to tell you what happened to Linnet at Westminster three days ago."

They turned down a narrow side street and stepped into the first tavern they found. It was dark and small, with rushes over a dirt floor and two unkempt customers asleep in the back corner. After getting their cups of ale, Jamie and Francois sat at a table next to the door where the air was not so sour.

"This could happen to no one else," Francois said after Jamie told him about the witches' cabal. Then he cursed in three languages Jamie could identify and one or two he could not.

Francois tilted his head back and emptied his cup, then signaled to the tavernkeeper. After the man refilled their cups, he raised his to Jamie.

"I love my sister with all my heart, but I pray to God she may become your trial soon."

"I hope so," Jamie said and clanked his cup against Francois's. "You're her twin. You understand her best. Am I right to deceive her as to my intentions?"

"For certain," Francois said with an emphatic nod. "Linnet is as stubborn as the day is long. She won't be pushed. You've a much better chance if she believes it is her idea."

"So, we shall make a pact, then, behind her back," Jamie said, raising his cup again.

Francois laughed as he touched his cup to Jamie's. "How she would hate it, but 'tis for her own good."

"I love her," Jamie said, "but as God is my witness, I cannot understand why she must do the things she does."

Francois dropped his usual smile and stared into his cup. "She wants justice in a world that is not just," he said after a time. "She wants to set things aright."

"Where was the justice in using me to punish your father?" Jamie could not help but ask. "Why did she not tell me about Pomeroy's offer and trust me to find a way?"

Francois leaned back and blew out a long breath. "The only person she trusts—besides me—is herself. She took all that happened to us when we were children harder than I did—being motherless, our father's neglect, losing everything when our grandfather fell ill. Even if she believes you care for her, she will not let herself rely on you."

"But what of my uncle Stephen and Isobel?" Jamie said. "She shares a close bond with them."

"She did learn to trust them, so there is hope for you." Francois waggled an eyebrow. "But as I recall, it did involve a life-and-death struggle."

"Aye, it did," Jamie said and shook his head. They sat in silence for a time before he spoke again. "Stephen says the two of you fought him like crazed animals when he and my father found you in Falaise."

"In sooth, I do not know what would have happened to us if Stephen had not taken it upon himself to act as our protector," Francois said. "I expect we would have been forced into a whorehouse."

That was precisely what Jamie's father said. Jamie hated to think about Linnet as she had been then—a breathtakingly beautiful girl, with no home, no money, and only a brother her age to defend her. It was hard to imagine it now, but Francois had looked almost as pretty as his sister at that age.

Francois sighed. "I fear, my friend, that you will need to prove yourself to Linnet over and over again," Francois said, then winked. "But she is worth it."

"She is, indeed," Jamie said, getting to his feet.

He was tired of talking, and even more tired of thinking about how to manage her and mold her to his will. All he wanted was to be with her, to have her safe in his arms.

He remembered to lift a hand in farewell to Francois as he went out the door. 'Twas past time to go. He'd been away from her far too long.

Chapter Fourteen

Linnet threw her arms around Jamie's neck as soon as he came through the door. "The bishop kept you far too long."

He kissed the tip of her nose. "Did you miss me?"

"I did," she admitted, since it was far too late to pretend otherwise.

"I missed you more," Jamie said. Then he gave her a kiss that curled her toes—and almost made her believe it.

She rested her cheek against his chest and sighed as he ran his fingers through her hair. The steady *thump-thump* of his heart brought her an unfamiliar sense of peace. In the happiness of the moment, she could almost forget the difficult tasks she had set for herself.

"Francois was here," she said.

"Hmm."

She felt a bit guilty for being glad the two had missed each other. But this was their last day in London, and she did not want to share what little time they had left even with her brother.

"Once we return to Windsor, we won't be able to be together like this," Jamie said, echoing her thoughts.

Being at Windsor would be like it was in Paris—kissing in darkened courtyards and making love between old pots and bags of grain in dusty storerooms. She suspected that what had seemed exciting to Jamie at eighteen would no longer sit well with him. Jamie was a man now, the sort who was used to living his life in the open, with nothing to hide.

Jamie took her face in his hands and smiled down at her with a soft look in his eyes. "We'll sneak off as often as we can."

The secrecy suited her; she was reticent to have anyone know her business. But Jamie was not as comfortable about "sneaking off" as he pretended.

One thing was different from when they were in Paris. While he was affectionate with her, no declaration of love ever passed his lips. She told herself this was good, that it would make it easier when he left her this time.

But she did not believe it.

"Let's not waste what time we have left here," Jamie said, lifting her chin. "Come upstairs with me."

She nodded. However long it lasted, she had him now.

Much later, when they lay entwined in her bed in the fading afternoon light, Jamie said, "I could not find the hidden door in the corridor at Westminster."

She disentangled her legs from his and got up on one elbow. "I thought you had an appointment with the bishop."

"I wanted to see the secret passageway before I met with him."

She sat up. "Did you not believe me? I am not some silly woman who sees things that are not there."

"You, silly? What a notion," he said, rolling his eyes.

"Nay, I never doubted you. In fact, I told the bishop all about the witches' cabal you witnessed."

Her cheeks grew warm. "How could you tell him what I saw? He is a churchman!"

Jamie laughed and ran his hand up her arm. "In sooth, I do not believe it is possible to shock the bishop. Though the pleasures of the flesh do not rule him, celibacy is not one of his virtues. He has a mistress, you know."

"But why would you tell him?"

"If witches are brazen enough to meet in the bowels of Westminster Palace, who knows what evil they are up to? You forget, our young king was in the palace when this happened."

"I suppose it is good to be cautious, but their interest did not appear to be . . . political," she said, thinking of the naked woman on the table.

Jamie sat up and grabbed both her arms.

"Going down that passageway alone was so dangerous, I still cannot believe you did it," he said, his eyes like blue fire. "What in God's name made you do it?"

She was not about to confess that she had thought she was following Alderman Arnold.

"We have discussed this already—or rather, you shouted," she said, arching her eyebrows. "It is over and done with."

Praise God she'd had the good sense not to tell Jamie the whole tale. If Jamie knew she suspected the wolf-man had seen her—and, God forbid, what he was doing at the time—Jamie would have gone into an even worse rage than he had.

"You are hurting me," she said, though he was not,

truly. When she looked pointedly at where Jamie's fingers were digging into her arms, he released his grip at once.

"Sorry, but each time I think of you down there alone with them, I want to kill someone." He looked away from her and narrowed his eyes. "I want to feel my blade buried to the hilt in that wolf-man's gut . . . or squeeze the life out of him with my hands around his throat."

Linnet suppressed a shiver as she remembered the wolf-man's eyes boring into hers. She felt so blissful—and so safe—with Jamie at her house that she had been able to push aside thoughts of the witches most of the time. When she awoke with nightmares, Jamie's arms were about her. His solid presence soothed her.

"Another reason I told Beaufort about the witches," Jamie said, picking up the thread of his conversation again, "is that I thought he might be privy to the secrets of the palace."

"Did he know of the hidden passageway?" she asked.

"The bishop says there was once a secret passageway, but he denies knowing where it was."

"What will he do about the witches?" Linnet asked.

"He'll keep his eyes and ears open for sorcery and any sort of treachery against the king," Jamie said. "And the bishop has a great many eyes and ears."

"You mean the monks and priests under his purview?" Linnet asked. "What will they know of demon-worshippers?"

Jamie lay back on the bed and put his arms behind his head. "The Winchester geese are the bishop's best source of information—the prostitutes hear most everything."

Linnet twisted a strand of Jamie's hair around her

finger as she debated whether to tell him. Finally, she said, "I learned something else the bishop might like to know."

As Jamie waited in silence for her to tell him, she ran her fingers in a slow circle over his bare chest.

"How well do you know Lady Eleanor Cobham?" she asked and felt Jamie's muscles tense beneath her fingertips.

"Why do you ask?" he said in a voice that was too casual.

She stopped her hand and looked him in the eye. "I heard something about her when I was in London before."

"There is always some gossip about Eleanor."

He spoke without meeting her eyes, and she did not like it.

"I made a purchase from an old woman who makes herbal remedies." Even under torture, she would not admit she had gone seeking a potion to make Jamie repulsive to her.

She waited for him to ask what her visit to a herbalist had to do with Eleanor, but Jamie's lips were shut tight.

"The old woman told me," she said, drawing the words out, "that Eleanor used love potions on Humphrey, Duke of Gloucester."

"Women waste their money on such 'magic' all the time," Jamie said. "The City and the church officials turn a blind eye to it so long as there is no allegation of sorcery."

"That is the thing." Linnet turned so that her legs hung over the side of the bed and began to swing them. "The old herbalist says Eleanor obtains her potions from Margery Jourdemayne, a woman who works in the dark arts. This Margery is known as the Witch of Eye."

Linnet wondered where the old herbalist was. When she went to her shop today, the door had been locked tight. Her neighbors said they had not seen the old woman in weeks.

"Tell me your curiosity did not move you to seek out this Witch of Eye," Jamie said, sitting up. "It would be just like you."

Linnet glanced sideways at Jamie. Despite his disparaging tone, his expression was uneasy.

"You know something about this," she said, turning to tap her finger against his chest. "And about Eleanor Cobham."

He ran a hand through his hair and looked at the door, as if contemplating escape.

"What is it?" she said.

"You will laugh and think me a fool."

Jamie looked like a boy caught eating cakes before supper.

"Perhaps I will," she said, "but tell me all the same."

He fidgeted some more, blew out a breath, and glanced at the door yet again before he finally spoke. "When I was in London two or three years ago, I went to bed with Eleanor."

His words stung like vinegar on a fresh cut. Jamie, however, showed no sign he noticed how his words made her wince.

"I had no intention of going with her, at first." Jamie shrugged. "When she made it plain she was inviting me to her bed—the woman was not subtle—I tried to find a way to politely refuse her."

"But you changed your mind," Linnet said, doing her best to keep the razor-sharp anger she felt out of her voice.

"'Twas strange," Jamie said, looking at his hands. "After having no thought except how to make my escape, quite suddenly, I wanted her. In fact, I wanted her so badly that ... well ..."

"Well what?"

He shrugged again, looking slightly embarrassed. "Well, I believe I took her right there in the corridor outside her chamber the first time."

He could not wait to get Eleanor into her room?

The *first* time?

"And you thought I would laugh at this?" Linnet said, her voice rising.

Jamie looked at her with wide eyes. "'Twas not my fault. The woman drugged me!"

Linnet turned her head away. "I am not your wife," she said through clenched teeth. "You need not lie to me."

"I swear to you, she must have given me a potion. No woman would have been safe from me. I was like a bull in spring, mindless to anything but rutting, rutting, rutting."

"How did you survive this trial?"

Somehow, Jamie failed to realize her question was rhetorical. Instead, the fool said, "In sooth, my cock was hellish sore for days."

Did he think she wanted to hear that? She wanted to throw something at him, but there was nothing close at hand on the bed.

"How long were you in that room with her, Jamie Rayburn?"

"Two, three days? 'Tis hard to say. I stayed until the madness passed." When he caught her expression, he raised his hands, palms out. "I could not leave and let myself loose on the rest of womankind in the state I was in."

"How chivalrous of you. The absolute height of chivalry, to be sure." She got down from the bed, flung her robe on, and pulled it tight around herself. "You should go now."

"You are angry?" he asked, his eyes wide and blinking. "Come, do not tell me you are jealous of a woman who had to drug me to get her way with me."

"Jealous? Why would I be jealous?" she snapped. "I had lovers, too."

It was almost true. She had very nearly done it. She'd wanted to. She'd meant to. She would at her very next opportunity!

Jamie dropped down from the high bed and grabbed her by the shoulders. The anger in his eyes was most gratifying. But whatever he was about to shout at her, he bit it back.

"You will follow our agreement?" he said with an edge to his voice. "No other lovers during our affair."

How dare he accuse her after what he'd just confessed? She twisted away from his grip and glared at him.

"If I do take another lover," she said, "I'll be sure to claim he slipped a potion into my cup."

Linnet was so angry Jamie could almost see the steam rising off her as she stood, arms folded and eyes blazing. He had to work to hide his smile. Ha! She was jealous of a woman he went to bed with more than two years ago— and against his will.

If that was not a good sign, he did not know what was.

Of course, he had wanted to shake her until her teeth rattled for that remark about her other lovers. That had scalded; he still felt the burn of her words in his belly.

He sucked in a deep breath. He could not change her past. What mattered was that he would be the last lover she ever had.

Because, by God, she would never have another.

Jamie pulled her into his arms. She was stiff as an iron pike, but he stifled her protests with a kiss. A moment later, her arms went around his neck, and she melted into him like butter on hot bread.

Aye, she was his for good. She just did not know it yet.

Chapter Fifteen

Joanna Courcy, the boldest of the queen's ladies-in-waiting, grabbed Linnet by the wrist and pulled her into the privy chamber behind the screen in the Great Hall.

"You must speak to her!" Joanna said, her voice high and shrill. "We are all at our wits' end."

Joanna could be speaking only of Queen Katherine.

"I shall help if I can," Linnet said. "What is it that troubles you?"

"The queen and that *Welshman*," Joanna hissed in her ear.

With a sinking feeling in her stomach, Linnet asked, "Has she been indiscreet?"

"She is all a-twitter over him," Joanna said, her hands fluttering in the air. "And he, a lowly commoner."

Which was entirely beside the point.

"We have dropped quiet hints, but she ignores them," Joanna said. "None of us can speak to her as you do."

Linnet hid her misgivings and patted the woman's arm. "Do not fret. I shall speak with Her Highness at once." And she would give that Owen Tudor a good tongue-lashing as well.

The journey from London had been long and tiring. All she wanted to do now was change her clothes, settle her things into her chamber, and then go off somewhere with Jamie. After the freedom they had in London, it had been hard to sit next to him for hours on the barge and not be able to touch him as she wanted to. The most she could do was occasionally touch her fingers to his arm.

But the queen needed her, so she would have to wait to have time alone with Jamie. Without stopping in her own chamber to change, she went to the queen's apartment.

Queen Katherine greeted her with a warm smile that lit up her eyes. "My dear Linnet," she said, taking her hands, "'tis good to have you back with us."

"Your Highness, what is this I hear about you and Owen? I begged you to be cau—"

"Sometimes I despair of you," Queen Katherine said, rolling her eyes heavenward. "No wasting time with 'How do you fare, Your Highness?' Or, 'Lovely gown you are wearing today, Your Grace.'"

"I am sorry," Linnet said, knowing the chastisement was just. She often forgot to observe the niceties expected in noble society. "You do look exquisite today, but I am anxious for you to tell me I've no cause to worry."

"No need to fret," Queen Katherine said with a sparkle in her eyes. "For 'tis too late for it to do any good."

"Too late?" Linnet asked, panic rising in her throat. "What can you mean?"

The queen leaned close and whispered next to Linnet's ear, "I've already gone to bed with him." When Linnet tried to lean back to stare at her, the queen pulled her close again. "And it was *wonderful*."

Linnet felt her eyes go wide. Good heavens, what was

she to advise the queen now? "Your Highness, I understand how...overpowering...that can be. It can cloud one's thinking."

That was the honest truth.

"I suffer no confusion," the queen said, smiling at her.

"You are infatuated," Linnet said. "'Tis a passing fancy. Nothing that merits taking a great risk."

"I am so happy, my dear," the queen said, taking Linnet's hands again and squeezing them. "Please try to be pleased for me."

Heaven help her, this could not be worse. Clearly, her friend could not see sense just now.

"Enjoy him for a time if it pleases you," Linnet said. "But I beg you, keep it quiet. No one must hear of this."

"Come, what do you think I have done?" the queen asked with a laugh. "Sent messengers to the four corners of the kingdom to proclaim the news?"

"If you insist on proceeding with this...this..."—Linnet wanted to say "foolishness," but thought better of it— "affair, then it must be done in secret. Your ladies and I can arrange clandestine meetings, if you wish. But you absolutely must not spend hours behind closed doors with Owen when the entire castle knows he is alone in there with you."

"Why must I hide my feelings?" her friend said, her eyes growing sad. "I only want what every woman wants."

Could the queen be thinking of a serious alliance here? An affair with one of her underlings would stir unwanted troubles, but marriage was utterly impossible.

"Perhaps someday you shall have all you want," Linnet

said, because this was the only hope she could truthfully give her friend. "But it cannot be now."

"How long must I wait?" the queen demanded. "When will the men who keep my son judge him old enough that a man who pays court to me is not a threat to their influence? Can you tell me, Linnet? Will it be ten years? Fifteen?"

What had happened to the meek princess who always did what was expected of her? This woman who leaned forward with her hands on her hips and anger sparking in her eyes was not the same.

"I cannot give him up," Queen Katherine said, her voice firm. "I will not."

"I see," Linnet said, though she was not certain she did. "If you are set on continuing this dangerous affair, then at least let me give you herbs to help prevent a pregnancy."

"But my dear," the queen said with a soft smile. "I want a child."

Linnet fell back a step and reached behind her for a chair.

"In sooth, I hope Owen and I will have many children," the queen said with a faraway look in her eyes.

"Then I shall pray for you, Your Highness." The fear rising in Linnet's chest made her voice come out low and choked. "I shall pray night and day, for the path you are choosing is a perilous one."

"It is a path I will not walk alone."

Linnet swallowed. "Tell me. Is Owen worth the risk you are taking?"

The queen met her eyes. "I love him," she said, as if that answered all.

"But you were married to King Henry. You loved him, did you not?"

"Aye, but in a different way," Queen Katherine said with a sigh. "Like everyone, I was in awe of him. Henry was a great man, a king for the ages."

Linnet had adored King Henry, who was like a king from tales of old. Owen was not a bad sort, but next to King Henry, he seemed so...ordinary.

"With Henry, everything came before me," the queen said. "He was always off fighting or occupied with affairs of state. But Owen wants only to be with me and make me happy."

"How long can he make you happy?" Linnet asked. "If Gloucester or the council find out, there is no telling what they will do."

"They cannot do worse to me than my own mother did in the years of my father's madness," the queen said. "She cared more for her spoiled dogs than for us children."

It was easy to forget that this delicate French princess had suffered a difficult childhood.

"While she entertained her lovers with lavish feasts on the other side of Paris," the queen said, her voice bitter, "we nearly starved because she could not be bothered to pay for our upkeep."

"I beg your pardon, Your Grace." Linnet took her friend's arm and led her to sit on the bench by the windows.

"I will not give him up," the queen said again.

Her friend seemed to have found her strength at last.

"All I ask is that you be cautious," Linnet said, taking the queen's hand in both of hers. "You do understand you must keep your affections a secret?"

After a moment, her friend nodded.

"As you are set on this course, I will do what I can to help you."

"Thank you," the queen said. "I hope someday you will understand that true love is worth any risk."

"Is it worth losing all you hold dear?" Linnet asked, her voice strained. "Your very life?"

"You are braver than I am in so many ways, my friend." The queen touched her fingers to Linnet's cheek and gave her a patient smile. "But you are a coward when it comes to love."

Chapter Sixteen

"Have you spoken to Owen again?" Linnet asked.

"Aye." Jamie kicked a stone out of the path. "And he is every bit as unreasonable as the queen."

A gust of wind blew cold and damp across the river. Linnet shivered and tightened her hold on Jamie's arm. Each afternoon, they walked this path along the Thames where they could speak without risk of being overheard. No one else came out strolling in this chilly weather.

"I have begged the queen to be discreet," Linnet said, "but she is poor at hiding her feelings."

"I am certain no one notices but you," Jamie said. "Owen's lowly status is a blessing, for who would believe the queen would have an affair with her clerk of the wardrobe?"

Linnet rubbed her forehead against a threatening headache. "Until the queen tires of him or comes to her senses, we must help them keep their affair a secret. I've let the queen use my cloak to pretend she is me when she goes to meet him, and—"

Jamie jerked her to a halt and whirled her around to face him. "Linnet, you cannot do this. I forbid it."

"You forbid it?" she said, arching an eyebrow. "Surely, you did not say that."

"Listen to me," he said, fixing eyes as hard as sapphires on her. "You owe the queen your good counsel, and you have given her that. But you cannot do more. You cannot help her with this deception."

"Why not?"

"'Tis far too dangerous." He pressed his fingers into her arms. "Can you not see? If their affair becomes known, it will look as if you promoted it. The council will want to avoid blaming the king's mother for flouting their will, but they will be happy to blame you—a foreigner—for encouraging her misdeeds."

"Let go of me," she said, but she did not argue.

She had learned through painful experience that she and Jamie held different views on what loyalty required. Discussing this further would change neither one's mind. The queen needed her help, and she would give it.

"Don't be angry with me." He caught her hand and raised it to his lips. "You know I am right."

"Ha!" Still, it was hard to stay annoyed with Jamie when he was only trying to protect her—and harder still when he was gazing at her with that hungry look in his eyes.

"Come," he said, tugging on her hand. "Let us find somewhere we can be alone and forget about those two for a while."

She could no more resist him than swim against a strong current. "Do you have a place in mind?"

"I do," he said with a glint in his eyes that sent a tingle all the way to her toes.

In the fortnight since their return from London, they

had made love in the buttery, the wine cellar, empty storerooms, and even the woods—a feat in late November. She would have met him in his bedchamber, but Jamie did not want her being seen going and coming from his room. He worried far more than she did about her reputation.

"I have claimed an empty guestchamber for our use." He held up a long iron key. "I stole this from the steward's key ring."

She laughed. "How did you manage that?"

"I shall never tell, but I expect I've committed an offense against the Crown." He pulled her against him. "For such a risk, I expect to be rewarded."

"You shall, I promise," she said, smiling back at him.

He dropped his arms and stepped away from her, as if suddenly recalling they were within sight of the castle.

"I don't care who sees us," she said. "I have no virtue to be 'tarnished.'"

"Don't speak that way." Jamie looked past her, his jaw set and his expression grim.

She put her hand on his arm and waited until his gaze returned to her face. "I am glad you found a place for us. Tell me where it is, and I shall meet you there now."

When he said nothing, she said, "Please, Jamie."

Her stomach fluttered as his eyes went dark.

"Aye," he said, "'tis past time I had you in a proper bed again."

They returned to the castle together, bid each other good-bye in front of several people outside the hall, and then made their way to the appointed guestchamber by different routes. Following Jamie's directions, Linnet skirted the Round Tower and entered the wing across from the royal apartments.

Her steps echoed as she hurried up the stairs to the second floor. At Christmas, this part of the palace would be filled with guests, but it was empty now.

She hoped the somber mood that had settled over Jamie by the river would not return before she reached the chamber. As soon as she tapped on the door, though, he pulled her into the room and kissed her with a fierceness that left no doubt of his passion for her.

How she wanted him! Every moment she was away from him, she ached for him. She leaned her head against the back of the door and closed her eyes as he pressed hot, wet kisses down her throat.

Strong hands roamed over her body, squeezing, stroking, as his mouth moved along the edge of her bodice.

Then his mouth was on hers, all hunger and want. He pressed his hard shaft against her, making her throb with need between her legs. When he cupped her bottom and lifted her, she had to tear her mouth away from his because she could not breathe. He bit her shoulder as he gripped her hips and held her against him.

How could it be like this every time? This mindless, aching need that took over every part of her—every thought, every hope—was a mystery she could not explain. For five years, she had felt nothing, needed no one. Now, all Jamie had to do was walk into a room and the pent-up desire of their years apart could knock her to her knees.

"Do you want me?" he asked, his breath hot in her ear.

"Oh, aye." She tried to speak the words but was not sure if she said them aloud.

He set her on her feet and held her face in his hands. Looking at her with eyes burning like blue fire, he said, "You do not want me as I want you."

"I do," she confessed. "More."

She heard the ping of buttons popping and hitting the floor as he wrenched her gown open and pulled the bodice below her breasts. When he lifted her up, she wrapped her legs around his hips. She clutched his hair in her hands and let her head fall back as he cupped her breasts and pressed his face between them.

Aye, aye, touch me, touch me. Sensations ripped through her as he rolled her nipples between his thumbs and fingers and planted hot, wet kisses along her breastbone.

She pulled at her skirts. There were layers and layers of cloth between them. She wanted him now. Right now, inside her.

She tried to speak. "Jamie, I want…"

"Wait," he said, his voice low and fierce against her ear. "I shall have you in a bed this time."

She kept her legs wrapped around him as he carried her to the bed.

In a strained voice, he said, "I have not seen you fully naked since we returned from London. I want to. I need to."

She nodded and released her legs.

"Is this a favorite gown?"

No sooner did she shake her head than he rent her gown in two, top to bottom, with his dagger. The burst of cool air felt good on her burning skin. He pulled the shreds of the gown off her, and she was naked.

He stood still a moment, his eyes raking over every inch of her. Then he closed the distance between them; his mouth was on hers, and his hand between her legs. *Aye, aye.* How she needed him.

His tunic felt rough against her breasts. She pulled her mouth away to say, "Your clothes, too."

He threw the bedclothes back with one hand as he lifted her onto the bed. Before getting in beside her, he shed his own clothes. How did men undress so quickly? The thought flitted through her mind and was gone before he climbed up the steps of the high bed. That and every other thought left her as he lay down beside her and pulled her into his arms.

"God in heaven, how I want you, Jamie Rayburn," she said.

In an instant, his mouth was on hers, and she felt the warmth of his skin against her, head to toe. Their tongues moved against each other in deep, hungry kisses. His hand was on her breast, and she moaned into his mouth as he took the nipple between his thumb and finger. When she tore her mouth away, he lowered himself to play with her other nipple with his tongue. She pounded the bed with her fist because it wasn't enough.

"Aye," she said on a breath as he finally took her breast in his mouth and sent sensations jangling through her every nerve. She arched her back, wanting more still, but his hand moving up the inside of her leg distracted her. When he cupped her, she gasped.

Jamie had magic in his fingers. He claimed her mouth again as they did their work, racking her body with an onslaught of pleasure and tension. *Not yet*, she was going to say, because she did not want this only for her...and then she didn't care.

"You are mine," he said against her ear, and she was.

She exploded into waves of pleasure.

Before she could catch her breath, he rolled her so that she lay on top of him. His shaft pressed against her, reminding her of his need and reigniting hers. One of his hands gripped her bottom and the other covered her breast as they kissed surrounded by the curtain of her hair.

She eased herself slowly down his body as she pressed kisses to his neck and chest. Straddling him, she turned her face to feel the hair of his chest against her cheek. He seemed to hold his breath as she ran her tongue down the center of his chest, tasting the salt of his skin. When she circled his nipple with her tongue, he groaned and gripped her hips.

She moved to one side of him and reached for his shaft, wanting to feel the hardness of his need for her. As she wrapped her hand around it, his moan echoed her own desire. She pressed wet kisses down his chest and stomach, letting her hair slide over him as she held his stiff rod in her hand. She wanted to please him, to pleasure him, to make him hers.

Her cheek brushed his shaft as she ran her kisses lower.

"'Tis more than I can stand," he said, but he did not stop her when she took him in her mouth. His hands were in her hair, and his hips rose to meet her as she moved her mouth up and down. His moans egged her on and made her ache between her legs.

Suddenly, he sat up, pulling her up with him. Strong arms lifted her onto his lap. "Wrap your legs around me," he said, his voice thick with desire. "I want to be inside you when I have my release."

Her womb tightened at his words.

"I want us to be one," he said.

His hands splayed over her back, holding her tight against him, as he took her mouth in hot, deep kisses.

She lifted herself to position the tip of his shaft at her entrance. The feel of him against her sent a spasm of anticipation through her.

She put her hands on either side of Jamie's face and looked into his eyes. Her emotions were so strong they choked her, overwhelmed her. She feared she might weep, though from joy or sadness she did not know. She wanted to take him inside her and make him a part of her forever.

She wanted to tell him she loved him, but she did not.

"Jesus, help me," Jamie cried between clenched teeth as she lowered herself onto him.

The sensation of him sliding inside her was so intense, she gasped and squeezed her eyes closed.

Hearts racing and breathing hard, they clung to each other, fighting to remain still to prolong the moment. When he reached between them to touch her, she was almost too sensitive to bear it. Then he began to move inside her. She felt the pressure build and build inside her until a burst of stars lit up her vision as waves of pleasure pulsed through her.

But he did not stop. With his hands gripping her hips now, he moved against her without mercy, his breath coming in ragged gasps. The tension built inside her again, and she rocked against him, her hands clawing at his back.

From a distance, she heard him calling out to her as jolts of sensation shook her again. This time, they were so strong that she screamed. She screamed his name.

He wrapped his arms so tightly around her she could not breathe and fell back against the bed, bringing her with him. She lay on top of him, both of them breathing hard, their skin glistening with sweat.

"Jesus and all the saints!" he said, as if in praise of the miracle that had occurred between them.

She rested her head against his chest. His heart was beating as fast as hers, urgent and insistent in her ear.

This could not be normal. Other people could not feel this.

At this moment, everything she was, everything she wanted was here with him. She forgot the queen and Owen. Forgot her enemies. When she was in Jamie's arms like this, all else faded to nothing. It frightened her that something so fleeting could make her forget everything else she wanted, everything she had worked so hard to achieve.

If she forgot them, what would she have when Jamie left her?

Linnet trailed her fingers down Jamie's chest and sighed. Sometimes after they made love, she could almost believe things were as they once had been between them. Almost.

But they were both wiser and more jaded now. In sooth, she had always been jaded. Perhaps it was growing up knowing she had a father who didn't care what happened to her. And from the time she was thirteen, men had told her lies and attempted to seduce her.

Jamie had thought himself worldly back then, being three years older and a warrior. And he was, in some ways. But at his core, he had been such an innocent.

Fighting had not taken that from him. She had.

She had been too young herself at the time to appreciate the purity—and, aye, the rarity—of his love for her. 'Twas a wondrous thing he had given her; she knew that now.

He desired her now as much as ever. If possible, the bedding was even better than before. He liked her, enjoyed spending time with her. But once, he had given her the kind of love that held nothing back, and she knew the difference. Jamie might feel some affection for her, but he would not give her his heart again. He would save it for the woman he wed.

She laid her head back down on his chest, needing to feel his warmth radiate through her.

How long before he decided he needed a wife? She knew him. Jamie would want a woman he could openly share his life with. How long would she have him before he left her for the quiet, staid life he wanted?

She swallowed and blinked against the sting in her eyes. He'd left her once. He would do it again. Everyone did, save for Francois.

It hurt her pride that she cared so much more for him than he for her. She was used to men trailing her, begging for her favors. But Jamie just had to give her that look and crook his finger, and she would follow him into a soggy field to make love against a tree in a downpour.

His breathing was the steady rhythm of sleep, so she got up on her hands and knees to look at him. Her heart hurt as her gaze drifted over the strong planes of his face in repose.

When he opened his eyes, the corners of his mouth curved up.

"You are a lovely sight to wake up to," he said and brushed his knuckles lightly against her cheek. Then he drew his brows together. "But why are you sad?"

She shook her head.

He pulled her down against him and gave her a melting kiss that eased the ache in her heart. Nay, she would not be sad. No matter how much it hurt her later, she would make the most of the time she had with him.

Chapter Seventeen

Jamie took a long ride along the river to get away from the chaos in the castle. After the quiet weeks of November and early December, Windsor had become abuzz with activity overnight. Servants scurried to and fro, hanging greenery and preparing chambers for the many guests expected to arrive for Christmas Court.

Jamie preferred the castle when it was quiet and nearly empty.

As he cantered past, a flock of ducks rose from the mist of the river and formed a V above him. He drew in deep breaths, filling his lungs with the cold, damp air, and felt better. A man was not meant to spend so much time indoors. What he wanted was an estate far from London—a place where he would know all his tenants and their families, as his parents did. He and Linnet could make a good life there.

The Duke of Bedford was bound to reward him for his services. Bedford had hinted at an estate in Normandy, but Jamie was holding out for lands in England. They were harder to come by, but England was home. He wanted his children to be born and bred on English soil.

"You needed this, too, didn't you, boy?" He patted Thunder's neck. A great warhorse was not made to be cooped up any more than he was.

Reluctantly, he turned Thunder around and rode back up the path. Windsor's huge, distinctive Round Tower loomed ahead as a constant reminder of what lay ahead of him: a month of endless talk, silly entertainment, and political maneuvering. He hated it. Give him a good horse and a sword in his hand, any day.

Everyone of importance was expected to make an appearance at Christmas Court. That meant Jamie would have to keep his eyes open for danger to the queen. Many of the wealthy merchants, and some of the nobles as well, suspected the queen of secretly supporting her brother's claim to the French throne.

As Jamie neared the castle, his squire came out the gate and ran up the path to meet him. Thunder's breath came out in white puffs as he reined in.

"Good boy," Jamie said and swung down.

"A message came for you, Sir James," Martin said, holding out a rolled parchment.

Jamie handed Martin the reins and took the parchment. "Thunder will need a good rubbing-down."

Jamie broke the seal and read the short missive. "Bedford has returned," he said as he rolled it back up. "He has taken up residence at Westminster. I am to go to him at once."

A few weeks ago, he had prayed diligently for Bedford's return to England. Now that he no longer wanted it, this was the one prayer God chose to answer. The mysteries of heaven.

With Bedford in England, Jamie's assignment to watch

over the queen was at an end. Bedford's authority was accepted, and his support for the queen was unqualified. His presence ensured her safety—at least from the risks known to Bedford. The queen's getting caught in an affair with Owen Tudor was not, however, among the hazards Bedford anticipated.

"She is the most unfortunate of women." That was what King Henry had said of his young queen on his deathbed—and Bedford still believed it. No one honored the dead king's memory more. Bedford would be surprised to learn the queen wished to share her bed with *any* man after the glorious Henry; the good man's heart might fail him if he knew she was bedding her Clerk of the Wardrobe.

Regardless, Jamie had lost his excuse to tarry at Windsor. It was time, then, to settle matters with Linnet. He had grown increasingly impatient with the way things stood in any case.

"Be ready to leave at dawn," he said to Martin as they entered the gate. "I want to reach Westminster before nightfall on the morrow."

He left Martin to return Thunder to the stables and marched across the upper ward. It was time to push Linnet to the wall and see what she would do.

He found Linnet waiting for him in what had become their usual meeting place—the empty bedchamber in the wing opposite the royal apartments.

After greeting her, he went to the narrow table against the wall where they kept a flagon of wine.

He spoke with his back to her as he poured a cup for them to share. "Bedford has returned from France."

When he turned, he caught no sign of dismay in her

expression. With an inward sigh, he went to join her at the window seat.

"Praise God, Bedford is here," she said, taking the cup from his hands. "No one else can control Gloucester."

Not the reaction he hoped for, but perhaps she did not yet grasp what Bedford's return meant for him and this affair of theirs.

"Aye, Gloucester will behave whilst his brother is in England," he said as he settled beside her on the bench. "The Council named Gloucester the Protector of England only in Bedford's absence—a wise move. Gloucester lost his authority the moment Bedford set foot on the English shore."

Jamie rested his hand on her thigh. If so much were not at stake, he would enjoy sitting and having a quiet talk with her like this.

"Bedford cannot be well pleased with his brother," she said. "First, Gloucester marries Jacqueline de Hainaut before King Henry was in the ground, when everyone knew the king had forbidden the marriage."

It was not Gloucester's marriage Jamie wished to discuss.

Linnet, however, was so incensed with Gloucester that she waved her hands about as she spoke. "He only wed Jacqueline because of her claim on Zeeland and Hainaut."

Gloucester's failed expedition to take Zeeland and Hainaut in his wife's name had diverted funds and men that Bedford badly needed for the war in France. Even worse, the expedition had nearly led to a break with Burgundy, England's critical ally in that war, because Burgundy also claimed Zeeland and Hainaut.

"If I were Bedford," Linnet said, her beautiful face as hard as granite, "I'd chain Gloucester in the dungeon for all the trouble he's caused."

"Lucky for Gloucester, his brother has a more forgiving nature than you do." Jamie smiled and squeezed her thigh. "You have heard that forgiveness is a virtue?"

"Hmmph." She crossed her arms. "A man who shows no repentance deserves no forgiveness."

No mercy for Gloucester. It was time to find out if she had any for him.

"Bedford has summoned me to Westminster. I leave early on the morrow."

He felt her stiffen beside him. With her eyes straight ahead, she said, "How long will you be gone?"

"I cannot say." He shrugged. "A few days, a week perhaps."

She turned and said, "I shall miss you."

He would have preferred, "Do not go," or "Take me with you." Still, it was better than nothing.

Then she put her arms around his neck and kissed him, and that was better still.

"Come to London with me," he said, nuzzling her neck. "We could stay at your London house, where we would not have to sneak about to be alone."

"I like sneaking about with you."

Well, he did not. He was damned tired of clandestine meetings and creeping about as if he were bedding another man's wife. That was fine in the days when he did occasionally bed other men's wives. But not now. Not with Linnet.

"I do want to go, but one of us must stay to watch over Owen and the queen," she said in a reasonable tone that grated on his nerves. "Left on their own, I fear they will never keep their secret."

How long could he keep his own secret? How long before she realized she was meant to be his wife?

"Come to bed," he said and pulled her to her feet.

Tenderness was not what she was going to get from him this time. But he was going to make damned sure she missed him.

Jamie hated the thought of being away from her, even for a few days. Through the narrow window, the sky was growing dark. Soon, they would have to dress and make their way—separately, of course—to their own chambers to prepare for supper.

'Twas poison in his stomach to leave without having matters settled between them. Christmas guests would start arriving. Soon the palace would be crawling with half the men of consequence in England.

"How many others have there been?" he asked.

Linnet lifted her head from the pillow to look at him. "Others?"

"Other men," he said between his teeth. "Other lovers."

"Would it matter?" She sat up. "How many women have you bedded?"

"Come, Linnet, that is hardly the same thing." Really, where did she get these notions?

"Not to you, of course." She turned her back to him and wrapped her arms around her knees.

"Tell me there has been no one else in England." He thought again of all the guests that would soon fill the castle. He could not bear knowing another man would look at her and remember the feel of her skin beneath his hands.

Blood pounded at his temples.

"There has been no one," she snapped.

Praise God for that. He folded his hands behind his head and drew in a deep breath. If she was lying, he did not want to know the truth.

"The same cannot be said of you," she said, turning to glare at him over her shoulder. "There was that horrid Eleanor Cobham, for one."

"I told you I did not want to bed her. I do not even recall it."

"Do not lie. You remember it quite well." In an undertone, she added, "Sore cock, indeed."

Linnet drew men like flies. They were drawn to her ethereal beauty—and even more to the wildness they sensed beneath it. God, how he hated to leave her.

He sat up, turned her toward him, and searched her face. "Can I trust you while I am gone?"

From the murderous look she gave him, she did not like the question. But he did not care. He had to know.

"Can I?"

"If you do not trust me, do not bother coming back."

He took that as a yes. But he wanted more than to know she would not climb into another man's bed in the few days he would be gone.

She tossed the bedclothes aside, retrieved her chemise from the bottom of the bed, and leapt to the floor. As she lifted her arms to drop the chemise over her head, his gaze preceded it down the graceful line of her back, her nicely rounded buttocks, and her long, long legs.

Lord above, she was beautiful.

She went to the window and stood, arms folded, with her back to him.

He followed her and spun her around so he could look into her eyes. "With Bedford returned, my duties are done here."

Her shoulders tensed beneath his hands. But if he was waiting for weeping and begging, he might be an old man before he saw them.

"I will return to Windsor for Christmas Court. But after that, I must leave."

She lifted his hands off her shoulders. In a cool voice, she said, "That soon?"

Good God, Linnet, give me something. He was tired of being patient and damned tired of waiting.

"Perhaps I'll not bother returning from London at all," he said. "It is time, after all, that I started looking for a wife."

She turned her back to him again and looked out the window. After a long moment, she said in a tight voice, "You should be here during Christmas Court to help divert attention from Owen and the queen. They are bound to forget themselves."

"Is it only for Owen and the queen that you wish me to return?"

With her back to him, she said, "What do you want me to say, Jamie?"

He sure as hell was not going to ask her to say it. If she did not want him, there was no use pushing her. He'd been down that road before.

He gathered his clothes from the floor and threw them on.

"I am sure you will do just as you please, as you always have," he said as he jerked his boots on.

Anger vibrated through him as he stomped across the room and snatched his cloak from the back of the door.

"And I shall do as I please as well." He turned with one hand on the door. "There are plenty of women in London besides Eleanor."

He let the door slam behind him.

Chapter Eighteen

The winter afternoon light was nearly gone by the time Jamie and Martin rode through the Great Gateway of Westminster Palace. After leaving Martin in the outer ward to see to their horses, Jamie headed for the privy palace to find Bedford.

Soldiers in tunics emblazoned with the royal herald of bright blue, gold, and red stood guard outside the Painted Chamber, which served as the royal audience and bedchamber. After giving them his name and business, Jamie settled on a bench to wait. A short time later, one of the heavy double doors opened a few inches and words were exchanged between someone inside and one of the guards.

"Sir James Rayburn," the guard said in a voice that could be heard at fifty paces. "His Grace the Duke of Bedford will see you now."

Jamie nodded to the guard as he passed through the door. Once inside, he stopped and gaped at the room like a peasant from the country. Now he understood why the Painted Chamber, along with Saint Stephen's Chapel, made Westminster rank as one of the most magnificent palaces in all of Europe.

The king's state bed, a magnificent piece of furniture built for Henry III, dominated the far end of the long, narrow room. There were paintings above and around the bed, which was situated with its head against the north wall, next to the fireplace. On the east wall, several feet beyond the bed, two elegant windows overlooked the Thames.

Jamie leaned his head back to take in the wood ceiling decorated with rows of carved moldings called lobed paterae. But then his gaze was drawn to the five-and-a-half-foot-high mural of the coronation of Edward the Confessor at the head of the bed.

Jamie heard someone clear his throat and turned to find Bedford beside him. Belatedly, he made his bow. "Your Grace."

"I take it you have not been in the Painted Chamber before," Bedford said with a warm smile. "I've seen it many times, and yet I am always struck by its beauty.

"I am sure you recognize these," Bedford said, gesturing around the room.

Jamie's gaze followed the series of wall paintings depicting Old Testament stories, which were interspersed with inscriptions and brightly painted heraldry.

"The paintings of Virtues and Vices are my favorites," Bedford said as he led Jamie to the paintings on the window splays on the south wall. "I am particularly fond of this one."

Bedford pointed to the painting of a woman in chain mail and crown, who was sticking a spear into a man while choking him with a stream of coins from a long leather purse.

"The Virtue of Generosity triumphs over the Vice of Greed?" Jamie asked.

"Very good," Bedford said with a smile.

A voice came from behind them. "Generosity is a virtue when done with a purpose."

Jamie turned to see the duke's uncle, resplendent in his bishop's robes of dazzling white with elaborate gold embroidery, entering through a side door.

"Your Grace." Jamie bowed low to Bishop Beaufort.

"I was just telling my uncle how valuable your reports were," Bedford said.

Jamie nodded, acknowledging the compliment.

Both men eyed him until he began to feel uncomfortable.

"Is there some service I can do for you now, Your Grace?"

Jamie asked the question of the duke, but it was the bishop who answered. "'Tis more accurate to say that we can be of service to each other."

"You are a good man," Bedford said, "in the mold of your stepfather, FitzAlan."

"Thank you," Jamie said. "There is no higher compliment you could pay me."

"My nephew does not say it to flatter you," the bishop said, "but to explain why we are offering you a most desired opportunity."

Jamie felt a prickle up the back of his neck. Only two things were certain about this "opportunity." One, it was sure to benefit the bishop and the Crown. And two, it would be nigh on impossible to refuse. When the two most powerful men in the realm wished to bestow a favor, a man refused it at his peril.

"Do you know Sir Charles Stafford?" the bishop asked.

When Jamie shook his head, Bedford said, "He paid sentage in lieu of serving, so you would not have met him in France."

Just because the law permitted a nobleman to pay a tax instead of providing the military service he owed the king directly, that did not mean he ought to. Unless this Stafford was too elderly or infirm to fight, Jamie knew all he needed to know about him as a man.

The bishop, however, disagreed.

"What is important to know about Stafford is that he has significant holdings in the north. And, *he has no male heir.*" The bishop's pinched expression suggested this was a serious failing on Stafford's part. "This means, of course, that his daughter will inherit."

Sweat broke out on Jamie's palms at the mention of a daughter. Discussion of unwed daughters generally led in only one direction.

"Not only are Stafford's holdings substantial, but they are near the Scottish border," the bishop continued.

"You will be pleased to hear," Bedford put in, "that the Stafford lands are not far from your uncle Stephen's estates."

Jamie felt like a tennis ball bounced back and forth between the two men; he wanted out of the game.

"Who holds these lands is a matter of importance to the Crown," the bishop said. "Naturally, we have taken an interest in the selection of a husband for Stafford's daughter."

With a warm smile, Bedford put a hand on Jamie's shoulder. "This seemed a perfect opportunity both to reward you for your service and to ensure these lands are in the hands of a man we can trust. Stephen and young Henry Percy could use your help in keeping the peace along the Scottish border."

Despite the chill of the room, sweat trickled down Jamie's back. This was a much greater honor than he expected. Turning it down was going to be difficult. Very difficult, indeed.

"I know you have need of lands," Bedford said. "Most of FitzAlan's are entailed and will go to your younger brother."

Bedford did not need to explain his situation to him. Although William FitzAlan treated Jamie as his son, he was, in fact, his stepson. As such, he could not inherit the entailed lands.

"Since you advised me you wished to marry and had no lady chosen," Bedford continued, "I spoke with Stafford on your behalf."

Damn. He could kick himself for telling Bedford he was looking for a wife. Of course, he had done it precisely to this end. He had hoped Bedford would facilitate a good match. Since he expected to wed a woman he hardly knew and did not love, why not a land-rich heiress?

At least that was what he thought before he set his mind on Linnet. Despite his angry departure, he was no less determined to make her his wife.

"Your Grace, I . . . ," he began.

"I understand you are anxious to meet the lady," Bedford said, misunderstanding him completely. "I've arranged for Stafford and his daughter to make the journey to Windsor with you."

Lord, help me. He would have to spend an entire day trapped with the girl and her father in a covered barge before he could get this sorted out.

Where was his mother when he needed her? Lady Catherine FitzAlan would know how to get him out of this with the least damage to the family's relationship with the royal family. He suspected Bishop Beaufort had a long, long memory for slights.

While Bedford appeared to take no notice of Jamie's lack of enthusiasm, his sharp-eyed uncle was more perceptive. "I can assure you Stafford's daughter is a devout and virtuous lady, if that is your concern," Bishop Beaufort said. "In sooth, it was her wish to join a convent."

God had heard his prayer! Putting his hand over his heart, Jamie said, "If that is what the good lady wishes..."

"It is not what her father wishes," the bishop snapped. "I assure you, the girl will marry."

"There is one matter, however, that must be addressed before the marriage can be arranged." Lines of worry showed on Bedford's face as it settled into a serious expression. "What is this I hear about you challenging Pomeroy to single combat?"

"Is it not enough we have to suffer such foolishness from Humphrey?" the bishop said.

The comparison did Jamie no good at all. Burgundy had been so enraged at Gloucester's military expedition into Hainaut that he had issued a personal challenge to Gloucester. Humphrey had accepted the challenge—then left his wife and set sail for England.

"We were able to persuade the pope to prohibit the two from dueling under threat of excommunication," the bishop said. "But we could lose France over this yet. Bedford has been working night and day to repair the damage with Burgundy."

"My challenge to Pomeroy could cause no such harm," Jamie said. "I thought it a measured response to a grievous insult, but I can see I should have just run him through at the time."

"You forget to whom you are speaking," the bishop said with a steely look that probably sent small children running. The bishop turned to Bedford. "I thought you said he was a man of good sense."

"James," Bedford said, "you will have to withdraw the challenge."

"I mean no disrespect, Your Grace, but you know I cannot do that. I am no coward."

"Such stupidity." The bishop raised his arms as if beseeching heaven. "To win a fight, young man, one must consider all the consequences."

The bishop then proceeded to lecture Jamie while pacing back and forth in front of him. "The most likely consequences of pursuing this course are that you will end up languishing in prison or with your head on a pike. In either case, you can hardly claim to have prevailed over your enemy."

"That may be true," Jamie said, acknowledging the bishop's point. "Still, it changes nothing. Honor will not permit me to withdraw the challenge."

Bedford cleared his throat. "My brother complains that you have sent his friend Pomeroy several letters repeating the challenge."

Jamie shrugged. There was nothing he could say to that.

"Am I correct in supposing," the bishop said, "that honor would require you to allow Pomeroy to escape alive if he concedes during the fight?"

"Aye, he can concede at any time," Jamie said.

"Perhaps we can convince Pomeroy to apologize," Bedford said. "Would that resolve the matter?"

Jamie did not like it. "I suppose it would have to do."

"Negotiating an apology will take time," the bishop said, steepling his hands and touching his fingertips to his chin. "Unfortunately, Stafford will not proceed with the marriage until the matter of this challenge is resolved. That was the one point upon which he insisted."

Praise God for that.

The bishop pursed his lips and looked at Jamie through narrowed eyes. "Still, I advise you to work the ground," he said, tapping his fingertips together under his chin. "I hear the ladies find you appealing. I suggest you put your mind to charming both the girl and her father when you accompany them to Windsor."

Jamie groaned aloud when he saw Gloucester, Eleanor Cobham, and their entourage preparing to board the royal barge at the Westminster wharf early the next morning. He stepped back, hoping he would not be invited to join them. God's beard, he wished he was riding back to Windsor with Martin.

He had heard whispers about Eleanor in the short time he was in the palace. Apparently, another lady had fallen ill after Gloucester had shown her favor.

Eleanor snapped her head around and caught Jamie staring. When he acknowledged her with a slight nod, she cast a speculative look at him, head to toe. God have mercy, Eleanor examined him as if she were a man choosing a woman in a whorehouse. His repulsion must have shown on his face, for the look she leveled at him now was pure venom.

"You must be Sir James Rayburn," a male voice said behind him.

Stafford. Jamie drew in a deep breath, then made himself turn to meet his traveling companions. Stafford was stout and had the florid complexion of a man who drank too much. Not a fighting man, that was for certain. Jamie had never seen a cloak that startling shade of green. He tried not to stare at the matching liripipe hat with its ridiculously long tail.

"Good day to you," Jamie said. "You are Lord Stafford?"

"I am!" the man said in a voice so loud Jamie wondered if he was hard of hearing. "And this is the prize, my friend."

Stafford turned and waved his arm at a young lady who stood a few steps back. "This is my daughter, Lady Agnes Stafford."

"A pleasure to meet you, Lady Agnes," Jamie said, making a polite bow.

She was not the sort of rare beauty like Linnet who made men stop and stare and forget where they were, but she was pretty, with very fair skin and dark, soulful eyes.

"Sir James." She gave no smile as she dipped her curtsy.

"Of course, the real prize is my lands," Stafford said. "She is just the bonus, eh?"

Good God, how could a man speak about his daughter that way? No wonder the girl did not smile.

"You look like a strapping young man who can give me grandsons! That's what I want from this, I don't mind telling you—a grandson to take over the Stafford lands one day."

Stafford appeared unaware that a prospective bridegroom might be offended by his happy anticipation of his future son-in-law's death.

Jamie's plan to make himself so unpleasant that Stafford would lose interest faded as the wretched man spewed on. He glanced at the girl, feeling more sorry for her by the moment. What must it be like for a young girl to have such an oaf for a father?

"I only got the girl, you see," Stafford said. He shook his head. "There is no greater disappointment to a man in this life."

This had gone on long enough.

"My parents have both sons and daughters," Jamie said before Stafford could hurl another insult at his daughter, "and, I can tell you, they greatly prefer the girls."

"They do?" Stafford asked, pinching his face as if he were tasting something foul.

"They say daughters are like the sun, bringing warmth and happiness to their home, while sons are like the winter storms, bringing chaos and trouble."

Jamie was making this up out of whole cloth, but he felt compelled to compensate for Stafford's churlish—nay, malicious—disregard for his daughter's feelings.

When Stafford opened his mouth to argue, Jamie said,

"The second barge is here. Let us board quickly so your daughter will have a seat near the brazier."

Eleanor Cobham was bringing such a large entourage to Windsor that several of her ladies and servants, along with a good many trunks, had been left behind to share the second barge with Jamie and the Staffords.

Stafford's head spun around to where the barge had just pulled up. "'Tis damp on the river. I must have the seat nearest the brazier for my gout."

While Stafford elbowed his way ahead of the others waiting on the wharf, Jamie held his arm out to the girl. She took it without offering him a word or a smile. After a short time with her father, Jamie no longer wondered at her dour expression.

There were two braziers on the barge. Seeing her father settled in the choicest seat by the first, Jamie found a seat for the girl near the second brazier. The boatmen worked quickly to batten down the heavy cloth cover that served to protect the passengers from wind and rain and keep the heat from the braziers within.

For some time after the boatmen eased the barge away from the wharf, Jamie and Lady Agnes sat in silence. She was such a tiny thing that he felt huge beside her.

The girl worked a kerchief in her hands. She seemed so desperately unhappy that he felt an urge to rescue her. Another man, however, would have to save her from her father. Still, he wished there was some way he could ease her misery.

The girl did not appear to have the skill most women had of filling awkward silences. Jamie was trying to think of something to say to her when she suddenly turned her dark eyes on him and asked him a question as if everything depended upon it.

"How many demons would you say are in hell?"

Jamie thought he must have misheard her. "What did you ask?"

This time she spoke slowly, as if she suspected he might be slow-witted. "How many of the angels turned against God to take their place with Lucifer?"

He blinked at her, trying to think of how to respond to such an unusual question.

"Most of the holy men agree," she said, her dark eyes intent on his, "that one in three angels fell from grace."

"Then it should be a simple calculation," Jamie said, feeling rather proud of himself, "provided you know how many angels there were to start with."

"That is just the difficulty," she said. "'Tis most distressing, but there is some dispute as to the precise number of angels at the time of Lucifer's revolt."

"So long as the good angels outnumber the demons two-to-one, what does it matter how many demons there are?" Oddly, Jamie was starting to enjoy himself.

"That is a soldier's answer," she said with a smile that quite transformed her face. "But you could as well ask why the ratio should matter at all when the good angels have the power of God on their side."

"'Twas your question to begin with," Jamie said, giving her an answering smile. "Tell me, why do you care how many fallen angels there are?"

She pursed her lips and gazed off into the distance, her expression intent once again. After a long moment, she said, "When I pray for the strength to resist demons, I would like to use the number."

"But surely God already knows how many there are."

She turned her large dark eyes on him again. "You are right, of course. Mother Therese—she is the abbess at Saint Mary of the Woods near my home—tells me I devote too much time to the contemplation of the small points of faith."

Jamie did his best to hide his smile. Mother Therese sounded like a wise woman to him.

"But when it comes to God," the girl said, "how can one say any point is small? Saint Paul himself said in his Epistle to the..."

As penance for his sins, Jamie spent the rest of the afternoon discussing the meaning of various biblical verses. He did not mind it so much, and it seemed to please her. Well, it did not please her, precisely, for she grew quite agitated as she made her points.

Truly, they should let the poor girl go to the convent.

One of the women, a commoner by her dress, shot dark glances at them each time Lady Agnes's voice rose. Eventually, the woman gathered her skirts and left the shelter, apparently preferring the drizzle and the conversation of the boatmen outside to their theological discussion.

Lady Agnes's eyes followed the other woman out. "That woman walks with the devil," she said in a low voice.

Jamie turned to stare at her. Truly, this young lady was a constant surprise.

"I advise you to wear a cross and say your prayers," Lady Agnes said. "For that one had her eyes on you, and it cannot be to good purpose."

"And I thought she was watching you," he said, trying to make light of it by teasing her.

"Aye, she was, but for a different reason." Agnes nodded, her face earnest. "I make her uneasy, for she knows Satan can gain no purchase with me."

Apparently Agnes did not think the same could be said of him.

Chapter Nineteen

Windsor Castle was filling up with guests, although none of the royals had arrived yet—if you did not count the queen, which no one did. Linnet stood looking out the narrow window of her bedchamber, wondering what could be keeping Jamie in London.

She never thought she could miss him so much. Why had she not gone with him when he asked her? Their angry parting left her with an uneasy feeling in the pit of her stomach. She was anxious to see him and make things right between them.

A movement caught her eye, and she turned her gaze eastward to find a line of barges coming up the river. Knowing Jamie would return by horse, she was only mildly interested in these new arrivals.

Her interest grew, however, when she saw that one flew the royal banner, the Lancaster lion and French fleur-de-lis. The first man off was Gloucester, his ermine-trimmed cloak and brilliant crimson, gold, and blue tunic proclaiming his royal status. The woman on his arm with her hood pulled up against the cold was likely his mistress, Eleanor Cobham.

Linnet was about to go down to join the formal greeting party when the second barge pulled up to the wharf. Because she was not eager to see either Gloucester or his mistress, she paused to see who would emerge from the other barge.

Her heart did a flip as a tall figure jumped to the dock before the boatman tied the boat. The winter sun glistened on the almost black hair blowing across his face. At last, Jamie was here. She picked up her skirts to hurry down, when she saw Jamie turn back toward the barge and raise his arms.

Linnet stood stock-still, skirts clenched in her hands, as Jamie put his hands around a petite woman's waist and lifted her off the barge. That was unnecessary; there were steps the lady could have taken. Then, in a protective gesture that sliced Linnet's heart, Jamie tucked the lady's hand into his arm. As the two crossed the dock, Jamie bent his head down to her as if intent on catching her every word.

Linnet dropped onto the stool next to her and pressed her hand to her chest, trying to breathe. Surely, she was reading too much into what she had seen. These were simple gestures of courtesy that any knight would show a lady in his company.

Yet, she felt so light-headed she had to lean forward and rest her head on her knees. What would she do if she lost Jamie again? In building her trade and plotting her revenge, she planned years ahead, anticipating each move as if it were a complex game of chess. Yet, when it came to Jamie, she lived day to day, moment to moment. Why?

She knew damned well why. Neither she nor her plans fit into the kind of life Jamie wanted. That was as true now as it was five years ago. She could never be the sort of wife he wanted: a woman who always behaved as she should, bowed to his "greater wisdom," and caused him no trouble.

And yet, she did not know how she could survive losing him again.

In her mind's eye, she saw Jamie hovering over the young woman on the dock. Had he given up on her already? Nay, he had no hopes to give up this time. Although he was drawn by the passion that burned between them, he no longer saw her as a woman he would want as his wife. And Jamie wanted a wife.

Her shortcomings seemed many and large. She swallowed back the tears that stung at her eyes. Feeling sorry for herself was not one of her usual failings. She stood up and snapped her fingertips against the skirt of her gown to straighten it.

She needed to decide what she wanted, and then she could go about getting it, as she always did.

But what did she want? She wanted Jamie. But she also wanted her boot on her enemy's neck until he begged for mercy. And that was the problem. Would Jamie wait for her while she settled her obligations from the past?

She would find this last man, the shadowy figure who was behind the scheme against her grandfather, and punish him. Once that was done, she would figure out what to do about Jamie.

She had time. Jamie had been gone but a week. He could not have become attached to another woman in so short a time. This helpless woman who needed lifting off boats could mean nothing to him.

Heartened by her arguments, Linnet hurried out the

door and down the corridor. Halfway down the staircase
that led to the Great Hall, she came to an abrupt halt. The
words Jamie had said when he first arrived at Eltham rang
in her ears: *I have come home to marry.*

Jamie deserved to have hearth and home with a loving
wife and children. No man would make a better father.
Why should the thought of him having what he wanted
tear at her heart like a jagged blade?

That day at Eltham, Jamie had told her he had reason to
hope Bedford would facilitate a desirable match for him.
And now, Jamie was returning from a visit to Bedford
with a young lady on his arm. He would want a woman
like the one on the dock. A woman he could hover over
and protect. A woman who would not embarrass him.

Noise from the hall drifted up to where she stood alone
on the staircase. Word of the arrival of the royal guest must
have spread, leading everyone to fill the Great Hall to see
and be seen. The Christmas festivities could now begin.

Linnet was not feeling festive.

A man emerged from the hall and walked toward the
stairs. When he looked up and caught sight of Linnet, he
smiled broadly and put his hand to his heart.

"The very woman I longed to see," Edmund Beaufort
called out to her as he ran up the stairs two at a time.

"Good day to you, Edmund." She offered him her hand.
"Did you come on the barge with Sir James? Perhaps you
can help me find him."

He kissed her hand and placed it on his arm.

"I came by horse, but I saw Sir James in the hall," he
said as they started down the stairs together. "You will
find him with his soon-to-be betrothed. He traveled here
with her and her father.

"Take care!" Edmund caught her as her foot missed a step.

Oblivious to her distress, Edmund leaned close and said in a low voice, "Frankly, 'tis a better match than anyone expected, given how modest his own holdings are. James Rayburn should count himself a lucky man."

And she was the most unlucky of women. For the second time, she had lost the only man she ever loved.

Chapter Twenty

Linnet craned her neck to look for Jamie over the crush of people.

"Come sit next to me." The queen linked her arm with Linnet's and led her to where large cushions had been placed on the floor in a semicircle.

"We are sitting on the floor?"

"'Tis the best place to view the men's dancing competition." The queen took Edmund's proffered hand and sank gracefully to the floor.

"I thought there was to be a mummers' play," Linnet said, not that she cared what the entertainment was tonight. Where was Jamie? She was intent on discovering if there was any truth to what Edmund had said. If he was looking for her, too, they should have found each other by now.

"Sit down, Linnet," Queen Katherine said with a laugh as she tugged at the hem of Linnet's gown.

The king would arrive with Bedford in just two days. The prospect of having her son in the same castle, albeit in a separate apartment and under the watch of another woman, had put the queen in a lively mood.

After casting another look around the room for Jamie, Linnet took Edmund's hand and sat on the cushion next to the queen.

Edmund dropped to one knee beside her. "I must leave you to join the other men for the competition," Edmund said, holding both her hand and her gaze for far too long. "May I ask for your favor?"

Linnet arched her eyebrows. "My what?"

"Your favor," Edmund repeated. "Say you will cheer for me to win the competition."

"Certainly. I shall clap the loudest."

He kissed her hand. Looking up at her with the devil in his eyes, he said in a hushed voice, "And what favor will you grant me if I win, sweet one?"

She leaned forward and whispered back, "I am not at all sweet, so do not expect to like what I give you."

"I shall take my chances." He grinned and winked at her. "A reward may be all the more delicious for not being sweet."

Before she could pinch him, Edmund ran off to join the young men who were gathering opposite the ladies on the floor.

The queen leaned over to whisper in her ear. "Owen claims to be a poor dancer, but I begged him to join the competition." She giggled like a girl and added, "It gives me an excuse to watch him. Does he not look fine in his new clothes?"

The short green tunic and orange leggings revealed Owen's muscular thighs to advantage.

"The tunic is a gift from you?" Linnet asked.

"As my clerk of the wardrobe, his appearance reflects

upon me," Queen Katherine said. "'Tis important he dress well."

That may be true, but Linnet doubted the queen's clerk would have received such a fine gift if he were a paunchy man of sixty.

Joannna Belknap, one of the queen's ladies who sat farther down the row, leaned forward to get their attention. "The dancers are ready! Here is the first one."

The ladies clapped enthusiastically as each young man took his turn, twirling around the circle and leaping over a candle set on a tall holder in the middle. The third man was Edmund Beaufort, who proved to be an accomplished dancer. When he leapt as gracefully as a hart over the candle flame with a foot to spare, the women whooped and stamped their feet in a most unladylike fashion.

After a final set of spins around the circle, Edmund took a running leap over the candle with his arms and legs extended. As he landed, he dropped to his knees and slid across the floor to stop just in front of Linnet. Linnet threw her head back laughing—until she felt a prickle at the back of her neck.

She turned to see Jamie leaning against the wall with some of the other men who were not participating. His eyes were hot on her, and he was *not* cheering. Perhaps all was not lost. Jamie looked as if he was torn between murdering her and ripping her clothes off. Linnet met his gaze and held it, not caring who noticed.

The queen elbowed Linnet in the ribs, drawing her attention back to the dancers. "It's Owen's turn!"

Edmund Beaufort remained where he was, half lying on the floor in front of Linnet, as the musicians began a new song and Owen took the stage.

Owen had a heavy, muscular frame better suited to a jousting contest than a dancing competition. Owen, however, was the sort of man who could risk making a fool of himself and laugh about it. This lightheartedness was part of what attracted the queen to him. Though Owen could not begin to match Edmund's performance, he danced with such lively good humor that the ladies soon burst into applause.

"Please do not appear so enthralled, Your Grace," Linnet whispered, though of course it did no good.

The music grew faster, signaling that the song and Owen's turn were coming to an end.

The ladies' cheering encouraged Owen to make a final round of the circle. As he skirted the side where the ladies sat, Linnet saw that the hem of someone's gown was draped across the floor directly in Owen's path. Before she could shout out a warning, Owen's foot caught on the fabric.

"Oh!" Too late, Linnet screamed as Owen flew through the air, sending the ladies scattering and leaping to their feet.

Linnet stared, not quite believing it. Owen had landed facedown ... in the queen's lap.

The music died on an off-key chord. The room went still as everyone stared openmouthed at the queen with Owen's face buried in her lap. The silence grew deafening as the guests waited for the queen to shout her outrage.

Instead, the queen slapped her hand over her mouth. Her eyes danced, and her shoulders shook.

"Owen, get up!" Linnet hissed, giving him a none-too-discreet kick.

Owen lifted his head—which, most unfortunately,

was still between the queen's thighs—and Her Highness fought against another burst of giggles.

Owen tried to get up, but his feet were hopelessly tangled in the queen's voluminous skirts. As if by magic, Jamie appeared and hauled Owen to his feet. The two men scraped low bows to the queen—and then were gone.

Chapter Twenty-one

"**A**re there no more dancers?" Linnet called out above the buzz of whispers in the hall.

When she gave Edmund a pleading look, he clapped his hands and shouted, "Music! Come, Sir Gerald, let us see if you can best me."

Linnet sighed with relief as a young man took to the floor and the music of flute, harp, and drum filled the hall.

"God bless you, Edmund," she said close to his ear. "Will you stay with Queen Katherine? I have something I must attend to."

"Anything for you, my sweet," Edmund said and kissed her hand yet again.

She really would have to have a talk with him, but not now.

As she made her way through the crowd, she caught bits of conversation and raucous laughter.

"Who was that in the queen's lap?"

"Don't know, but I'd say it was not the first time he's been there!"

God help her, this was a disaster. With everyone looking

for signs of an improper liaison between the queen and Owen, the truth could readily be discovered.

By the time Linnet reached the foyer, Jamie and Owen were nowhere in sight. After a quick look in the nearby rooms, she ran across the upper yard without a cloak. The chamber where she and Jamie usually met had most likely been given to one of the new guests, but she would check it anyway.

An instant after she rapped on the door, Jamie filled the doorway, towering above her.

"Where is Owen?" she asked as she scurried past him. Odd, but the room was warm, as if the brazier had been lit for some time.

"Don't trouble yourself about Owen," Jamie said. "He is safely out of the way for tonight."

Linnet threw her hands up in exasperation. "How can the queen be so foolish over him?"

"It must be that she loves him," Jamie said with an edge to his voice.

"What kind of answer is that?" Linnet said, turning around to face him. "She risks both their lives with this affair."

"For a woman in love, no sacrifice is too great," he said. "Or so I have been told."

His tone was hard and angry, and she did not understand why.

"I did not wait here half the afternoon to talk about Owen and the queen," he said.

Jamie had been waiting for her? Had he meant to break the news of his betrothal to her alone?

"And now, I want to know what in the name of all the saints you have been doing with Edmund Beaufort," he said, his voice steadily rising. "Tell me, did you send for him to take my place the moment I was gone?"

His eyes were blazing. When he took a step closer, she had to fight the urge to step back.

"Could you not go a week without a man in your bed?"

This must be what he looked like when he charged at an enemy across a field. But now, she was just as angry. It welled in her chest and pounded in her ears.

"By what right," she said in a low voice that could have cut steel, "do you believe you can question what I do?"

"Was that silver-tongued Edmund Beaufort man enough for you, or did you bestow your gifts upon others as well?" He took a step closer, and this time she did step back. "You did say one man might not be able to satisfy your needs."

She could not believe she was hearing this.

"How dare you!" She slapped her hand to her chest, saying, "I am the one who is wronged here."

"You, the one wronged?" he thundered. "You, the innocent?"

"You have a lot of gall, Jamie Rayburn, to ask me insulting questions about other men, when you have gone behind my back and gotten yourself betrothed."

From the way Jamie's mouth fell open, he had not expected her to know about his betrothal yet. What kind of fool did he think she was?

"Did you think I would not hear of it?" she asked, her voice going perilously high and thin. "You could not be bothered to tell me first? You must bring her here to Windsor to surprise me with the news?"

The anger seemed to have gone out of him. Guilt could

do that. He reached his hand out to her, but she lifted her arms and stepped back from him.

"How could you, Jamie?" she said, tears stinging her eyes despite herself. She hated crying. Hated, hated, hated it. She clenched her fists and turned her back to him.

"I knew all along you would leave me," she said, trying and failing to control the shake in her voice. "But I thought you would be kinder in how you did it this time. We had an agreement, remember? When you wished to end it, you were to tell me first."

He came up behind her and put his hands on her shoulders. As soon as he touched her, her body began to convulse in silent sobs.

"Just go!" she said in a choked whisper. She could not bear to have him see her like this, weak and sniveling.

"I am not betrothed," he said, his breath against her hair. "I would have told you."

"Edmund says it is all arranged."

"It is true that the bishop and Bedford suggested the connection," he said. "But that is all."

She wiped her nose on her sleeve, even though it was very bad for the velvet.

"What will you do?" she asked, managing to keep her voice steady this time.

"I am the sort of man who needs a home, a family. A wife."

It shouldn't hurt this much to hear him say it. But in her heart, she knew this was true about him. She had known it since the day he left her in Paris. Tears were flowing so hard now that she did not bother swiping at them with her sleeve.

"I want more than a lover," he said. "I want a woman

who will make a life with me and be the mother of my children."

He was leaving her.

She had to hold her breath to keep from breaking into loud sobs like a five–year-old. Misery twisted at her gut; at the same time, she felt faint and nauseous.

"I love you, Linnet, but 'tis all or nothing with me," he said. "You will make your pledge to me, or I will find another."

Jamie loved her.

As she turned to face him, his arms came around her. She rested her head against his chest. It had been such a long, long time since he had told her he loved her.

"Don't leave me," she whispered. "Don't ever leave me."

"There are promises I need from you," he said.

"Just don't go," she said, closing her eyes and holding him tighter. "Don't leave me again."

She did not care what promises she had to make. All she wanted was to be here in his arms.

"I must have your word—"

"We can speak of this later, can we not?" She dropped her hands to his buttocks. "I missed you something fierce."

His stern expression softened. "You did?"

"Every moment," she said, her voice growing husky.

He pulled her closer and brushed his cheek against hers. Against her ear, he said, "I missed you, too."

She leaned back so he would see the desire in her eyes when she told him what she wanted from him. "I want you to tell me you love me again, when you are inside me."

Her words had precisely the effect she hoped.

Jamie crushed her against him and kissed her with a

fierceness that set fire prickling beneath her skin. Without lifting his mouth from hers, he backed her up until she leaned against the bed. He cradled her head in his hands, his fingers splayed in her hair, and gave her an open-mouthed kiss of such hunger she wasn't sure there would be anything left of her—and she didn't care.

When he finally lifted his mouth from hers she gasped for breath—and sucked it in again when he cupped her breasts. His groan of need echoed her own as he buried his face in her neck. She gripped his hair in her hands as he pressed hot wet kisses down her throat.

He spun her around and began unfastening her gown. As his fingers worked the buttons, his ragged breath was in her ear and his shaft hard against her buttocks. Then his mouth was on her bare shoulder. Gentler now, he eased her gown and chemise down together, kissing her bare skin in its wake. She swallowed against the surge of desire when he gripped her hips and nipped her bottom.

A shiver of pleasure shot through her limbs as he ran his tongue up her back. When she turned in his arms, Jamie enfolded her in an embrace that warmed and comforted her, even while it made her heart pound with anticipation. He lifted her onto the bed and then broke away just long enough to strip off his clothes.

She opened her arms to him as he joined her on the bed. When his mouth found hers this time, it was a slow, lingering, open-mouthed kiss. They melded into each other, tongues moving in a sensuous rhythm that was a prelude of what was to come.

Praise God, Jamie was back with her. This was all she needed. *He* was all she needed.

His hand moved up her thigh, and she could not

breathe. She ached for him. Ached to have him touch her, to be inside her.

When he touched her center, she was wet with desire for him. She felt the warmth of his breath in her ear as he worked his magic with his fingers.

"Jamie..." She tried to speak, but could not. When she tugged at his shoulder, he understood and rolled on top of her.

At last she felt the tip of his shaft against her. She lifted her hips and gasped with the rush of sensation as he plunged into her. He paused when he was deep inside, and they clung together, both breathing hard. Then he rose on his elbows to look into her eyes. The warmth in them enveloped her and made her heart swell with joy.

"I love you," he said. "I've never stopped."

Her body clenched around his shaft inside her.

"I love you, too," she said.

He began moving inside her, with excruciating slowness at first, and then with an urgency that matched her own. They were as one in their passion, their need, their love.

"I love you," he said in a harsh gasp against her ear, and they came together in a pulsing release that staggered her with its violence.

Afterward, she lay adrift, resting in the circle of his strong arms. When at last she roused herself to lift her head and look at him, he gave her a wide grin.

"You did miss me, didn't you?"

"Mmmm-hmmm." She smiled and closed her eyes. "Perhaps you should bar the door. With so many guests in the castle, someone might wander in looking for an empty chamber."

"You don't fool me. You just want to look at my bare arse."

It was true; she did enjoy the view when he went to bar the door. And when he turned around, he looked like a Greek god with the golden light of the brazier shining on the lines of hard muscles of his chest and arms. 'Twas a shame a man who looked like that ever had to wear a shirt.

She sighed with contentment as he lay down beside her and drew her into his arms again.

"'Tis good to have you back at Windsor, Jamie Rayburn."

"So you did not fill your time with Edmund?" he asked, and she knew he was only half joking.

"You are the only man I want," she said, pressing her face into his neck. "It's been that way for me from the day you rode into Paris with the king."

"You didn't like me much before that, when we met in Caen," he said with a smile in his voice.

"I was thirteen!"

"I remember you at thirteen," he said, stroking her cheek. "You were so full of fire, and already so lovely, I am certain you attracted all manner of inappropriate attention."

She had hated the way men leered at her.

Jamie brushed the hair back from her face and kissed her forehead. "I did not mean to make you frown."

When she smiled up at him, he lowered his mouth to hers. She sighed with pleasure at the feel of him over her, his hard chest pressed against her breasts. As they kissed, she ran her hands over the long line of his back to the rise of his buttocks and back up again.

His body was more familiar to her than her own. Her fingers went to the scar where a blade had caught him in the side. Each of his battle scars, in an odd way, reassured her that Jamie could face whatever danger fate threw at him and survive. He was the very best of fighters.

After they made love again, she lay awake, waiting for him to renew his demand for pledges and promises. She would agree to what she must.

How much would she have to give up for him? How far would she have to go to keep him?

Jamie told himself he should take it one step at a time. She had told him she did not want him to leave her, ever. That should be enough for now. But it was not. He was done with pretense. He was finished with taking what he could get from her.

He should have pressed his advantage and insisted on an answer before he took her to bed. But seeing her vulnerable made him weak. When she said she missed him, he was ready to forgive her anything. Hearing her say she wanted him inside her sent lust roaring through him. Nothing mattered then except having her naked beneath him. His thoughts were drowned in sensation; making love to her was all he wanted, all he knew.

But after the endless kisses, after the joining of bodies that felt like a joining of their souls, his questions returned. He would have her answer. Her pledge. He did not want her as a lover or mistress—though he most definitely wanted her in his bed. When a man was off fighting, he needed a home to return to. He wanted his to be with her.

"Linnet, it is time we settled matters between us."

She turned on her side and ran a finger down his chest. "You spoke of promises before," she said, fixing those deceptively innocent pale-blue eyes on him. "What do you ask of me?"

That was one of the things he appreciated about her: She looked you right in the eye no matter how hard the question.

"I want us to marry." His heart thundered in his chest as he waited for her answer.

"Are you certain you want me as your wife?"

"'Tis not the first time I've asked, as you may recall."

"This is a serious matter. Something we should discuss dressed, I think."

With that, she got up from the bed and slipped her chemise over her head. What was in the woman's head?

"'Tis a simple question," he said from the bed. "It requires a simple answer, yea or nay."

He got distracted for a moment as she pulled long, silky strands of her hair out from her chemise.

"How soon do you want to marry?" she asked, crossing her arms.

She was asking when; he took that as a good sign.

"As soon as it can be done."

"Must it be soon?" she asked.

"Aye, it must."

She nodded but then bit her lip. Not the joyful bride he hoped for.

He got up from the bed and went to her. "What is it? Tell me what worries you."

She gave him a long, assessing look before she spoke. "I have put a great deal of effort into building my trade," she said. "You would not expect me to give it up c pletely, would you?"

He could not help smiling, because it was so like her. She could not simply say she would be his wife; she must negotiate the terms. Well, he had one term he would insist upon as well.

"I have no objection, so long as it does not require us to live in London."

"A long visit once or twice a year will do."

The radiant smile she gave him lifted his heart. At last, she seemed happy about their marriage.

"In another year," she said, clapping her hands together and rising on her toes, "I shall have enough saved to buy your lands for you."

What was she talking about? "I don't need my wife to buy lands for me."

"I do not mean to offend you." She rested the flat of her hand against his chest, which had an unexpected calming effect on him. "You have need of lands, and I have the means—or will have soon. You would think nothing wrong in marrying an heiress for her lands. Why should this be different?"

Was this the reason she wished to wait?

"I can provide you a home," he said. "Eventually, we will have a finer one, once Bedford grants me lands for my service."

She had distracted him from what he meant to say.

"But there is a promise you must make to me," he said, "or we shall not marry."

Her smile faltered. "What is it?"

"You must give up these senseless grudges. You must promise me—absolutely—that you will cease to seek

person you believe to have wronged
you were a child."

ood cause," she said with that stubborn

"I do not care if you do. It is dangerous, and I will not have it. How could I leave to do my duty in France, knowing you are home in England provoking men to violence at every turn?"

More than that, he could never hope to make her happy until she gave up this obsession of hers.

She pressed her lips together and narrowed her eyes at him, as if judging whether there was any room to negotiate.

"I'll not move an inch on this, Linnet." He folded his arms across his chest. "I will not be the man who has to tell his children their mother is in the Tower for murder—or worse, that her body was found floating in the Thames."

She looked off to the side, tapping her foot. This was hard for her, and he knew it. He waited her out.

Finally, she blew out her breath and said, "All right. I agree."

"I will have your solemn promise on it."

She looked as if she would rather eat worms, but he was not budging. In sooth, he would have liked to ask her to write the promise in blood. But he was a reasonable man.

She sniffed and tilted her chin up with all the dignity of a queen being asked to relinquish her crown.

"I shall pray fervently that God punishes those who wronged my grandfather and left my brother and me to starve," she said, her voice edged with bitterness. "I shall pray that they suffer in this life and burn in hell for all eternity in the next."

"And?"

She took a deep breath and let it out. "I swear I shall cease to pursue the godforsaken demons myself."

There, she had said it. He had won. He took her hands and lifted them to his lips.

"I have something to give you." Jamie lifted the medal of Saint George, the dragon slayer, from around his neck and slipped the silver chain over her head.

"But King Henry gave that to you," Linnet protested. "I cannot take it."

"It is a saint for soldiers," he said, smiling down at her. "But with the trouble you get into, I would feel better if you wore it."

Linnet lifted the medal from where it rested between her breasts and touched it to her lips.

"Thank you," she said, blinking back tears. "I shall never take it off."

He cupped her cheek in his hand. "Now it would be nice if you told me you love me and want to be my wife."

"I do love you." She threw her arms around him and buried her face in his neck. "I could not give you up again."

Joy and a quiet sense of peace settled over him as he held her in his arms. She was his now.

Then she leaned back and looked up at him from under her lashes. "I have a confession to make."

Damn. He didn't want to hear this. He tensed, hoping her confession would not make him have to kill Edmund Beaufort.

"I like to listen to the tales of your victories."

He laughed. "Now I believe you love me."

"I love you with all my heart, Jamie Rayburn."

Jamie held her to him and closed his eyes. Five years he had waited for this. At long last, Linnet was truly his. All he wanted would be his.

Chapter Twenty-two

Linnet clapped with the others as the mummers cavorted through the hall in their masks. All through yuletide, there had been lavish entertainments, from dancing bears to acrobats. In the lower ward, there were cock and dog fights, which she despised, but those were easily avoided.

The sounds of harp, flute, and tabor floated down from the gallery as people milled about, stretching their legs and making conversation before the next round of entertainment.

Linnet and Queen Katherine stood side by side with their backs to the wall. Speaking in low voices, they gossiped good-naturedly about various nobles and merchants in the Great Hall.

"That young squire of Sir James's is going to have all the ladies sighing in a year or two," the queen remarked.

"Martin has such a pure heart. I wonder if he'll notice?" Linnet said with a laugh. "I've grown quite fond of him."

"A pure heart—likely he's the only one in this room you could say that of," the queen said with a sparkle in her eyes. She took Linnet's hand and squeezed it. "'Tis good to see you so happy, my dear."

It was true. Joy filled her heart and lightened her step. She had floated through the days of holiday festivities in a feathery cloud of bliss. The prospect of marriage was unexpectedly...freeing. Instead of making her feel confined, it brought her a sense of contentment.

At least it did most of the time.

But now and then, the twin vices of anger and guilt dug their talons into her. Justice had been denied her. The man responsible for ruining her grandfather's last years still enjoyed the fruits of his thievery. He had robbed her of everything that protected her and left her at the mercy of the worst sort of men.

She thanked God every day that Jamie's uncle Stephen had saved her and Francois. And she would never forgive her father for failing to do so. Of course, he had failed her long before that.

"When will you become formally betrothed?" the queen asked.

Linnet was grateful to the queen for diverting her. It was difficult, but she was determined to keep her word to Jamie and not dwell upon the past.

Queen Katherine, dear friend that she was, was giddy over their upcoming marriage.

"As soon as Christmas Court ends, we will travel to Ross Castle to make our betrothal pledges in the presence of his family."

Despite Jamie's reassurances, she felt anxious about how his parents would receive her. She had met the Fitz-Alans briefly in Normandy when she was a girl; both had seemed formidable. Once before, Jamie had led them to expect she would be his wife—only to come home empty-handed. She suspected that would be hard for a parent to forgive.

"It will be an adventure for you, living in the country and becoming part of a large family."

"Although I used to tease Jamie about wanting this sort of life," Linnet said with a broad smile, "it is what I want now, both for me and our children."

It comforted her to know that her children would grow up within the protection and warmth of a large extended family.

The thought of having a child lifted her heart. It was such a hopeful act. She had never allowed herself to think of having a child before. Although she refused to admit it to Jamie or Francois, she did know her efforts involved some danger. Besides, children were about the future, and she had been absorbed with the past.

"I should like nothing better than to raise my son in the country," the queen said with a catch in her voice. "They will take him from me again soon."

"I am sorry for it," Linnet said.

"At least I have Owen," the queen said. "And a time will come when we, too, shall marry."

"Do not speak of it here, please!" Though the queen had spoken softly, Linnet looked quickly about her to be sure no one had overheard.

The queen seemed perilously close to tears. Desperate to divert her, Linnet said, "There is that awful Lord Stafford and his daughter."

Queen Katherine touched a kerchief to her nose. "I do hope they are not coming this way."

"What could Bedford and the bishop have been thinking, attempting to pair Jamie with Agnes Stafford?"

"Nothing could be simpler to understand," the queen said, in control of herself again. "Lady Agnes is a land-rich heiress, and Jamie is a strong warrior from a family with close ties to the Lancasters."

Though Jamie had told her—repeatedly—that it was a delicate situation, it nagged at Linnet that he had not poured cold water on Stafford's expectation of a marriage offer for his daughter. Jamie wanted to seek his parents' counsel. His mother, he assured her, would know how he could extricate himself without damaging his family or humiliating the young lady.

"The Stafford girl is quite pretty, but with a little effort, she could be a beauty." Queen Katherine made a disapproving tutting sound with her tongue. "She wears the most unflattering gowns. And a smile would do her no harm."

Linnet was in no mood to hear this.

"*Mon Dieu!* Here they come." The queen pasted a regal smile on her face.

"Your Highness, Lady Linnet." Stafford made a bow and greeted them in a voice that easily carried above the noise of the hall.

Stafford's orange and red tunic and matching hat and hose were so bright Linnet blinked. Perhaps his daughter wore such somber colors to avoid drawing more attention to them.

The queen appeared too stunned by his attire to speak.

"Where is Gloucester?" Stafford demanded, as if the queen were her brother-in-law's keeper. "Haven't seen him all evening."

"Did you enjoy the mummers and the acrobats?" Linnet asked, seeking safer ground.

"Actors and acrobats are ungodly men and women," Lady Agnes said. "I averted my eyes as best I could."

Linnet was afraid to meet the queen's eyes for fear of laughing.

"The money would have been better spent as a donation to the church," Lady Agnes added.

The girl seemed unaware that she was judging the wisdom of royal expenditures—and to the queen, no less.

"Surely God would find no harm in a little entertainment," Linnet said with a smile.

Lady Agnes looked at her as if she had spoken a foreign language.

"Lord Stafford," the queen said, "I hear you must leave us soon."

Praise God for that.

"I must take my leave on the morrow, but my daughter will remain here in Lady Elizabeth's care."

Poor Lady Elizabeth.

"You see, my health is not good. I..."

Linnet could not decide which was worse: hearing about Stafford's digestive problems or listening to his daughter preach at her.

When the pair finally left them, Linnet leaned against the wall to recover. Before she could catch her breath, Edmund Beaufort glided between several people to join them.

"Your Highness," Edmund said as he made his low bow, then turned to Linnet. "And the bewitching Lady Linnet. When will you run away with me?"

"Never." When he paused too long over her hand, Linnet tugged it free. At least he had not started writing poetry to her. But then, Edmund only pretended to be a romantic.

She did not see Jamie until he stood beside her, scowling at Edmund as if he would like to rip him limb from limb. To Edmund's credit, he did not step back.

Jamie gave Edmund a curt nod and clamped his hand on Linnet's arm. "Excuse us, Your Highness. Lady Linnet and I have an urgent matter to discuss."

Jamie's jaw was clenched as he steered her across the room. He waited to speak until they were behind a pillar in the anteroom.

"If that man looks at you like that again, he will regret it."

"Like what?" Linnet said, though she knew precisely how Edmund looked at her.

"Like he is imagining you naked in his bed," he said. "Did he ask you to be his mistress again?"

The vein in his neck was pulsing.

"He believes your motives are the same as his, since he thinks you are about to wed Lady Agnes," she said, because Jamie deserved a little goading. "Edmund is a good sort, really."

Jamie made an indecipherable sound that could not be interpreted as agreement. Truly, he had no sense of humor about some things.

A servant going by with wine offered them a cup, which Jamie took.

"The stars were aligned in your favor the day we met again," she said, leaning back against the pillar. "Otherwise, you might have actually married that Agnes Stafford. Mercy, a duller woman I have never met."

Linnet could jest about it now that she knew nothing would come of it.

"Do not speak harshly of Lady Agnes," Jamie chided.

"There is much I respect and admire about her. She will make some man a fine wife."

For men, there was a long distance betwixt respect and desire. However, Linnet chose not to mention the obvious.

"For such a godly woman," she said in a low voice, "she has big breasts."

Jamie choked on his wine and wiped his mouth on his sleeve. "Linnet, leave the poor woman alone!"

She narrowed her eyes at him. "You noticed her breasts, didn't you?"

"Aye, of course I did." Jamie shrugged. "They are a fine feature—a God-given feature, I might add. Where you got the notion a godly woman cannot have an attractive shape, I could not guess."

The conversation had ceased to be humorous. "You find this Agnes attractive? Very attractive?"

"Are you jealous?" he said, grinning like an idiot.

He leaned down and blew in her ear, sending a ripple of tingles down her spine. Then he whispered, "Why would a man choose a plain oatcake when he could have an apple tart with clotted cream?"

She burst out laughing, her ill humor gone in an instant. "So I am your apple tart, am I, Jamie Rayburn?"

"Wait a few moments, then follow me," he said next to her ear. "I am going to steal a bowl of clotted cream from the kitchen."

She leaned back and raised her eyebrows. "You cannot mean..."

He winked and nodded.

She rolled her eyes, but she said, "Where shall I find you?"

"Meet me downstairs in the undercroft. We'll find an empty storeroom."

His eyes went dark as he ran a finger slowly down her arm. Such a small gesture, and yet her pulse beat wildly. She would go anywhere with this man.

"Count to two hundred," he said. "I'll be waiting for you."

Linnet only got to thirty-five.

She picked up her skirts as she hurried down the stone stairs. With her mind occupied with thoughts of Jamie and clotted cream, she almost ran headlong into two people coming up the steps.

The black-clad figure was Hume, the priest who served as Eleanor Cobham's clerk. Whatever was he doing down here? He could have no more business in the undercroft than she.

Even more surprising, the priest was in the company of Margery Jourdemayne, the Witch of Eye. All the ladies in Eleanor's circle used Margery for their medicinal needs, from love potions to headache powders. Since Margery's arrival at Windsor, however, Linnet had not heard a whisper about her providing anything but these ordinary remedies.

Consequently, Linnet had dismissed the old herbalist's dire warnings about Margery practicing dark magic and consorting with the devil. All the same, something in the woman's penetrating stare sent a shiver up her spine.

"Good day to you," Father Hume said.

Who was he to give her that malevolent look? She arched an eyebrow and swept her gaze over him.

"Good day," she said and then continued down the stairs at a brisk pace, as if she had an important errand to attend to—which she did.

She continued along the low arched passageway wondering where she would find Jamie. With all the guests, servants would be in and out of the wine cellar, so he would not choose there. Farther down, the door to the spicery was ajar. That was odd. Because spices were as valuable as gold, the room was usually locked up tight.

Was this where Hume and Margery had been? The spicery would be a treasure trove for a woman in Margery's trade. After glancing up and down the corridor, Linnet slipped inside.

Pungent smells surrounded her. She stopped to draw in a deep breath, trying to identify them. Rosemary, mint, lavender, sage, cinnamon. The rich, intermingled scents were intoxicating. Which had Margery come for? Mint leaves for the headache? Mustard for a poultice? But why would Father Hume come with her?

There was a drop of some substance on the long table used to mix or pour spices into smaller containers. Linnet put her nose to it and sniffed. It had a strong, tangy odor. She rubbed her finger over it, then touched her finger to the tip of her tongue. Her tongue went numb—an analgesic of some sort? Father Hume seemed young to be suffering from aching joints.

She ignored the herbs hanging from the ceiling and went to examine the rows of bottles, jars, and pots. A small cloudy jar that sat alone on the corner of a high shelf caught her eye. It looked as if it was kept apart so it would not be mistaken for another.

She found a small stool underneath the table and stood on it to take a closer look. From the light dust, she could see the bottle was not quite in the circle where it had been.

She lifted it off the shelf and put her nose to it—the same strong, tangy smell. Carefully, she put it back in its place.

What could it be? Perhaps it was something for Eleanor, though it hardly seemed like an ingredient for a love potion.

She jumped as the door to the spicery swung open.

"There you are." Jamie gave her a devilish grin as he kicked the door closed behind him. "I brought the clotted cream."

He set the bowl on the long table and sniffed as his gaze drifted around the small room.

"Are the smells not wonderful in here?" she said.

"I do like a touch of spice with my clotted cream," Jamie said with a glint in his eyes.

He dipped his finger in the bowl and brought a large dollop of clotted cream to her lips. She licked it off his finger and closed her eyes with pleasure as the rich flavor filled her mouth. When he took her in his arms and kissed her, the taste of him mixed with the sweet taste of cream. Heady smells filled her nose as he laid her back on the table.

She decided she could tell him later about Margery, the unlocked door, the mysterious potion...

Chapter Twenty-three

Christmas Court was nearly at an end. After so many days of drinking and feasting, the crowd was boisterous. Linnet could barely hear the music of harp, flute, and tabor above the hum of conversation in the Great Hall.

Linnet caught sight of Martin talking with some other squires and touched his arm to pull him aside.

When he turned, his eyes went wide.

"L-L-L-Lady Linnet." After a delay, he swept her a formal bow, bumping a man behind him in the process. The man swore at him, but Martin did not appear to notice.

Linnet sighed inwardly. Surely, the lad should have grown accustomed to her by now.

"Have you seen Sir James?" she asked as she peered through the crowd.

"H-he took Thunder out for a gallop."

Someone moved, and a glint of silver near the floor caught her eye. She stood stock-still, unable to breathe. In the gap between men's leggings and the skirts of gowns, the silver-clawed bottom of a cane shone bright against a black square of the tiled floor. Her vision narrowed like a tunnel to fix on it through the crowd.

Linnet swayed on her feet, hit by a wave of dizziness as the memories burst into her head. She and Francois holding hands as they hid under the bed. The men arguing. All she could see were the men's feet...and that distinctive silver lion's paw on the base of the cane.

Where are his grandchildren? Where are they?

The raspy voice had been angry, insistent. With each word, the silver-clawed paw thumped on the floorboards. The memory of the sound made her stomach tighten and her palms go damp.

"M'lady, are you well?" Someone had taken hold of her arm and was speaking to her. She shook the hand off her.

Slowly, she lifted her gaze from the silver base of the cane to take in the man who held it—the man she had been seeking for so many years. She saw a flash of green brocade, but then the crowd moved and her view was blocked.

"Leave me," she said, shaking off the hand that had fastened onto her arm again.

With her heart thundering in her ears, she began walking toward her enemy. Mychell had lied to her, given her the wrong name. The man with the cane was not dead. He was right here at Windsor. Mychell must also have lied when he claimed the man was just an intermediary, a lackey like himself.

The fiend's back was to her. She took in the fine brocade stretched over a broad back gone to fat, and the elaborate liripipe hat with a long tail drawn forward over his shoulder.

He was talking with Gloucester and Eleanor...and Pomeroy. But she barely took note of the others; even Pomeroy did not matter. She had made a vow that day as she hid under the bed. At long last, she had found her enemy. Ten years she had waited. And now he was hers.

Her heart pounded in her ears, blocking all other sounds, as she started toward him through the crowd. A glimmer of reason broke through her trance: *Not here.* Not here in the hall before all these people.

But she needed to see his face. Making a wide circle, she worked her way around the room until she stood behind a pillar opposite him. She closed her eyes and leaned her head against the pillar while she gathered herself. Despite all her efforts to find him, her enemy had hidden from her at every turn. Now, finally, she would know who he was.

Would she recognize him? Would he be an old friend of her grandfather's, as the others had been?

The advantage was hers now. She must not forewarn him that she knew who he was. And that she intended to destroy him.

She drew in a deep breath and walked around the pillar.

The group had shifted so that Pomeroy once again blocked her view. All she could see of the man was dark hair and a fat cheek, pink with good health. In her memory, his voice was an old man's. But here the villain was, in the prime of life, with years before him to enjoy the fruits of his unearned prosperity.

All thought of carefully choosing her timing, of working by stealth, went out of her head when the man threw back his head and his hearty laugh rang out above the noise of the crowd. How dare he enjoy his life after destroying her grandfather? How dare he, after leaving her and Francois to face the world alone and penniless?

She remembered the fear of getting caught stealing and losing a hand. She remembered hunger clawing at her belly when they did not manage to steal enough. She remembered the English soldiers cornering her and Francois in their empty house in Falaise. She remembered the lechery in the soldiers' eyes that she did not fully understand and yet made her ill with fright.

All of it happened as a consequence of this man's acts against them. Red rage grew in her until her body pulsed with it. She could not bear that he should walk this earth another day, another moment.

As she moved toward him, she felt for the thin blade she kept strapped to the inside of her forearm. She gave her arm a snap, and the blade slid loose from its sheath and fell into her cupped hand. As she folded her fingers over the hilt, she imagined sticking it into the middle of her enemy's chest.

She needed no plan. His time had come.

Justice was hers.

"Quickly. She is there," Martin said.

Jamie followed his squire's gaze and saw Linnet. She was moving through the milling guests like a hunter stalking forward, her eyes on her prey.

"You were right to fetch me," Jamie said without taking his eyes off Linnet. God's beard, what was she doing?

Jamie eased his way around an elderly couple, then quickened his pace. But a massive woman in red velvet stepped in front of him, and he lost sight of Linnet behind the woman's expansive headdress. He stepped to the side and looked over the heads of the noisy crowd, tension thrumming through him. Where in the hell was she?

A moment later, he saw her emerge from behind a pillar. Her eyes were fixed dead ahead, and she took no notice of the people who attempted to speak to her as she brushed past them. Jamie had seen that same fierce expression on the faces of warriors charging into battle.

But who or what was she charging toward? As he plunged through the crowd again, he followed the direction of her gaze . . . to Pomeroy. Damnation, he didn't know Pomeroy was here. Good God, she was headed straight for him. What in the name of all the bloody saints did she plan to do?

Jamie pushed his way through the guests as quickly as he could without knocking anyone to the floor. When she was but five feet from Pomeroy, Jamie stepped in front of her. She gasped and looked up at him, her eyes wide and unblinking, as if he'd wakened her from a dream. Taking her firmly by the arm, Jamie wheeled her around and marched her toward the door.

"God's blood, Linnet," he hissed in her ear. "I told you I would take care of Pomeroy."

When he finally got her out of the crowded hall, he kept going. He intended to take care of Pomeroy once and for all this time. But he would deal with Linnet first.

He marched her all the way up the stairs to her chamber, shoved her inside, and slammed the door behind them.

"I swear, you will be the death of me," he shouted at her. "What were you about to do to Pomeroy? You had murder in your eyes."

"Nothing," she said in a voice that still sounded dazed. "I was not going to touch Pomeroy, I swear it."

He took hold of her shoulders and gave her a shake. "I told you I would take care of him."

She was shaking so violently that he ground his teeth to make himself stop yelling at her.

"It was not Pomeroy," she said.

"For God's sake, do not lie to me. I saw you."

"But I—"

"You broke your promise to me!" He slammed his fist on the table beside them, making the jars on it rattle. "In the name of all that is holy, why can you not see how dangerous this is? What will I have to do to keep you out of trouble? Chain you to the floor? Leave a guard of twenty to watch you?"

"I felt as if I were possessed," she said, sounding more bewildered than contrite. "I knew 'twas not the place nor—"

"Not the place? For God's sake, you were about to attack him in front of three hundred people. And that is not the worst of it. The Duke of Gloucester was standing next to Pomeroy. If you brandished a blade near Gloucester, I'd never get you out of the Tower."

"Who was the third man talking with them?"

Was she finally beginning to see the gravity of what she had done? "God's wounds, Linnet, that was the mayor of London. You could hardly have chosen a worse group to assault if you tried."

"The mayor?" She blinked several times, as if trying to absorb this news. "But you told me he was a good and honorable man. Are you quite certain of his character?"

"What does it matter what sort of man the mayor is?"

When he rubbed his forehead against the blazing headache she was giving him, she stepped closer and put the flat of her hands on his chest. His skin sizzled beneath her touch.

Hurt and love and anger surged through him in a ball of emotion too strong to contain. He slammed the bar across the door. This time, he did not care who might have seen them enter her bedchamber. Let them all know he was here in her bed.

He gripped her face in his hands and covered her mouth, letting her feel his anger. His shaft throbbed with need. He wanted to claim her, subdue her, finally make her his.

For she was not his. Not yet. Despite her promises, her pledges. She had not truly given herself to him.

Why could she not love him enough?

He would take her now, because he could. Because he wanted her. He clenched the silky strands of her hair in his fingers and kissed her until she sagged against him. When he pulled away, her lips were swollen, and her skin was pink where his whiskers had rubbed against it.

She looked so fragile in his arms. But Linnet was no delicate flower. She tore through life, leaving a burned trail behind. He both loved and hated her fiery nature, her strength, her unwillingness to follow the rules of her class and her sex and do as she ought.

He wanted to bend her to his will. Possess her.

When he lifted her, she wrapped her legs like a vise around him. Their mouths were locked as he slammed her back against the door. She made little cries against his mouth as he covered her breasts with his hands and squeezed the nipples through the cloth. When she tore her mouth away, he sucked on the skin of her neck, leaving his mark. The smell of her hair in his face made him mindless with desire. He wrenched her skirts up and ran his hands up her bare thighs. Gripping her rounded buttocks, he held her tight against him. Despite the layers of cloth between them, he could feel her heat.

Gasping, he leaned his forehead against the door and moved against her. Jesus and all the saints, she felt good.

But not as good as he would feel inside her.

"Jamie, please," she said against his ear.

He claimed her mouth again as he frantically untied his braies. When her hands found bare skin under his tunic, the breath went out of him. Finally, he freed himself from his braies and leggings. He paused with the tip of his cock just inside her and closed his eyes, savoring the unbearable rush of desire that pounded in his ears and pulsed through every vein.

Then he plunged into her. And he was home again. All he wanted was to be here inside her right now. Again and again, he thrust deep inside her, as she clawed at his back and made those sounds in the back of her throat. As she screamed in his ear, he came in an explosion of lust and anger and so much desire that it staggered him.

Using the door as support, he slid to the floor with her before his knees gave way. Christ, what this woman did to him!

When he could move again, he lifted her off him and stood to tie his braies.

She stumbled to her feet and threw her arms around his waist. "Please, don't be so angry with me. You don't under—"

He pushed her away and forced himself to say it.

"You must choose. I will not have a wife who will take a blade to a man in the middle of Windsor Castle, in the presence of half the royal family."

"But he—"

"I cannot chase down and kill every villain you provoke into threatening your life! And it will not be just your own life you put at risk, but our children's as well." He leaned close and shook his finger in her face. "I will not have it. I told you, I will not pledge myself to you unless you let the past lie."

Tears streamed down her face, but he would not be moved. Not this time.

"You. Must. Choose," he said, tapping his forefinger against her chest with each word. "Continue this battle or be my wife. For I swear to you, Linnet, you cannot do both."

Chapter Twenty-four

Jamie found Sir Guy Pomeroy gambling in a small, well-appointed room in the Curfew Tower at the far corner of the palace grounds. A brazier glowed too hot on one side of the room. On the other, several noblemen sat at a table with their sleeves rolled up and cups before them. A young squire stood behind each man, ready to pour more wine or run an errand.

All the men looked up as Jamie entered, and several hailed him. One was Sir John, a big man from Northumberland who knew his father well and had fought with them in France.

"Do you wish to join the game, Jamie?" Sir John called out. "Sir Guy brought cards from France."

The cards, which were not yet available in England, must have cost a small fortune. Each card was an elegant miniature painting with gold highlights.

"Just what we Englishmen need," another man joked. "One more way to lose our coin."

Jamie did not join in the laughter. "I believe I have all the vices I need."

Something in his voice caused the room to go quiet.

Anger roiled through him as he met Pomeroy's cold black eyes across the table. He was going to wipe that sneer off the pompous bastard's face.

"Speaking of your vices, how is Linnet?" Pomeroy said. "I must say, her behavior in the hall today was bizarre even for her. But what can you expect of a woman raised by a merchant?"

Jamie drew his sword from its scabbard and slammed the flat of the blade in the middle of their game, scattering cards and sending coins rolling to the floor. Hands went to sword hilts all around the table, but Jamie kept his eyes on Pomeroy. Jamie had a well-earned reputation with a sword. With the point of his aimed at Pomeroy, it was unlikely anyone else would attempt to interfere.

Jamie put his other hand on the table and leaned across it. "I will give you the benefit of the doubt, Sir Guy, and assume you did not receive my challenge."

Pomeroy had the gall to say, "What challenge?"

This was a private dispute; Jamie made it public now only to force Pomeroy's hand. If Pomeroy had the sense to remain quiet, Jamie would have refrained from saying anything more in front of the other men.

"What challenge?" he said, his eyes burning into Pomeroy's. "The challenge I delivered to you a full two months past at Westminster. The challenge I repeated in messages delivered to you every week since."

At this, the gazes of the other men shifted from Jamie to Pomeroy. A man might seek a peaceful resolution to a challenge, but he could not simply ignore it—at least he could not and retain the respect of his peers.

"Come, Rayburn, I thought you were jesting," Pomeroy

said. "I could not credit that you would risk your life over a woman so common."

Pomeroy was a hairbreadth from having Jamie's blade in his chest. 'Twas a shame it would be dishonorable to cut the godforsaken man down while he sat in a chair.

"I have waited nearly two months for you to name the time and place," Jamie said, biting out the words. "I will have satisfaction this day. Two miles upriver there is a wide bend in the Thames. Meet me in the field on the south side in two hours, or I shall come find you and strike you dead for a coward."

Pomeroy raised one black eyebrow. "I warned you before, she is not worth what this will cost you."

Jamie lifted his sword and brought the sharp edge down with a crack, cutting a half dozen of the valuable cards with one stroke. He lifted the sword and leaned forward until the point touched Pomeroy's tunic over his miserable heart.

"All you need to know," Jamie said, "is that saving that lady a moment's concern is worth more to me than your life."

Pomeroy kept his composure; Jamie had to give him that.

"Is defending her"—Pomeroy cleared his throat—"*virtue* worth your life?"

"Be in the field at the bend in the river, or I shall come find you," Jamie said. "If I have to chase you down, I promise you, I shall show no mercy."

Jamie straightened and sheathed his sword.

"This is a personal matter between Pomeroy and me." He let his gaze travel to every man at the table. "If men hear of it beforehand and take sides, it will feed into the current political strife. That will serve no one."

There were several grunts of agreement around the table.

"Can I rely upon you men to keep quiet until the matter is settled?"

"That you can," Sir John said in his deep voice. "To be certain, we shall remain together until it is done."

Jamie nodded his thanks.

"What say you to riding out to observe the fight?" Sir John said to the others.

One of the men slapped the table and grinned. "This is a fight I'd like to see."

This was followed by nods and "ayes" all around the table. Men loved to watch a fight.

Jamie gave Pomeroy a long look before he turned on his heel and left. When he stepped out of the tower, he drew in a deep, cleansing breath of cold air and started across the lower ward.

"You gave Pomeroy no means to avoid the fight," Martin said as he caught up to him.

Lord, he'd forgotten the lad was with him.

"'Tis too late for that now," Jamie said without turning his head. In the messages he had sent Pomeroy over the weeks, he had hinted that Lady Linnet might be willing to accept a formal apology and a sum of money—large enough to be painful to Pomeroy—as compensation for the harm done.

But that would not satisfy Jamie now. This sort of fighting was so much more complicated than war. He must put the fear of death into Pomeroy, without actually killing him.

Jamie preferred the rules of war. He wanted Pomeroy's blood.

"Was that wise, sir?" Martin asked. "To provide no opportunity for a peaceful resolution?"

"'Tis the only way."

"But Sir Guy is well-known for his fighting skills," Martin persisted.

"What kind of father do you have that I must explain this to you?" Jamie exploded.

Christ give him patience! He'd had enough talk for one day. The lower ward was huge and took so long to cross he wished he'd brought his damned horse. Just when he thought the boy had the good sense to be quiet, he spoke again.

"My mother devoted herself to teaching me the virtues of knighthood," Martin said, sounding as though he had given Jamie's last remark careful thought. "But perhaps my father would have taught me the more practical aspects had he not died when I was a babe."

Damn. Why did he not know the boy's father was dead? Martin was his squire. If the boy had no father to teach him what he ought to know, then it was Jamie's duty to do it.

"The matter with Pomeroy is a simple one," he explained. "Pomeroy poses a threat to Lady Linnet. As she is my future wife, I cannot allow that."

"You are to wed her? That is the best of news, sir."

Jamie was not feeling particularly joyous about it at the moment. But he was determined.

Martin was quiet until they passed the guards at the gate by the Round Tower that separated the lower and upper wards.

"Are you certain you will prevail, sir?"

"Aye." There was no other choice.

"May I be your second, sir?"

The boy's offer broke Jamie's sour mood. "You are a good lad, but I will not need a second," he said, slapping Martin on the back. "But there is something I would have you do for me."

"It would be an honor, sir."

"I want you to tell Lady Linnet I had to leave Windsor on business for Bedford."

"You want me to lie to her?" Martin's eyes went wide. He did manage to refrain from reminding Jamie that a knight is honest and true—though Jamie could see he wanted to.

This time, Jamie laughed out loud. "Trust me, this is not the sort of thing you tell a woman until after it is done."

Martin appeared to think this over, then nodded. "I see. 'Tis more gallant to save the lady what might be needless worry."

Or, in the case of my beloved, it is best to give her no opportunity to interfere.

"When shall I say you will return?" Martin asked.

When I've put the fear of God into Pomeroy.

Likely as not, Jamie would end up with a few bumps and scrapes. He was quick to mend, but he might not be in fit shape to be seen today.

"To save her needless worry," Jamie said, a smile twitching at his lips, "tell her not to expect me before the morrow."

When they reached his chamber, Jamie set Martin to polishing his shield and cleaning his boots. He sharpened his sword and dagger himself, as he always did, and slid an extra blade into his boot. As he strapped on his sword, he looked up to find Martin watching him with an earnest expression.

"I begin to feel insulted by your lack of faith."

"'Tis not that," Martin was quick to assure him. "But I fear that a man who would insult Lady Linnet cannot be trusted to follow the rules of chivalry in fighting either."

"A good observation," Jamie said with a nod of approval. "Sir John thought the same, which is why he made sure he and the other men will be there to serve as witnesses."

Martin blinked at him. "You know Sir Guy has no honor and yet you will fight him?"

What nonsense had the boy's mother put into his head?

"Believe it or not, Pomeroy will not be the first man I've fought who was not a man of honor," Jamie said, suppressing a smile. He put his hand on Martin's shoulder. "If you find yourself often fighting men of honor, you must ask yourself if you are on the wrong side."

He was ready to go. Martin went with him to the stables to help him with Thunder. Once he was mounted, he looked down at his squire, who was still holding on to his horse's bridle.

"May I come to watch, after I tell Lady Linnet the lie?"

"Aye." The lad could use the experience of watching a rough fight or two before Jamie took him to France.

"Take care, sir."

The lad looked so anxious that Jamie had to laugh.

"You're a good lad, but you fret like an old woman."

Jamie leaned over to give Martin a friendly rap on the head. "My father taught me well, as I shall teach you. I am well prepared for the likes of Sir Guy Pomeroy."

The conversation with Martin cheered him considerably, and he enjoyed the ride along the river. Fighting was not something he worried much about. He had been trained by the very best—his father and his uncle Stephen. In a fair fight, he was any man's match. In an unfair fight, chances were just as good he would prevail.

As he approached the wide bend in the river, he saw the lone horseman waiting in the middle of a field shorn of its summer harvest.

Pomeroy. Jamie's light mood vanished.

He should have dealt with Pomeroy a long time ago. He had been hard on Linnet—not that she didn't deserve it. But he had been angry with himself as much as with her. After today, Pomeroy would know better than to come near her.

If Jamie let him live.

As he rode closer, he saw four other horsemen near the hedge that separated the field from a wood. He recognized the big man who lifted his arm in greeting as Sir John.

Pomeroy wore full armor. For one-on-one fighting, Jamie thought this was a mistake. A coward's mistake, but a mistake nonetheless.

"A fine afternoon," Jamie said to Pomeroy.

"'Tis filthy cold," Pomeroy said and rammed his helmet on.

Jamie shrugged. "Not so cold as to freeze the ground. The gravediggers should have no trouble with your grave."

As he waited for Sir John to join them in the center of

the field, Jamie examined Pomeroy's horse, weapons, and gleaming armor.

"In fairness, I must tell you," Jamie said. "The armor is a mistake. I'm willing to wait while you remove it."

"You insolent bastard of a traitor! You dare instruct me on how to fight?"

Jamie shrugged again. "I warned you."

Sir John rode up between them and cut off Pomeroy's string of curses.

"Each of you will ride to the far end of the field and await my signal for the combat to begin," Sir John said. "It ends when one of you concedes or is dead. Agreed?"

"Aye," they both answered.

Jamie cantered to the edge of his side of the field and turned Thunder to face their opponent. His great warhorse danced sideways, as ready for a fight as he. Jamie fixed his eyes on Pomeroy. Cold, hard anger filled him as he let himself remember Linnet on her knees with the fiend's hand coiled in her hair.

You will pay for the humiliation you caused her, for the fear in her eyes, for that cut on her cheek.

"Sirs, are you ready?" Sir John shouted.

"Aye!"

"At my signal," Sir John barked out. He raised his sword, then swung it down, shouting, "Commence to fight!"

"Aaarrgh!!!" Jamie shouted his battle cry. Thunder's hooves pounded beneath him as they charged across the field. He and this horse had been through so many battles together that they read each other like brothers. At his signal, Thunder galloped head-on at Pomeroy.

At the last minute, Pomeroy's horse tilted left. Jamie hit

Pomeroy with his shield with a loud *thwack* as he passed, but Pomeroy stayed on his horse. On the next pass, Jamie took a heavy blow with his shield and struck Pomeroy across the back with the flat of his sword.

So long as they were on their horses, Pomeroy's armor gave him the advantage. Dislodging Pomeroy from his horse, however, was proving more difficult than he had anticipated.

"I do not know where you got your reputation for fighting, Pomeroy," Jamie shouted. "You must have been at the back with the carts and the mules, for you would not have lasted a day fighting at King Henry's side."

Pomeroy galloped toward him with a roar and swung his sword at Jamie's side with all his force. Jamie felt the wind of the sword on his back as he flattened himself against Thunder's neck. Then, in one movement, he rose up and slammed the flat of his sword across Pomeroy's back. Pomeroy was already half off his horse when Jamie turned Thunder around and flung himself onto Pomeroy's back.

They crashed to the ground amid flying hooves. As soon as Jamie stopped rolling, he leapt to his feet, sword at the ready. He waited for Pomeroy, who was slower, hampered by his armor.

After that, the fight did not take long. Without the armor, they would have been a close match, for Pomeroy was powerful and skilled. Jamie was all that, but he was also agile and quick.

Finally, Jamie slammed Pomeroy to the ground, straddled Pomeroy's chest, and wrenched off his helmet. Battle rage rang in Jamie's ears. As he looked into the man's black eyes to his blacker soul, it was all he could do not to draw his dagger across Pomeroy's neck.

But a knight was expected to show mercy, not kill a countryman, after he had disarmed and defeated him in single combat.

"If you ever touch Linnet again," Jamie hissed through his teeth, "I shall rip off your arms and legs and eat your heart."

Pomeroy's eyes had fury in them, too. "I concede," he said through clenched teeth. "Now get off me."

Jamie thought of the thin line of blood on Linnet's fair skin and could not let the man go unmarked.

"First, let us see if you are as brave as she is." Jamie picked up Pomeroy's sword from where it had fallen and brought the shining blade to Pomeroy's cheek.

Pomeroy's demeanor changed instantly. His eye twitched and sweat beaded on his brow.

"Do not cut me," Pomeroy said in a low voice.

"What is it?" Jamie demanded. When Pomeroy said nothing, Jamie pressed the flat of the blade harder against Pomeroy's cheek without quite breaking the skin.

"Stop!" Pomeroy swallowed when Jamie eased the pressure. In a low rasp, he said, "There is poison on the blade."

"You would stoop to poison?"

Jamie's hand shook with the effort not to kill the man for the affront. The devil stood on his shoulder, urging him to slice the poisoned blade across Pomeroy's cheek. The devil whispered in his ear that no one would suspect Jamie knew the blade was tainted. The blame would fall on Pomeroy himself. A man who chose so dishonorable a means to win a contest deserved an ignoble death.

But Jamie's father had taught him that his enemy's behavior did not guide his own. A knight did not take a man's life by poison, no matter how richly the death was deserved.

Grinding his teeth against his rage, Jamie forced himself to toss Pomeroy's sword aside. Holding Pomeroy by the throat, he pulled his own dagger.

"I should cut out your eyes just for looking at her," he spat out. "But I shall settle for this."

Pomeroy clenched his jaw, but he did not cry out when Jamie drew the edge of the blade across his cheek. It was a deep cut that would fester and leave a scar.

"When you look at your reflection, I want you to remember that I could have killed you this day," Jamie said. "Know that if you ever threaten Linnet again, I shall."

Chapter Twenty-five

"There is a rumor on the wind about you, Lady Linnet," Gloucester said.

Linnet raised an eyebrow. "Only one, Your Grace? 'Tis disappointing to learn I am so little remarked upon."

Gloucester guffawed and slapped his knee. "I do like a clever woman. Never fear, dear lady, there is always a good deal of talk about you—especially about your beauty."

She expelled a dramatic sigh. "*That* is not very interesting."

Neither was Gloucester. When he crossed the hall to sit beside her on her bench by the window, there was no escape. One simply did not walk away from a man who was the king's uncle and third in line to the throne, tedious though he may be. Just yesterday, she would have done it anyway. But after how angry Jamie had been with her, she was determined to be more circumspect in her behavior.

"There is also speculation as to whom you've taken as your latest lover." Gloucester leaned closer. "But I, for one, am more interested in learning who will be your next."

Linnet did not like the direction of the conversation—or the way the duke was staring at her chest.

She cleared her throat. "But that is not the rumor you first spoke of?"

"You are quite right."

His sweet scent was going to make her sneeze if he did not move farther away. She glanced about the room, hoping someone would rescue her.

"What I heard is that you are looking for a particular man," Gloucester said in a low voice. "A merchant you suspect of cheating your family many years past."

Linnet's heart leapt in her chest. He had her full attention now. Trying to keep her voice steady, she asked, "Do you know who this man is?"

"Not at present. But if it is important to you, *mon cherie...*" He shrugged one shoulder and lifted his hands. "I could be persuaded to apply a bit of pressure here, a hint of a favor there..."

As a member of the royal family, Gloucester had means to obtain information she would never have. And more, he was the darling of the London merchants. If Gloucester let it be known that he required certain information, he would get it.

Linnet leaned forward, her breath coming fast. "You would do this for me, Your Grace?"

"The task could prove...enjoyable," he said with a slow smile. "Who knows what we might discover together?"

She sat back and folded her hands in her lap. Gloucester liked to play at being chivalrous, but he expected payment for service. Of course, she should have known there would be a quid pro quo. All she needed to do was think of something he wanted—other than herself.

His heavy scent made her nose twitch dangerously as he leaned close again. "There are too many ears here in the hall. Come to my rooms in an hour, and we can discuss how best to pursue your mysterious merchant."

"Will Lady Eleanor be joining us?" she asked, playing innocent.

He gave a bark of laughter. "Eleanor knows I like to share my goodwill."

Which was probably one of the reasons Eleanor remained his favorite.

"All the same, let us keep this...arrangement...to ourselves," Gloucester said, giving her a wink. "I suspect Sir James Rayburn would not be pleased if he learned of it."

And there was the rub.

While she was not going to let Gloucester lay a finger on her, let alone get into bed with him, Jamie would be furious if he learned she was still pursuing her revenge. She had not meant to. Truly, she had every intention of giving up the search. But with Gloucester dangling the means of discovering the identity of her worst enemy, she could not turn away.

She would have the name in no time.

And Jamie need never know.

She got to her feet. As she dipped her curtsy, she gave Gloucester a slight nod. Then she picked up her skirts and left him without a backward glance.

The question of what to pay Gloucester for the favor was already settled in her mind. It was well known Gloucester overspent his income. His lavish support of the arts, among other indulgences, left him perpetually short of cash. Gold coin she had aplenty.

Gloucester was like a fish on a hook. All she had to

do was get him in her net without falling into the water. She would make this a business deal, and they both would walk away satisfied. From what she heard, that was more than could be said of his lovers.

He would give her the name of her enemy. Once she had it, she would crush the villain like a soft pebble beneath her heel. Then all would be as it should be: the evil would be punished, the honest and hardworking rewarded.

Jamie called it revenge, but she called it justice.

To leave her past behind, she must do this one last thing. And then, she would begin her new life with her beloved.

An hour later, Linnet presented herself at Gloucester's rooms. She was covered head to toe in hood and cape and carrying a purse filled with gold coins. She was expected. After a brief glance at her face beneath the hood, the guard opened the heavy door for her.

She could not make herself go in at first.

For the hundredth time, she told herself Jamie need never know. Sweat broke out on her palms as she stepped into the room—not from any fear of Gloucester, but because she felt guilty for deceiving her future husband— the man she loved with all her heart.

"Jamie, I promise I shall never deceive you again," she whispered under her breath. "But I can have no peace until I avenge my grandfather and right the wrong done to us."

Chapter Twenty-six

Jamie was starving. 'Twas always that way after a fight. As soon as he cleaned himself up, he went to the hall hoping to find some supper. He could eat an entire wild boar himself.

Supper was finished, but when he hailed a servant, the good man brought him a tasty venison pie and a loaf of bread. Ignoring the people milling about the hall, he sat at a trestle table and made quick work of his meal. When he was done, he got up to look for Linnet.

Food was not the only thing a man hungered for after a fight. He was randy as hell.

The Virgin protect him. Eleanor Cobham was heading straight for him like a hound on the scent of a fox through an open field. Jamie glanced to the left and the right, though he knew full well it was too late to escape.

"Lady Eleanor," he said, making his bow. "You look striking tonight."

He spoke the truth—Eleanor looked as if she might strike anyone who stood in her path.

She narrowed cold gray eyes at him and demanded, "Do you know where your lady friend is?"

How much jewelry could a woman wear? Gloucester could have financed another foray against the Flemish with the gold and glittering stones hanging off his mistress.

"My 'lady friend'?" he asked in a mild tone, knowing damned well it would annoy her.

Eleanor leaned forward, hands on her hips, and he smelled the strong wine on her breath.

"Do not play the fool with me, James Rayburn. You know very well I mean that fair-haired French bastard who puts on airs as if royal blood ran through her veins."

In a flash, Jamie's own blood was pounding in his ears. "If you were a man, Eleanor, I would beat you senseless for that remark. As it is, I will ask you to curb your tongue."

"Men are such fools," she spat out. "Shall I tell you where the woman you are so gallantly defending is at this very moment?"

Unease settled in his gut. He cursed himself for letting this corrosive woman make him doubt Linnet. She had pledged her love, given him an eternal promise. She would not play him for a fool.

Not again.

"Lady Linnet is with the queen and her ladies in the queen's apartment," he said.

Eleanor clenched her fists and stamped her foot. "She is with Gloucester!"

"You are mistaken," he said, fighting the insidious doubt that was seeping into his heart. "But if she were in his company, I am certain it would be for some innocent purpose."

He just could not imagine what. Linnet had little

patience for people she disliked. She would avoid Gloucester like the plague, unless...unless he had something she wanted.

Jamie rubbed his temples with one hand as he found himself walking down a long corridor beside Eleanor. The woman seethed with malice. Why was he letting her lead him to Gloucester's rooms? It was wrong of him to doubt Linnet.

The question kept going through his mind: What could Gloucester give her?

Anything she wanted.

Jamie had a moment of panic as he followed Eleanor into an empty bedchamber. Had he completely misunderstood her? He tried to recall if his wine had tasted unusually sweet.

Eleanor, however, marched across the room without a backward glance. When she reached a door on the opposite side, she stopped and pressed her ear to it. Jamie's heart beat faster as he realized the door must connect to Gloucester's apartment. Eleanor waved impatiently for him to join her. When he did not, she lifted the latch, pushed the door with her fingertips, and stepped back.

Jamie watched in horror as the door slowly swung open to reveal the scene in the next room. Gloucester was half-dressed, his chest bare in the wide gap of his open robe.

And Linnet was on his lap. In his arms.

Time stopped as the sight before him stole his trust, killed his faith, and destroyed the future he had imagined. His heart froze and shattered into a hundred pieces at his feet.

Linnet looked up, startled, and pushed Gloucester away. But there was guilt in those pale-blue eyes.

"How could you, Linnet? How could you do this?"

He slammed the door and turned on Eleanor. Anger roiled in him, pounding through his veins and blurring his vision.

"You are an evil woman," he said, stepping toward her. "One day God will punish you for it."

"You should blame your lover, not me," she said when he had her backed against the wall.

"I know you poisoned other women you found with Gloucester," he said, wrapping his hand around her throat. "If I hear Linnet has had so much as a bad stomach after this, you shall regret it."

"No one can prove I poisoned anyone."

"Did I say I would attempt to prove it?" he said. "Do I seem the sort of man to waste my time in court?"

Eleanor's eyes went wide as he brought his face down close to hers.

"Pray Linnet stays well," he hissed through his teeth. "For if she falls ill, I will sneak into your bedchamber in the dark of night and slit your throat."

With this last duty discharged, he turned and left.

As he marched down the corridor, Linnet caught up to him. He did not look at her.

"Jamie, that was not what it seemed. I—"

"I hope you got whatever it was you wanted, Linnet. I hope it was worth the price you paid."

"I did not—"

"Another woman will value what I have to offer. She will not sacrifice my affections and sell her honor."

"I did nothing wrong."

Jamie came to an abrupt halt and turned to face her. "Nothing? Nothing!" he roared. He had to clench his hands to keep from grabbing her and shaking her. "I find you sitting on the lap of a half-naked man in his bedchamber, and you call that *nothing*?"

"It was nothing, I promise. You are the only man I love. The only one I want."

"And that is the worst part of it," he said, shaking with emotion. "To get something you wanted, you would go into the arms of a man you detest. By God, you are a cold-hearted woman."

"Jamie, I only meant to—"

"There is nothing you can say that will make a damned bit of difference to me," he said. "I am done with you."

She started to speak again, but he had already turned away.

Chapter Twenty-seven

"The queen will meet you again tonight." Linnet's eyes followed Jamie crossing the hall with Agnes Stafford as she spoke to Owen. Agnes's hand was tucked into Jamie's arm.

"How?" Owen asked.

"What?"

"How will Katherine get away and where shall I meet her?"

"Half an hour after supper, I will cross the upper ward wearing her ermine-trimmed cape and hood, with her ladies in tow." Linnet tried to concentrate, but it was hard with Jamie and that woman in the same room. "At the same time, the queen will slip out the side door in my cape to meet you at the place in the wood."

"Who knew love would prove so difficult?" Owen said with a sigh. "You do us a great favor by the risks you take on our behalf. I wish I could do the same for you."

"Jamie stays at Agnes's side like a dutiful dog," she said. "Is this farce meant to teach me a lesson?"

Owen shrugged. "Jamie says he intends to wed her."

"He could not be that foolish." Truly, he could not. "They would hate each other inside a month."

"Jamie says the lady's religious devotion is sure to make her a good and faithful wife."

"A good and faithful wife," she snapped. She folded her arms and glared at the two of them. "No mortal man would tempt Agnes, that is for certain."

It made her so angry to see him parading around the hall with the paradigm of virtue. He meant it as a slap in her face, and she felt the sting.

"What Jamie says is certain," Owen said, "is that he will always know where Agnes is."

Linnet tapped her foot furiously. "And that is enough for him?"

"So he says. I pray he comes to his senses before it is too late."

Linnet swallowed back the tears that threatened to break through her anger.

"Surely you are not going to let him make this disastrous mistake?" Owen said, nudging her with his elbow. "If you do not save the fool from his own poor judgment, you will both regret it."

"He is not ready to listen to me yet."

"Ready or nay, you have no more time. He intends to leave Windsor on the morrow."

Owen was right. If she was going to win him back, she could delay no longer.

"I believe Jamie would sacrifice anything for you," Owen said, turning serious, "if he could be sure of you."

"I fear it is too late. I've hurt his pride twice, and he'll not forgive me that."

"'Tis unlike you to give up so easily," Owen said. "You are usually like a terrier."

She squeezed Owen's arm. "Wish me well."

Jamie might pretend he was not aware of her presence, but she knew better. As soon as she started toward him across the vast hall, his eyes were on her. His expression was hard, but he looked at no one else.

A few men tried to halt her progress, but she brushed past with a smile and a nod, set on her mission. When she reached Jamie's group, she stepped into the circle beside him and proceeded to greet each person.

"Sir Frederick," she said, nodding to the handsome man on her other side who wore a forest-green tunic and matching liripipe hat. "That is an exquisite velvet."

The cloth was fine; it came from her own stores.

"Lord Stafford." She gave him a broad smile, thinking what a difficult father-in-law he would make. Jamie almost deserved him.

"Good day, Lady Agnes." The lack of interest in the young lady's dark gaze surprised—and relieved—Linnet. The lady may be tedious, but she was an innocent in this drama.

Linnet completed the circle and turned at last to Jamie. He was working the muscles of his jaw, and his face had angry red blotches.

"Sir James. How very pleasant to see you." She gave him a placid smile she had learned from the queen. "Are you well? You look a trifle...flushed."

"I have never been better," Jamie bit out.

"The musicians are a delight, are they not?" she said to the group. "I can tell you, there are none to match them in Paris."

This remark led to a lively conversation, as she knew it would. The English loved nothing better than to hear that they outmatched the French in some cultural accomplishment.

While the others were thus engaged, she said to Jamie in a low voice, "We must speak."

He fixed his gaze above the head of the man opposite him. "We have nothing to talk about."

"You can leave with me now, or we can talk here in front of everyone," she said. "You know how little I care for what people think."

She could almost hear him grind his teeth.

"I will come," he said, "because it would be unkind to allow you to embarrass Lady Agnes."

"If you ask me, she will be relieved to have you gone." She raised her voice then to speak to the others. "If you will forgive us, the queen bade me bring Sir James to her. She has something she wishes to ask him."

Jamie narrowed his eyes at her, as if wanting to confirm that she was lying. She gave him her placid smile again to let him know she was, and that he could do nothing about it. Would he call her or the queen a liar in public? Nay, he would not.

Linnet waved her fingers at the others and took Jamie's arm. Feeling the heat and tension of the muscles beneath her fingers made it difficult to maintain her calm facade. They did not speak again until they were outside in the cool of the upper courtyard.

"Shall we take a walk by the river, or would you prefer we talk in your bedchamber?" she asked.

"The river."

He pried her hand from his arm—a telling gesture for

a man in whom courtesy was ingrained—and stomped ahead of her toward the gate.

"You do not have to be rude," she snapped.

The sun was out, but the ground was still muddy from the last rain. She soon wished she wore boots rather than the delicate slippers that matched her gown. His long strides made it impossible for her to keep up.

"Damn it, Jamie! Slow down."

She was getting more and more vexed with him as she trudged behind him, despite her need to convince him that he still loved her and should marry her.

"Do you believe Agnes would not complain if you treated her like a serf, expecting her to follow behind the great warrior?"

He turned on his heel. "You dare to criticize me for a lack of *courtesy*? After what you have done?"

"I made a misjudgment, that is all," she said. "I admit I should not have gone to meet Gloucester in his apartments."

"Misjudgment! Misjudgment!" he shouted, raising his arms.

"Nothing happened with Gloucester," she said. "How can you think I would ever let him touch me?"

"Not let him touch you? God's blood, Linnet, you were sitting on his goddamned lap!"

"All right," she said, fighting for control. "I already admitted it was a mistake to go to his bedchamber, but I did nothing wrong. He grabbed me before I knew it. Men do that to women sometimes."

"Nay, it does not happen to other women," he bit out.

"Not to virtuous women, you mean?" she said, leaning

forward with her hands on her hips. "Women like Agnes Stafford?"

"Precisely."

"I suppose she is just the sort of woman you want." She clasped her hands under her chin and batted her eyelashes. "One who will sit at home meekly awaiting your bidding."

"I will for certain not have to worry about finding her in other men's bedchambers, doing God knows what!"

His words were like a blow. She stepped back, tears stinging at the back of her eyes. In a low voice, she said, "I would never bed another man."

"But you damned well would let him think you would," he hissed at her. "What man wants a wife who lets other men believe she will bed them? Or who will let them get that close?"

He was so angry she could hear his ragged breathing.

"You could not have believed I would accept your going alone to Gloucester's bedchamber," he said, his eyes burning holes into her. "Nay, you just thought I would never find out."

The truth of his words cut through her. Still, she tried to defend herself. "If you understood my need to find justice for my grandfather, I could have told you. But you never wanted to listen. You never wanted to hear it."

"The dead do not want or need your justice," he said. "Could you not sacrifice this dangerous obsession for me? For the life we could have together?"

"And what sacrifice would you make for me?" she asked in a choked voice. "Must all the sacrifice be mine?"

"You have sacrificed nothing!" The bite of bitterness was hard in his voice. "I will not have a wife who will lie to me and bring shame upon my family and upon my children."

The harshness of his judgment made her spirits drop so low that her limbs felt heavy and weak. Still, she forced herself to step closer and touch his arm.

"Jamie, is there no hope for us?"

He jerked his arm away as if her touch had singed him.

"How could I do my duty and return to France? I cannot be wondering who my wife will cozy up to as part of some foolish scheme of hers while I'm gone.

"And I will warn you," he said, narrowing his eyes and jabbing his finger at her. "You may find that when you lead men to water, there are some who will insist on taking a drink."

He spun away from her and began striding back toward the castle. Linnet had to hold her skirts high and half run to keep up with him.

"What else did you keep from me?" he spat out without turning to look at her. "How many ways did you make a fool of me this time?"

"'Twas just the one time, I swear it." She held on to her headdress with one hand as she trotted beside him. "And I did not make a fool of you. You know there is no one else."

"What I know is that once again there was something more important to you than the bond between us."

"'Tis not true."

"More important than the life we could have had together."

"Nay, I—"

"More important than keeping your word to me."

"But I also made a pledge to my gran—"

"More important than me."

"Nay, not more im—"

"And there always will be something more important than me."

"But I love you," she pleaded. "I love you with all my heart."

He halted and turned on her, his eyes blazing. "I've seen how it is between my mother and father, and between Stephen and Isobel, and I can tell you this: True love does not come last. 'Tis not what you consider after every other blessed thing."

He lifted his hands palm out and began stepping backward. "I am done waiting for you to put aside the hate that will surely destroy you. I am done with all of it. I am done with you."

Choking back tears and clenching her fists, she said, "Then you deserve a dull wife like Agnes who will bore you to death."

"Lady Agnes is exactly the sort of wife I want," he shouted back at her. "A woman who is predictable and faithful. A woman who will be a steady influence on our children."

"For all her virtues," she said, her anger rising, "I'll wager she'll not go cheerfully to your bed."

From the way his face went scarlet with rage, she had hit a sore spot. Fine, she meant to.

"I am certain Lady Agnes will be a good wife in *every* way," he said. "And I will not open doors to find her in the arms of another man."

She wanted to beat her fists against him, to shout at him, to hurt him as he was hurting her.

"Will it make you proud to have a wife who is only faithful because she finds bedding men distasteful?"

Anger made her reckless. She squeezed her eyes shut, scrunched up her face, and said in a high, false voice, "Not again, m'lord husband! Did we not do it just last month? I beg you, be quick about it!"

When she opened her eyes, his fists were clenched and the vein in his neck was pulsing.

"That is enough," he said in a low growl. "Stay out of my sight."

He turned and started again for the castle with a determined stride. But almost at once, he halted and uttered a long string of curses beneath his breath.

Linnet dragged her gaze from Jamie to look up the path. When she saw the couple standing but a few yards away, her mouth fell open. Of all the times for Jamie's parents to appear, it had to be just as she was screaming the most vile things to him. Jamie's mother's eyebrows were so high they almost touched her headdress. Lord Fitz-Alan's expression was stern.

"Mother, Father," Jamie said as he went to meet them.

Linnet closed her eyes and prayed God would remove her to somewhere else. How long had the two been listening? Recalling her imitation of Agnes in bed, she felt hot and nauseous.

Her embarrassment, though, was nothing compared to the desolation and despair that took hold of her.

Somehow, everything had gone wrong. She had been intent on making Jamie understand her for once. And she had been certain that when he saw how much she loved him, he would forgive her. Because he had to. Because she needed him. Because she could not lose him again.

She knew with utter certainty that something irrevocable had just happened between her and Jamie. A sob caught in her throat at the thought that Jamie never wanted to lay eyes on her again.

I have ruined it all. Neither of us shall ever be happy again.

Chapter Twenty-eight

Jamie and his brother Nicholas exchanged amused glances across the table.

Their sisters were mercilessly teasing Martin, something they never seemed to tire of. Martin, an only child, had been so stiffly polite at first that he had sent the girls into gales of laughter. By now, he was accustomed to their lively banter. Worse for him, if he wanted any peace, the girls had adopted him as a favorite.

Three-year-old Bridget, the youngest, ran into the hall with her nursemaid chasing behind her.

"I am sorry, m'lady," the maid said.

"'Tis not your fault," Lady Catherine said, waving her off. "Bridget, sit down. Quietly."

"It's my turn to sit by Martin!" Bridget said, pulling at Elisabeth's arm.

"You are late, so you lost your place," Elisabeth said, grasping the edge of the table.

Martin looked a little wild-eyed at being the subject of such violent devotion. Jamie and his brother Nick, shared another amused glance across the table. It was lucky for Martin that the two eldest girls were wed and gone.

The other girls took sides and joined the argument between Elisabeth and Bridget, then Bridget gave a loud shriek.

His father banged his fist on the table. "Enough!"

Silence fell on the FitzAlan hall.

"Am I raising wild heathens or young ladies?"

All five girls lowered their eyes, for every one of them hated to disappoint their father.

Without a word, Martin lifted Bridget onto his lap to end that particular dispute. A wise lad.

"Did God give us so many daughters to punish us?" his father said to his mother.

His mother gave her husband a sideways glance and smiled, for everyone knew Lord FitzAlan doted upon his daughters.

Ah, it was good to be home. There was no better place to heal than amid this laughter and chaos.

But even after a month with his family, Jamie still felt raw. He ignored the chatter that floated around him as his thoughts drifted back to Windsor, as they so often did. What a fool he had been to believe he could change Linnet—or make her love him.

He had left Windsor the day of his fight with Linnet, ahead of his family. He could not bear to be under the same roof with her another hour.

Soon, he would travel to visit Stafford in Northumberland and offer for his daughter. He told himself it did not matter that he was having trouble recalling Agnes's face.

And yet, he could not forget one inch of Linnet. He could see her naked now, the candlelight glinting on long strands of silky white-gold hair and revealing each tantalizing dip and devastating rise of her long, lean body.

And her face. Men would go to war for a woman with a face like that. Soft-blue eyes, straight nose, full bottom lip, high cheekbones. Each part was perfect, and the combination was enough to take a man's breath away. Such delicate features for a woman as strong as the best-made sword.

"Jamie."

He looked up when he heard his mother call his name and was surprised to find he and his parents were alone at the table.

"Come up to the solar," his father said. "We have something to discuss in private."

With all that had happened, he had forgotten about the messages his parents had sent to Windsor urging him to come home. Chances were good they wished to discuss the very topic he wished to raise with them: his plans for marriage.

They had been patient and not pressed him after he had come home devastated from Paris. But it was time now. He needed to know what he would bring to his upcoming marriage. Most of the family lands were entailed and the girls all needed dowries. Still, Jamie expected his father had some small estate he could grant him.

As soon as they were settled in the family's comfortable solar, Jamie made his announcement. "You will be happy to hear I have decided to become betrothed at last."

His mother raised her eyebrows and gave him a long, penetrating look. "I would be happy for you, if you seemed pleased yourself."

"I am pleased," he said in a firm voice. "Very pleased, indeed."

"Who is the lady you have in mind?" his father asked.

"Lady Agnes Stafford."

His parents exchanged a look.

"You know her?" Jamie asked.

"After you left Windsor, we had the 'pleasure' of speaking with Lady Agnes and her father. That Stafford is an insufferable idiot."

His mother cleared her throat.

"Lady Agnes is a...a lovely young woman, though perhaps a trifle...fervent," she said, speaking slowly as if choosing her words carefully. "But we had reason to believe your affections lay elsewhere."

Jamie clenched his teeth and waited to speak until the blood ceased to pound in his ears. "You were misinformed."

"From what I saw, son, 'tis Linnet you want," his father said.

"Linnet is not the sort of lady I wish to make my wife," Jamie said, keeping his voice steady with an effort.

"Perhaps you should give yourself time before rushing into a marriage with someone else," his mother said, "so soon after your...disappointment."

"I am not disappointed. I am relieved to have escaped marriage to a woman who lacks every virtue a man would wish in a wife." His voice had grown louder than he intended, so he paused to take a deep breath before continuing. "I intend to leave soon for Northumberland to make the arrangements with Lord Stafford. I have reason to believe he supports the match, as I hope you will."

"No need for haste," his father said. "You've been gone a long time. Nicholas and the girls are just getting to know you again."

"We all missed you," his mother said, giving him

a warm smile. "Surely this can wait a few weeks, or months."

"Waiting will change nothing, Mother. I am set on this."

A long, tense silence followed this declaration.

"Before you embark on marriage, there is something we must tell you," his father said. "It is what we called you up here to discuss."

His mother turned away from him to look into the fire. When he saw how pale she was, the icy hand of fear gripped his heart. God forbid that she was with child again at her age.

He rushed to her side and knelt beside her. "Mother," he said, taking her hand, "are you unwell?"

Her hand felt clammy to his touch. As he rubbed her fingers against his cheek, he regretted every day he had been away. He and his mother had a special bond. In the unhappy days before William FitzAlan came into their lives, they had been through harrowing experiences that had not touched her other children's lives. He had been so young he could not be sure how much of his recollections were real. But he still had dreams in which he heard her screaming.

She brushed his hair back from his forehead, a gesture from his childhood. "Truly, I am well."

He closed his eyes against the surge of relief that coursed through his body and gave a silent prayer of thanks.

"This cannot be about Father's health," he said, glancing at his father. "He still looks as if he could slay dragons for breakfast."

When this old family joke about his father did not bring

a smile, Jamie looked from one to the other of his parents. "What is it, then?"

Like many old soldiers, his father still wore his hair cropped short, in the style made popular by their dead king. When he ran his big hand through it, Jamie noticed it had almost as much white as bronze in it now.

"It is my story, William," his mother said. "I will tell him."

His father was always more a man of action than of words. After giving her a searching look, he nodded. "If you are certain, love."

She cleared her throat. "You have always known that William is not your true father."

Jamie drew in a breath and let it out. After all this time, his mother was finally going to tell him. He got up off the floor and settled himself into the chair opposite her.

William FitzAlan took his place behind his wife and put his hand on her shoulder.

"I never wanted a different father from the one who raised me," Jamie said, meeting his eyes. "I know I could not have had a better one."

"Stephen told you some years ago that Rayburn, who was my husband at the time, also was not your father."

His mother's speech was uncharacteristically hesitant. He should tell her it did not matter, he did not need to know, but he had waited too many years to hear the truth of his birth.

"I thought...I had reason to believe...that the man with whom I conceived you..."

Hell, this was awkward. He did not want to think about his mother "conceiving" with a man, as she put it, particularly with a man who was not William FitzAlan. He ran his hand through his hair, conscious that this gesture—like so many of his—mirrored those of the man who raised him.

"You thought what, Mother?"

"I never told you about him, because I believed he died shortly after you were born."

Why did it matter just when the man died?

"I received a message from a monk, who advised me that ... your father had come to his monastery gravely ill."

His mother leaned back in her chair, looking exhausted.

"The monk wrote that the young man hung on the edge of death for days and did not recover," she said. "But we learned a few months ago that he did survive. The monks thought it a miracle."

Jamie sat up straight.

"He never left the monastery," she said. "After he recovered his health, he took vows and joined the brothers."

"Are you telling me he has been alive all this time?" Jamie demanded. "And that he is a *monk*?"

"He was alive when we first sent for you," his father said. "But he took a sudden fever sometime before Christmas and died."

Jamie got up and began pacing the too-small room. It should not matter to him if the man was alive or dead—this monk had been nothing to him.

"How did you learn of this?"

"You remember Isobel's brother, Geoffrey?" his father asked.

"Aye, we were friends in France," Jamie said. "He left to join a monastery in Northumberland."

"When we last visited Stephen and Isobel, we went to

see Geoffrey at his abbey," his father said. "There was a monk working in the kitchen garden as we passed. We paid no notice of him, but he saw your mother."

"Afterward, he asked Geoffrey about us," his mother said, picking up the story. "He was quite upset, and he ended up confessing who he was to Geoffrey."

"It was not the sort of news to tell you in a letter," his father said.

Jamie did not know what to think. "Why would he disclose himself after all these years, when he never bothered to make himself known to us before?"

"Geoffrey says he kept his secret out of respect for your mother," his father said. "He did not wish to cause her difficulty."

"I suppose a child born of a man not your husband could present 'difficulty,'" Jamie said, turning to his mother. "You haven't told me all of this yet, Mother."

"Mind your tongue when you speak to your mother," his father said, stepping toward him.

His mother stood and put herself between them, a palm up on each of their chests.

"Sit down," she said in a voice that brooked no argument.

"I apologize," Jamie said, regretting his harsh words. He knew too much of what her life had been like with her first husband to judge her.

His father pulled a stool up next to her chair, and the three of them sat.

"I did what I had to do to save myself." His mother spoke in a clear, forceful voice. "And I have never once regretted it."

She drew in a deep breath and let it out. "I should have

told you once you were old enough to understand, but the time never seemed right. I did not realize how the question of your father's identity hung over you."

He had not lost sleep over it. FitzAlan had married his mother when Jamie was three, and their bond was as close as any father and son. All the same, Jamie had wondered about the nature of the man who sired him—and how he could have left his mother.

"What was this monk's name?" Jamie asked, because he wanted to know the name he should have been called.

"Wheaton," his mother said. "Richard James Wheaton."

James. So his mother had given him what she could of the man's name. She must have had some regard for him.

"He told me he had considered joining a monastery in his youth, and so I am not surprised he became a monk," his mother said, using that careful voice again. "But from what Geoffrey told us, Richard Wheaton's life was unusually . . . contained, even for a monk. He took great comfort in the routine of monastery life."

"Are you saying something was wrong with him?" Jamie asked.

His father shrugged. "Wheaton's brother—your uncle, I suppose—can tell you a good deal more than we can. He's written several times expressing a desire to meet you."

"His name is Sir Charles Wheaton," his mother put in. "He is most anxious for you to visit. His estate is in Northumberland, within a day's ride of Stephen and Isobel's."

The three of them sat in silence for a long time, lost in their own thoughts.

Finally, his father said, "You have unfinished business. 'Tis best to settle it before you take on a wife."

"I do not see what is unfinished about it," Jamie said, "but I suppose I can pay a visit to Charles Wheaton when I travel north to see the Staffords."

"See Charles Wheaton first, before you make an offer of marriage." His mother leaned forward to touch his arm. "The visit may help you decide what to do."

She could not say more plainly that she believed he was making a mistake in choosing Agnes for his wife.

"Mother, my decision is already made."

Jamie leaned his elbows on his knees and rubbed his temples. Too many thoughts jumbled in his head at once. The man who fathered him had been a monk. He had a new uncle. And his mother, whose opinion mattered more than he liked to admit, disapproved of his marriage choice.

Before he could get his bearings, his father gave him news of a different sort.

"We received a message from Bedford today." His father pulled a rolled parchment with a broken seal out of his tunic and handed it to him. "The Council fears there will be riots if Parliament is held in London, so they have decided to hold the next session in Leicester."

Since leaving Windsor, Jamie had hardly given a thought to the political strife that still threatened the country.

"So, Bedford has not yet succeeded in forcing his brother and uncle to settle their dispute?" he asked.

His father shook his head and pounded his fist on his knee. "That damned Gloucester."

"If King Henry were alive," his mother put in, "Gloucester would never dare cause such strife."

"Will the Council still have the young king open Parliament?" Jamie asked.

"Aye," his father said. "'Tis all the more important that the king be seen."

Jamie tried to hold back the question, but he had to know if Linnet was headed into danger. "And the queen?"

"She is already on her way north."

Chapter Twenty-nine

The city of Leicester was in chaos. Linnet pulled back the flap of the carriage to look out as they lurched through the crowded street that ran beside the church to the castle's main gate. Drunken men with clubs and bats filled the streets.

"I am greatly relieved that His Grace the Duke of Bedford sent his own guard to escort us," the queen said, her voice high with tension.

Linnet, too, was glad to be traveling today with an escort of twenty men-at-arms and royal banners flying.

"When the duke warned us there could be trouble here," Linnet said, "I had no notion it would be as bad as this."

"Nor I," the queen said, clasping Linnet's hand. "I wish Owen could have ridden inside the carriage with us."

Linnet chose not to respond. Nothing could have been more inappropriate than to have the queen's lowly clerk of the wardrobe travel in her carriage all the way to Leicester Castle.

Linnet and the queen were thrown against each other as the carriage rumbled and swayed over the uneven slats of the castle's drawbridge. Without pausing, the carriage continued through the barbican and gatehouse. After crossing the expansive bailey yard at a fast clip, the carriage finally pulled up before what looked to be the castle hall.

Linnet pressed her face to the gap in the carriage cover.

"Jamie is here!" she cried out.

There he was, on the steps right before her. After longing for him every hour for the past month, she could not quite believe he was here.

He and an older knight, both in chain mail, were running down the steps two at a time, shouting to their escort and waving the carriage on. Mercy, he looked wonderful in his knightly garb, hair flying behind him, as he sprinted to the carriage.

The carriage tipped alarmingly as Jamie and the other knight leapt onto the outside of it. The carriage lurched forward, throwing Linnet against the back of the seat. Before she could grab hold of anything, she fell against the queen as the carriage careened around first one corner, and then another. Finally, it jerked to a halt.

Linnet untangled herself from the queen and attempted to straighten her headdress. Through the gap in the cover, she saw they were stopped beside a low building attached to the back of the castle hall.

The carriage door burst open, and a huge, formidable man with a hard, handsome face and fading tawny hair blocked Linnet's view of anything behind him. It was Jamie's father.

"Lord FitzAlan," Linnet said. "What has happened, sir?"

He gave her a quick nod as he offered his hand to the queen. "We must make haste, Your Highness."

FitzAlan lifted the queen down from the carriage as if she weighed no more than a rag doll. Then Jamie took his father's place at the carriage door. He looked every inch the gallant knight come to save her, from the determined line of his jaw to the glint of the sword in his hand.

The tension of Jamie's stance, alert to every danger, showed he expected trouble. She was so frightened now she wanted to throw herself at him.

"Out. Now." He spoke in a sharp voice as he looked to the left and right of the carriage.

She grasped the hand he held out to her and found herself almost flying through the air. Then his arm was about her waist, holding her tight against his side. Her feet barely touched the ground as they followed the queen and FitzAlan through a low doorway. Judging from the low arched ceiling of the passageway, they were in an undercroft.

"We are in the kitchens?" she heard the queen say.

"'Tis the safest route, Your Highness," FitzAlan said.

Smells of roasting meats and warm bread wafted out to them as Jamie hurried her past the noisy entrance to the kitchen.

"What is the danger here?" she asked him.

"Hurry now." Jamie kept one hand on her and held his sword in the other as he moved her along. All the while, his eyes searched side to side and behind them. Linnet caught glimpses of barrels and pots and sacks of grain as they continued along the passageway past various storerooms.

"But what is happening?" Linnet said. "Tell me."

"Not now."

They came to a narrow servants' staircase. FitzAlan led the way and helped the queen after him.

"You first," Jamie said, a firm hand at her back.

She lifted her skirts and ducked her head. The dark, enclosed stairwell seemed to have been made for smaller people. When she looked over her shoulder, she saw Jamie taking the first steps backward, his sword at the ready.

Dear God, what was this? Linnet gave her arm a sharp shake, so that the handle of her thin dagger fell into her palm.

After climbing three flights without pausing, she was perspiring. Whether it was from exertion or fear, she could not say. The sounds of the men's boots and her own labored breathing echoed in her ears in the enclosed space. When FitzAlan opened a door above her, the sudden noise of a great many voices startled her.

As FitzAlan held the door and waved them forward, Linnet stepped over the stone threshold and ducked through the low doorway on the queen's heels.

She found herself in a half-open corridor or gallery. Shouting filled the air, echoing off the walls and ceiling. Linnet went at once to peer over the railing. Below her was a vast hall filled with people. They were yelling and raising sticks in the air.

Jamie grabbed her by the arm and snatched her back from the railing. "Along here," he ordered, pointing ahead. "Stay close to the wall."

FitzAlan was at the other end of the gallery, holding another door open for them. The queen gave Linnet a terrified look over her shoulder before ducking through the doorway.

When Linnet followed her, she felt as if she had stepped into another world. She was in an oak-paneled room with tall, cheval-glass windows on one wall and exquisite tapestries on the others. Through the doorway opposite, she could see several connecting rooms.

"Where are we?" She tilted her head back to take in the elaborate ceiling with its even rows of carved paterae.

Queen Katherine looked about her and heaved a sigh. "We are in the queen's apartments."

"You'll be safe here," FitzAlan said. "We have guards posted at all the doors."

"I will advise His Grace the Duke of Bedford that you have arrived," Jamie said to the queen. "He will want to explain the situation to you himself."

"You are not leaving us, are you?" the queen said before Linnet could get the words out. "After frightening us half to death, you cannot abandon us."

"My father will stay with you while I—"

"My son will stay with you," FitzAlan interrupted. "Jamie, I have other matters to attend to now that we have them away from that crowd."

"Why were all those men carrying sticks and bats?" Linnet asked.

"Jamie can explain." Tilting his head toward the door they had come through, he said to Jamie, "I'll send a few more men up to guard the servants' entrance."

With that, FitzAlan dipped his head in the general direction of the queen and Linnet and departed.

"Your father is a man of few words," the queen remarked.

"That was a long speech for him," Jamie said, shrugging his shoulders in a gesture that was so familiar it sliced through Linnet's heart.

She longed to step into his arms and rest her head on his chest. In the month since he had broken their marriage plans and left Windsor, she had been miserable. She could not even summon an interest in pursuing her enemies. While she still read the reports Master Woodley sent her, she had not returned to London. Instead, she had remained in the quiet of Windsor, where she and the queen could comfort each other for their losses.

She wanted to ask Jamie a thousand questions. Was he still angry? Did he suffer as she did? *Was he betrothed to Agnes?*

Instead, she asked, "What is happening here?"

The queen, however, did not wish to discuss the turmoil taking place outside the doors of this quiet apartment.

"King Henry loved to come here," she said before Jamie could answer. A soft smile touched the queen's lips as her gaze moved around the room.

Linnet sensed her friend's sadness and bit back her impatience to question Jamie. "You were here with the king?"

The queen nodded. "This castle brought back fond memories of his grandfather, John of Gaunt."

"They say he was closer to his grandfather than his father," Linnet said.

The queen took her hand and squeezed it. "'Tis true. Of course, his father was often off fighting when Henry was young."

Henry Bolingbroke, forever known as the Usurper, had favored his second son, Thomas. When he was in England, it was Thomas he took to court with him. He left his

heir to spend time either with his grandfather or at Oxford
under the tutelage of his half uncle, Henry Beaufort. Linnet was not alone in believing Henry was a better king
for it.

"This was one of John of Gaunt's favorite castles," the
queen said.

John of Gaunt not only ruled on behalf of his nephew,
Richard II, during Richard's minority, but he was also
the richest man in England in his time. A look around the
opulent room made it easy to believe.

Both women turned at the sound of boots and male
voices. A moment later, the door swung open and the
Duke of Bedford entered.

"'Tis good to see you, dear sister," Bedford said, leaning over the queen's hand. He gave Linnet a polite nod,
then continued, "I've sent a messenger to intercept the
king's carriage. There is no point in his coming to open
Parliament until things are quiet here."

"I will not see my son?"

Bedford's eyes crinkled at the corners in a kindly
smile. "I hope he can be brought here soon."

Linnet watched as the queen worried the kerchief in
her hands. Would she not complain? Would she not shout
and demand to be with her son? Surely, the queen could
bring some pressure to bear? Make threats, promises,
whatever it took.

Linnet found it hard to understand her friend's passive
acceptance of her loss of control over her child. But then,
Linnet had not been raised in a royal household, where
such things were understood from childhood.

"Where are my trunks?" the queen asked.

Her trunks? She is separated from her only son once

again, and she asks after her trunks? And the queen put the question to Bedford, as if he were one of her servants and not the effective ruler of England and France.

The duke, however, showed no offense. "Your clerk of the wardrobe is overseeing their removal from the wagon."

Linnet now understood why the queen had asked: Owen was likely to be wherever her trunks were. Rather than fight her situation, she sought Owen to comfort her in her distress.

"Sir James," the duke said, interrupting her thoughts, "your presence will reassure the ladies. Stay and keep them company."

Damn his father and damn the duke for leaving him to cope with the women. Now that he'd seen Linnet—and the queen, of course—to safety, he wished to be gone.

Linnet turned to him and his breath caught in his throat.

"Tell us now," she said. "What is happening here?"

Once again, the queen diverted the conversation. "I shall rest until Owen comes. The events of the day have been rather trying."

"I will help you get settled," Linnet said.

The queen held up her hand and gave Linnet a wan smile. "Stay with Sir James. I know you are anxious to hear the news."

Jamie watched the queen pass through two adjoining rooms before entering the third and closing the door behind her.

He was alone with Linnet, which was the last thing he

wanted—or rather, the last thing he needed. Was every-one conspiring against him?

"Well?" Linnet folded her arms and tapped her foot, in that way she had. "Are you going to tell me?"

It took him a moment to recall where he was and what she was asking about. "Gloucester and the bishop are still at each other's throats. The King's Council feared Glouc-ester's supporters in Parliament would incite violence, so they banned the members from carrying weapons."

"I take it they did not foresee the need to include wooden bats in the ban?"

"They did not," he said, amused by her remark, despite himself. "With the merchants and Gloucester's other supporters up in arms—or bats—nothing can get done. Bedford is threatening to cart his fractious family off to Nottingham and force them to come to terms."

At the sound of a door scraping behind him, Jamie turned to see Stephen Carleton duck in through the ser-vants' entrance.

"Stephen!" Jamie called out as he went to greet him. Stephen, who was just ten years older than he was, was more like a brother to him than an uncle.

"You think I came to see you?" Stephen said. "Nay. I heard the exquisite and delightful Lady Linnet was here."

Stephen opened his arms to Linnet. When she ran into them, Stephen swung her in a circle.

"You devil, Linnet, why have you not come to see us?" Stephen said. "Isobel told me to give you a most severe scolding."

"Where is Isobel?" Jamie asked, interrupting what seemed to him an excessively warm greeting. "Did she not come with you?"

"She cannot travel now," Linnet said in a tone that suggested he was an idiot.

"She is with child again," Stephen said with a broad grin.

With a warm smile that shone in her eyes, Linnet said, "How happy she must be. I am sure Isobel is the best of mothers."

Jamie reminded himself that Linnet did not want to be a mother; she wanted to murder men who had wronged her family.

"I just arrived, but there is no point in staying if Parliament can get no business done," Stephen said. "I intend to turn around and go home. The two of you should come visit us until this is settled."

Linnet's cheeks turned pink and she dropped her gaze to the floor. Jamie did not believe for a moment that Stephen had not heard he and Linnet had parted ways. When Jamie glared at him, Stephen merely smiled and looked at him expectantly.

Jamie cleared his throat. "I will come for a few days, as I have matters to attend to nearby."

"What matters?" Stephen asked, knowing damned well Jamie did not wish to discuss this in front of Linnet.

"I believe you know of my errands."

"I heard your mother told you about the monk who was your father, and that you intend to visit the monastery where he lived."

Linnet gasped aloud. Jamie ignored her; he did not want to hear—or answer—her questions.

"Apparently you are not my only uncle," Jamie said. "The monk's brother wishes to see me."

"Sir Charles Wheaton," Stephen said. "I know him. He is a good man."

Jamie sighed. In addition to Stephen's uncanny ability to hear news before anyone else, he seemed to know everyone.

"You have other business as well?" Stephen asked.

Jamie told himself there was no reason not to say it; it was no secret. Still, he was careful not to look at Linnet as he spoke. "I intend to visit Lord Stafford to arrange my betrothal to his daughter."

Stephen's brows shot up. For once, Jamie had surprised him. Stephen took a step closer to Linnet, as if taking sides.

So much for blood ties.

Chapter Thirty

"Hold your shield higher," Jamie instructed.

He was practicing with Martin in the enclosed court-yard behind the palace.

Martin lifted his shield, and Jamie gave it a good crack with the flat of his sword that sent Martin back three paces.

"That is the way," Jamie called out when the lad came back swinging.

Martin had a natural skill with the sword and was improving daily. But instead of following through as he should, Martin checked his swing and dropped the point of his sword.

"What is the matter?" Jamie said. "I did not call a halt."

Martin widened his eyes and began making an odd motion to the side with his head.

"By Saint Wilgefort's beard, Martin, just say it!"

"She is here," Martin said in a whisper loud enough to carry a mile.

There was only one woman who could make his squire act like the village idiot.

That made two of them.

Jamie steeled himself to see Linnet before turning around, but his effort was for naught. The sight of her made him wretched with longing. Aglow in a cream and gold gown, she looked like an angel sent from heaven to brighten the world for lowly man.

He reminded himself she was no angel. This was Linnet.

From the corner of his eye, he saw Martin make his escape. No lesson needed; the lad knew when to beat a hasty retreat.

Was Linnet here to attempt to change his mind? He told himself she could not do it...but he knew he lied. One brush of those long, slender fingers, and he would weaken. He missed her like the devil. Her absence was an ache that never left him. Perhaps he was wrong to hold out against her. Would he suffer more with her than he did without her?

"If you'll sheathe your sword," Linnet said without a hint of humor, "I would speak with you."

Clearly, she was not here to pledge her undying devotion and beg him to take her back. He heaved a sigh as he slid his blade into the scabbard at his belt. Then he folded his arms to indicate he was ready to listen.

"Something unexpected has happened," she said, her voice pitched high with tension.

What was this? Linnet was clutching her skirt, and her knuckles were white.

"Unexpected?" he asked.

"I cannot speak of it here," she said, glancing up at the dark windows overlooking the empty courtyard. "We must be somewhere private."

He narrowed his eyes, taking in the rigidity of her stance, the lines of tension in her face. Something had upset her enough to swallow her pride and come to him.

It seemed unlikely anyone could overhear them in the courtyard—but apparently it was not private enough for what she had to tell him. His curiosity grew.

"There is an old armory off the courtyard that is no longer in use," he said, gesturing to a weathered wooden door. "No one will hear through the stone walls."

The door creaked as he opened it for her. In the gloomy light that filtered in from the small windows near the roof, he saw broken shields and other weapons beyond repair piled against one wall. Two long benches were covered in a thick layer of dust.

"I have no cloak for you to sit on." Puffs of dust filled the air as he swiped at one of the benches with his sleeve.

"I don't wish to sit, thank you."

What made her so nervous? It was so unlike her. He watched her closely as he waited for her to tell him. As her gaze flitted around the room, a thought began to grow in him.

When she still did not speak, he prompted her. "You had something unexpected to tell me?"

"Aye, quite unexpected. At least to me." Her gaze came back to rest on him for a moment and then flitted away again. "I thought you would want to know. That you would want to help me. You see . . ." She paused to lick her lips. "You see . . ."

It hit him like a thunderbolt. Jesus and all the saints protect him. Linnet was with child. *His* child. A swell of joy and wonder rose up in his chest, almost lifting him from the ground.

"This changes everything," he said, because it did. "You see that, don't you?"

He never thought he would be a man who would keep his wife under lock and key, but he would do what he must to keep her safe until the child was born. Surely she would settle down once she had a babe in her arms?

"Aye, it changes all," Linnet said, wringing her hands. "The difficulties are boundless."

She took a step toward him. Her soft blue eyes were full of worry.

"A child should not be cause for despair, but of hope," he said.

Her fine-boned shoulders relaxed a bit, and she graced him with a tentative smile that lanced open all his wounds.

"That is what the queen says," she said. "But how did you guess the reason I came to you?"

"You told the queen about the child before telling me?" This hurt more than he could admit to himself.

She furrowed her brows and examined him. A moment later, her eyes flew open wide.

And they both knew the mistake he had made. It was not Linnet who was with child, but the queen.

Jamie rubbed his temples, trying to roll back all the thoughts and plans that had suddenly formed in his head.

"Could you be with child?" he asked, because he needed to know.

She bit her lip and shook her head. His chest tightened as he thought of the children he would never have with her. He looked away; he could almost hear that door close forever.

"Your future wife would not have been pleased with such a surprise," she said in a tight voice.

His wife? God help him, he had forgotten all about Agnes. He never could think of another woman when Linnet was near.

"A man takes care of his children," he said, his anger with himself making his voice hard. "Lady Agnes would accept that. As an obedient wife, she would respect my judgment."

"Hmm." The sound she made conveyed disagreement, which he chose to ignore.

"You were right to come to me," he said, trying desperately to focus on the problem she had brought to him. "'Tis no simple matter to find a place where Queen Katherine can have the child without anyone discovering her secret."

"Hertford is among the properties the Council granted the queen for her own use," Linnet said. "She says it is out of the way and too small to accommodate many visitors. She could be left alone there."

He nodded. "That might do. An even more difficult task will be finding someone trustworthy to raise the child."

"The queen will not give up this child," Linnet said. "She and Owen intend to marry."

"God's beard!" Jamie ran his hands through his hair. "That Owen has bollocks, I'll say that for him. I pray we don't see him drawn and quartered before the babe is christened."

"'Tis the queen who surprises me," Linnet said in a soft voice. "She believes that if she has children with someone as lowly as Owen, she will be allowed to keep them."

"'Tis an awful risk for her to marry without the

Council's permission," he said. "But now that there is to be a child, one can hardly blame them."

"Her confessor has agreed to marry them in secret at Hertford. She wants you to be a witness to their marriage." Linnet dropped her gaze to the dirt floor. "It is dangerous, but one day they may need someone to attest to it whose word will be trusted."

Dangerous, indeed. He could be accused of treason.

"I have business in Northumberland that cannot be delayed," he said. "But I will come directly to Hertford as soon as it is concluded. It should take me no more than a week."

She startled him by touching his arm. It was just a light touch, but it sent a rush of hot lust through him.

"Pray, do not wed Agnes Stafford," she said, her eyes bright with unshed tears. "There is no lack of women who could love you. Yet, you seem bent on marrying the one who cannot."

It was so hard not to believe she cared enough to change for him when she was looking at him with so much warmth and longing in her eyes. She was so close he could smell her skin and hair. His fingers itched to touch her.

Linnet had taken hold of him as a young man—heart, body, and soul. So long as they both lived, he would want her. He understood that now. But once he gave his vow to another, he would not succumb to the temptation. By the Virgin, he needed to get himself wed as soon as possible. He would send Martin home to visit his mother and leave with Stephen on the morrow.

"Is it not enough to punish me?" she asked, her touch scorching through him again. "One of us should be happy."

He took one last look at the face that could make him forget every other thing that mattered to him in this world.

"Tell the queen I shall join her at Hertford." He lifted his gaze to the trees on the far side of the river. "I shall be betrothed when next we meet."

Chapter Thirty-one

"*P*raise God you are here." Linnet threw her arms around Francois's neck as soon as he walked through the door of her London house. "I could not live through this without you."

Francois patted her back and asked, "What has happened?"

"Jamie is getting married," she said into his neck. "To someone else."

Francois blew out a deep breath. "I feared as much."

He unhooked her arms from around his neck. "'Tis your own fault. Twice now you have tossed out the best man you will ever have."

"I did not toss him out." Indignation helped her fight the sting of tears at the back of her eyes. "Jamie left me. Both times."

"Christ above, Linnet," Francois said, raising his hands into the air. "You had to know Jamie would not stand for what you did with Gloucester."

"I was trying to get information, nothing more."

"Just because you can dangle men from your fingers, does not mean you should do it," Francois said. "And did it have to be Gloucester, second in line to the throne? What was Jamie to think?"

She crossed her arms and tapped her foot. "He should have trusted me. I can manage Gloucester."

"You can manage Gloucester? Then how is it that Jamie found the two of you grappling in the duke's damned bed-chamber?"

She should not have told her brother that part.

"You are supposed to be on my side." She turned away, angry that her lower lip was trembling.

Francois heaved a sigh and put his arm around her. "Sorry, sweetling."

She swallowed. "I cannot let him marry Agnes, truly I cannot. The woman has no spark at all." 'Twas simply wrong for Jamie to be with a woman who would not appreciate his passion. If only . . .

"Come, I have news of my own to share with you," Francois said. "You'd best sit down for this."

The grave expression on Francois's usually cheerful countenance sent a tremor of foreboding through her. Once they were sitting side by side on the bench under the window, he pulled a thick stack of folded parchments from inside his tunic. The edges were curled with age.

"I've arranged them with the oldest on top," he said as he flattened them on his knee.

She touched his arm. "But what are they?"

"Letters." Francois cleared his throat. "Letters from our father to our grandfather."

The breath went out of her. She looked into her twin's face, unable to form the question.

Francois pressed his lips together and nodded. "Aye, he did not forget us as we thought."

All these years, she had believed they did not merit the slightest consideration from their father. But here was proof to the contrary—proof that he had at least remembered them from time to time. Tears streamed down her face. From the time she was little, she had told herself she did not care that he had forgotten them. But it had always been a scar upon her heart.

"What does he say in the letters?" she asked.

Francois set the stack in her lap. "The ink has faded, but you can read most of them."

She untied the twine that held them together and picked up the first one. As soon as she unfolded it, she recognized Alain's seal and signature at the bottom. The parchment was torn along the fold, and her eyes blurred when she tried to make out the words.

"Tell me, Francois."

"He asks Grandfather to send us to him," Francois said in a quiet voice. "He also writes that the messenger carries enough money to pay for our journey—or for our upkeep, should Grandfather refuse again."

"Again?"

"Apparently, these are not all of the letters," Francois said. "Only the ones he sent to London."

Francois pulled a bulging leather bag out from under the bench and untied the strings that held it closed. Gold coins glimmered and clinked as he poured them onto the low table in front of them. Two or three lone coins spilled over the side and rolled across the floor.

"Grandfather had this much gold here in London?"

Francois nodded, his expression grim.

"But...we could have paid our debts. We would not have had to flee in the middle of the night. We..." She closed her eyes and touched her fingertips to her forehead. All that suffering for naught.

"Grandfather was a wealthy man and did not need our father's money—not for a long time, anyway," Francois said. "By the time we did need it, he likely forgot he had it."

She nodded. "His memory grew worse and worse those last two years." After a long moment, she said, "But why did Alain never tell us he did this?"

"Pride, perhaps." Francois shrugged. "He may not realize we did not have the benefit of the funds."

Linnet rested her hands on the letters scattered in her lap. If she had known, how would her life be different? She had been angry for as long as she could remember. Angry that her father left their mother pregnant without a backward glance. Angry that he did not deem his bastard children worthy of his notice, much less his support.

She would not trade her early years with her grandfather for the constrained life of a nobleman's daughter. But if she had known about the letters, surely she would have made different choices these last years. If she had known of his attempts to support them and to bring them into his household, she would not have felt compelled to punish him for failing her.

Perhaps she would not expect everyone important to her to desert her. Everyone except for Francois, of course. He was the one person she had always believed loved her enough not to leave her.

Perhaps she would have trusted Jamie.

"He told me he tried to find us after Grandfather died," Francois said. "When he could find no trace of us, he assumed we died during the siege."

"Where did you find the gold and the letters?" she asked.

For the first time since he gave her the letters, Francois grinned. Eyes twinkling, he said, "Do you recall that curly-headed little girl you found in Mychell's house?"

"Aye, his daughter Lily."

"Well, Lily and her sister Rose appeared at your door while you were in Leicester," he said. "They had your ring."

Linnet laughed. "Lily found the letters, didn't she?"

"Aye, she did. They were hidden in a hollow in the wall of the shop, behind a brick."

"What a sharp-eyed girl." Linnet shook her head. "How did she know they belonged to us?"

"Her sister can read, if you can believe it."

"Not half as surprising as her thieving father naming his daughters after flowers."

"Lily, the little scoundrel, wanted to return the letters and keep the gold. She tried to convince her sister that you had so many coins you would not miss these."

Linnet laughed and clapped her hands. "Is she not wonderful?"

"Rose, however, insisted that all be returned."

"I hope you rewarded the girls."

He nodded. "I gave them half."

"Half? That seems more than generous..." She narrowed her eyes at her brother. "This Rose is not a little girl, is she?"

"I would call her petite," Francois said, a smile tugging at the corners of his mouth.

"Nay. Do not tell me. Let me guess. This Rose is eighteen and as pretty as her younger sister?"

Francois looked off into the distance and rubbed his chin, as if considering the question. "Nineteen. And prettier than her little sister."

"Did she take the money you gave her?"

He shook his head. "The lovely Rose kept two coins as a reward, one for herself and one for her sister, and insisted I take back the rest." He paused. "But I slipped the rest to Lily, who hid them under her cloak."

"This Rose has enough trouble having Mychell for a father, without you adding to her grief."

"Me?" Francois said, slapping his hand against his chest. "Add to a young woman's troubles?"

"That is what you do," Linnet said. "Have a care, Francois; this is an unsophisticated girl. You cannot—"

"You've no cause to chide me. I've done nothing," Francois said, holding up his hands. Then he added, "But I cannot help it if she wants me."

She rolled her eyes.

Francois's expression turned serious again. "I am sorry, love, but I have more news to give you." He took her hand and squeezed it. "'Tis unhappy news, this time."

"So long as you are safe and here with me, the tidings cannot be too unhappy."

"I must return to France at once."

"To France? But why?"

"An urgent message came three days ago from our father's steward."

Her heart began to beat faster. "From the steward, not Alain?"

"Alain was not well when I left a few months ago," he said in a gentle voice.

"Why did you not tell me?"

He raised an eyebrow but did not answer. If he had told her, she likely as not would have said she wished Alain were already burning in hell.

"I am sorry, sweetling, but the steward wrote to inform me of Alain's death." He patted her knee. "He was nearly sixty, you know. He had a long life."

"I am a wicked, wicked person." Linnet covered her face, overwhelmed by guilt and an unexpected sense of bereavement.

Alain had made mistakes from the moment they met—constantly correcting her behavior, attempting to make her conform to his notion of how a protected young lady of noble birth should act. But she had not been protected, and she could not fit that mold.

She would have refused to conform in any case, simply because it would have pleased him. Anger and resentment had gripped her soul; her burning need to punish him had blinded her to aught else.

And now, it was too late to make amends. Too late to attempt a reconciliation. Too late to ever truly know her father.

"I was bitter about the time you spent with him," she said, wiping a tear away with the back of her hand. "Now that we know the truth, I can see how very wretched that was of me."

"The fault lay with him as much as you," Francois said. "He'd no notion of how to treat a daughter, especially one like you. You weren't raised to be a simpering lady—and living in Sir Robert's household those last two years did not help matters."

When Stephen and Isobel left for England, they had put the twins in the care of Sir Robert and his wife. The couple had imposed no rules and delighted in Linnet's independent nature. Linnet had adored them.

"Though you drove him mad, our father was fond of you, in his way. When I saw him last, he asked a hundred questions about you."

She sniffed. "That makes me feel both better and worse."

They sat in silence, listening to the sounds of carts passing in the street below.

Finally, Francois said, "I must leave at once to take over the estates."

"At once?" She swallowed.

"I thought you would be with Jamie, that you and he would..." Francois's voice faded. "I hate to leave you here alone, especially now."

She covered her face with her hands. "Now that Jamie has abandoned me, you will do the same?"

She was being childish and unfair, but she hated being parted from him so much she could not help herself.

"You forget you left me first to marry," Francois said.

"That made no difference between us, and you know it."

Francois put his arm around her and patted her back.

"I am sorry to be horrid about it." She wiped her face on her sleeve and attempted a smile. "I know it is ridiculous, but I thought I would always have you, that we would always be together."

"You can come with me."

She ran her hand over the letters that still rested in her lap. "I missed my chance to reconcile with our father. It may be too late for me with Jamie, as well, but I cannot leave England until I am certain."

"I thought that was what you would say," Francois said, then he gave her one of his broad winks. "Jamie is the one who will not have a chance. What man could refuse you?"

She thought of Jamie's last words to her: *I shall be betrothed when next we meet.*

"Pray I am not too late," she said, gripping her brother's arm. She would see Jamie at Hertford soon, and she would know then.

"The day Jamie weds another, I will board a ship for France."

Chapter Thirty-two

"'The Lady Agnes cannot be the cold fish she seems to be," Stephen said, putting his arm around Jamie's shoulders as they walked out of the Staffords' hall. "When you get her alone, 'tis a different story, aye?"

Jamie glanced over his shoulder to be sure they were out of earshot. "She is an innocent virgin," he hissed. "You think I would violate her?"

Of course, Linnet's virginity had not stopped him. He felt a twinge of guilt over that, but he could not pretend to regret it.

"I'm not accusing you of deflowering Agnes." Stephen gave Jamie's cheek a playful slap. "But surely a bit of license is called for before shackling yourself for a lifetime?"

Jamie had taken more than a bit of license with Linnet when she was younger than Agnes. But then, Linnet's virginity had not stopped her any more than it had him. It did not even give her pause. She had given herself to him wholeheartedly that first time—even urging him on when he argued they should wait. What a wonder that first time was. He remembered how she looked beneath him, her face flushed and her legs wrapped around him...

"Come," Stephen said, jarring him from his thoughts, "tell me you've at least kissed Agnes senseless a time or two."

"Agnes?" Jamie was having difficulty pushing images of Linnet, naked and writhing, from his mind. He rubbed his forehead, trying to clear it, and found it was damp.

"Aye, Agnes," Stephen said, sounding exasperated. "By Saint Peter's bones, if you are not tempted to kiss her and a good deal more, you should not have come to see her father."

The sooner he had another woman in his bed, the sooner he would stop thinking of Linnet.

"'Tis a shame Stafford is not here," Jamie said. "Did you not deliver my message to him?"

Stephen waved his hand. "'Tis fortunate Stafford happened to be called away." Then he waggled his eyebrows. "You should use the opportunity to find out if you and Agnes are 'well suited.'"

"Are you suggesting I drag her under the bushes while I am a guest in her father's home?"

"'Tis damp beneath the bushes this time of year," Stephen said. "Behind a door would do."

"We are here but a few hours," Jamie protested.

Stephen lifted his hands, palms up. "If you do not find her appealing..."

"Of course I do. I am a man and she is a woman. And a very pretty woman, at that." He felt like punching his uncle. "Even if I meant to do it, I could not get her alone."

"If you wanted to get her alone, you could manage it,"

Stephen said with a shrug. "That is what we men do. 'Tis why having a daughter frightens me half to death."

As much as it annoyed Jamie to hear it, Stephen's words had the ring of truth. Those weeks in Paris, he and Linnet had kissed—and more—behind doors, under stairs, in the mews...

"And if a woman wants a man, she will make it easy for him to find her alone." Stephen spread out his hands. "It has been that way from the beginning of time."

Jamie thought of Linnet's eagerness. How many times did they make love on the floor because they could not wait to reach the bed? He would miss that fiery passion.

He did miss it.

He tried not to think about the ache in his chest as he and Stephen walked across the windswept meadow outside the gates of Stafford's manor house. Spring came late here in Northumberland. It would be several weeks before the ground they walked would be planted with rye or wheat.

The wind flapped at Jamie's clothes as they stopped to watch the dark clouds rolling in over the hills. Living here would suit him. He liked the open spaces and clean smells—and Northumberland's distance from the politics of London.

Neither of them had spoken since they left the gate, but Stephen broke the silence now.

"Most men are satisfied with a bride who brings a fair dowry and has the skills to manage a household," Stephen said. "If their wives do not suit them, most men are content to keep mistresses and get their pleasure from other women."

After a long pause, Stephen said, "But we are not like most men."

Stephen was right. If Agnes was to be his wife, 'twas past time he kissed her. Once he set his mind to it, it was nothing to get her out a back door of the manor house. Taking her hand, he began walking her toward the woods. He did not intend to roll on the wet ground with her, but he wanted privacy for this.

He had bedded a good many women to forget Linnet the first time. Since he was going to be a married man, this time he would have to forget her with only one. No easy task, but he was determined. He knew what he wanted: a calm and steady life. What he did not want was a wife who was always at the center of tumult and mayhem—and usually the cause of it.

Agnes's hand was dry and cold in his and did not clasp his back. He was undeterred. He was going to prove Stephen wrong and kiss her senseless. He would make her sweat. Sweaty and breathless. She would beg him not to stop. But he would stop, because he was an honorable man. A true knight.

"Sir James, please slow your pace."

He turned to find Agnes's hood had fallen back and her cheeks were pink with exertion. She was a pretty woman, really.

She gasped as he pulled her close. He cupped her cheek and looked into her grave eyes. Innocent as she was, she had to know he was going to kiss her now. Instead of softening or becoming nervous, as he expected, her lips thinned into a line of disapproval.

But that was only because she hadn't been kissed before. Not by him, anyway. He leaned down to brush a kiss on her cheek and blow a soft breath into her ear.

Nothing. No indrawn breath. No sigh. No soft breasts pressing against his chest.

He sucked in his breath. In for a penny, in for a pound.

This time, he put his lips to hers. How was he to feel lustful when she did not move? An uneasy feeling settled in his stomach, as if he were doing something wrong. It made no sense. Hell, he'd kissed girls since he was twelve and never felt a shred of guilt for it.

He was relieved when she pulled away.

He reminded himself that they were almost strangers, and she was an innocent. In time, he would awaken passion in her.

"You do know what husbands and wives do to have children?" He ran a finger down her arm and gave her a slow smile. "You want children, do you not?"

She nodded, her expression solemn. "I pray I will have many children to give to the church," she said. "They shall serve God as I was not permitted to do."

"You want them all to be nuns and priests?" He was almost too surprised to get the question out.

"I prefer the boys be monks."

Jamie wasn't sure he liked the idea of one of his daughters spending her life in a nunnery, but it was hard to know with girls. Boys were another matter.

"My sons will be strong knights in the service of the king. None will choose to wear a cleric's robe. They will be fighters, every one."

Agnes folded her arms across her chest and narrowed her eyes at him. "As we are speaking plainly, Sir James,

I wish to know if you intend to follow the church's guidance regarding marital conjugation."

Jamie felt his eyebrows reach almost to his hairline. She could not mean what he thought she did. Surely not.

"The church admonishes us that the only righteous purpose of conjugation is procreation."

"But no one follows the church's guidance on this," Jamie said, raising his hands into the air. "I doubt even men who are repulsed by their wives follow it, unless they are very, very old."

"Celibacy within marriage is a great virtue."

"'Tis not healthy for a man." He was shocked at the very notion of it. "These silly rules do not come from God. They are made up by priests who dislike women—or who have no notion what they are asking a man to go without."

Agnes's face was flushed. "You criticize the judgment of men of God?"

They were having a real argument now.

Jamie took a deep breath. She was speaking from ignorance. Once she experienced "conjugal relations," she was bound to change her mind.

"While the church encourages husbands to forgo their marital rights," she said in a calmer voice, "it does permit the activity on more days than is necessary for procreation."

Jamie remembered laughing about this with his friends. One long evening during a siege, they had attempted to count the prohibited days as they sat around their campfire drinking. They had stopped at three hundred.

He was not laughing now.

Agnes sniffed. "That is the church's preference. A wife, however, is not permitted to refuse her husband."

Just to be contrary, Jamie said, "Under the law, a wife may demand her conjugal rights as well."

Agnes made a very unpleasant sound through her nose.

"I shall have to discuss this with the abbess at length when next I see her." She furrowed her brow, apparently lost in contemplation of sin and marital conjugation. "It seems unfair that I should be tainted by my husband's sin if he is weak. And yet, it would be a sin to wish my husband would satisfy his carnal lust elsewhere."

Jamie swallowed. "Avoidance of sin is the only reason you would not want your husband to lie with other women?"

She blinked several times, as if she was trying to puzzle through some great mystery. "What other reason could there be?"

"Time for us to return to the house." He took her arm and started walking, determined not to think about what she had said.

As they crossed the field to the house, he felt as if stones weighed on his chest, making it hard to breathe.

Chapter Thirty-three

Linnet heard a knock on the front door, followed by her maid's feet on the stairs. There was not one person in all of London she wished to see. When her maid appeared on the solar's threshold, she held her breath, waiting to hear who it was.

Lizzie clenched her skirts and darted her eyes about the room. "A priest is here, m'lady. He says he must speak with you."

Linnet wondered at her maid's unease. Though she could not imagine why a cleric had come to see her, she could think of no harm in it. She revised her opinion when she went down and saw the black-robed man waiting outside the door. What did Eleanor Cobham's clerk want with her?

"Father Hume." She dipped her head slightly, but she did not invite him inside.

She had forgotten meeting him and Margery Jourdemayne on the stairs to the undercroft at Windsor almost as soon as it happened. The memory of it now made her uneasy. She'd never liked this sinister priest, who followed Eleanor like a shadow.

The priest glanced up and down the street before he spoke. "I have come to bring you a warning from a friend."

Linnet raised her eyebrows. "Lady Eleanor considers herself my friend?"

"I did not say it was Lady Eleanor," he said through tight lips.

So it was Lady Eleanor. "What is the warning my mysterious 'friend' wishes to give?"

"There are rumors traveling about the City that you are engaged in sorcery and witchcraft."

"What?" Her hand went to her chest, and she was unable to keep the tremor of alarm from her voice. "I have heard nothing of this."

"But others have heard the rumors. Powerful people. Men in the church," the priest said, drawing out the last word.

Fear clawed at her belly. After Pomeroy accused her of killing her husband with sorcery, she had lived under the shadow of the accusation for months. She remembered how the villagers backed away and made the sign of the cross when her carriage passed. The memory of the black fear on their faces sent a frisson of terror up her spine.

Now she understood her maid's unease and furtive glances.

"They are saying," the priest said, leaning forward, "you used sorcery to make the queen fall in love with Edmund Beaufort."

Her mouth went dry. This had to be Pomeroy's doing.

"Sir James Rayburn's family is a powerful one. While you were 'under his protection,' certain persons were afraid to act." The priest cleared his throat. "They are no longer afraid."

"I have means to protect myself," she said.

"They will prove insufficient. Your friend recommends you leave at once for your homeland."

"Leave for France?" she asked, startled.

"You haven't much time."

As a child, she had been forced to flee London in the dead of night. She was sorely tempted to do so again. But she could not leave England until she saw Jamie again.

Or heard news of his marriage.

Besides, she had done nothing wrong. She would not let her enemies force her to leave this time. She had no intention, however, of sharing her plans with this weasel of a priest—or his keeper.

"You can thank my 'friend' for her counsel," she said as she eased the door closed.

"They will arrest you tomorrow." The priest stopped the door with his foot to give her his parting words. "And here in England, they burn witches."

Linnet paced her solar, considering what to do. It seemed foolish to stay. Jamie wanted a wife who could give him a quiet life and a peaceful home. Even if she were not arrested, tried, and burned, she could never persuade Jamie she could be that sort of wife—not with accusations of sorcery whispered about her.

Who was behind this? At first, she assumed it was Pomeroy. But now, she wondered if she had ruffled too many feathers among the powerful London merchants. They were suspicious of her, just as they were of the queen.

As a foreigner, she should have walked softly. Instead,

she had fanned the flames of their resentment by her success in trade. And then, she had used the leverage her success gave her to pursue one of their own.

Whether it was Pomeroy or the merchants spreading these accusations, she would not just sit here, waiting for her enemies' next move against her.

"Lizzie!" she called, wanting her maid to help her change.

When Lizzie did not answer, Linnet went looking for her. After finding no one belowstairs, she went behind the house to the kitchen. Carter, the rough man Master Woodley had hired to escort her about the City, sat on a stool eating an apple. Master Woodley must have hired Carter for his size alone, for the man was huge.

"Where is Lizzie?" she asked.

Carter cut a slice from the apple and ate it off his knife. "The other servants are gone."

They must have heard the rumors of sorcery. Apparently Carter was too surly to be frightened.

Fighting back the sour taste of nausea at the back of her throat, she said, "I will need you to escort me to Westminster in an hour."

Carter nodded but did not get up. "I shall be here."

Linnet went to her chamber to dress for the occasion. She would dare them to make the accusations to her face. Damn them! She was so angry that her first instinct was to wear a bold, blood-red gown. Instead, she made herself think carefully about the impression she wished to make.

She was well aware her looks could be both an advantage and a disadvantage. Rather than the red, she chose a delicate eggshell-colored gown embossed with intricate embroidery. The trim was a warmer shade of the same creamy white shot through with silver threads. A thin ribbon of the trim ran along the top edge of her bodice, while wider bands were sewn at the high waist, at the wrists, and along the bottom of the gown.

It was not easy getting into the gown and matching headdress without a maid, but when she looked at herself in her polished steel mirror, she was satisfied. The snug bodice, set off by the trim, subtly showed off her breasts and the whiteness of her throat. When she walked, the trim along the hem drew attention to the movement of the skirt and made it appear to float about her.

Coils of fair blonde hair were visible through the delicate silver mesh on either side of her face. Most important, a heavy silver cross rested just above the top of her bodice. Everyone knew witches could not wear crosses. On a longer, more delicate silver chain, Jamie's pendant hung out of sight between her breasts. She touched it and closed her eyes, wishing with all her heart that he was here.

Never in her life had she felt so alone. Jamie was gone. Francois, too. She could not call on the queen without putting her in danger. It was up to her to save herself, as it had always been.

After slipping on her cloak with the silvery-gray fur trim, she took one last look in the mirror. She was ready for them.

She was no angel, but she looked like one.

Chapter Thirty-four

"'Tis good to see you," Geoffrey said, pounding Jamie on the back.

Geoffrey was a big, barrel-chested young man who would have been mistaken for a warrior, save for his tonsured hair and habit.

"What shall I call you now?" Jamie asked. "Brother Geoffrey?"

"That will do," Geoffrey said with a broad smile. "I have my prior's permission to accompany you to your uncle's, since he is an important benefactor of our abbey. But first, I thought you would want to see where your father spent much of his life."

"Do not call him my father," Jamie said.

"Brother Richard, then," Geoffrey said, ever the peacemaker. "Visitors are not permitted in the dormitory or the chapter house, but I can show you the church and grounds."

The abbey was situated in a lovely spot next to a river bordered by giant yew trees. Despite its beauty, impatience tugged at Jamie as Geoffrey led him behind the kitchens to show him the gardens.

Geoffrey stopped before a desolate piece of ground no more than twenty feet by ten. "Brother Richard spent most of his time tending this herb garden, when he was not in prayer."

Jamie stared at the small plot tucked between the kitchen block and the ditch that carried water from the river into the abbey.

After a long silence, Geoffrey said, "There is not much growing now, but you should see it in high summer."

"This is where he spent his days? For more than twenty years?" Jamie was appalled. In the name of heaven, the man was once a knight.

"I understand he took care of the goats during his first years here," Geoffrey said. "But their unpredictability distressed him."

"Goats? Goats distressed him?" He would have accused Geoffrey of jesting, but the sympathy in his friend's eyes stopped him short.

"I believe Brother Richard was content here," Geoffrey said in a quiet voice.

Jamie's gaze roved over the brown stubble of the miserable patch. Content? More like, half dead.

"Come, his brother lives a short distance from the abbey." Geoffrey put a hand on his shoulder. "We must leave now if I'm to be back before compline."

A tall, strongly built man with a warrior's stance met them at the gate. "I am Charles Wheaton, lord of this castle," the man said. "And your uncle."

"That is yet to be seen," Jamie said.

"You would call your mother a liar?" Wheaton said. "I'd heard better of you."

If Geoffrey had not been so quick to grab him, Jamie would have planted his fist in the man's face. "Take care how you speak of my mother."

Wheaton did not turn a hair. "Calm yourself, laddie; I was not the one who called her a liar."

"I never said she lied," Jamie said, temper prickling at his skin. "But she could be mistaken."

"I wanted to see you to be sure myself," Wheaton said. "You're a right bit more handsome, but the likeness between us is there for any fool to see."

From the first moment, Jamie had been trying to ignore that Wheaton had the same unusual shade of blue eyes that he did. Wheaton's hair was streaked with gray, but it must once have been as black as his.

"If you've forgotten what you look like, son, I can have a mirror brought out for you."

Jamie was not amused. "I have fought in France since I was fifteen. Do not call me son. Or laddie."

Jamie flinched as the older man put a heavy hand on his shoulder. "Since the only two people who could know the truth said it was so, you may as well accept it."

"I do not see where it is any business of yours what I believe."

"Come, Jamie, give the man a chance to explain," Geoffrey said. "Let us go inside and talk over a cup of ale."

"Thank you, Brother Geoffrey," Wheaton said and turned to lead them across the bailey yard.

The castle had an old square keep, but it was well-maintained. Jamie scanned the walls and outbuildings and saw that these, too, were kept in good repair. Charles

Wheaton may be a disagreeable character, but a man who took good care of his property merited some respect.

They settled into the hall, which had a blazing fire in the hearth, an impressive display of weapons on the wall, and clean rushes on the floor.

"Charles, you should have told me they were here."

Jamie turned at the sound of a woman's voice behind him. A frail woman, who looked to be about his mother's age, had come into the hall and was walking toward them, leaning heavily on the arm of a servant.

Wheaton rushed to her side and took the servant's place. When he turned back to face them, Jamie was startled by the transformation in the man's expression.

"Meet my wife," Wheaton said, beaming down at the delicate woman. "A better woman, God never made."

"Charles, please," she said.

She had a light, sweet voice that reminded Jamie of music from the high strings of a harp. But her pallor made it plain as day that Wheaton's wife was in poor health.

"This is your aunt, Lady Anne Wheaton," Wheaton said, then quoted Chaucer: "'Any man worth a cabbage all his life ought to thank God on bare knees for his wife.'"

Anne Wheaton's hand was icy and as light as a feather in Jamie's as he bent over it, but there was warmth and laughter in her hazel eyes.

"We have waited a very long time to meet you," she said.

Jamie was confused. "But I only just heard…"

"Of course, dear," she said. "But we knew about you all along."

"Then why—"

He did not finish his question because she began to

cough. It was not a delicate cough, but one that racked her frail body and made Jamie wince.

"Let me take you upstairs, love," her husband said. "I am sure these young men will wait while you rest an hour."

She shook her head. "Just let me sit by the fire, and I shall be fine."

Wheaton helped her into a chair, then placed a cushion behind her back and tucked a blanket around her. "How's that, love?"

Jamie could not help softening toward Wheaton as he watched the big man hover over his sickly wife.

"Do not fret, Charles. I do not intend to let God take me today," she said, smiling up at him. Then she turned to Geoffrey and Jamie. "Please, take a seat. We do not often have visitors these days, so this is a great treat for me."

"For me, as well," Jamie said and meant it. He took the chair opposite her, though the heat from the roaring fire was going to make him break out in a sweat.

"A gallant young man," she said, turning to her husband. "Just like Richard."

Wheaton patted her hand.

"Can you tell me about him?" Jamie asked, finding it easier to ask her than his uncle.

"It did not surprise me that your mother trusted him, for 'twas easy to see that Richard had a pure heart," she said, a smile in her eyes. "He was the kindest man I knew."

"If he was so kind, how could he leave my mother with that man?"

"He did feel guilty, but what could he do? That man was her husband," she said. "Meeting your mother affected him deeply. If she had been free, he would have offered for her. He was very troubled and prayed often for her safety."

"Hmmph. He should have fought for what he wanted," Wheaton said. "Instead, he used the abbey as an escape from life."

"But all turned out well for your mother," Lady Anne said, a smile lighting her pale face. "When we met them, it was clear that she and Lord FitzAlan are devoted to each other."

Jamie nodded.

"We did not contact your family sooner, out of respect for Richard's wishes," she said. "It would have...upset him."

Jamie cleared his throat. She smiled so sweetly at him that he felt like an oaf pressing her. "I am very glad to meet you, but why did you wish me to come here? I am a stranger to you."

"Because you are the only child of our dear Richard, of course," she said, as if that should be answer enough for anyone. "And you are my husband's closest kin, as well."

"Closest kin?"

"What she is saying is that you are my heir," Wheaton said. "Or you would be, if the truth were known about who your father was."

Jamie felt like the ground was shifting under him.

"I don't know if it makes me a bastard to be fathered by one man while my mother was married to another, but I am certain I have no legal claim to your lands. Nor would I attempt to press such a claim."

"But we have no one else," Lady Anne said in a small voice. "I have told Charles he must take a younger wife after I'm gone, in hope of getting an heir, but he refuses to consider it."

"Annie, don't," Wheaton said, squeezing her hand.

She began to cough again. It made Jamie's chest hurt to hear it. This time, Wheaton lifted her up in his arms and carried her off.

A short time later, he came down looking drawn. He took his chair and drained his cup of ale.

"I won't wed again," he said in a heavy voice. "There could be no other woman for me after Annie. But I could not sire an heir, in any case. I had something of a wild youth before I married. So far as I ever heard, none of the women ever conceived."

After a long silence, Jamie said, "Your lack of an heir, sir, does not mean I have any claim to your estates."

"Better that I decide who shall have my lands, than that they go to the Crown for Bishop Beaufort to choose," Wheaton said. "I've hired a lawyer to find out how it can be done."

Jamie did not know what to say. To have his own lands was something he had dreamed of for years.

Finally, he said, "You are a fit man. You've a long while yet to make a decision."

"When I lose Annie, I will take my brother's place at the abbey." Wheaton poured himself another cup of ale. "I'll grant you the lands then."

Jamie knew Wheaton would not appreciate false comfort, so he gave none. "I am truly sorry your wife is unwell. Has it been a long illness?"

"Her health was fragile from the day we wed," he said. "I count myself blessed for every day I've had with her. I've had a good life. The best life. No regrets for me."

No regrets. The man had no children, and he had been watching his beloved wife die from the beginning of their marriage. And yet, Jamie believed Charles Wheaton would not have exchanged his life for another.

"'Tis a fine estate," Jamie said finally. "I would do my best to keep it as well as you have."

"I could tell that from the way you looked at it," Wheaton said. "'Tis a comfort to me."

The three of them talked for a while of crops and cattle, but it was growing dark and time for Jamie and Geoffrey to go.

Wheaton walked them out to the gate.

"We will welcome you to our brotherhood when the time comes," Geoffrey said to Wheaton.

"I hope I may visit you and your wife again. And... thank you," Jamie said, unable to find an adequate way to express his gratitude.

"Make the most of what life gives you," Wheaton said, clasping Jamie's shoulder. "Don't live a life of regret like my brother did."

Chapter Thirty-five

Linnet entered Westminster Hall through the grand ceremonial north entrance, with its vaulted porch portal and flanking towers. After passing through the twenty-foot-high wooden doors, she paused beneath the great arched window.

As always, her gaze was drawn upward to the hammer beams and braced arches of the massive timber roof. It had been commissioned by Richard II and was said to weigh more than 650 tons. Richard had never been one to economize. Still, Linnet judged the new roof worth the expense—as had his cousin and usurper, Henry IV, who completed it.

Linnet was well aware of the gazes that drifted toward her as she scanned the room for the bishop. Ah, there he was. Though the bishop's back was to her, his pristine white robes stood out amid the colorfully clad nobles and wealthy merchants.

Men drew in their breath as she strode past them, her chin held high. The bishop turned around just before she reached him, as if he had eyes in the back of his head—which some said he did.

The bishop arched an eyebrow ever so slightly. "Now I see what caught everyone's attention."

"Your Grace." She sank into a low curtsy.

When she rose, Bishop Beaufort said in an amused tone, "A special evening, is it?"

She returned the smile. "In sooth, I am hoping for an uneventful time ahead."

"It will be more difficult for anyone to overhear us if we walk," he said in a low voice. As she fell in beside him to stroll the length of the room, he said, "I suspect I know what you wish to speak with me about."

"I swear to you, these rumors about me are false," she said in a hushed voice.

"'Twas risky—but very clever—to come here tonight and put your accusers off their guard." A faint smile touched his lips. "I must say, that large cross and... heavenly... gown are nice touches."

"Thank you, Your Grace."

"Your enemies will have to think twice about proceeding after such a public display of your virtuous nature," he said. "But tell me why you seek me out."

"Because my enemies are yours, Your Grace," she said. "The most dangerous rumor against me is that I used sorcery to cause the queen to have an affair with your nephew."

"This is the reason I am willing to speak with you, of course," he said with a thin smile. "I am glad we understand one another."

"I will do all I can to protect the queen and Sir Edmund," she said. "Can you advise me?"

"I cannot prevent your arrest," he said, and Linnet's heart sank to her feet. "But I've a better chance of keeping this quiet and controlling the outcome if you are tried by an ecclesiastic court."

The bishop nodded to a group of well-dressed men Linnet did not recognize.

"If I send you a warning," he said, "get yourself to a church with all haste and claim sanctuary."

"God bless you, Your Grace."

"God blesses those who use the wits He gave them." The bishop stopped walking and said in a voice loud enough for those nearby to overhear, "Where do you get such exquisite cloth? I know it comes from Flanders, but you must tell me the weaver."

Bishop Beaufort, clever man, was using his well-known interest in the cloth trade with Flanders to mislead others in the hall as to his reason for speaking with her. She was happy to play along.

"The weaver's name slips my mind, Your Grace." The bishop knew very well the name was a well-guarded secret. "Whoever does the embroidery on your vestments is highly skilled...almost as skilled as the woman who does mine."

When she held out her sleeve for him to examine, his expression soured, for hers was finer.

"It would be a great honor for me to provide your new cardinal's vestments, if that would be permitted," she said. "After all, a cardinal's vestments should be the very best."

"That would make an excellent offering to the church."

Linnet tried not to smile as she asked, "Would it count against my tithing?"

"From what I hear, you can afford the additional donation."

The richest man in England certainly knew how to squeeze a coin.

"I wish to make a donation as well to the chancery you are building in honor of our late and glorious King Henry."

The bishop pressed his lips together and nodded, and she knew her gesture touched him. It was well known that the bishop had been exceedingly fond of his nephew, the great King Henry V.

Linnet was about to take her leave when he spoke again.

"I believe I saw you talking with Sir James Rayburn the last time you were here at Westminster Palace. Could you be the reason he showed a singular lack of gratitude when we offered him marriage to a wealthy heiress?"

Linnet felt herself color and dropped her gaze to the floor. "He is grateful now, I assure you."

"Does he have any notion how much wealth you would bring to a marriage?"

She shook her head. "I fear it would not balance my faults on his scale."

"Then something is wrong with his scales." The bishop pursed his lips. "He does place a rather high value on his honor, so I suppose you must have damaged his pride in some way. 'Pride goeth before a fall.'"

That could be said of her as well.

"I've accomplished what I came for," she said, "I think it best for me to leave now."

"Mind whom you trust," the bishop said by way of farewell.

"Your Grace," she said, dropping a curtsy.

She made her way through the crowd toward the south

entrance, where she had arranged to meet Carter. Before she reached it, she caught sight of Eleanor Cobham whispering with two men in an alcove. From their gestures, it appeared they were having a furious argument. As Linnet passed them, Eleanor stormed out of the alcove and almost ran into her.

"'Tis nice to meet a 'friend' tonight," Linnet said.

"I am not your friend, but I will tell you this," Eleanor said. "You waste your time here. The bishop's star has fallen. Leave while you can."

"I will give you advice as well—you underestimate the bishop at your peril." Linnet gave her a tight smile and continued toward the door.

When she did not see Carter waiting for her outside, she assumed he had left to respond to nature's call. She decided to take the opportunity to go to Saint Stephen's Chapel. She wanted to see the progress made since her last visit to the chancery being built in memory of their beloved dead king.

The chapel was built perpendicular to the Great Hall and jutted out to the east, toward the Thames. To get to it, Linnet had only to walk down a short covered walkway.

Her breath caught as she paused at the entrance of the long, narrow chapel. Light from a dozen tall candles reflected on the colored glass in the windows and shone warm light on the intricate carvings and painted seats. As she marveled at the chapel's beauty, the tension of the last hours seeped from her muscles. Hope stirred in her heart; all things seemed possible again.

Without warning, she was lifted off the ground as someone grabbed her from behind.

She tried to scream against the damp cloth pressed

against her face. Almost at once, her lips went numb, and there was a metallic taste on her tongue. She struggled against the thick arms that held her, but the man had muscles like steel beneath her fingers.

Even as she tried to fight, a fog settled over her. Her arms ceased to follow her commands, flopping uselessly at her sides. She could not feel her legs at all.

Darkness took her.

Chapter Thirty-six

Jamie felt as if he had stepped into the light. Everything was clear now. He could have a safe and ordered life, or he could have Linnet. No matter how much havoc Linnet caused, nothing would ever be right without her.

He had come perilously close to choosing the path of the man who sired him: a life that was predictable and safe... and small. A paltry existence. Instead, he intended to take all that life had to offer, the pain with the pleasure, and live it to the fullest with the woman he loved.

Jamie waited in the bailey yard, anxious to make his farewells and leave. He looked up as Stephen came out with Isobel and helped her down the steps of the house.

"How long do you expect to be in London?" Stephen asked when they reached the bottom.

"As long as it takes to convince Linnet to be my wife."

"Be quick about it." Isobel gave him a broad smile and patted her enormous belly. "If you are to be this babe's godparents, you need to return with her in time for the christening."

Isobel gave her husband a sidelong glance.

"I'll see what's keeping the groom with your horse," Stephen said. "Meet you at the gate."

Isobel took Jamie's arm, and they began to stroll toward the gate.

"At least you need not worry about hurting Lady Agnes's feelings," Isobel said.

"That is for certain." Jamie laughed. "As soon as I left her house, she ran away to the nunnery."

"It was kind of you to stop to see her there before leaving."

"She is hell-bent on remaining at the nunnery," he said with a smile. "If the abbess fails to persuade her father through reasoned argument, Agnes intends to chain herself to the altar."

Isobel held her belly as she chuckled. "Pray, do not make me laugh, or I may have the babe right here in the yard."

As they walked, Isobel's expression grew thoughtful. "Tell me, what went wrong with Linnet this time?"

Jamie blew out his breath. "Simply put, Linnet wants revenge for something that happened years and years ago more than she wants me."

"I see," Isobel said and nodded to herself.

"Tell me, how can I convince her to forget the past?"

Isobel stopped and turned her serious green eyes on him. "Did you never consider helping her settle her old scores?"

"What? Help her with such foolishness?"

Isobel raised her eyebrows at him and then began walking again. "'Tis not foolishness to her."

"But it is foolish nonetheless—and dangerous besides." He ran a hand through his hair. "Why can she not leave it alone and be happy to be a wife and mother like other women?"

Jamie turned in time to catch Isobel rolling her eyes.

"If she were like other women, she would not be the woman you love," she said. "Try to understand her. If you felt a great wrong had been committed against, say, your mother, could you rest?"

Isobel knew precisely how protective he felt toward his mother; she always made her points with razor-sharp accuracy.

"But Linnet promised me she would let the past be." Breaking her word to him still rankled.

"You know how it was for her," Isobel said. "When Stephen and William found her and Francois, they were living by their wits, stealing food and protecting themselves with an old sword. It cannot be easy for her to forgive the men who put them there."

"But she thinks nothing of poking a stick at these men," he said, raising his hands in the air, "no matter how powerful they may be."

"All the more reason she needs you," Isobel said.

Who knew women were such bloodthirsty creatures? "I suppose I shall have to help her. God knows she cannot do it alone, no matter what she thinks."

Stephen caught up to them then, leading Jamie's horse. "My wife put you on the right path?"

"Do you doubt it?" Jamie put his arm around Isobel's shoulders and gave her a squeeze. "Wish me luck, for I fear we shall have our wedding in the Tower."

Isobel grinned at him. "At least you shall be together."

He bid them a final farewell and mounted his horse.

As he made the long journey to London, Agnes's strange words of parting nagged at him, drawing his mind again and again, like an infected wound.

"Pray for God's protection," Agnes had said, "for I have seen demons hovering over the lady you seek."

Chapter Thirty-seven

$\mathcal{L}$innet was beneath the water, rocked by the motion of the sea. Her heart began to race because the sea was too dark for her to see the surface, and she did not know which way to swim.

Gradually, she realized the rocking motion was not the sea, but someone carrying her. Her head pounded. She recalled someone grabbing her from behind...and the strong medicinal smell of a cloth over her face. She sniffed. Damp wool now. Was she wrapped in a blanket? She felt confined, swaddled as tight as a babe.

A voice came out of the darkness. "Any trouble?"

"None." She felt the rumble of the deep voice of the man carrying her.

The voice sounded familiar...A jolt of indignation ran through her: This was Carter, the very man she had hired to protect her.

She forced herself not to struggle. There was nothing she could do wrapped up like this—and letting them know she was awake might squander a later opportunity to escape.

"The others are waiting," the first man said.

He spoke in vernacular English, but his voice was cultured. An educated man, someone of the noble class or in frequent contact with the nobility.

"You take her an' give me the rest of my money now," Carter said. "I already risked more'n I like. I don't want nothin' more to do with you lot of devil-worshippers."

Devil-worshippers?

"Put her in the wagon, and you can go."

She bit her lip to keep from crying out as she was tossed through the air. A sharp pain shot through her shoulder as she landed with a hard thump. Wooden slats creaked beneath her as the wagon rocked from the impact of her weight.

"Mind you keep your mouth closed," the man with the cultured voice said. "I warn you—I know spells that would leave your cock limp for the rest of your days."

Carter spurted a string of oaths. Then she heard the clink of coins, following by receding footsteps. The wagon rocked again, this time with the weight of someone getting in the front. With a lurch, it moved forward.

As the wagon bumped along, she rocked herself from side to side, intent on rolling off the back of the wagon. Once, twice, she rolled over, and then...damn, she hit the side of the wagon. She gathered her strength and bounced herself. She was wrapped so tightly, it was slow going. Inch by inch, she moved until her feet fell off the end.

"Halt, John!"

At the woman's shout, the driver brought the wagon up sharply, which sent Linnet sliding forward away from the end of the wagon. She wanted to scream in frustration.

The next thing she knew, there was someone beside her, unwrapping the blanket from her face.

She saw a flash of starlit sky, and then a cloth was over her face. It had the same distinctive odor as before.

"Noooo!" Her scream was muffled by the cloth. In vain, she struggled against the bindings that held her fast.

Linnet awoke with a blazing headache. For a long moment, she lay on her back, staring at the ceiling with no notion of where she was or what had happened to her. Yet her skin prickled with the knowledge that she was in danger.

Slowly, it came back to her. How long had she been in the wagon? How many times had they reapplied the cloth? She had no sense of either.

She lifted her head and had to grit her teeth against the throbbing pain in her head. A hint of light filtered in around the edges of a single barred and shuttered window, and even that hurt her eyes. She was lying on a pallet in a narrow room. The weight she had felt on her hands and feet were chains. When she tried to sit up to see better, she was hit by such a wave of dizziness that she was forced to drop her head back down.

A tear slid down the side of her face into her hair. What was she doing here? Kidnapped, drugged, and chained like a dog! If she had listened to Jamie, done as he begged her, they would be at his parents' castle now, planning their wedding feast.

But nay. She had to poke her stick into the hornet's nest once more. After that disastrous encounter with Gloucester, however, she had done nothing to pursue her enemies. She had been too despondent to care. Once Master Woodley confirmed the mayor's spotless reputation for honesty, she had no notion where to look next in any case. Regardless, her earlier actions must have threatened someone powerful—and evil.

No matter what she'd done to bring this on herself, Jamie would come save her if he knew. No matter his wretched betrothal to someone else, no matter his fury with her, no matter his determination never to cross paths with her again—Jamie would come if he knew she was in danger.

To keep her courage up, she imagined Jamie coming down a long corridor to reach the door to this tiny room, fighting his way past twenty men. Such a warrior he was! How magnificent he would look, his sword swinging left and right, high and low, as he struck down one after another.

Then he would kick the door open with a great crash. He would stand for a long moment in the doorway, his chest heaving, praising God he had found her still alive. And finally, he would drop to his knee beside her narrow cot, take her in his arms, and—

Click. Click. Click.

Linnet turned her head toward the sound of a key in a lock. Her heart stopped in her chest as the door latch slowly lifted.

Chapter Thirty-eight

"Someone put it about that Lady Linnet was doing witch-craft," Mistress Leggett said. "Black witchcraft."

This was the third time Jamie had heard this since he arrived in London to find Linnet gone and her house empty. There had been whispers for months about nobles in the highest circles being involved with witchcraft and dark arts, but he'd never heard a word about it in connection with Linnet. Until today.

"I didn't believe it for a moment," Mistress Leggett said, fanning herself, though the room was far from warm. She sat with her knees apart and her bulk overflowing the small stool on which she sat. "But if any noble lady was going to be accused of sorcery, 'twas bound to be her."

"Why Linnet?" he asked.

"She doesn't act as men think a woman ought. And she won't pretend they know better. That's enough to put a woman at risk." Mistress Leggett's jowls shook as she nodded her head. "Believe me, I know."

Jamie tapped his foot, but Mistress Leggett took no notice of his impatience.

"I praise God I wasn't born with her sort of beauty,"

Mistress Leggett said as she refilled his cup from the pitcher of ale without asking. He refrained from shaking her as she refilled her own and drank down half of it. "Such rare looks can lead men to a dangerous sort of lust."

Mistress Leggett wiped her mouth with the back of her hand and shook a thick finger at Jamie. "Then, if she won't have him, the man will go half mad. And you can bet a pretty penny, he'll blame her for it. Next thing you know, he'll be saying she bewitched him."

"Are you saying you know who is behind the rumors? Who accuses her?" Jamie asked, still hoping she might give him something useful.

She puckered her lips as she pondered his question. "All the men looked at her, so 'tis hard to say. But where I heard the rumor was at the Guild Hall. I'd start there, if I were you."

God's beard! Any merchant in London might visit the Guild Hall. Jamie stood to leave.

"'A course that won't help you find her."

Jamie waited, nerves taut, halfway to the door.

"People say she caught wind she was going to be charged and got on a fast ship for France," Mistress Leggett said. "Must be true, for she was gone when the guard went to arrest her two days ago."

Jamie returned to Linnet's house, determined to search every inch of it. Master Woodley wrung his hands and followed on Jamie's heels, while Jamie searched from room to room.

The clerk cleared his throat as Jamie rifled through

Linnet's shifts and stockings. "Should you be looking through her...personal things, sir?"

"Goddamn it!" Jamie shouted. "She must have left a clue here somewhere."

He had looked everywhere—even under the floorboards—for something, anything, that might tell him where she had gone or who might have taken her.

"Lady Linnet would not leave London without telling me," Master Woodley said. "She is very good about keeping me informed—unlike her brother, I must say. When she goes, she always provides precise instructions on how I may exchange messages with her."

Jamie returned to the solar and dropped down onto the window seat amid Linnet's colorful pillows. *Where was she?* He held his head in his hands, trying to think.

"Truly, this is most unlike her, Sir James."

Fear gnawed at his belly, for all evidence suggested Linnet did not leave by her own choice.

Jamie looked up as Martin came into the solar, his young face taut with worry.

"I found nothing in the kitchen," Martin said. "No hidden letters, nothing out of place."

Damnation. "Tell me again, Master Woodley, what did she have you looking for regarding her grandfather's old business?"

"I was following the trail of gold," Master Woodley answered. "The path his fortune traveled—and through whose hands—all those years ago."

"What did you find?"

"The trail forked and forked and forked again. No matter which route I took, I came to a stone wall." He raised a finger. "But the same stone wall, mind you, which is telling."

"Can you not save time and simply tell me what you know? Lady Linnet may be in danger."

"All trails led to the Mercer's Hall. That is the stone wall."

"That is the oldest and most powerful of the London guilds," Martin put in.

"I am not a foreigner. I know what the mercer guild is." Jamie blew out a breath, annoyed with himself for snapping at the two of them.

The old clerk cleared his throat. "The lad is correct. Why do you suppose the mayor is most often a mercer?"

"You cannot mean the mayor of London is behind this shady business with her grandfather," Jamie said. "I know Mayor Coventry, and I do not believe it."

"I did not say he was." The way the little man raised his white brows reminded Jamie of his old tutor. "But I believe the man behind the scheme was a mercer—and a powerful member of the guild."

"Then I shall go to the Hall of the Worshipful Company of Mercers," Jamie said, rising to his feet, "and knock some heads together until someone tells me what I wish to know."

"But Sir James...," the clerk said behind him as he headed down the stairs, but Jamie was done with talking. He needed to do something, and knocking mercer heads together seemed as good as any.

Just as he reached the front door, someone pounded on the other side. He flung it open to find two girls on the step, looking up at him as if he were a wolf about to eat them.

Who the devil were they? Sisters, that much was clear, though one was still a child and the other all voluptuous curves. Their faces, however, were like mirror images, ten years apart.

He forced himself to take a deep breath and to say, "Good day to you."

"We are here to see Lady Linnet," the older one said. Her voice was breathy, and she leaned forward as she spoke.

"We've come to warn her!" the younger one shouted over her.

Perhaps the clue he'd prayed for had come in the form of these two big-eyed girls.

"Come inside, quickly," he said.

The older girl was staring at him with her mouth slightly open. When she took a step forward, the younger girl grabbed her arm and held her back.

"We do not know him," the younger girl hissed at her sister. Then to Jamie she said, "If Lady Linnet is not here, we are willin' to speak with her brother."

"He is not here either, but I am Sir James Rayburn, the man Linnet is going to marry." *If he ever got his hands on her again.*

"Then we've no time to waste," the younger girl said, pulling her sister over the threshold past Jamie. "Not if you want a wife who is aboveground."

Once they were in the solar, the girls, whose names he learned were Rose and Lily, told him what they knew.

Rose, the older girl, spoke first. "Our father agreed to help Lady Linnet."

"She had him over a barrel, 'tis why he did it," Lily put in.

Rose smoothed her skirts, then looked up at Jamie from under thick, dark lashes. "Since Father is a member of the guild and she is not, he sold her cloth under his own name for a percentage of the profit."

"He cheated her, 'a course," Lily added.

Rose gave her sister a sideways glance, then cleared her throat. "He also agreed to make inquiries—"

"Nose about, she means," Lily said, nodding. "But he never meant to."

"You do not know that, Lily," Rose said.

Lily crossed her arms. "Ha. Father lies like a—"

"Girls, please," Jamie said, putting his hands up. "Tell me what you know."

"We overheard Father talking to a man," Rose said.

"We hid under the stairs to listen," Lily said, "like we always do."

Rose's breasts rose and fell as she heaved a sigh. Jamie glanced at his squire, who was staring with open-mouthed admiration at the older girl.

"Father said that frightening Lady Linnet wasn't likely to work," Rose said.

"Aye, he says 'the only way to stop that one is to have her restin' on the bottom of the Thames,'" Lily added. "''Cause she is stubborn as an ox.'"

Rose cleared her throat again. "Father asked the other man how he wanted it done, but the man said he did not need Father's help."

"That's when the other man starts talkin' 'bout witches and sorcerers," Lily said, her eyes wide.

"Is this true?" Jamie fixed his gaze on Rose, though he knew in his soul it was.

"Aye, sir, I swear it," Rose said.

"What does this man who came to see your father look like?" Jamie asked.

"We was sent up to our bedchamber before he comes," Lily said. "An' we can't see much from under the stairs."

"But he had an old voice," Rose said.

A mercer with an old voice. God have mercy on him.

"Did he use a cane?" Master Woodley asked.

Lily nodded so vigorously, her curls bobbed. "A fancy one. All's I could see was the bottom, but it was all silvery and carved like a cat's paw."

"Could it have been a lion's paw?" Master Woodley asked.

Lily nodded again.

Where had he seen a walking stick like that? At the edge of his mind, he could see a cane and a glint of silver...

"Lady Linnet was looking for a man with a cane like that," Master Woodley said.

Jamie had believed it was Pomeroy she was intent on murdering that day at Windsor, despite her denials. But perhaps it had been someone else—this man with the silver-clawed cane.

"Who might know who this man is?" Jamie asked the clerk.

The clerk shook his head. "At Lady Linnet's instruction, I tried to bribe a couple of the others who had been involved in the scheme."

"Others? I thought you said there was one man?"

"I am persuaded that one man planned it. A very clever man. I suspect he parceled out just enough of the gold and goods to the others to get the cooperation he needed."

"Give me a name," Jamie said.

"While I could not find where the bulk of the gold went, I did discover that a small portion of it went to Alderman Arnold and to"—he cleared his throat—"Master Mychell."

"Where is your father now?" Jamie asked the girls.

Both shook their heads. Giving up their father was too much to expect of them.

"Come with me, Woodley," Jamie said, rising. "We are going to find a certain alderman."

"Wait," Lily said, leaping to her feet. "We've more to tell you!"

"Quick. Out with it."

"The man with the cane said he knows someone who'll pay *him* to get his hands on the lady. 'And once this fellow has her,' the man says, 'the whoring bitch will be no more trouble to anyone.'"

"Lily!" her sister scolded.

"That is what he said!"

Jamie squatted in front of Lily and took hold of her arms. "Did he mention this other man's name?"

"Aye, but 'twas a noble name what's hard to remember," Lily said, scrunching her face up. "Pom-o-tee? Pom-o-ray?"

Pomeroy. A chill went through Jamie, and he heard Mistress Leggett's voice in his head talking about a man driven by mad lust. Somehow Pomeroy had become connected with these merchant thieves.

"God bless you two," Jamie said, putting his hand on top of Lily's red curls. "Martin, see the girls home safely."

"We should return alone, same as we came," Rose said,

rising to her feet. "If I'm seen with a young man, Father is sure to hear of it and ask questions."

Jamie was surprised to hear that Mychell was a watchful father. But then, even rats cared for their young.

"You could use a second sword," Martin said, slanting his eyes toward the elderly clerk.

Martin was young and had no fighting experience, but he did have sharp eyes, a good sword arm—and no fear at all. And most persuasive of all, Jamie had no time to get anyone else.

"Come then," he said. "You can watch the door for me while I pay an unexpected visit."

Chapter Thirty-nine

As best Linnet could tell, two days had passed since she awoke in this room. All she had to mark the passage of time was the appearance of her keepers every few hours to bring her food and water and empty her chamber pot. There were three of them: goat, pig, and fox. At least, those were the names she gave them because of the masks they wore.

It gave her hope that they bothered with the masks. If they meant to kill her, why would they care if she saw their faces? She pushed away the thought that they might wear them to hide their identities from one another.

The first day she had made herself hoarse with screaming. When her keepers did not bother to admonish her, she understood no one could hear her and saved her strength. She made herself eat for the same reason. If they gave her a chance to escape, she would be ready. How she would escape with her leg shackled to the bed by a four-foot chain she did not know. At least her wrists and ankles were no longer tied together.

Her keepers moved about silently, ignoring her questions and entreaties as if they were deaf. They never spoke a word, until the last time they brought her a tray of food. Then, for the first time, she heard them whisper to each other.

"Tonight is the full moon."

"'Tis time then. He will come."

Who would come?

Which of her enemies would it be? Would it be the merchant she had been looking for? Though she did not know him, he would know her. After she had cornered Mychell, she had made no secret of who she was or her intention. That had been a mistake. She should have pursued him with stealth, as she had done with the merchants in Falaise and Caen. But she had grown impatient.

But how had she come to be held by witches? What was the connection between the merchants she had upset and these silent creatures in masks?

One thing was certain. Her drive for revenge had brought her to this place—alone and chained to a bed in the dark. Both Francois and Jamie had warned her again and again that her efforts were dangerous. But she had wanted justice.

Nay, she had wanted more than justice. She had wanted revenge. Was this her punishment for attempting to serve the final reckoning that belonged to God?

In the long hours on this narrow cot, she had ample time to dwell on her actions. What had she been seeking, truly? She thought she understood it now. Ironically, what she had wanted was to feel safe.

All these years she had been trying to put back the pieces of her grandfather's business—as if that would bring back her grandfather and the safety of her early childhood. His death had left her at the mercy of every sort of evil the world had to offer. She and Francois had each other, but a child needs more than another child.

Ironies abounded. By fighting to regain something lost to her forever, she had closed the door on the love and security Jamie offered her. But the truth was that she had expected to lose Jamie from the start. After losing so much else in her life, she had been afraid to let herself believe Jamie's love could be lasting.

But was it? If he did love her, why was he about to wed someone else? She tossed and turned on the narrow cot. How could he do it?

She must have eventually drifted off to sleep, for she awoke abruptly to the sound of the door closing. She sat up, her skin prickling with awareness. Someone was inside the room with her; she could feel him staring at her in the darkness.

"Who are you?" she demanded. "Show yourself."

She heard a whoosh and gasped as a flame appeared inches from her face...on the palm of an outstretched hand. The flaming hand appeared to float in the darkness, unattached to any human form. As her eyes adjusted, she discerned a sleeve above the hand and then the outline of a figure in cloak and hood.

Linnet tried telling herself it was all trickery and illusion, but her hand shook violently as she crossed herself.

The figure's hood was pulled low, making him appear faceless. Using the flame rising from his palm, he lit the candle next to her bed. Then he closed his hand in a fist, and the flame was gone.

"A marvel, is it not?"

The figure's deep voice was male and familiar. With a sweep of his arm, he threw back the hood to reveal his face. This was not a new enemy. Nay, this was the man with the oldest grudge against her.

Sir Guy Pomeroy.

"You look rather pale, my dear. Did I surprise you?" Pomeroy said. "I cannot tell you how gratifying that is."

"I should have guessed you were involved in this," she said, doing her best to keep her voice calm. "But devil-worshippers, Sir Guy? After you accused me of using dark arts to kill your uncle, that is a trifle unexpected."

"How better to divert suspicion than to accuse you of my crime?" he said, his teeth gleaming white in the dim light.

"Divert suspicion?" She sucked in her breath. "Are you saying you..."

"In ten years, it never occurred to you that I had a hand in my uncle's death?"

Why would it? Her husband seemed to have one foot in the grave from the time she met him.

"He enjoyed torturing me—parading you in front of me, when he knew how much I wanted you," he said, his voice seething with bitterness. "Then he would say you made him feel so 'young' that you were bound to be with child soon."

Linnet had no notion her husband had provoked Pomeroy with such lies. In sooth, he had been a sickly man who rarely pressed his attentions upon her during their brief marriage.

"I could not risk losing my inheritance, could I?" Pomeroy said. "You should be grateful I did not poison you as well."

"I suppose the death of a healthy sixteen-year-old would be more suspicious," she said.

"Precisely," he said, his black eyes gleaming. "That is what saved you, my dear, for I was very angry with you at the time."

Her heart pounded in her chest, for she could think of no reason that would stop him this time.

"There are those in our coven who have high ambitions—exceedingly high ambitions," he said. "To gain his assistance for what they seek, the dark angel will require a blood sacrifice of the highest order."

"You believe in this foolishness?" she blurted out.

"You have always underestimated me." Pomeroy clenched his fist and leaned so close she smelled the onions on his breath. "Do not do so now. You will soon see that all is possible when we call upon the great Lucifer and his demons."

He was serious. Her hand went to her chest. "Tell me you have not given your soul to the devil."

"I hold the power of life and death in my hands," he said, holding his hands out, palms up. "I can obtain all that I desire. First, my uncle's lands. Then, the friendship of the powerful. But I had to be tested again and again to prove my commitment before the dark lord would grant me my last desire. The thing I wanted most."

His eyes burned into her like glowing coals. "But now, at long last, I have you."

Sweat broke out on her palms, her forehead, and under her arms.

"When you learn how to call upon the dark lord," he said with a ghostly smile, "you, too, shall have all that you desire."

"Nay," she whispered. "I shall never do it."

"Your pathetic tools cannot bring you the vengeance

you seek," he said. "For all your efforts, you do not yet know who hatched the scheme against your grandfather, do you?"

When she could not find her voice to answer, he leaned close again and shouted in her face, "*Do you?*"

She swallowed and shook her head.

"But I do." He straightened and spoke in a calmer voice. "The man you seek used subterfuge and layers of intermediaries. While many merchants were aware of the scheme, only three knew who pulled the strings. So when you came to London asking questions, he was content to stay hidden and bide his time."

Linnet could not help herself. "Who were the three who knew him?"

"Leggett, Mychell, and Alderman Arnold."

No wonder the man had felt safe. Leggett was dead, Mychell hated her for driving him into debt, and Arnold would fear losing his position as alderman if his part was revealed.

"Others knew bits and pieces, but they were afraid to talk," Pomeroy said. "Besides, you were a foreigner with close ties to the queen. Everyone suspected you both of being spies for the dauphin."

Pomeroy's eye twitched as he gave her a thin smile. "But when you went to Gloucester, my dear, that changed everything. Gloucester asked a few questions. Suddenly this merchant had reason to fear the hidden threads would be revealed and spun together ... and lead to his door. He delivered you to me on a platter."

Linnet licked her lips. "How ... how did he know you wanted me?"

"Let us say, we have mutual acquaintances." His eye

twitched again. "But I shall turn on the man who gave you to me, as a serpent turns and bites his own tail, for your enemies shall be mine now."

She crossed herself again. *Mary, Mother of God, protect me.*

"Some of my brothers and sisters in darkness are angered by my decision to take you. They fear your disappearance could draw attention to us."

Was one of them Eleanor Cobham? Was that why Eleanor gave her warning?

"Others want to use you as our blood sacrifice, but I have refused them," Pomeroy said, his voice steadily rising to fill the small room. "For you are meant to be my bride in darkness, the goddess to my priest."

He was mad.

She told herself that if he meant to rape her, he could have set upon her as soon as he entered the room. Chained to the bed, she could do little to fight him. He talked of her being a bride. Did he want a ceremony of some kind to justify the deed?

"I shall never be a bride of yours," she said.

"I tell you, you are worthy," he said, his eyes glowing. "Even I did not see your special power until these last weeks. But I was right when I called you sorceress all those years ago. I see that now. I have watched how you pursue your enemies and know we are kindred spirits."

"Nay, I am not like you."

"Are you not? What has driven you? Love? Mercy?" He gave a harsh laugh. "Nay, you are filled with hatred, as I am."

But she did love. She knew with utter certainty she would give her life to protect Jamie or Francois.

Yet, the hard truth was that she did not put their happiness first. She meant to, once she had punished those who had hurt her and righted the wrongs of the past. Jamie's words came back to her, choking her: *Love is not what you consider after every other blessed thing.* She wanted to weep for her failings.

"When you cross over into darkness, we will be one with the great Lucifer," Pomeroy said, his eyes wide and staring, "and one with each other."

"If you harm me, Jamie Rayburn will kill you." Her own words surprised her, and yet as soon as she said them she knew them to be true.

Pomeroy's fingers went to a deep scar across his cheekbone that she did not recall him having before. As he traced it with his fingertips, his eyes scorched over her.

Then he lunged for her. She screamed and tried to scramble to the far side of the bed, but he caught her and hauled her toward him. Bile rose in her throat as he held her with his face against hers, his greasy hair pressed to her cheek.

"Tonight I shall cast the spell, and you will accept your place at my side," he said, his hot breath in her ear. "Until then, I shall have to restrain you."

"Jamie!" she screamed.

The cloth was over her mouth, the distinctive medicinal odor filling her nose and mouth and numbing her lips.

"James Rayburn will be dead soon," he said against her ear. "And you will think of him no more."

Chapter Forty

Jamie rode across the City, his mind on that day in November when he and Francois had seen Linnet approach the fat alderman in Westminster Hall. That was also the day he and Linnet had begun their affair. Those few days in her London house had sealed his fate. Though he had tried to fight it, he was hers from that time forward.

Nay, he'd been hers since Paris. He had loved the girl who defied convention and dragged him behind the shrubbery...the girl who looked him in the eye and told him she loved how he touched her...the girl who ignored her father's attempts to restrict her and refused to meet his expectations.

But the girl was nothing compared to the woman Linnet had become. She was fierce in her loyalty, awesome in her determination, courageous, clever, and witty. None could match her. God had given him a second chance with this beautiful, avenging angel of a woman, and what had he done? He'd left her at the first sign of trouble.

Please, God, let me find her. Once he did, he would never let her out of his sight again.

"Master Woodley," he called over his shoulder to the

clerk, who followed on a pathetic mule, "where precisely in the Cheape is Alderman Arnold's house?"

"Not far from Saddlers' Hall and Saint Paul's Cathedral."

When they reached the alderman's house, a prosperous-looking, three-story wooden structure, the servant who answered the door insisted Arnold was not home.

Jamie pushed past him, saying, "I shall see for myself."

"Sir, you cannot—"

"Martin, hold him while I have a look about," he said without looking back.

Other servants trailed him as he went from room to room searching for his quarry; none made the mistake of attempting to stop him.

When he entered the largest bedchamber on the second floor and found it empty, he cursed in frustration. "Damnation, where is that overripe snipe!"

He turned to find a maid with a saucy look about her leaning in the doorway. She slanted a look toward the huge wooden-framed bed and pointed at the floor. Jamie nodded his thanks and motioned for her to leave. Dropping to one knee, he reached under the bed and hauled the alderman out by his tunic.

"God's blood, you are a sorry excuse for a man," Jamie said as he held the alderman against the bedpost. "Tell me who was involved in the scheme to destroy Lady Linnet's grandfather."

"That was ten years ago," the alderman said, his eyes darting about the room. "You cannot expect me to recall it."

"I can and I do." Jamie lifted the man off his feet. "If

you want to live, you will tell me what you know. I want names."

"You would not dare harm me. I am an alderman!"

Jamie slammed him against the bedpost. "I am a desperate man, Alderman, and I've killed better men than you. Pray, do not test my patience further."

Good God, the man was wetting himself! Jamie dropped him and took a step back in disgust.

"It was Brokely, the mayor's father-in-law, who was behind it all," the alderman said in a high voice. "The rest of us played small parts or turned a blind eye—and profited very little."

"Did Mayor Coventry know of this?" Jamie demanded.

The alderman shook his head. "Coventry was not mayor then, of course. But he would not have countenanced it, if he had known. No one knew his father-in-law was behind it, save for me, Mychell, and Leggett."

"But you led others to believe the mayor had been party to it, did you not?"

When the alderman was slow to answer, Jamie pulled his dagger and touched the point to the man's throat.

"Aye, we did," the alderman squeaked.

"And when Lady Linnet came asking questions, you spread the word that there would be trouble if the truth came out."

"And it would cause great trouble, indeed," the alderman said, raising his eyebrows. "The King's Council will take any excuse to remove the restrictions on foreign merchants, and that would destroy us."

"Where can I find the mayor's father-in-law?"

"Brokely retired to his estate a few miles outside the

city several years ago. He is in poor health and travels little."

"All the same, he visited Mychell's house recently, did he not?"

The alderman's eyes shifted from side to side. "I would not know about that..."

"Do not leave your house tonight," Jamie said, jabbing his finger into the man's chest. "And for God's sake, wash yourself before I come back for you."

Jamie sent Master Woodley to wait at Linnet's house and left Martin to watch the alderman's house.

"If he leaves, I want to know where he goes," he ordered. "But do not follow him inside any buildings. You are to stay out of trouble, stay out of sight, and keep your distance. Do you hear me?"

Martin nodded.

Jamie rode at a full gallop for Brokely's estate, cursing himself for not helping Linnet get to the bottom of the plot earlier. She could squeeze their purses, but some men only did as they ought with a blade at their throat.

It was growing dusk when he finally reached Brokely's enormous manor house on a quiet stretch of the Thames. Since a house this size would have a great many servants and guards, he could not push his way through the front door as he had at the alderman's. Instead, he tied his horse and worked his way to the house through the shrubs and tall reeds along the riverbank. The wind still held the bite of winter, but there was a hint of spring behind it.

The growing darkness put him on edge, and a sense of urgency nipped at his heels. Soon—he must find her soon.

Here in the heart of England, defenses were minimal

and guards lax. On his second try, Jamie found an unlocked door and slipped inside. He had learned from his uncle Stephen that if you acted as though you had a right to be in a place, no one was likely to question you.

Jamie passed some men talking among themselves as they put their tools away for the day. They barely spared him a glance as he crossed the yard and entered the house from the back.

'Twas a different matter when he burst through the doors to the hall. Every servant turned to stare as he stood at the entrance, his sword in his hand. An old man sat alone wrapped in a blanket next to the hearth.

"Brokely, your son-in-law sent me," Jamie said, deciding to get the information he needed through subterfuge this time. "I suggest you send the servants away while we talk."

"How did you get into my hall? Who are you?" The old man pounded his cane on the floor as he shouted. It was a distinctive silver-clawed cane.

"The mayor believes you know the whereabouts of Lady Linnet," Jamie said.

Brokely's eyebrows flew up. A moment later, he waved the servants off with his swollen, knobby hands, saying, "Shoo! Shoo!"

Jamie sighed. Pressuring old men and soft merchants was unpleasant. Give him a good fight against a worthy opponent any day.

"Your son-in-law has learned of what you did to Lady Linnet's family," Jamie said.

"'Tis high time Coventry knew and gave me proper thanks," the old man said, banging his cane again. "If not for my fortune, he would not be mayor today. And I'm not ashamed of what I did to get it. 'Twas only because my daughter insisted, that I kept quiet."

So the mayor's wife knew—and the mayor did not.

"Was it she who gave you that fine cane? It must have cost her a pretty penny."

"She, at least, is grateful for all I've done for her."

"Then she must be grateful to her husband as well, for she gave him a cane just like it," Jamie said.

"Bah. I don't know why she set her sights on that prattling dog. But 'twas my money that bought him for her."

"Money you stole from an honest man who had fallen ill," Jamie said. "Have you no shame for that?"

"He was a foreigner who made far too much profit than ought to be allowed on English soil." Brokely shook his head. "I only wish I could have done it sooner. But that foreign devil was a clever bastard."

"The mayor says that if you wish to see your daughter and grandchildren again," Jamie said, taking his lie a step further, "you will tell me what has happened to Lady Linnet."

"He would not dare."

"You know damned well he would," Jamie said. "I suspect that is why your daughter kept it from him all these years."

"Coventry always did have a pole up his arse, the self-righteous fool." The old man spat on the floor. "The ungrateful son of a—"

"Tell me now!" Jamie shouted. "What have you done with Lady Linnet?"

"I'll tell you, but it will do you no good now." Brokely turned his gaze to the darkened window. "'Tis the full moon tonight. You are too late."

*   *   *

Linnet heard the chanting in her dream before she awoke. The pounding rhythm pulsed through her, increasing the violent pain in her head. A familiar dankness clung to her skin and was heavy in the air she breathed. She came to full wakefulness in a sweat of fear, knowing where she was: behind the secret door at Winchester Palace, where the witches met.

At first, she was too frightened to open her eyes. The flicker of candlelight and shadows played against her eyelids. She took in a slow breath, then opened her eyes a crack.

Even though she expected to see them, she gasped at the sight of the figures whirling and twisting within a ring of candles on the floor. As before, the figures wore grisly masks and animal hides.

She lay outside the circle, on the dirt floor against the wall. The chill of the ground and the sweat of fear caused goose bumps to rise on her skin. When she looked down, she saw that she was draped in a thin red silk cloth. She swallowed; she was naked beneath it.

Nay, she would not let herself think of how she had become undressed, of what hands had touched her. Not now. All her thoughts must be on escape. So long as they did not drug her again, she could hope to get away. It was a thin thread of hope, but she held on to it.

In the deep shadow against the wall, she could watch the circle unnoticed. In the center, there were two tables, one large, one small. The larger one was covered in black cloth, as before—except that no naked woman lay on it this time, praise God. On the second table, steam rose from a pot cooking over a small brazier.

Linnet drew in a sharp breath as a tall figure entered the circle from the far side of the room. *The wolf-man*.

She dug her nails into her palms as the wolf-man lifted a wriggling rabbit in one hand and a long black-handled knife in his other. With a sweep of his arm, he sliced the animal's head off.

Mary, Mother of God, protect me. Over and over, she repeated her prayer as the wolf-man used the bleeding carcass to draw a triangle in blood along the ground. His voice rose above the others in the chant as he performed the ceremony.

A chill went through her—she knew that voice. The wolf-man was Sir Guy Pomeroy.

Pomeroy took a white-handled knife from the table and cut herbs of some kind into the boiling pot. While he worked, the others gyrated around the circle, singing. Pomeroy lifted the pot with long metal tongs and poured the steaming liquid into a painted wooden bowl. Then he walked around the larger table dribbling liquid from the bowl onto the ground.

When he completed the circle, he held the bowl high over his head and turned in a circle, calling out "earth," "air," "fire," "water," in each quadrant. Then he poured the remaining liquid onto the ground.

There were two entrances, both at the far corners of the room, beyond the circle. Linnet intended to get to one of them and escape. Her limbs felt sluggish from the bitter liquid she remembered someone pouring down her throat, but she was unbound. She rolled onto her stomach and began to inch her way over the ground.

Her attention was drawn back to the center of the circle as a woman joined Pomeroy. Linnet remembered the woman's bird mask and black curls. This was the woman who had lain naked on the table last time—the woman who had had sexual congress with the wolf-man right before Linnet's eyes. God have mercy, she did not want to see that again.

And now, Linnet knew who the woman was—Margery Jourdemayne, the Witch of Eye.

Linnet began crawling faster. Then, without warning, Margery fell prostrate on the ground. Linnet went still as the room fell silent and all the dancers stopped to watch Margery.

Pomeroy raised his arms. In a deep voice that reverberated against the walls of the cavelike room, he called out, "*Conjuro te!*"

Margery thrashed about on the ground making strange sounds. Then she grew still. Slowly, she lifted her head, her eyes bulging. In a voice that sounded more like an animal's growl than human, she said, "*Adsum!*"

Linnet knew just enough Latin to know this meant, "I am present." But who was present? She ignored the shiver that went up her spine and set her mind to slipping past the group while their attention was on Margery.

"What fate awaits the bishop with tainted royal blood?" Pomeroy called out.

Why would he ask about Bishop Beaufort? And just who was he asking? And then she knew: The witches were conjuring the dead. In addition to their other sins, they were necromancers.

"John of Gaunt's bastard shall wear the red cardinal's hat," Margery said in her rasping animal voice, "and die an old man."

Linnet could not wait to hear more, from the living or the dead. She crept forward, her belly just off the ground.

Pomeroy's voice rang out above her. "What of the boy-king? What is his fate?"

Linnet halted in place and held her breath. Asking this question of the dead was not just heresy, but treason.

"He shall go mad and be king two times," Margery said in her slow, rough voice. "He shall die with a pillow to his face."

King twice, mad and murdered?

"Spirit, can you tell us the day and hour of his death?"

Linnet's blood froze in her veins at the menace in Pomeroy's voice. For a certainty, these sorcerers meant the child harm.

"Many years! Many years!" The words spewed forth from Margery's mouth as she fell to thrashing about on the ground again.

There was a rumble of low voices and shuffling of feet; the witches were not pleased with this last answer.

Linnet scooted forward a few more inches. From the corner of her eye, she watched Pomeroy go to the small table and stick his blade into the steaming pot. When he lifted it, a waxen shape was skewered on the end of it.

With a flick of his wrist, he flung the waxen image to the ground and shouted, "Cut short the life!"

Suddenly, voices swelled and filled the room. "Cut short the life! Cut short the life!"

This was an evil Linnet could not fathom: a wish to hasten a child's death. And the child they wished to harm was the great King Henry's heir, his only living legacy. Her friend's four-year-old son.

This evil must be stopped before they harmed the young king. She must escape and give warning.

The chanting echoed in the room and inside her head, repetitive and pulsing as she crept behind them. She moved slowly, hampered by the effort to keep the flimsy red silk wrapped about her.

"Descend into the darkness and the burning lake!" Pomeroy shouted in a voice like thunder.

Linnet dropped flat on her stomach as silence descended upon the room once more. She prayed none of the witches noticed that she was several feet from where they had left her.

Into the silence, a woman said, "To change so strong a prediction will require a blood sacrifice."

An argument ensued, with repeated calls for a "blood sacrifice." Then a single voice—Pomeroy's—rose above all the others.

"Bring the prisoner to the altar!"

Chapter Forty-one

Jamie rode hard for Winchester, the bright moonlight on the London Road serving as a constant reminder of the danger Linnet was in. Sorcerers and witches! He crossed himself and beseeched God to protect her.

When he reached the bishop's palace, the guards recognized him and let him in.

"Where is Edmund Beaufort?" he asked.

"In the privy chamber," one of the guards answered.

"I know my way," Jamie said and hurried past them.

Edmund stood to greet him. After one look at Jamie's face, he dismissed the men who were with him. As soon as they were alone, Edmund asked, "Have you news of Lady Linnet? We expected her to seek sanctuary, not disappear."

"She is in dire danger," Jamie said. "There is no time to explain, but I must know how to enter the secret passage in Westminster Palace. No matter what your uncle told me, I believe he knows how to gain entry to it. I pray to God he shared the secret with you."

While Jamie spoke, Edmund poured two cups of wine from a silver pitcher on the table.

"Even if I could admit to having such knowledge," Edmund said as he handed one of the cups to Jamie, "you cannot expect me to tell you."

Red wine splattered across the table and against the wall as Jamie knocked the proffered cup from Edmund's hand.

"Did you not hear me? She is in danger!" he shouted. "Pomeroy and a cabal of witches have her in the bowels of the palace. If you know how to enter the passageway, for God's sake, tell me!"

Edmund's rapid blinking was the only sign he was taken aback by this extraordinary news. "If someone has taken her there, then a member of the royal family has shared the palace secrets," Edmund said. "I promise you it was not a Beaufort."

"I suspect Gloucester told his mistress, and that Eleanor told Pomeroy," Jamie said. "These are devil-worshippers, Edmund. I must get to her without delay."

Edmund blew out a breath. "If Eleanor is involved in some way, it would be...unfortunate...if either I or my uncle's men were the ones to discover her. With the tension between Gloucester and my uncle, matters could quickly get out of control."

At the moment, Jamie did not care if all of England went down in flames.

Edmund paused, then said, "What I'm asking is, if I get you into the secret passageway, will that be sufficient help?"

"Just get me in, Edmund. That is all I ask," Jamie said. "Now we must go."

When they stopped for Martin on their way to Westminster, Master Woodley informed Jamie that his squire had never returned to Linnet's house.

Where in the hell was Martin? He should have returned hours ago. It wasn't like the lad to disappear. As soon as Jamie rescued Linnet, he would have to go looking for his squire.

Damn and blast, he needed a lookout.

Jamie looked down from his horse at the elderly clerk. Clearly, God was testing him—making him prove his worth by giving him such unlikely tools to work with. He held his arm out to Master Woodley and hoisted him up behind his saddle.

They rode on to Westminster. In the distance, Jamie heard the chimes of Westminster Abbey ringing for matins.

It was midnight.

At the sound of a loud commotion outside the doorway, the chanting came to an abrupt halt. Linnet fell back to the ground, hope thrumming through every vein. *Somehow Jamie has learned of my capture and has come to save me. Please, God!*

Several of the witches ran out in the direction of the noise. From her place on the floor, Linnet watched the doorway through half-closed eyes, her every muscle strained with tension. Over the thunder of her heartbeat, she heard sounds of a scuffle outside, followed by shouting.

A short time later, a new witch in a dog's pelt entered. The others came in behind him, holding someone in their midst. Linnet was so startled to see who it was that she nearly shouted his name aloud.

"Who is this intruder?" a woman in a goat's hide asked.

"I know him." Pomeroy's commanding voice was cold with anger. "How, pray tell, did Sir James's squire find the river entrance to the passage?"

"He must have followed me."

Linnet recognized the voice as Alderman Arnold's, though he wore the dog's pelt, rather than his usual colorful attire. "Sir James paid me a visit earlier and must have left his squire to keep an eye on my house."

"You fool!" Pomeroy said. "Where is Sir James? Did you lead him to us as well?"

Linnet prayed with all her might that Jamie would charge through the doorway behind them.

"Sir James shall come," Martin shouted as he struggled against the men who held him. "And when he does, he shall kill every one of you."

Give her a blade, and Linnet would help him. Gladly.

"We shan't be seeing Sir James this night," the alderman said in a self-satisfied tone. "I sent him on a fool's errand miles outside of London."

Linnet's spirits plummeted like a boulder down a cliff.

"Bind him," Pomeroy ordered.

Poor Martin! He fought like a young lion, but there were a half dozen on him and soon they had him bound.

"It appears we have our blood sacrifice after all," Pomeroy said.

God no, not this sweet young man.

A burst of righteous fury burned through Linnet as two of the devil-worshippers tossed Martin's trussed body on the ground next to her as if he were an animal carcass. She wanted to rip these masked devils apart with her bare hands.

Martin landed with his face just inches from hers. She looked into his wild eyes and wished she could pull him into her arms and comfort him.

She waited to speak until their captors began their chanting again. "Hold still while I work on your ropes. They must believe I am still asleep from the drug they gave me."

He nodded a fraction to show he understood.

The fools had tied his hands in front of him. She felt for an end of the rope and began to work it loose.

"You must close your eyes and ears if they take me," she said. "Whatever they do to me, they do not intend to kill me."

"Sir James will come," he whispered. "I know he will."

"That is why you must wait to act, no matter what you think they may be doing. Do not risk wasting your chance before Jamie comes...unless they come for you."

She stared into his eyes until he gave her a reluctant nod.

The chanting grew louder, making her head throb as she worked feverishly on the knots.

"Goddess! Goddess! Goddess!"

The new chant sent frissons of terror through the taut nerves of her body. Soon they would come for her.

Finally! The first knot came loose, and she began to work on the second. She nearly had him free when Martin hissed between his teeth, "Lady Linnet."

Just in time, she stilled her hands and closed her eyes. Her heart thundered in her chest as arms draped in animal skins grabbed hold of her. She moaned and let her head flop to the side as the two men in smelly furs lifted her.

"Goddess! Goddess! Goddess!"

By what perversion did they think her goddess?

The tops of her bare feet scraped on the rough dirt floor as they dragged her to the center of the circle. All about her, the voices shouted, "Goddess! Goddess! Goddess!"

Linnet awoke, dazed, lying on her back on the table at the center of the circle. They must have held the cloth to her face again. She struggled to shake off her grogginess and sit up, but her hands were tied to the table. When she tried to move her legs, she found that they were tied, too, so that her knees were bent.

A current of cool air touched her skin...

It could not be so. She slit her eyes and saw her own bare breasts, the nipples erect with cold. She closed her eyes.

The Virgin protect her. They had her naked. Never had she felt so vulnerable. Even when she and François were children and cornered by rough soldiers in an empty house, she had not felt this helpless. Or so utterly alone.

She fought to keep her features smooth, though she wanted to wail and weep in her despair. From beneath her lashes, she watched Pomeroy refill the bowl from the steaming pot on the brazier. The others were doing their mad dance around the circle again, their eerie shadows playing on the cavelike walls behind them. Their chanting filled her head, pounded through her veins.

God give her strength! She remembered the rest of the

ceremony all too vividly. She recalled precisely what the wolf-man had done to Margery while she lay on the altar table. But Margery had been a willing participant in the play.

Pomeroy turned and lifted the bowl high above his head. As he walked toward her, panic welled up in her chest and shot through her limbs. He came to a halt beside her. His burning eyes scorched over her skin, taking in every intimate curve and line.

I am strong enough to live through this. I will survive until Jamie comes. I will!

It was too late to save her from what Pomeroy was about to do to her, so she devoted her prayer to Martin. *Please, God, let Jamie come before they kill the boy.*

Pomeroy rested the warm wooden bowl on her belly, then went to stand at the base of the table. Tied down as she was, she could not fight him. She lifted her gaze to meet his and let him see the loathing in her eyes.

"I curse you to hell for this," she said between her teeth.

"You shall know who defiles you," Pomeroy said, his voice rising. "Who fills you with the spirit of a demon. Who weds you in the sight of the great Lucifer himself!"

The others in the room gasped as the wolf-man pulled off his mask and flung it across the room. But Linnet had known who the wolf-man was all along.

Sir Guy Pomeroy, gone mad.

The witches took up their chant again. Amid their rising voices, Linnet began to shake. Nay, she could not do this.

Pomeroy raised his arms out like a massive bird,

spreading the wolf skin wide. Beneath it, he was naked, his member swollen and erect. Linnet bit her lip and tasted blood.

Pomeroy's glowing black eyes locked with hers as he shouted, "I shall make you my goddess!"

Chapter Forty-two

"The steps are steep," Edmund warned as he held the secret panel open for them. "God go with you."

"I'll not forget this." Jamie clasped Edmund's arm before ducking through the doorway.

Edmund glanced up and down the hall as Jamie helped Master Woodley through. One day Jamie would laugh at how he'd gone into the battle of his life with only an old man as his comrade in arms. But not today.

Edmund closed the door, and Jamie heard a distant, eerie chanting.

"Remember," Jamie said as he fixed his torch into the brace in the wall, "you are to wait here at the top of the stairs. If I do not return, go to Edmund Beaufort."

Jamie clambered down the long flight of stairs and hit the dirt floor at a run. Almost at once, he lost the light from the torch and had to slacken his pace. He followed the chanting through the darkness, Linnet's description of the witches' sabbat vivid in his head.

Lord, let me be in time to save her.

The tunnel must be taking him close to the river. A

dank smell filled his nose, and he was splashing through puddles.

There was now light ahead. The passageway opened up into a larger area, lit by flickering candlelight, just as Linnet had described it to him. As he approached, he slowed his steps and pulled his sword. He paused in the shadows outside the entrance to observe his enemy before making his attack.

God in heaven! Rage and fear roared through him at the sight of Linnet lying naked on the table. Every muscle screamed to charge in blindly, sword swinging. But he forced himself to keep his head, because he must to save her.

In a flash, he took in the rest of the room: the dozen fiends thrashing and swaying to their blasphemous chant; a woman prostrate on the floor, arms outstretched; a man in wolf's hide and mask, at Linnet's feet.

He scanned the room for weapons. Four swords leaned against the wall opposite, next to a second entrance. Only four, though some of the devil-worshippers could have shorter blades hidden beneath their strange attire.

Jamie's goal was simple: to put himself and his sword between Linnet and her captors. These foul demon-lovers would have to kill him to get to her. And he did not intend to die today. He was going to grow old with that woman on the table.

He took one step forward before a movement near the far wall caught his eye. What he had thought was a pile of clothing was a second captive.

His heart froze. God in heaven, how did Martin get in this place? Rescuing the two of them would not be easy.

The wolf-man raised his arms and shouted. Jamie could not hear the words above the chanting; he did not need to.

The wolf-man would be the first to die.

The chanting suddenly changed to shouts of alarm. Linnet turned her head in time to see Jamie leap into the room, sword flashing. The witches scattered before him like boys before a charging bull. In an instant, he was beside the table, facing outward, sword in one hand and dagger in the other. With a slash of his dagger, he cut the rope that bound her right wrist.

"Take it," he said without turning, and she felt the weight of the hilt of his dagger in her palm.

As soon as she closed her hand around it, Jamie drew a second dagger from the back of his belt. His sword whistled over her, and a scream pierced the air as it sliced someone reaching for her from the other side.

Linnet cut through the rope holding her other wrist and sat up to free her ankles. As she worked, Jamie moved around the table, slashing at any who dared come close. She severed the last rope and yanked at the black drape beneath her, intent on covering herself from the filthy eyes of the devil-worshippers.

Jamie's cape fell over her. A rush of gratitude choked her as she touched her fingers to his back. "Thank God you have come."

Jamie had found her. They were outnumbered and surrounded by black-hearted men and women who consorted with the devil. But with Jamie here, all else was possible.

The sorcerers began closing in, their numbers giving

them false courage. But where was Pomeroy? It worried her that she could not see him, for he was by far the most dangerous.

A man in a sheepskin took a step too close and fell with a gurgling scream, blood pouring from his neck and soaking his white fleece red. Another grabbed at her from behind. No sooner did she feel the man's hand clasp her arm than Jamie's sword struck the man's side. The man dropped to his knees, his mouth moving like a fish caught onshore.

Jamie was a deadly, whirling force, whipping his sword back and forth as he moved around the table. By now, the witches stayed well back to escape his blade.

But Pomeroy had not fled to the river. He and three other men pushed past the other sorcerers, carrying broadswords. These four were not soft-bellied merchants unused to fighting. Nay, they carried their swords with the practiced ease of warriors.

Four swordsmen. Linnet did not like the odds.

She got to her knees and whispered close to Jamie's ear. "Pomeroy is their leader. If you take him, the others may lose heart."

He nodded a fraction. "He is a dead man."

Linnet knew she was a hindrance; Jamie would not leave her to attack Pomeroy while the others were circling her.

"We must back up to the wall where Martin is," Jamie said in a low voice. "I will hold them back while you cut his ropes."

Suddenly, there was a shout and a blur of movement as Martin shot out across the room. He barreled into several of the witches, taking them to the floor with him. Before anyone else could act, Jamie reached into the heap of bodies and pulled Martin out by the back of his tunic.

Linnet had not seen Jamie use his blade, but two more men in hides lay screaming and bleeding on the floor. Three female witches, including Margery Jourdemayne, fled out the doorway that led to the river.

"Guard Linnet," Jamie ordered as he handed Martin his sword. "Now get your backs to that wall."

Now was not a time to argue. Linnet slid down from the table and, holding Jamie's cloak about her with one hand and his dagger in the other, backed up to the wall with Martin.

Her heart was in her throat. Jamie stood alone with only his short blade as the four swordsmen came toward him. In one quick move, Jamie lunged for the alderman and then tossed him through the air at the four swordsmen. Pomeroy sidestepped in time, but two of the swordsmen fell back as the alderman slammed into them. As soon as the alderman gained his feet, he scrambled toward the doorway that led to the river.

"The alderman will get away!" Martin said, but she grabbed his arm.

"Jamie said to stay here."

The other sorcerers who were still standing—save for the four swordsmen—exchanged glances and then scurried out behind the alderman.

"I will find you and kill you!" Jamie shouted after them.

Linnet felt the tension of the four swordsmen as they moved as a group toward Jamie. Pomeroy was on the far left, a silver-handled sword gleaming in his hand.

Though Jamie faced them with nothing but a short

dagger, he showed no fear. Nay, he was angry. Seething with it.

"Martin, take her out," Jamie ordered without turning around. "Get her to safety, and I will take care of these foul Satan-lovers."

"I will not leave you!" she cried.

The swordsmen's eyes went to her, and Jamie sprang forward. In an instant, he drove his dagger into the belly and up under the breastbone of the closest swordsman. Just as quickly, he withdrew the dripping blade and stepped back with the man's sword in his other hand.

As Pomeroy and the other two inched closer with their swords raised, Jamie again positioned himself in front of her and Martin.

"Kill the boy, and hold the goddess for me," Pomeroy told his companions. "We must complete the ceremony before dawn."

"You wanted to see Lucifer," Jamie hissed. "And now you shall—for all eternity."

When Jamie attacked, fighting all three in a whirl of shining blades, Linnet could not take her eyes off him. Despite the danger, she was captivated by the sheer beauty of Jamie in motion. He was a warrior's warrior, a fighter of grace and strength, with honed skills and controlled fury.

In contrast, the sorcerers were hideous, half-naked heathens in dark hides.

Jamie's sword was a blur, first high and then low, left then right, in front and behind. Not one of them could get past him. Then he lunged, and Pomeroy went down with a scream that made the hairs on Linnet's arms and neck stand up. Pomeroy dragged himself a few feet, leaving a dark swath of blood behind him, before collapsing for good.

Linnet stared at his still form, bleeding out on the dirt floor, not quite believing it. After all these years, she was safe from him forever.

A table crashed, drawing her attention back to the fight. Jamie and the two remaining swordsmen went up and down the room, swords clanking. When they came near, Martin raised his sword, ready to enter the fray.

"Stay with her!" Jamie roared. "If one gets past me, you must be ready."

A moment later, Jamie got caught between the two. He ducked in time to avoid a fatal blow, but blood dripped from a long gash down his side. Linnet felt as if a hand squeezed her heart as he stumbled and shook his head to clear it.

Enough of this. "Martin, which one shall we take?"

"The one on the left."

"Aaargh!" She and Martin shouted as they ran forward together.

The man turned at the sound, and Jamie's sword hit his throat with such force it nearly severed his head from his body. As the last man charged from behind, Jamie spun around and impaled his dagger in the man's chest.

Linnet stood in the middle of the room, clenching her dagger in her fist. But it was over. Bodies littered the floor around her.

The dagger fell from her hand, and she dropped to her knees. She covered her face with shaking hands. God be praised, they were all three alive.

Jamie rested his hand lightly on her head. "'Tis all right

now, love," he said in a soft voice. "Come, let us leave this evil place."

He sheathed his sword and lifted her to her feet.

"No matter how long it takes, I shall track down every one who escaped and punish them for what they did to you," he said, holding her face in his hands. "I shall gouge out the eyes of every man who saw you before I cut his throat."

"Please, Jamie," she whispered, "I just want to leave it behind me."

"I swear," Martin said, and Linnet turned to see that he was stepping back up with his hands up. "I did not look at her when she was naked. Not once."

Jamie did not ask how the lad knew she was naked, but he gave Martin a look that would skin a cat.

"Let him be," Linnet said, putting her hand on Jamie's arm. "Martin did well here today."

"You and I will talk later about how you failed to follow my instructions," Jamie said to Martin, then pointed toward the passageway that led into Westminster. "Master Woodley is waiting at the top of the stairs. Run ahead and tell him all is well before his heart fails him."

Jamie enveloped her in his arms and buried his face in her hair. "God forgive me, I was almost too late to save you both."

"I knew you would come."

When she slipped her arms around his waist, her fingers touched the wet stickiness of blood, and the breath went out of her.

She leaned back to look at him. "Are you badly hurt?"

"Nothing worse than a usual day's fighting," he said, giving her a cocky grin.

Reassured, she started to smile back—and then screamed. Pomeroy had risen from the dead and was charging toward them with his blade leveled at Jamie's back.

Jamie grabbed the back of her neck and pushed her hard to the floor. She fell flat on her stomach. The black-handled knife was before her face, where it had fallen when the table crashed. She moved on instinct. The knife was in her hand as she surged to her knees with her arm outstretched.

She fell backward from the impact as her blade met Pomeroy's belly. Pomeroy swayed above her, his face ashen and blood seeping from between his lips.

Reaching his bloody hand out to her, he whispered, "You were . . . meant . . . to be . . . my goddess . . ."

As she watched, the life left his eyes. Then his body spun sideways and fell with a thump on the ground beside her.

A second blade was in his chest.

"I had him," Jamie shouted as he hauled her to her feet. "By all the saints, Linnet, what were you doing?"

She swallowed back the tears that suddenly choked her. In a high voice that shook, she said, "I was trying to save you."

Jamie wrapped his cloak more tightly around her and pulled her against him. How close he had been to losing her. He breathed in the smell of her hair and closed his eyes.

She was trying to save him. What was he to do with a woman who would act like that? A woman who would throw herself in the way of danger for him without a second thought?

He would love her forever. That was what he would do.

Chapter Forty-three

*L*innet rested her head on the edge of the wooden tub as Jamie sat behind her, running an ivory comb through her hair. After an hour of soaking, the smell of her captivity was gone from her skin, and she felt almost clean.

"You make a fine lady's maid," she said without opening her eyes.

Jamie stopped combing her hair to pour a fresh bucket of steaming water into the tub, then moved his stool to the other end of the tub and began kneading her foot.

"That feels heavenly," she murmured.

The hot water and Jamie's ministrations were the perfect antidote to her ordeal with Pomeroy and the witches.

"'Tis almost dawn," he said. "We should get you to bed."

Linnet had insisted on waiting at Westminster while Jamie took some of Edmund Beaufort's men to track down Alderman Arnold and Margery Jourdemayne. After finding them, he had awakened the mayor to have them arrested.

"We shall have to testify against them," Jamie said in a quiet voice. "The mayor assured me, however, that it will not be a public trial. Everyone—the mayor, Gloucester, the Beauforts—has an interest in keeping this quiet."

Jamie took her hand, encompassing it in the warmth and strength of his own.

"I should have helped you set things right before." Jamie looked away, clenching his jaw, then brought his gaze back to her. "I will do whatever you ask to remedy it now."

"What could I have you do?" She gave him a soft smile. "Take away Lily and Rose's house? Ruin Mistress Leggett's trade? Malign the good mayor's character? They are innocents. Even if they profited from the wrong, it would give me no satisfaction to punish them."

Jamie pressed his lips together and nodded. "Brokely is dying, so we shall have to leave him to make his accounting to God. The mayor, however, has offered to make whatever compensation you think just for what his father-in-law did."

Linnet shook her head. "There is nothing I want from the mayor."

She thought of how her enemies had joined forces against her and covered her face with her hands. "How did Brokely and Pomeroy find each other?"

Jamie gently pulled one hand free and pressed a kiss to her palm. "Most likely it was the alderman, as he was both a member of the coven and party to the merchant conspiracy." He paused, then said, "Yet I suspect Eleanor Cobham played some part in bringing them together. She knew Pomeroy through Gloucester, and she is closely tied to Margery Jourdemayne."

"I cannot prove it, but I believe Eleanor and that priest of hers are involved with this sorcery," Linnet said, and then she told him about Father Hume's warning to leave for France. "Eleanor must have disagreed with Pomeroy's plan to kidnap me out of fear it would go wrong and expose her."

Jamie poured another bucket of steaming water into the tub and began to rub her calf.

"What will happen to the alderman and Margery?" she asked.

"They and the others who are caught will be held in royal custody at Windsor," he said. "It does not seem near enough."

"I hope you do not feel you must gouge out the alderman's eyes and slit his throat," she said, attempting a smile. "He is too pathetic to be worth the trouble."

"I would do it if it would help you forget what happened tonight," he said. "I would kill them all for you."

"I've wasted too many years seeking revenge," she said. "Vengeance will not satisfy me."

"What then?" he asked, brushing his knuckles against her cheek. "Whatever it is, I will do it."

"If I promise to be a staid wife who never causes you trouble or worry, will you marry me?"

He shook his head. "The only woman I shall marry is the wild and troublesome one I've loved since she was a girl."

She got up on her knees and embraced him, soaking his shirt. She tasted the salt of her tears in the water that dripped down her face.

"I shall try not to vex you so much in the future," she said into his neck.

"My family will be gravely disappointed if you do

not," he said. "They fear that without you to prod me, I am bound to grow dull and tedious."

"You shall never be that," she said.

"Since I don't expect you to change..." He leaned back and pulled a pendant on a silver chain from the pouch at his belt. "I want you to wear this again. I've mended the chain."

She swallowed against the well of emotion that closed her throat and made her eyes sting. It was the medal of Saint George he had given her before.

"I found it on the ground near Saint Stephen's Chapel," he said as he slipped it over her head. "An angel must have guided my footsteps."

Jamie always had the angels on his side.

"After we go to Hertford and see Owen and Queen Katherine married, I'd like to take you to Northumberland to meet my new uncle and his wife. If you like Northumberland, we will make our home there."

"Wherever you are shall be my home."

Jamie wrapped a towel around her and rested his hands on her shoulders. "I will stand between you and any threat of harm, and I shall be at your side in times of joy and sorrow."

She felt the warmth of his breath on her cheek as he kissed her. "Now 'tis time for you to rest."

Linnet wiped her teary face on the towel. "You asked what you could do to make me forget what happened."

"Anything."

"Then take me to bed," she said. "Give me a child."

He made love to her slowly, with a tenderness he had not shown her since their days in Paris. With every touch, he made her feel she was precious to him. There would always be times when their passion would run hot and urgent, but this sweet tenderness was what she needed now.

Afterward, she lay in the arms of the man who would be her ballast in stormy seas and her shelter in times of trouble.

"Tell me a tale of one of your victories," she murmured against his chest.

As Jamie told his tale, she imagined him in his graceful warrior's dance, swinging high and low with his sword, the strongest and most handsome knight on the field.

Dawn was bright in the window as she drifted off to sleep, her heart at peace at last.

Epilogue

Northumberland
1431

When Jamie crested the hill and saw the square keep that once belonged to Charles Wheaton, contentment spread through him like warm honey. Tenants working in a distant field waved a welcome to their lord returned from France.

"A new babe, I see," he said to a young mother who smiled and bowed to him as he passed her cottage.

Jamie took in the fresh whitewash and new thatch. He had married an industrious merchant wife, and their estates prospered. Of course, he would have to spend the next fortnight calming his tenants. While they were fond of his wife, they did not always take well to her attempts to change how they did their work. If their fathers had done something a certain way, that was good enough for them—but not for Linnet.

Linnet must have had the men watching for him, for she and the children were waiting at the gate to meet him. As always, his breath caught at the sight of her. Sometimes he still could not believe his good fortune. To him, she seemed more beautiful each time he returned home.

As soon as he dismounted, she flew into his arms. He held her against him and, for the moment, ignored the little hands that pulled at his leggings.

"I am home for good," he said next to her ear. "I shan't go to France again."

He turned and rubbed his son's head. "Have you been taking good care of the womenfolk, John Alan?"

John Alan nodded with such a weary expression on his four-year-old face that Jamie had to laugh.

When his daughter Annie held her arms out for him to carry her, something inside him shifted. With her mother's fair looks and headstrong nature, this one was bound to cause a father heartache. Annie shrieked with pleasure as he lifted her onto his shoulders.

"Francois and Rose are well and send their love," Jamie said as the four of them headed to the keep. "They will visit in the autumn and may stay in England through the winter. Things are...difficult in France. This business with Joan of Arc has left a sour taste in all our mouths."

The young woman's courage and single-minded determination reminded Jamie too much of his wife for him not to admire her.

"You have news from London as well?" Linnet asked.

"Aye. The new Duchess of Gloucester is increasingly unpopular. 'Twas foolish of Gloucester to marry Eleanor, for she makes enemies at every turn."

Jamie only wished he had found proof of Eleanor's connection to the sorcerers.

Linnet patted his arm. "Eleanor will pay the piper one day."

They entered the hall, where a large cup of ale and a platter of cold meats and warm bread waited for him on the table. He made quick work of the meal, despite having a wiggling child on each knee.

When he finished, he kissed his children and set them on their feet. "I have new stories for you, but I must talk alone with your mother now."

After their nursemaid had taken the children out, he set a packet of letters on the table. "Mistress Leggett sent these and said business is going well."

Mistress Leggett and her sons handled the day-to-day business of Linnet's trade. While Linnet still visited London once or twice a year, she seemed more interested these days in managing the castle's large household and estates.

"And how is Lily?" Linnet smiled as she asked, for Lily was a favorite.

"Poor Martin! Somehow, she got him to agree to bring her here after he visits his mother. He can face any man in combat, but he has yet to learn how to say nay to a female. If my sisters come as well, he'll have no peace at all."

"Poor Martin, indeed." Linnet did not sound sympathetic.

"Lily says she wants to gather a special healing herb that grows north of here," he said.

Lily had surprised them all by apprenticing herself to the old herbalist.

"I do hope they all come," Linnet said, her face shining. After growing up with just her brother and grandfather, Linnet loved having extended family and friends about her.

"Did you hear any whispers in London about the queen

and Owen?" Linnet asked. When he shook his head, she laughed. "Surely, the Council must know about them by now? When last we visited, she was enormous with their second child."

"Humphrey and the Council either do not know or choose to pretend they do not," he said. "Either way, let us pray they continue to ignore them."

Linnet put her hand over his on the table. "Shall I send word to Stephen and Isobel that you are home?"

There was only one thing Jamie liked better than to sit and talk with his wife. He leaned forward to smell her skin and whisper in her ear. "Let me have you to myself for a time. I want to spend a week in bed with you."

"I hoped you would say that," she said in a husky voice. "I missed my passionate knight."

"Come, love," he said, pulling her to her feet. "I have been away far too long."

Historical Note

Henry V's widow, the French princess Katherine de Valois, had four or five children with Owen Tudor, her clerk of the wardrobe. Six hundred years later, many facts about their relationship are not clear—if they ever were. One story commonly told about them is that the queen fell for Owen after seeing him bathing naked. Another is that Owen caused a stir at court by falling into her lap while dancing.

It is generally believed that Owen and the queen secretly married, though there is no record of it. I consolidated events a bit and set their marriage in 1426, when it probably took place closer to 1429.

Prior to her relationship with Owen, the queen was rumored to have had a flirtation with Edmund Beaufort. This is probably what prompted Gloucester, the young king's uncle, to persuade Parliament to prohibit the queen from marrying without permission.

Despite the law, the queen and Owen lived in seclusion with their growing family at Hertford for several years. Their quiet life came to an end in 1436 when Owen was imprisoned on a charge of treason, probably at Gloucester's instigation. Queen Katherine "retired" to Bermondsey Abbey, where she died after giving birth to their fourth or fifth child. Some say she died of heartbreak.

The queen's death marked a turning point in Gloucester's influence over the king. Henry VI, now fifteen, ordered Owen released and elevated his Tudor half brothers, Edmund and Jasper, to earls. Owen lived until 1461, when he was executed as a Lancaster supporter in the War of the Roses.

Owen and Katherine's eldest son, Edmund Tudor, married Edmund Beaufort's cousin Margaret. Margaret was already widowed when she gave birth—at the age of thirteen—to their son Henry. It was this child, the grandson of Henry V's widow and her clerk of the wardrobe, who would later usurp the throne to become Henry VII and begin the Tudor dynasty.

Eleanor Cobham, the daughter of a mere knight, became Gloucester's mistress while serving as lady-in-waiting to his wife. After Gloucester's first marriage was invalidated, she became his duchess. Once Gloucester's older brother died, making Gloucester next in line to the throne, Eleanor could almost see the crown on her head. It appears she decided to act before the king married and begat an heir.

In 1441, Eleanor Cobham was convicted of using sorcery and witchcraft against Henry VI, after one of her close associates, John Hume, turned informant. Eleanor admitted to witchcraft but denied the allegations of treason. For her penance, she was made to walk through London with a lit candle and then was imprisoned for life on the Isle of Man. Because Eleanor allegedly used sorcery to trick him into marrying her, Gloucester was conveniently "unmarried" a second time.

Eleanor's co-conspirators did not fare so well. Margery Jourdemayne, who had been imprisoned for sorcery once before, was burned as a relapsed heretic. Thomas Southwell, a cleric and physician, died in the Tower before a sentence could be carried out. Roger Bolingbroke, a cleric and well-known Oxford scholar, was hung, drawn and quartered; afterward, his head was displayed on London Bridge.

As passion ignites and
danger closes in, Catherine and
William must learn to trust in each
other or risk losing everything that
truly matters to them . . .

❦

Please turn this page
for an excerpt from

Knight of Desire

Book One in the
All the King's Men Series

Available now

Prologue

"Tomorrow I am to be married."

The surge of disappointment in William's chest caught him by surprise. Although he was told the castle was crowded because of a wedding, it had not occurred to him that this achingly lovely girl could be the bride.

"I do not expect this will be a happy marriage for me," she said, lifting her chin. "But tomorrow I will do what my father and my king require of me and wed this man. From that time forward, I will have to do as my husband bids and submit to him in all things."

William, of course, thought of the man taking her to bed and wondered if she truly understood all that her words implied.

"Lady, I would save you from this marriage if I knew how."

He spoke in a rush, not expecting to say the foolish words that were in his heart. He was as good as any man with a sword, but he had no weapon to wield in this fight. Someday, he would be a man to be reckoned with, but as a landless knight, he could only put her at risk by interfering with the king's plans.

Impulsively, he reached out to trace the outline of her cheek. Before he knew what he was doing, he had her face cupped in his hands.

Very softly, he brushed his lips against hers. At the first touch, a shot of lust ran through him, hitting him so hard he felt light-headed and weak in the knees. He pressed his mouth hard against hers. Dimly, through his raging desire, he was aware of the innocence of her kiss. He willed himself to keep his hands where they were and not give in to the overpowering urge to reach for her body.

He broke the kiss and pulled her into his arms. Closing his eyes, he held her to him and waited for the thundering of his heart to subside. God have mercy! What had happened to him? This girl, who trusted him blindly, had no notion of the danger.

Swallowing hard, he released her from his embrace. He could think of no words, could not speak at all. With deliberate care, he pulled her hood up and tucked her long hair inside it. Then he let his arms fall to his sides like heavy weights.

"I did not want his to be my first kiss," she said, as though she needed to explain why she had permitted it.

She took a quick step forward and, rising on her tiptoes, lightly touched her lips to his. In another moment, she was running across the yard, clutching her cloak about her.

For many years, William dreamed of that night. In his dreams, though, he held her in his arms by the river in the moonlight. In his dreams, he kissed the worry and fear from her face. In his dreams, he rescued her from her unhappy fate.

In his dreams, she was his.

THE DISH

Where authors give you the inside scoop!

♥ ♥ ♥ ♥ ♥ ♥ ♥ ♥ ♥ ♥ ♥ ♥ ♥ ♥ ♥

From the desk of Margaret Mallory

Dear Readers,

Am I unkind? I made Sir James Rayburn wait until the third book in my All the King's Men trilogy to get his own story. First, as a toddler, he watched his mother find love with her KNIGHT OF DESIRE, William FitzAlan. Then, as a young squire, he played a supporting role to his uncle Stephen, the KNIGHT OF PLEASURE, in his quest for true love. And now, when I finally give this brave and honorable knight his own book, I let the girl he loves stomp on his heart in the prologue.

After that unfortunate experience, all Jamie Rayburn wants—or so he says—is a virtuous wife who will keep a quiet, ordered home waiting for him while he is off fighting. Instead, I give him the bold and beautiful Linnet, whose determination to avenge her family is bound to provoke endless tumult and trouble. Worse, this heroine is the very lady who stomped on Jamie's heart in his youth.

Why would I do this to our gallant knight? After he has shown such patience, why not reward him with the sweet, undemanding heroine he requested?

Although that heroine might prove to be a trifle dull, she would be content to gaze raptly at our hero as he told tales of his victories by the hearth.

Truly, I meant to give Jamie a softer, easier woman. But when I tried to write Jamie's story, Linnet decided she *had* to be there. And when Linnet sets her mind to something, believe me, it's best not to stand in her way.

Besides, Linnet was right. Who better to save Jamie from a staid and tedious life? No other woman stirs Jamie's passion as she does. And what passion! If our handsome knight must contend with murderous plots, court intrigue, and a few sword-wielding sorcerers before he can win his heart's desire, then so be it.

I am sure Jamie forgives me. Our KNIGHT OF PASSION knows a happy ending is worth the wait—and it's all the more satisfying if it doesn't come easy.

I hope you enjoy reading Jamie and Linnet's adventurous love story as much as I enjoyed writing it!

Margaret Mallory

www.margaretmallory.com

♥ ♥ ♥ ♥ ♥ ♥ ♥ ♥ ♥ ♥ ♥ ♥ ♥ ♥ ♥ ♥

From the desk of Cara Elliott

Dear Readers,

Oh, dear. Just when all the gossip about Lady Sheffield and the Mad, Bad Earl of Hadley (you may read their story in TO SIN WITH A SCOUNDREL)—has died down, the Circle of Sin series is once again in danger of stirring up scandal. This time, it's Lady Sheffield's fellow scholar, the lovely and enigmatic Alessandra della Giamatti, who is caught up in a web of lies and intrigue.

Well, luckily for her, Hadley's good friend, the rakish "Black Jack" Pierson, comes to the rescue in TO SURRENDER TO A ROGUE (available now). A decorated war hero, Jack is also a talented painter . . . not to mention highly skilled in the art of seduction. (Apparently, he is intimately acquainted with all the creative ways a man can use a soft sable brush to . . . er, I really ought to allow you to discover those colorful details for yourself.)

At first blush, archeology might not seem like a subject that inspires heated passion. However, I chose to plot my story around an excavation of ancient Roman ruins in England because I have always been fascinated by how, throughout history, the idea of buried treasure has resulted in both serious scholarship and serious skullduggery. In Regency times, the "science" of archeology was in its infancy. Napoleon deserves credit for taking a host of scholars with him to Egypt, along with his invading army, and encouraging them to preserve artifacts of the past for academic study. On the English side, Lord Elgin carefully crated up marbles from the Parthenon in Athens and removed them to London, where they became the nucleus of the British Museum. (Today, there is quite a vociferous debate between Greece and Great Britain about whether the artistic treasures were, in fact, looted from their rightful home—but that is a topic I shall leave to the diplomats to decide.)

In TO SURRENDER TO A ROGUE, things really heat up as the digging begins outside of the spa town of Bath, which is, in fact, set on the site of an ancient Roman outpost. Someone is threatening to expose a scandalous secret from Alessandra's past if she doesn't betray all the principles she holds dear. Does she dare confide in Jack? She has good reason not to trust handsome rogues, so it's no wonder that she views him as dangerous. *Oh so dangerous*. But if ever a lady needed a hero to fight for her honor . . .

And speaking of dangerous men, Alessandra's cousin—that unrepentant rake otherwise known as the Conte of Como—is rattling his own sword . . . so to speak. Not content with playing a secondary role in my first two books, Marco saunters into an adventure of his own in TO TEMPT A RAKE (available in winter 2011). As you know, he is a rather arrogant, abrasive fellow, and he is used to having females fall at his feet. So when the free-spirited Kate Wood-bridge—the most rebellious member of the Circle of Sin—resists his flirtations at a country-house party, he can't help but be intrigued. Like her fellow "sinners," Kate is both beautiful and brainy—and hiding a dark secret that occurred in her past. When things take a sinister turn at her grandfather's estate, seduction is no longer a game, and she is forced to decide whether a rakehell rascal can be trusted . . .

Please visit me at www.caraelliott.com, where you can sneak a tantalizing peek at all three books in my Circle of Sin series.

Cara Elliott

♥ ♥ ♥ ♥ ♥ ♥ ♥ ♥ ♥ ♥ ♥ ♥ ♥ ♥ ♥

From the desk of Robyn DeHart

Dear Readers,

Who out there isn't fascinated by the lost continent of Atlantis? The legend is as compelling as Jack the Ripper and El Dorado, those unsolved mysteries that have been perplexing people for hundreds of years. But it was Atlantis that captured my attention for the second book in my Legend Hunters series, DESIRE ME.

With Atlantis, you have a little bit of everything—Greek mythology, hidden treasures, and utopian societies.

I couldn't help but add my own flair to the myth and make my Atlantis home to the fabled Fountain of Youth. Add in an ancient prophecy, a lost map, and Sabine Tobias, a heroine who is a living, breathing descendent to the Atlanteans—and you've got a recipe for adventure coupled with plenty of trouble.

But what does any damsel in distress need? A good hero. A sexy-as-hell, smart-mouthed hero who is, shall we say, good with his hands. That is, he's handy to have around when you're stuck in an underground chamber or when you need to slip into an old estate without being seen. Enter Maxwell Barrett, legend hunter extraordinaire and expert on all things Atlantis.

With DESIRE ME, I return to my series about Solomon's, the exclusive gentleman's club of Legend Hunters. This book was, at times, harrowing to write, but not nearly as dangerous for me, the writer, who sat safely at home in my jammies with my faithful kitties to keep me company. Poor Max and Sabine, though, are on a perilous race against time, trying to solve the ancient prophecy before a nasty villain destroys them both. But they find themselves neck deep in trouble about as often as they find themselves wrapped in one another's arms.

Visit my website, www.RobynDeHart.com, for contests, excerpts, and more.

Robyn DeHart

Want to know more about romances at Grand Central Publishing and Forever? Get the scoop online!

GRAND CENTRAL PUBLISHING'S ROMANCE HOMEPAGE

Visit us at www.hachettebookgroup.com/romance for all the latest news, reviews, and chapter excerpts!

NEW AND UPCOMING TITLES

Each month we feature our new titles and reader favorites.

CONTESTS AND GIVEAWAYS

We give away galleys, autographed copies, and all kinds of fun stuff.

AUTHOR INFO

You'll find bios, articles, and links to personal websites for all your favorite authors—and so much more!

THE BUZZ

Sign up for our monthly romance newsletter, and be the first to read all about it!